Murder Music and Mayhem

By Donna Emerich & Bella Reign Flanagan

Murder Music and Mayhem

Murder Music and Mayhem

Acknowledgements

To my family in Colombia. Thank you for your love and support through the process of bringing this manuscript to life. For Marissa Elisabeth Sparkle on, baby girl. We love you. For baby Emilio You are my sunshine

For anyone who has ever had to endure the manipulations of a Narcissist.

For Valeria

You hit like a bitch!

Prologue

I idolized Elvis. I got the singing bug after performing solos in church. I decided I would become a star. Only problem was, life and people got in my way. They only want to saddle me with an average life. I would not stand for an average life! Women are nice for a while, but ultimately they get in the way. Honky-tonkin' is the best way to get heard, to be a star you have to be on stage. The road is calling me. No one will stand in my way, be they alive or dead.

Life started in the usual way. I joined our family at birth but always needed special attention. I was the apple of my mother's eye. My father was not a pleasant man. He was always whispered about behind closed doors. His father was a mean drunk who beat his mother. My dad caused too many problems to deal with, so he was sent away. I assumed from what I had heard, my dad was afraid he would become violent, so he would not discipline his children. He put all his energy into hard work. He met my mother. Slaved away on a farm. Hard work was a common thread between them. Being different was hard. I couldn't drink cow's milk. Dad had to get a goat he did not want because of me. Dad took several kinds of physical labor jobs but that's all I knew he could get. He never finished school. There was no need. The same was true for my mom. Hard work and family was all she knew. She preferred things that way. Having brothers and sisters was okay. The first things I learned were how to shoot a gun and to fish. I enjoyed animals. They needed me. That was important to me. Animals seemed to have an unending love, an admiration for me. I loved being the center of attention which truly showed when I sang with the chorus. When I started school, I was always trying to be a star with art work and music. I needed to be noticed. Learning by books was not important to me but I enjoyed the notoriety that came with being sent to the principal's office. Getting a reputation as a trouble maker got me noticed but unfortunately the principal knew me by first name. My dad decided to try to focus my attentions on athletics. He was a fan of baseball. He would cut church to watch sports on Sunday. This angered my mother. It set a bad example for us kids. My brother was a bit of a wise guy. He swiped hub caps, stole cars and kept a pack of Lucky Strikes rolled up in his t-shirt sleeve. He quit school early, became a mechanic. My older sister had quit school by eleventh grade to get married. No one was interested in getting an education. I discovered I had talent as a singer after my solos in church, when I was noticed by the girls. Singing charms the girls. I was so cool. I had a church girlfriend for church activities, and a school girlfriend to do my homework. I started myself a little gang. The guys in my neighborhood took orders from me. Of course, I had to prove myself. First I had to prove I could handle myself. We had a neighborhood kid that harassed me. I stood up to him. My father encouraged me to punch the other kid. My mother was so angry! She said it was wrong to fight! He told her, "Shut up! He has to fight to be a man!" Once, my dad had me pick a fight with the biggest kid on the block. I'd better win!! Or else! My mother had always done all the discipline. You would think with all her opposition to violence, she would have been gentle with punishment. Never! She laid into you with the first thing handy. I dove under the bed for protection. My brother picked up the bed so she could beat me! Nice brother! To earn the respect of our neighborhood gang, I had to prove that I wouldn't tell on them. Being a kid, I was willing to do what it took. I got put up to robbing my sister's wedding! You could hear her bawling at me running out of the church screaming. "Gene, you will be sorry for this!" Those shits told her I did it! I had spent my hard earned money on them. Those assholes watched me get beat with metal coat hangers and a metal rod! My sister was screaming. "Jesus! Stop it! You're going to kill him on my wedding day!" I never told on them, that's why I was the leader of our gang. By the time I was ten, I had a pack a day habit and was sneaking hard cider. I was earning a bad reputation.   I loved that girls would turn to me for protection, but others considered me a bully. I was pleased with my newly earned status. By fourteen, I did whatever I pleased. My parents had no control. When the cops brought me home, my mother would give them hell. Reminding them of all their indiscretions growing up got them to lay off of me. As I said, I was my mom's favorite. My younger sister was annoying, but she had many cute friends who were willing to do anything for a future star! My friends and I thought nothing of slipping a little LSD in their lemonade.   I went to school high most of the time. Our principal found out and thought he was "man" enough to take a swing at me. Wrong move! Me and the boys handled him. He wouldn't be using that arm to swing at anybody for a long time. It would take several months for his arm to heal. Of course, I was the only one who got suspended. The principal said I started the whole thing! I always got blamed for everything! I decided no one could tell me what to do. I wanted to see the USA! I threw a dart at a map and that's where I headed. I helped myself to my mom's savings and was on my way. The town was quiet for a while. I sent my parents postcards with pleas to send me food money. I learned how to hustle on the street real fast or die. I was quick with my fists. Women would offer me food and other comforts. I learned to use my age to my advantage to keep out of jail. By the time I arrived back home, my innocence was gone.

Murder Music and Mayhem

I tried to go back to high school but I had aged ten years in the time I was hitchhiking around the country. I had discovered my love for drugs on the road. Drugs helped pass the time. The 1960's were full of free drugs and love and I enjoyed as much of them as I could. But high school was a bore. I was sixteen and in the eighth grade. I was ready to get a car. I had become friends with a band of traveling Romani's (gypsies) and they taught me many things. I learned about the school of seven belles. They take a mannequin and place seven bells throughout the clothing. If you can pickpocket the mannequin without setting off the bells, you are ready to work a crowd. This is a helpful skill if you are starving. But I felt comfortable around them. I didn't really have many friends, so my attraction to the criminal element had been present in my childhood. By seventeen, I had a criminal record. My mom, ever my defender, gave me the idea that I was indestructible. The local judge did not agree. I was given an option. Military service or prison. I willingly went to the military. I considered this a new adventure to sharpen my skills with guns and looked for a way to earn points with my upper classmen. We had a guy get sickly during a march. Drill sergeant never bothered to check on him so I let my superior know the guy was sick. I officially made an enemy of my drill sergeant. We squared off several times during my first five weeks of basic training. I always made sure if we squared off, it was in front of my squad. Proving I had no fear of anyone. I told that prick off, always making sure I did it in proper form. Most of the guys that joined enjoyed partying as much as I did. Inspections never stopped me. We knew about them in advance, so we hid the stash. I would always find the weakest guy in case I

needed someone to blame. But we got busted doing LSD.

It was cool during live night fire. My buddy jumped up to

fight with the cops so I did not end up catching the heat.

It wasn't my first time in legal trouble. Rehab was fun. I

loved getting sent there. I did not take orders well.

Instead of guard duty, I left base to party and showed up

again before the holiday was over. I whined to the

chaplain so I could get out of church service early. It did

not work out as I had planned. They sent me to a hole in

the wall base to await my discharge.   I was excused from

service because I had drug issues. But they figured they

would see if I would do better in a base further away

from civilization. Ha! I went to church so I had more

freedom to do what I wanted. Fuck, I didn't last six

months. I couldn't wait to get out and become a country star! That was my heart's desire.

Fans. Women to take care of me. Money. Yes, that's the life for me. Unfortunately, I had to get a day job. I went back to what I was taught. Roofing and black topping. Scams and easy money. The elderly are easy to convince. After reconnecting with my buddy, Danny we started working together. We did lawn work, roofing, black topping and other easy money jobs. We'd make enough money to party for a few days while our old ladies collected welfare for the kids. After a few weeks, we had a system going. Standing out on the back lawn of a customer enjoying the sun, I noticed a girl. She was young and beautiful. I immediately started thinking of how I was going to get in her pants. I had not had the best luck after my stint in the service. I took up with a girl named Denise. I got a factory job so I could honky tonk at night. She had a job and a daughter. I thought this was ideal. She needed a man in her life. She would be grateful to have me. The relationship lasted long enough for me to get a girl of my own. Her mother just needed steady income. She played the game better than I did. She got child support. I got constant jail time. She made me sound like a monster. That was untrue. I treated her better than she deserved. This girl looked promising. I made friends with her brothers and put on parties for them to gain their trust.   I convinced her youngest brother to introduce us. Lynette had been in several foster homes because her mom couldn't collect welfare for her. I thought she was eighteen. I had the hots for her and her brother gave permission to ask her out. Just as I thought things were going great, there were red lights flashing and lots of police cars in the driveway. Strolling down there with a pounding headache, I asked what was going on. It seems she had escaped from another foster home. She was fourteen, but could easily pass for twenty years old. As they took her away, the throbbing in my pants was controlling my thoughts. If I could get her brother to apply for temporary custody of her, I would be able to get her to like me. My plan worked! While the county reviewed the application for temporary custody, Lynette got to stay with her brother. I spent all my time taking her out and buying her gifts. She was falling for me. I started feeling as though Lynnette belonged to me! I would be her first and only.

Every time they would take her away, she would find me. She would never give me up! Upon her last escape, her mom decided she deserved money from our relationship. I was told that I could have her daughter if I paid her bills. Raising my future wife had perks. When I stopped paying, she had me arrested for rape! So, I went back to paying her to stay out of jail. Then, Lynette ended up pregnant so there was a shot gun wedding! I figured it was worth it to have such a "young" wife. Unknown to me, she had some emotional issues. Add in raging hormones and Lynette became a raging lunatic. Her fits caused discord between us on a constant basis. I spent all my free time in the bars so I did not have to go home. There were plenty of ladies in the bar to hang out with. I would have to sneak in after she went to bed. I could not stand her! I sent her packing back to her mother until she dropped that baby. After getting a call, I headed to the hospital, drinking all the way. I walked in, blurry-eyed but anxious to see a miniature me. Little Gene Allen, Jr. Damn, I did a hell of a job if I do say so myself! Lynette got worse, not better. She was a mental case. I would have signed her into a psychiatric hospital if she would have stayed in one place long enough. A short time later, I got a call. "Come get your boy. He isn't getting proper care." She only cared about the next man she could snare into her web. So, here I was with a baby. I truly was not father material but your kid has to worship you, right? Maybe he will help me get women. He would make a pretty handy tool to get the ladies to notice me. But what was I going to do with him? I really didn't have my own place, since both Denise and Lynette left me. Guess we'll have to live with mom and dad. They will have to help me raise Gene Jr.

Both sisters were convenient babysitters. I needed to get my music career going. I took a day job to help fund my gigs in bars around all the local counties. A lone country singer was appealing to a lot of lonely women. Everyone wanted to be the inspiration of my next song. Fights over women and money landed me in jail more often than it should have. I met Genevieve. She was a single mom who thought she would give me a little class. She came from a "loaded" family. I was a kept man and I enjoyed it. I even let her meet my son. She covered

his expenses too. She loved to throw money around.

That included buying drugs. Our relationship ended

on a sour note. I did not need more kids. I truly

needed to keep my mind on becoming a star. We

went back to my mom's house.   I tried to teach

Junior all I had learned, but we started butting heads

from the time he could talk. I hit the road to make

money and soon noticed that you got more exposure

if you were part of a band. Being a front man, I had

charisma, charm and all the ladies loved me. Men

were jealous of my talent and great looks. Country

girls seemed more willing to take care of a man.

City girls wanted to be kept in all the latest fashions.

I was the one who deserved to be kept in all the

finer things. I would become a star! No matter what

I had to do or who I had to walk over to get there.

My band practiced. Or what we considered

"practice" was a jam session when we were

drinking, which was often. My buddy and I went to

a bar where this chick he liked worked. He

introduced me to Agatha- "Aggie" for short. Aggie

was not interested in Jessie, but she definitely had

"eyes" for me. When I asked about Jessie, She said

he was okay as a friend, but nothing else! I went

back to the same bar. She was in the same spot.

With a smug smile, I sauntered over. "What are you

waiting for, Aggie?" "You, Gene!" While going

through a few pitchers of beer that she paid for, we

talked about her being divorced and her kids. I told

her I had a son. She said I could come by and meet

the kids. While walking her home, all I could think

was 'this will be an easy score.' I knew she would give in. But I thought better of it. I needed her to believe I was a great guy. A great catch for her. On Saturday, Junior and I went to meet Aggie's family. Walking to her place, I told Junior he needed to be on his best behavior. "Do not screw this up and you could end up with a new mom!" I knocked. Aggie answered, inviting us in. Only one of her kids lived with her. I showered her girl with gifts. I needed to prove what a great man and father I would make. As planned, we were invited to move in. Junior really liked having a family. Aggie came to the bars and watched me play for the crowds. Living in town just would not do. To be a country star, I had to live the country life. We hunted and fished. We didn't have enough money though. Guess I would have to take a "normal" job. Aggie didn't mind living poor. But that would never do for me. I kept exotic pets for the status. The only time I was happy was being on stage and drinking. I spent my free time swilling beer and having band practice. Boys being boys, my son did some crazy stuff.Aggie was not herself. I thought Junior's bullshit was making her sick. His behavior got worse the more I beat him. I was getting frustrated with the whole situation and it showed. I drank more. Aggie bitched. We fought. Aggie decided there was something going on with her kids. Questioning Kat, she just said that she and her friend were teasing Junior. That he had picked up a knife and screamed "Don't touch me!" When I asked him what happened, he started telling me that Kat's friend used to lock him in her bedroom.

25

Further explaining that every time she came over, she did bad things to him. I never believed it for a minute. I thought he was lying to ruin my easy street. I figured I should hear the rest of his story, in case it could blow back on me. I said, "Go on." "Kat's friend Gena used to touch me here" he said, pointing to his dick. She made me touch her boobies and her pussycat. She kept touching my wiener until it got stiff and hurt. Then, she made me lie on the bed, put her legs on both sides of me and sat on my wiener." Crying, he said he was afraid to tell me. I asked him, "Did you find my porn magazines and movies?" "What is porn, Dad?" "I cannot believe you made up this story so that Aggie throws us out!" "So what was Kat doing while her friend touched you?" "She laughed at me and told me to

26

be quiet or she'd tell on me." With a back hand slap, I hissed, "Don't you speak of this to Aggie! It's your fault she's sick. She's sick because you are a nasty, bad boy! No one could love a boy like you!" Aggie explained it to me. "Gene, he has problems. He should see a counselor. Maybe he needs medication." "Fine, I will take him!" Talking to the school guidance counselor, I was given the name of a child specialist. For the first session, he had Junior draw pictures. "I'm spending good money so he can draw pictures?" "These pictures show that he has been sexually abused by someone older than him." "Bullshit! You have no idea what you're talking about!" Grabbing Junior by the hand, I dragged him back to the car. Revving the engine, I pulled out, laying rubber. I pulled over and grabbed my son by

27

the shoulders. "I have no idea why you are lying but you are never to talk about this again! Do you hear me?" "Yes, Sir!" "If you get us thrown out of her house, you will be sorry!" Once we got home, Junior ran for his bike. With tears streaming down his face, he peddled towards the creek. Slamming the kitchen door as Gene walked in; Aggie asked "How is Junior?" "That counselor is crazy! He saw a bunch of shit in the kid's pictures! It's all a bunch of shit!" "You're wrong, Gene." Aggie felt a sharp sting across her face. "He's my boy! I'll decide what he needs!" 'I run this house! Do your job and I will do mine!" This was not the first time I'd raised a hand to a woman. No woman knows more than me, on any subject! Slamming the door on his way out, Gene headed for a local dive he considered his sanctuary. The more he drank, the angrier he became with his son. Full of rage, he headed back to Aggie's to vent his anger on Gene Jr. Falling through the kitchen door, he screamed "Where is that lying little prick?!" "He's not here, Gene. Your sister took him to your mom's. Just go to bed." Bouncing off the walls, he found his way to the back bedroom. "Come join me honey!" It was time to get the girls up for school. After a few minutes, there was loud snoring coming from the bedroom. Everything was safe for a while. Aggie put her fingers to her lips to hush Kat and Gena. "Did he pass out?" "Yes, where's the kid?" "He's hidden at his Aunt Dana's house." "How long will he be gone?" "Until Gene calms down. He's back to second shifts, so things will go back to normal."

"Hey, what did the doctor say?" "I have an aneurysm, or so he thinks. More tests to follow." "Wow, can they give you something to dissolve it?" "Not sure what he will do, but I'm not ready to tell Gene yet. He will take it as a weakness and really turn into a prick. He will make my health problems all about him!" "I think once he starts working steadily, he will calm down." "Bull, Mom. He can't hold a job for more than a month. He has delusions that he's a country music star! He sucks, his music is ancient, boring and out-of- touch." "Eat your breakfast and go to school!" About noon, Gene came out of the bedroom groggy and hungover. "Here, start with some coffee and toast while I make your eggs and bacon. Clothes are in the bathroom for your shower. You start work today.""You seem to be excited about the idea of me going to work. Why?" "You seem to need something to keep you busy. Gigs are only on weekends. Plus, a weekly paycheck will help cover your expenses." "Are you saying I don't pay my fair share?!" Well, consider the fact that you can afford a hotel room and good beer on gig nights." "Okay, that's a beautiful start to a paycheck." But it was a lot of up and down hills to get to work.   After a couple weeks of work, it wasn't all that bad. I was ready for the weekend. Four twelve hour days gave me a three-day weekend. Aggie had come back from the doctor. She was prescribed medication and rest. Gene Jr had trashed his bike in an accident. While Aggie patched him up, Gene berated him telling him what a loser he was. Slapping him in the

31

head with his fist as a reminder not to have a bike accident. Breaking down into a fountain of tears, Aggie screamed "Stop it! I can't take it anymore!" Full of faux concern, Gene asked what was wrong. Aggie explained about her condition and the need for medication and rest. Telling Aggie to go sit and put her feet up, he turned his anger outward at Kat. He commanded she was to do all the housework and cooking. Grabbing Junior by his neck, he marched him outside to the garage. He screamed, "You made Aggie sick! This is your fault! Because you're such a bad boy! You do not deserve a mother!" Punching him repeatedly, "It's your fault! I told you to behave. This is all your fault! Pull yourself together! Stop blubbering! Go clean up your face and help Kat with the housework." "At your age, my dad had me doing man's work! I'm too

soft on you! Get going!"

Running to the bathroom, little Junior hid there,

cleaning up his face. Gene kissed Aggie gently. "You

stay home and rest. The boys and I have a gig tonight."

Changing clothes and putting on enough cologne to

knock out a prostitute, he grabbed his guitar and headed

out. Kat knocked on the bathroom door. "It's okay Junior.

He is gone." Opening the door, Kat looked into the

saddest eyes she had ever seen. "It's not your fault Mom

got sick. You did nothing wrong. You're a normal kid

whose father is a fucking asshole!" Packing his head and

face with ice, she told him to sit on the couch. Aggie said,

"Oh, my little boy! I'm so sorry he treats you this way.

He should never have blamed you for my being sick. I

love you like my own son!" Aggie hugged him gently.

"Mom, maybe he needs to go to his aunt's again. Gene is

going to kill him!" "Kat, Junior is the only reason his

family helps him out. He uses him as a tool to worm his

way into women's homes!" "Dana should call a

caseworker or someone! I think he holds something over

their heads so they don't narc him out" announced Kat.

"Mom, are you sure Genes smacking you around isn't the

cause of your health problems?" "What would make you

say such a thing!?" screeched Aggie. "You cannot deny

that he's hit you. You have never had health problems

before." "I am fine. Blood clots are common. My blood

pressure is up." "Did you ever think Gene is the problem?

Nanna and Pop don't feel he's good enough for you.

You've screamed at him over the way he treats his son.

He's a dirt bag. Lives off us, cannot keep a job and thinks

he's gonna be a big star! You need to throw his sorry ass out!" "He will calm down. This happens when he isn't able to go on gigs all the time. He resents having to have a day job" replied Aggie. "Even the coolest rock stars had day jobs before they made it big! He is just lazy. He thinks women should support him!" Still ranting, Kat was loudly bitching about Gene going through their savings. "Christ, Mom if he knew you had a life insurance policy; he'd make sure you had an accident." "No, Kat, he would never hurt me!" "He already has, Mom! Just like he'd never hurt his son because he "loves" him! I guess love and pain are the same in Gene's eyes. He only loves himself." "I am too tired to debate this with you, Kat." "Okay Mom. You need to rest." She kissed her mother on the head. Unknown to Aggie, Gene Sr. was standing outside the back door listening to the whole conversation.

Smiling his evil grin, thinking about the insurance policy.

She will be dying soon so I should benefit of course

because I'm the one taking care of her. This will help me

out immensely! When she dies, I will get the money

since we got married. Her kid will collect benefits from

her death and it will all go to me! Gene diligently took

care of Aggie, but kept blaming Junior for her declining

health. Every time he'd come home, he was looking for

Junior to take his anger out on. He demanded Junior try

to stand up to him and fight. Junior was passive and

mild-mannered so he ran and hid.   Even though he

loved Aggie, he wanted to go back to the safety of his

grandparents where he knew his father wouldn't beat him.

On many occasions Gene's own family had turned him in

for the abuse he perpetrated on his young son. But out of

fear and a worse reprisal, Junior always said he had fallen

or had a bike accident. Gene would keep Junior from school until he healed. He would bring him to the party house he hung out in. His eldest sister had come to his parents' house to find a party happening and her nephew alone upstairs with a creepy looking man. Grabbing her nephew, she marched him out of the house. The house was cleaned up before his parents arrived. They never believed Gene would do such a thing. After a few weeks of working second and third shifts, he did his due diligence and called home at dinner time. When there was no answer, he started bitching to himself. "Goddamn kids! Took off and left her alone again." Heading home, he found the door unlocked. He walked in and yelled for Aggie. The kids were asleep. He found Aggie unconscious. He tried to revive her. He screamed so loud the kids woke up and called 911. She gurgled her last "I love you" as the paramedics took her away. Screaming at Junior, I told him this was his fault for behaving so badly. My parents took him home with them. After the police took my statement, I was released to go to the hospital. The doctor explained there was nothing anyone could have done. The clot went into her brain. After speaking with her family, I was invited to the police station. They kept me for hours. Finally, I decided I may need a lawyer. Seems Kat told her family I might be after Aggie's insurance money! Her family immediately cleaned out the house, even taking things that didn't belong to Aggie. Her family buried her under their family name. Even with the coroner's report in hand, her family said that the aneurysm was caused by my abusing her. Because of this, the insurance company refused to pay out. I was forced to move back in with my parents. I let my job go. My plans were ruined. I drank constantly for the next year. I played

up the grieving husband routine. The gigs were starting

to come back in. I went back on the road while the boy

stayed with Mom and Dad. I needed to line up my next

mark! Out on the road, I ran into an old friend. We'd

hook up in between partners. After she watched a few

gigs she suggested we try dating. She had a job, so I

figured she could take care of me! Hopefully my kid

doesn't fuck this one up! I need to get to Nashville. All

true country stars make it there. Lacy promised to be my

manager and get me to Nashville, just as Aggie had.

Women have never understood what a privilege it is to

help me become a star. Let's see if Lacy will be worthy

of my interest. The relationship started out alright. Her

daughter idolized me. I thought I could bring my son into

the mix. Free child care so I could honky tonk. As I

started performing more, Lacy became my manager and like Aggie, promised to help me get to Nashville. The band practiced at Laci's house. She went to the bars to watch me play.   Lacy paid for everything, so I had no financial responsibilities. After moving in, to pad my hand I asked Lacy to be my wife. She happily agreed. My son was fourteen, so he had friends and pretty much his own life. This was fine with me. Her child pretty much had her own life. Things were going perfectly. I'd get to Nashville this time. Looking into music companies, I had great plans!   I got a phone call from my daughter. Seems she decided she wanted to be with her "dad". I didn't know this girl, so I made her prove she was related to me. You can never be sure. Stalker fans will lie to be with you. One of my buddies took me to the train station to pick her up. She greeted me with flowers and a family

Bible. More proof, in her mind that I should love her.

When I brought her home, Lacy treated her like family.

But soon, we noticed she was in the family way! Lacy

did her best to be good to her. She even bought baby

things. But all the attention I showered on my

"supposed" daughter disturbed Lacy. Jealousy became a

problem. I explained to Lacy "I am man enough to make

both of you happy!" That earned me a punch in the face,

but it was the truth!   My girl started blossoming. Soon

she would be a mother. She had blossoming breasts,

heavying and full. This drove Lacy into a deep

depression. She just couldn't compete with my "girl."

The last row came when I told her I would not throw out

a pregnant woman just because my wife was insecure.

Lacy left after calling the county and said I was sleeping

with my daughter! They had issues with her age and I

had to prove she was pregnant before she arrived on my

doorstep. My "girl" became the woman of the house.

She did everything for me. I helped her bathe my

"grandchild." Our relationship was close, so close that

the town began to talk. I could sleep with whoever I

wanted to! My son had problems with me being that

close to his sister. He found us in bed together, packed up

and went to my mother's. My son could not accept the

fact that in many primitive tribes, it was acceptable to

sleep with your daughters. I saw no problem with their

line of thinking. The county made her get her own place

with her boyfriend. I didn't mind sharing her, but those

government types just don't understand "family" like I do.

Lacy had me arrested for breaking our court order. Seems

we just could not live in the same town. While in jail,

through friends I met my next girlfriend/victim. Ruby

had been a fan of my music and my band. Once I was released, I looked Ruby up. I allowed her to sing back up in my band to give it a fresh sound. When I asked her out, she blew me off. Said I would have to pass the ultimate test! I have never been afraid of a challenge. This will be a cake walk. I can make anyone like me! There are many ways but bribery works best. The kids all liked me, except a pint size version of my daughter. This kid made me sweat bullets. She was more intimidating than the D.A. She grilled me over Aggie's death.   She expected me to have a job and not to take her mother's money or time. But I convinced her to trust me. So I began dating Ruby. She spent all her time with me and the band. She also became my manager. She had the chops to go through all the work to get me to Nashville, where all the best country stars go! I wanted to play at the Grand Old

Opry and smoke grass with Willie Nelson! Ruby thought we needed to move down south to make this a reality for me. This included dragging all the kids with us. Her kids got money because their dad had died. So their money was my money. But Ruby needed to earn us more money so I could be the star that I am. Ruby truly believed in my talent so she started sending in rough tracks of my solo stuff to everybody and their uncle. She got a list of every record company in the USA to send them to. She found a company that would produce a CD of my music. Of course, I had to pay for it. "Not!" They were offering a contract. But now I had to come up with money for this adventure. I refused to put up my own money. Everyone should want to do this for me! Ruby went to work putting together a benefit in my honor. You would have thought I was God, the way I was portrayed as a star. With the needed funds donated by local fans, I was ready to

conquer the country music capital. Paying to play was the

only way I could get record companies to give me the

time of day. The made me pay for the CD's to be

produced. I could do whatever I wanted with them.

Marketing was my problem. It was the same as a vanity

publisher. You pay to play. Nothing more than wanting

to be a star was on my mind. After "the big trip," Gene

believed he had become a star. He started selling his

CD's at shows. His band was having none of his

egotistical bullshit.   The end of his band started him on a

solo career. Track shows with Ruby made him popular.

Ruby's idea of moving to a southern state came to pass.

Gene had sent his music to overseas radio stations and

was well received. Doing personal shows via the internet

helped him get noticed. But he never felt obligated to

help. So while Ruby and all the kids including his son moved, Gene went to a resort to play music and party. Ruby headed for the Ozarks. Selling anything that was not needed for gas money, they headed out. During this time, Gene had discovered other uses for the internet. During his "supposed" tour, he shacked up with a woman he met on the internet. The only person who saw any of his earnings was his mom because she had supported him. While Gene played the resort and partied, Ruby held several jobs to support the kids. Ruby started looking for a permanent career with or without Gene. Pulling herself together, she bought into a restaurant, working day and night she became self-sufficient. About two months into her new career, Gene came back. He worked too hard at the resort, so in his view she could support him for a while. Between what she made and the pension for the kids he'd be able to relax and write songs. He'd even watch the kids for her so she could work more hours. For Gene's amusement, they went to rodeos and other activities to cement his popularity. Another favorite pastime of his was to set Ruby's son up to fight Gene Jr. demanding that they inflict maximum pain upon each other. Ruby came home and caught Gene taking bets on the fights! She informed him that he needed to find some gigs to occupy his time. He was not babysitter material. Getting together with his buddy from up in his neck of the woods they tried many business ventures but ended up drinking instead. He didn't feel he should. "I deserve to be adored and party like a rock star. Everyone should want to support me because I'm a star." I started doing small shows to make Ruby happy, but I felt she should be happy to pay for me. After a while, Gene decided that

Ruby was ungrateful for the privilege of dating him. Trolling the internet, he would look for women online. Preferably ones with enough money to keep him comfortable. The restaurant business fell through because Ruby wasn't smart enough to run a business. Under the guise of wanting to see her older children, we headed north. She couldn't get away from me fast enough. Who cares?! I have friends that will help me out! Back in the old home town, I discovered it was lonely with my parent's accolades to help my bruised ego. With my cheerleaders gone, I had to rely on the charity of friends. I discovered band mates did not truly appreciate me. I could freeze to death and they had no concern. Being made to sleep outside was a rude awakening. I figured one of my buddies would allow me to crash on their couch. I said, "Can I come in and get warm for a few minutes?" His wife did not want me in "her" house.

Roddy should "learn" to keep his bitch under control.

Seems all my old pals are pussy whipped! Finally I

figured out that I would get no sympathy or help so I

moved on. I shared a place with an old friend. She

always wanted a physical relationship but there was no

way you could cover her face or her stench, so it was an

absolute "no." But she loved to drink and always kept me

in booze. I stayed with her family, but you weren't

allowed to drink around their children. I used the phone

to arrange gigs to get back on the circuit again. After

staying at several places, I decided I needed to find

myself a lady to take care of me. I had a female cousin

who worshipped me. I'm sure I could wrangle an invite

to stay with her. After a phone call of sweet talk, I fished

out an invite to stay in a resort area. Ricki took me

around, showing me off with the star status I deserved!

People from my dad's side of the family gave me all the

accolades I needed. Taking me to dinner, buying me

drinks. Asking me to sing and play for them. It felt like I

was home again. Ricki and her boyfriend helped me find

a day job and arrange local gigs. Another cousin took me

out to meet his friends. Bikers were fun to hang out with.

They appreciated my music and bad ass attitude! Having

connections in this area was good. I could always use

some muscle. Never know when you need to have

"someone" taken care of. People were treating me right.

Then Ricki thought I needed to meet a lady. We went to a

local Legion. Ricki introduced me to a shy but damaged

girl. After the introductions were made, I learned just

how damaged she was. Abused and mistreated, she was

the perfect mark for a guy like me! Bonus, she had a job

and liked to be needed. The more I saw of her, the more

attached she became. She was extremely clingy. Buying

me clothes for outdoor work and showing up at my

cousin's place. Ricki started acting jealous, like she

wanted to sleep with me too! I would, but her boyfriend

might get a little pissy. I think its fine to sleep with your

cousins. My shy girl, Patsy was calling. She was begging

me to take her away from her horrible life. But she had

baggage that would come with her, in the form of her

mother that just wouldn't die and she needed to. Plus a

tiny annoying "kick me" dog. If I wanted access to her

money and credit cards, I had to take all of them. But to

pull this off, I would need to bring her back to where I

could control all aspects of her life. First things first,

I needed to remove an obstacle: her husband! I needed to

get him out of the way. Permanently! We loaded Patsy,

her mom, dog and anything else we could carry into her car and my truck and headed back to my town. Once I got her into an efficiency apartment, I started planning how I would get rid of her husband. I asked my friend to keep an eye on Patsy and her mother while I took a two day trip back north. I waited for him in his favorite watering hole. The man was nothing if not punctual. After buying him a few rounds, his tongue loosened up some. He started bitching that his "wife" had run off, no more extra spending cash. I asked him how he kept her in line. "She responds well to a good punch. A little Russian roulette kept her mouth quiet. When her mom got lippy, I put my tube steak between her lips. That kept her mouth quiet. The old lady worked in public so I had to be careful on where I taught her lessons on minding her manners! Gotta hit the head, be right back." Watching him wander toward the men's room, I loaded his beer with a "mickey." I thought to myself, this should slow him down. Tim returned, downed his beer and headed home. Tim asked Gene if he wanted to come by his house for a night cap. "Sure!" Tim's words slurred. Then came the blurred vision. Gene said, "Maybe I'd better drive!" Pushing Tim over to the passenger side, Gene grabbed the steering wheel with gloved hands. His plans were coming together perfectly. Carrying Tim into the house, Gene dropped him on the couch. With a quick call, Gene invited the motorcycle club over to give Tim a special kind of "love." After removing all traces of Patsy from the trailer, the boys had some fun with Tim. After being sodomized orally and anally to teach him a lesson, Gene pissed in his face. He won't bother my property/Patsy again! He headed home with a broad smile back to Patsy. Welcoming Gene home, Patsy asked, "Can we look for a place to call our own?" "Yes, dear. Let me grab the paper." As we moved into the new place, I noticed Patsy's mother looking at me with wide questioning eyes. After my friends had moved in the furniture, we cracked beers. Putting away dishes and clothes kept Patsy busy. Things fell into place. Patsy's world revolved around pleasing me. Just the way I liked it. When Patsy was leaving work, she found state police waiting by her car. Curious, she asked, "May I help you?" "Yes ma'am. We were told this car was stolen." Patsy reached into the glove compartment and showed them the vehicle's registration and insurance documents, proving ownership. "Your husband has made some serious claims against you." "Well, let me call my boyfriend. He can bring the paperwork proving the abuse

I suffered." "Ask him to meet you at the police station, along with a lawyer." Making the call, she instructed Gene where he would find all the pictures and documents. They entered the police station with three file folders of evidence and handed it to the investigator. "This should prove to you who is lying!" Her lawyer tried to calm her, saying,"Let me handle this." Crying, Patsy said," It's like he's beating me all over again! He wins again!" Gene left the room grumbling, "He doesn't learn! I'd have thought my lesson would be ingrained in his head. Guess we were too subtle! I won't be that nice again! Releasing Patsy, the cops apologized for putting her through this ordeal. After the trip home, Gene was informed that they had been making too much noise and had too many dogs. They were evicted. They found a place in the country where they had room to grow. Patsy had noticed things!

55

She believed she was expecting! Gene was less than impressed with this idea. He was on the path to stardom. This would put a wrench in things! But after several trips to the doctor, they said her issues weren't physical. They were mental. Oh, shit! I picked a real great one. She's "fucked" in the head! She was sent for tests and psychological services! How do I get rid of this chick? I was awarded the "Rising Star" award! Now I'm stuck with this crazy broad? With a diagnosis and prescriptions in hand, I had her apply for disability, figuring she could help support me financially. I hired a lawyer to help her get disability and to file for divorce. She was entitled to half of everything. That would help me out financially. I thought to myself that if I wanted access to her wealth, I should divorce Lacy and marry her! Once Patsy started taking all those medications, she started having seizures.

More problems! This broad's a nightmare! Patsy had

always been straight-laced, not much of a drinker. She

soon discovered that she liked beer! Proving I was still

the knight in shining armor, I asked Patsy to marry me.

"Oh yes, Gene! You are the most wonderful man in the

whole world." The wedding was done in a quiet

ceremony without a splash. The combination of alcohol

and psychotropic drugs caused her more seizures. I

suffered through it for as long as I could take it. The

money just wasn't worth it.   She was told to stop the

drugs or she was history. Cutting down on her scripts,

she began smoking pot! This I could control! I gave her a

job, for her self-esteem. I allowed her to book gigs for me.

This appeased her, and I collected her disability checks.

As long as I controlled the women in my life, I was

happy. The more awards I won, the more indestructible I

felt. I was a star! God knows I deserved the applause. I do not need to be humble. I am a "great singer and songwriter." People should accept this! I did live shows on the internet. Not only to expand my fan base, but also to expand my groupie pool. Patsy started questioning my weeks on the road. Complaining that I was on tour but drinking more money than I made! She found credit card receipts for specialties in my hotel room. What the hell? You can't bribe teenage girls to sleep with you unless you can afford to finance their bling addiction. The more Patsy complained, the more I thought about her needing to go away "permanently."

Then I would get her checks and she would stop breathing. It should be an accident. I play the grieving husband so well! Since she had no children, everything she had would be mine! Maybe I should take her on a late honeymoon to relax her suspicions. Maybe a trip to Graceland. She always had a thing about the King! Time to make plans. But first, I need an insurance policy to make it all worth it! I will have to keep my kids at a distance.   I called my friends from Ozark to set up a couple's get away. As I explained how I wanted Patsy to feel "loved." Frank thought it would be great for his wife Gertie too. Using Patsy's money, I put my plan into action. I had taken out life insurance policies on both of them. $250,000 apiece. I figured it would seem sketchy if he only took one out on Patsy. I planned the perfect getaway. Touring Graceland, beauty spas and makeovers. Patsy and Gertie spent time shopping in the best western apparel stores and going to country shows in the evening. I treated Patsy like a queen! Frank gave Gertie the royal treatment. Enjoying her honeymoon, Patsy thought Gene had changed back to the man she had first met. The nightly lovemaking was a treat as Gene had become distant since he had started touring on his own. Gertie asked Patsy if this behavior was out of character for Gene. It sure was for Frank! Thinking deeply for a moment, Patsy said, "Come to think of it, yes it is." "Do you think Gene has a girlfriend?" "I don't know, but after all the hotel receipts I found, I am concerned that he has been sleeping with underage groupies." "Don't take this the wrong way, Patsy but I have never trusted Gene. Frank and I always fight when he's around. It's like he enjoys watching the fireworks whenever we fight!" This plagued Patsy's mind so much she started acting like she needed her meds again. This was exactly what Gene planned on! If she needed her meds again, she could have an accident.

Standing in front of the full length mirror in her hotel room, Patsy stared at her reflection. The woman staring back at her was someone she didn't recognize. Looking back at her was a woman who had changed. She had become heavy, dumpy and looked very bloated. The medicines and beer had slowed her body down. She was no longer the fit, vivacious woman Gene had met two years before. Between the seizures and the drugs, her brain felt clouded. Beer made her feel like she belonged! Anger filled her heart. Gene and the doctors did this to her! But then again, her ex-husband had done his fair share of damage to her mind, body and soul. Was Gene looking to upgrade? Putting her out to pasture? 'I will not allow this to happen! He will love me or else!' Gene's plan was working better than expected. He was planting all the seeds of doubt in her heart. The hole in her heart was opening wider with each thought of Gene playing with groupies while on tour. Heading into the bathroom, Patsy lit up a joint. Gertie came bounding in. "Patsy, I thought we were going out?" "I needed to relax because if I saw Gene right now, I'd punch him in the face! I know he's up to something, I just can't get it out of my mind!" Gertie smiled. "I could use a hit off that. Frank is up to no good too. I heard them talking about going out on tour together! Men are snakes." The pot helped calm Patsy's urge to start a fight with Gene. This was their late honeymoon. There would be time for fighting when they got home. Gene figured if he planted the seeds, she'd explode and end up back on her happy meds. Once she was back on the meds, he could control the circumstances around the accident! Just another small push and she'd be over the edge. During their dinner,

Gene and Frank were chuckling about going on tour together, leaving Patsy alone. Brooding the rest of the evening, Patsy was quiet. Lethally quiet. Saying goodbye to their friends, they packed to head home in the morning. Gene then "accidentally" dropped a receipt from buying a teenager a "teddy" from a lingerie store. Patsy found it, screaming "What the fuck is this, Gene?" "It must have come from housekeeping. Let's hit the rack. Long drive back home!" That was the final straw, after the meltdown Patsy had; Gene knew she would need that trip to the psychiatrist when she got home. It was exactly what he wanted to happen. The trip home was long and tawdry. Patsy had three seizures and spent hours in the emergency room. By the time they got home, she needed to be sedated! A trip to the psychiatric center got her admitted for a week. When she was finally released,

Patsy came home with a fist full of prescriptions. Just the way Gene had planned. Because of her setback, Gene was put in charge of her disability checks. She was no longer considered mentally competent. This gave him the control he needed over Patsy. Her demise would come soon enough. Planning a tour with Frank and solo with his band, Gene was on cloud nine! With all the groupies, this tour would be fun. The more Patsy listened to his plans, the bigger the hole in her heart became. Why live if Gene didn't love her anymore? He got what he wanted, her disability checks and his fame. Being depressed, all she wanted to do was sleep. Her mother realized she had given up.   While Gene and the boys were on a supposed tour, Patsy's mother tried to get her to go to therapy. Marge opened the new batch of mail and discovered Gene's insurance policies! Now things were beginning to make sense to Marge. She demanded that

Patsy get the hell out of bed. "Leave me alone! I am so

tired." "Wake up! You need to see this!" Patsy sat up,

rubbing her eyes. "Okay, this had better be good!" "I just

opened this letter. Seems that no good for

nothing husband of yours took out insurance policies on

both of us!" "You're lying to me, Mother!" "Read for

yourself! Seems he has been pushing your buttons so you

would need psychiatric care again and he would be put in

charge of your disability checks! "That son-of-a-bitch!

He's planning on killing me!" "No, he's planning on

killing US!" "Oh my God! It all makes sense now. His

taking me on a honeymoon. The head games. All so I'd

go crazy and he could kill me off for insurance money!"

"Now, let's get you an appointment with a therapist."

While Marge brought Patsy back to life, Gene was going

from town to town singing in bars. After a few shows,

Frank and the boys went back home. But Gene went on,

the next gig was in a large city with plenty of young

groupies who would do "anything" he wanted. Gene was

booked as an International Star of Country Music. After

his first set, a group of young girls approached him,

asking for autographs. Smiling, he signed for all of them.

Then a beautiful girl caught his attention. She was

whispered about in the bar. Gene smiled, asking if she'd

like a drink. "I can't get served in here" she whispered,

"But could we go to your room?" "Sounds good, let me

finish this last set." After picking up his pay, he met

Candy outside. Sneaking her past the front desk at the

hotel, Gene brought Candy to his room. Inviting her in,

he shut the door. "Can I pour you a drink, Candy?" "Yes,

please!" "So, where are you from?" "Out west."

"Really?" "Truth be told, I left home to become a singer." "How old are you?" "I'm thirteen. But I'm not a kid. I took care of my parent's house while they worked." "Why did you leave home?" "Problems with my stepfather." "I see, said Gene. "So, how have you been getting by?" "I sang. I cleaned for people. Stuff like that. Do you think you could help me, Gene?" "Let's hear you sing." Picking up his guitar, he played a well-known song. Candy began to sing along. "Not bad" said Gene. "But what can you do for me?" Gene asked with a sly grin. "Whatever you want me to, Gene." "Let's see how grateful you can be." Going towards her, he lunged at her growling. "I thought you would be grateful to me. Now, let's see what else you can do with those pretty pink lips!" Unzipping his fly, he grabbed her by her hair and pushed her down towards his fly. His flaccid member showed no interest in Candy. "I said put those lips on it! Bring it to life!" After twenty minutes of giving him oral sex, Candy announced, "You have "whiskey dick." Nothing is bringing that thing to life." "You aren't grateful! You should be thanking me. I'm a star. You're a whore!" Lumbering toward her, Gene grabbed her by the throat, throwing her against the wall. Candy slid down the wall. "Now, tell me how grateful you are that I, a country music star allowed you to suck my dick! You were not worshipping me the way I deserve. Now tell me!" He slapped Candy across the face. No response. "Bitch, I said praise me!" Shaking his head, he dropped on the bed, passing out. After six hours of sleep, Gene awoke with cotton mouth. Looking over at Candy, he noticed her lips were a pale shade of blue gray. Gene crawled off the bed. Walking over to her, he touched her neck for a pulse. There was nothing but pale, blue skin.

"Oh, fuck! She died before I could fuck her!" Calling

Frank for help, he screamed "NOW!" Frank arrived to

find a dead Candy and Gene panicking. "What the hell,

Gene?" "Did you bring the refrigerated truck?" "Yes!"

"Let's take her down the back stairs before daylight."

Carrying Candy down the stairs and putting her in the

refrigerated truck, Frank put a lock on the door with a

seal around the back, Cops wouldn't break the seal.

"Take her to the desert and dump her. I will clean up the

room and leave. I have another gig, so I need to get

myself together. Do it the way I told you and I will share

my payday with you.""You're my friend; I know you

can't afford a scandal. I'll help you, but this is the last

time." Smiling, Gene said "You always say that, Frank."

Frank pulled out of the parking lot just before day break.

69

Gene cleaned up the room, bathed and headed out for a big breakfast. His conscience was clean. He felt nothing. On to the next state!   Pulling into St. Louis, Gene smiled. There will be another pool of adoring fans. As he was setting up for his gig, the local bar flies started filling up the bar. Casey asked the bartender, "Who is this guy?" "He's supposed to be a country music star. But I've never heard of him before." Once Gene started to play, she said, "Oh, I've heard of this guy, he won some kind of award." "He's not so great" complained Betsy. Hearing this discussion, Gene tuned on all his charm. Buying them drinks and flirting. But no sale on the merchandise. Gene started to feel that these women should be praising his talent. Instead, he was made fun of and belittled. As he packed up, one of the local working girls offered him a date. He offered to meet her out by his van in twenty minutes. Collecting his pay, he looked at this local girl with disdain. Her face filled him with anger. Walking outside, the air was filled with humidity and rain. A sudden clouded burst filled the street with a heavy downpour. Gene offered for Casey to get in the van. "I need a drink" boomed Gene. "Hop in the back and grab the bottle of Jack for me, would you?" "Sure." Pulling over outside of town, Gene joined Casey in the back of the van. Taking a large pull off the bottle, Gene smiled. "That's better." "So, what shall we do, Casey?" "What do you like, Gene?" "How about this?" Leaning over, Gene gave Casey a gentle kiss. Casey smiled, "That's nice." Gene reached his arm around Casey, putting his hand on the back of her head. He pushed her face toward him for what she thought was going to be another kiss. Surprise! He pushed her face into the mattress on the floor, pinning her by putting his knees in her back. He turned her over to face him. "So, what do you expect from me, Casey?" "Gene, I normally get paid for sex. I am a professional." "Really, Casey? You should pay for the privilege of being with me. I'm a country star!" "Well, let's see what you've got, Gene! With pride, Gene dropped his pants. Casey stared at him with a confused look. "Well, where is it?" she questioned. With a sweet smile, Gene punched Casey with such force that she choked on her own teeth. As he strangled her, he explained that she wasn't worthy of sucking his dick! He laid her limp, lifeless body down gently before jumping in the driver's seat and driving away. He smiled to himself. Now she knew what a privilege it was! Now, let's find a place to bury her. Texas works. No one cares about dead whores there. Now it's time to head home and finish off Patsy! But first, a few more gigs. New Mexico

should be fun, lots of country music fans for me to thrill.

Nice town, lots of desert, so plenty of places to dig a hole.

Setting up for the gig, Gene noticed a pretty little girl.

She had deep brown eyes and long, thick black hair. She

had ample breasts and hips. Her lips were the color of

fresh strawberries. Smiling at her, she blushed under

Gene's deep, penetrating gaze. He told the waitress to ask

her what she'd like and to put it on his bill. Being that

she was fifteen, she ordered a pop and a sampler platter.

A quesadilla, tacos, rice and beans. Gene sang every one

of his ballads while gazing at this Mexican beauty named

Marissa.   During the break between sets, Gene

sauntered over to Marissa. "Was the food to your

liking?" "Oh, yes. Might I say what a wonderful voice

you have!" "Why, thank you! What's your name, Miss?"

"Marissa, Sir." "What's this Sir stuff? My name's Gene."
"Will you stay for my next set?" "Yes, sir." "No sir, just
Gene." After a set of fifteen songs, Gene started tearing
down. After settling his tab and collecting his pay, he
asked Marissa if she would join him for some late night
supper. Ordering room service, he took Marissa up the
back stairs so she wouldn't be seen by anyone at the front
desk. He showed her the bathroom so she could wash up
and brought in the room service cart. He set up the meal
and spiked Marissa's Shirley Temple. He lit candles and
softened the overhead lights.   Sitting down to dinner,
Gene began asking Marissa about her family and school.
She explained about her large family. Because they had
little money, the kids had to pick fruits and vegetables to
sell. Finishing school was okay for the males in the
family. Girls were married off to older men with means.

"So, who have your parents chosen for you to marry?" "I will finish school and become a doctor. I want to open a clinic in my hometown." "This drink tastes funny, Gene." "Maybe it needs to be stirred since all the fruit is on the bottom." Marissa guzzled the drink down, shaking her head. Standing up, she staggered and headed for the restroom. Gene put the cart outside the door and hung the do not disturb sign on the door. Preparing for his conquest, he called out, "Are you okay?" After some gurgling sounds, Marissa answered, "I'm fine. Be out in a few minutes." Realizing that there was more of a kick to her drink than she was aware, Marissa made herself vomit to help with the dizziness. She knew Gene was planning to take advantage of her and maybe even kill her. Thinking hard, she decided that if she acted drunk, he'd figure it wasn't worth it. Stumbling out of the bathroom, "Here, let me help you, Marissa" Gene said, leading her over to the bed. "Are you okay?" "I feel so wobbly." Smiling, Gene said in a hushed voice "Lay back on the bed and rest." While pretending to close her eyes, she watched Gene preen himself in preparation for his attack. Once he had given himself a final look over in the mirror he approached the bed. Cautiously, he climbed up next to her, touching her black, silky hair. He caressed her right cheek. It was warm to the touch. He skin was like porcelain. Unbuttoning the top of her dress, he reached inside to find a set of plum sized breasts heaving to his touch. Smiling, he removed her blouse so he could bask in the glory of her plum sized breasts. An evil smile spread across his lips, smacking with delight as he sucked each of her breasts. His thoughts headed south to the mysterious triangle of pleasure between her thighs.

Removing her shirt ad panties, he smiled in delight hoping to be her first. Caressing her inner folds, he moaned with pleasure. Using his tongue, he opened her like a flower waiting to be plucked Stripping down; he mounted her, shoving his manhood deep inside of her. To his anger, he was not her first. He expected her to at least tell him how good he was. He shook her and demanded that she praise him. She opened her sleepy eyes, looked into his old, wrinkled face and said, "Are you done yet? I'm bored." "You fucking bitch! You're nothing but a filthy whore!" He punched Marissa in the face repeatedly. "How dare you!" Grabbing her face, he covered her nose and mouth with one hand, putting pressure on her face causing her to bleed. He used his other hand to squeeze her neck. The color drained from her face as he let go, knowing that he had taken another life. Thinking fast, he decided to drop her body in a ditch outside of town.

Composing himself, Gene cleaned up any evidence of

Marissa from the room. Carrying her body down the back

stairs, he put her body in the back of the van. He then

went back upstairs to his room. Taking a shower, he

planned to dispose of Marissa's body and head home to

Patsy. He paid his bill and left the hotel. Starting the van,

Gene started talking to the voices in his head. Who did

that little girl think she was? Telling me she was bored!

Women beg for the chance to pleasure me! I fixed her!

She's dead! No one will care about a Mexican whore!

Ten miles out of town, Gene pulled to the side of the road

and rolled Marissa's limp body into the ditch. Speeding

away, Gene again felt invincible! Waiting several

minutes until she knew he was gone, Marissa climbed out

of the ditch sore and bruised. "Shit, for such a "bad man"

he hits like a bitch!" "Now I'll show him which one of us is the bitch!" Traveling four days to get home, Gene was tired and his wallet wasn't as full as he thought it should be "I had fun." Pulling into his driveway, he looked at the house. It was dimly lit, quiet and warm. Quietly opening the door, Gene looked around. Something isn't right here, he thought to himself. Going from room to room, Patsy and Marge were nowhere to be found. Having to bring in his own luggage was a bummer. Throwing his dirty clothes in the washer was his idea of covering his ass. Looking into the fridge, he found his shelf filled with cold beer. Thinking out loud, "She's learning!" Grabbing a beer, he sauntered over to the kitchen table to look through the mail. He should have her disability check. It was, after all the third of the month! Finding the empty envelope, Gene growled, "That's MY money!" At the bottom of the pile of mail, Gene discovered a hearing

notice that was dated the first of the month. Reading the

letter, Gene discovered that Patsy's therapist had

petitioned the court to reinstate her as payee of her

disability checks. "Fuck! Can't leave her alone for a

minute! If she's in charge of her disability checks, the

only way to get her money is to remove her from the

picture!" But, she can't know that I have the insurance

policies! Gene often found comfort in answering the

voices in his head. Hearing the sound of Patsy's car

pulling in the driveway, Gene quickly put the mail back.

Then, putting himself in his recliner, he turned on the

T.V. The sound of laughter came through the open screen

door. Gene reached over and turned on the overhead light.

Hello, ladies. Where were you?" "Oh, we had free passes

for the show at the casino. Then we had a few drinks and

gambled some. I even won $2,500.00 on a slot machine. So, how was your tour, honey?" "Fine. I cut it short to check on you. I was worried about you." "Mom and Dr. Sebastian have been taking good care of me. Dr. Sebastian has taken me off all meds except Zoloft and we have sessions three times a week. I trust Dr. Sebastian. I tell her "everything." Marge piped up, "I was concerned because she's a woman shrink. But she's one smart cookie!" "Well, ladies, I'm exhausted! Good night." When Gene closed the bedroom door, Marge whispered, "He's been through the mail!" "I figured he would be looking for my check." "You can't trust him, Patsy!" "I realize that, but we are safe for the moment." "Did you give the doc copies of everything?' "Yes, Ma, I did." "Doctor Carla Sebastian will be our saving grace. Remember to call her so she knows Gene is home from his tour." "I will. Lock your bedroom door, Ma." "You should sleep in my room" complained Marge. "Look, if I don't sleep in "our" room, Gene will know something's up." "Okay, just be careful, Patsy!" "I will, Ma. Goodnight."   Patsy let the dogs out before bed. Opening the bedroom door to grab her night shirt, she saw Gene. He was snoring and lost in a deep slumber. With a long sigh, Patsy relaxed. She knew Gene was out for the night. Smiling to herself, "Let the games begin!" Patsy finally fell asleep but tossed and turned all night. She had dreams of Gene smiling while strangling her. Is this going to be the way he gets to me? Paranoid delusions? Patsy would not let Gene have the last laugh! She was up at 6:00a.m to make Gene breakfast in bed. Gene gorged himself on pancakes, bacon and eggs. Gene ate quietly while Patsy prepared his bath.   While Gene bathed, Patsy called her doctor's office leaving a desperate message. "He's home!" After doing dishes Patsy asked Gene, "What are your plans for today?" I am going to see the guys and catch up." "What do you want for dinner?" Smiling, Gene said, "One of your stuffed pork chop dinners and apple pie for dessert." "Anything you want, honey. I will start on it after group today." "Group?" "It's a women's group for survivors of abuse." "Okay, I understand" smiled Gene. "Have a good day! Later!" Once he had been gone several minutes, Patsy got ready to head to the meeting. "Mom, if Gene comes home early, call me at Dr. Sebastian's office." With Marge starting Gene's dinner, Patsy was free to head out. Before the meeting started, she met with her doctor. "So, how was it to see Gene?" "Scary because we knew he'd been through the mail. He knows about the hearing to make me payee again. He knows I'm not on any meds but Zoloft and that I am in therapy. "Does he know you found out about the insurance policies?" "No, Doc but I am sure that he is going to hatch a plan to kill me and my mom off." "I have copies of the policies. You're not on any heavy meds, things should be alright. I'm going to introduce you to someone in group. She will be your sponsor, so she will be in contact with you constantly. That should keep Gene off guard. Shall we join the others?" "How do I explain a sponsor?" asked Patsy. "She will be a sober companion to talk to about your feelings of self-worth." "Group, this is Patsy." "Hello, Patsy!" Each member stood up and gave a brief summary of their reasons for being in the group. After listening to their stories, Patsy discovered she wasn't the only one who had survived abuse. Dr. Sebastian introduced Patsy to Patricia Valerie Simpson. Patricia sits Patsy down and recounts her story. "My husband was an abusive drunk. He hid behind his success as a real estate broker to the rich and powerful. He sold houses to Hollywood actors and rock stars. He had Hollywood elites on speed dial. No one knew that he was an abusive prick. If we had to attend an A-list party and I had bruises, he would call in a makeup artist to cover them up for him. Finally, after years of being told "they" could do nothing to help me, I knew I had to protect myself. One night, he had done an eight-ball of coke and downed a bottle of Scotch. He was out of his mind. We had an argument and he attacked me. I defended myself. We wrestled. His gun went off. He died. But not before I lost the vision in my right eye and sustained brain damage, causing a stroke and paralysis on my right side. Hence, the need for my metal legs. So, you see, I do understand how you feel, Patsy. Dr. Carla

Sebastian gave me some background on you. I wanted to

make sure that I was a compatible match as your sponsor.

Here are my rules:

1. You call me twice per day

2. I make surprise home visits. This will keep us

honest

3. If I feel it necessary, I will deal with family

members I feel are toxic to your recovery.

If any of these rules are a problem, say so now. "No,

Patricia." "Good, so let's have your address and phone

number. Here is the number you call for your check-ins.

This is for emergencies. It goes to our legal advocate,

police department and the on-call social worker. We start

tomorrow. If you get scared, call my number. Better safe than dead! Any questions? Good. We will talk. Have a great night!" Patsy hurried home to fix Gene's special dinner. Once home, Patsy explains to her mother about her new sponsor. Marge thought carefully before she spoke. "Honey, Gene won't like this, but I am sure Dr. Sebastian is trying to protect you. Since Patricia does surprise visits, it will keep his behavior above board. Surprise visits and call-ins will make it harder for him to plan to murder us. So, this could be a good thing. Gene's not going to appreciate this." Just then, Gene came slamming through the front door. "How are my two favorite ladies?" "Just as sweet as can be" smiled Patsy. Gene gave each woman a kiss, laced with the scent of beer and Jim Beam. "Wash up, dinner will be ready soon." While Patsy made Gene's plate, they exchanged pleasantries. "So, how was group, Patsy?" "Well, Dr. Sebastian assigned me a sponsor to help me with my recovery. I have call-ins and surprise visits to keep me honest. And elimination of toxic influences." "Sounds like AA to me" smiled Gene. After pie, Gene retired to the front porch. Lighting up a cigar, he pondered what Patsy had just told him. Smiling, he said aloud, "Sounds like good old-fashioned game of cat and mouse. Can I kill them under the sponsor's nose? This should be rather fun! Plans to make" cackled Gene. "Oh boy, he took that news too easy" whispered Patsy. In a low toned voice, Marge said, "I agree. He is up to something." "Yes, he is planning our deaths!" "I don't believe he will stand much of a chance with Patricia! He has met his match. She won't be sweet talked." "I am pleased. We may survive this after all." Hearing the door rattle, Marge announces loudly, "I found a new crochet pattern for a blanket set."

"We need to start projects for the holidays." "I just got

four new craft magazines for us to go through" smiled

Marge. Walking up behind Patsy, Gene slithered his

arms around her ample waist. "How about showing me

how much you missed me?" cackled Gene. "I missed you

too, sweetie." "I will be waiting" he said, heading toward

the bedroom. He flopped down on the bed, remote in

hand. Putting on his favorite Playboy channel and after

some huffing and puffing, Gene was done. He passed

out on the bed before Patsy even arrived. This was a

common pattern. If she waited long enough, he would

entertain himself and fall asleep. Brewing them a cup of

tea, Marge looks into her daughter's tired face. "How

long can you keep him at bay before he demands that you

fulfill your wifely duties?" This was a prelude to him

asking for the money from the casino. "He will want all of it, for some nonsense" whined Patsy. "Give him part of it", replied Marge. "That won't satisfy him, he will demand it all!" "Hide our craft money. Give him the rest." "He hasn't paid bills in two months. I had to cover them. He needs to support his groupies. I refuse!" "

Let's hope he stays mellow." Before Marge realizes it, Patsy is asleep in front of the T.V. Marge covers her baby girl with a blanket and locks up for bed. Patsy wakes to a crash. She ambled toward the bedroom with her mom following close behind her. Patsy pushed the door open, "What are you doing, Gene?" "Looking for my wallet!" "It's right there on our dressing table." "I will start breakfast." "Let your mom do it. I need to speak with you." "What do you need, Gene?" "The band needs some stuff. I need the money from your win at the casino." "I used some of it for our craft projects for Christmas and I paid the bills you conveniently forgot about for two months." "Are you bitching about doing your job?!" "You need more money for your groupies, I suspect!" Knocking Patsy to the floor and grabbing her purse, Gene tore through the purse, ripping the fabric. "Where is it, bitch!?" Patsy finally got to her feet. Heading out the door, she made a dash for the kitchen. Marge hands Gene a cup of coffee which he grabs, throwing the hot liquid in Patsy's face. Screaming in pain, Patsy began to cry. "Well, we wouldn't have to go through this if you gave me the money!" Just as Gene lumbered toward Patsy again, a voice boomed from the living room, "Is there a problem here!?" "Who the fuck are you?" "I am Patricia, Patsy's sponsor." The cloud of anger flew across Gene's face. Composed, he extended his hand. "I'm Gene, Patsy's husband." Shaking his hand, Patricia felt the instant need to bathe with lye soap. "Patricia, this is my mom, Marge." "Pleased to meet you. Looks like coffee is on!" "What do you take in your coffee?" asked Marge. "Milk, sugar and facial skin, please." Gene shot Patsy a glare that could have melted steel. After several sips of coffee under a deafening silence, Gene announced that he was heading for the shower. Once Patricia was certain that Gene was showering, Patricia turned on one heel, marched into the kitchen and asked Patsy, "Are you alright?" "Yes, Patricia." "Good." Smack! "What the hell was that all about?" Meekly, Patsy asked "What do you mean?" "I have been here long enough to know that your husband is a narcissistic sociopath who lives to have women praise him because he is a star. He lives off women because he doesn't feel he should have to work for a living. He is abusive too. Did I miss anything?" asked Patricia. "What caused this row?"

"Well, Patricia, Patsy and I won $2,500.00 at the casino. Gene wants it. Expects Patsy to surrender it" complained Marge. "I see", smiled Patricia. "How much is left?"

"Not sure. We paid the house bills that he never paid and bought craft supplies." "Tell him you put it into a ninety-day CD to earn interest. That will buy you some time. Since you don't lie well, I will take you to the bank to get the CD." "Let's get you ready to go," Patricia says with a soothing tone.   With tears in her eyes, Patsy spoke softly. "He destroyed my favorite purse." "We will find you a new one" cooed Marge. While helping Patsy get ready, Marge decided that she needed to speak with Patricia. Sneaking away, Marge asked Patricia to speak with her alone. "You need to know that Gene took out a life insurance policy since Patsy got her disability back. He has no access to her money, so he will try to get rid of us. If you read the file, you know about the drugs and him having her put in a psychiatric facility. Now that she is straight, she's a threat to his lifestyle." "Thank you for telling me, Marge. I will do what I can to help your daughter." Walking into the kitchen Gene announced "Guess I don't get breakfast this morning!" Marge smiled. "Sit down. I'll have it ready in just a minute." "So, Patricia, what makes you qualified to be a sponsor?" I survived an abusive, merciless psychopath. I am sober and I am here to help other women thrive in their lives." Marge stifled a hearty laugh at Gene. Patsy emerged cleaned up and dressed for a nice day in town. Looking at Patsy, Gene scrunched up his eyebrows. "Dressed awfully nice to clean the house, aren't you?" "I have

therapy and paperwork to fill out at the bank." "Excuse

me!" replied Gene. "Bank?" "Yes, I put the money we

won into ninety-day CD's to earn interest. Patricia is

teaching me about interest bearing CD's." "If you needed

financial advice, you should have discussed it with me"

complained Gene. Cocking her head to one side, Patricia

said, "I understand you're a famous country star." "Yes I

am. Have you heard my music?" "Yes, I have checked

out your music and career. Someone should have given

you financial advice! Apparently you aren't even worthy

of a recording contract or a real tour! You're just a

wannabe country star!" Choking on his coffee, Gene

growled, "Who do you think you are!?" "I'm someone

who's got your number, Gene!" Patsy's face turned an

ashen white while her sponsor went toe-to-toe with her

abusive husband. Marge sat back, enjoying the show.

Gene inhaled deeply, letting it out slowly, and then

announced "I will be speaking with your doctor. Seems

to me you need a different sponsor and better meds." "Be

my guest, Gene. Remember, she chose me to be your

wife's sponsor! I'm good. My record as a sponsor speaks

for itself." Gene stomped toward the door. Patsy called

out after him, "I booked you a great gig for this weekend,

honey!" Once Gene had squealed the tires and splattered

rocks around, Patsy said, "Wow! He is seriously pissed at

you, Patricia. "He will hurt you! "Tell him to bring his

'A- game' He doesn't scare me! We need to get to town.

Go to the bank then head to Dr. Sebastian and advise her

of what has transpired."   After the trip to the bank,

Patsy had her therapy session. Looking more relaxed,

Patricia handed Patsy a gift. Opening it, she broke down

96

in tears. "It looks just like the one that Gene destroyed!"

"Your mom told me where to find it." "Oh, thank you!"

"Patricia, a word? So, how unhinged is he?" "Bad, Doc."

"You are baiting him. Making yourself a target." "If he

blows up at me, he will go to jail and Patsy will be safe."

"Careful. She lives with him. She is alone with him. She

needs to tread lightly. He is not balanced." "He intends to

show up here and demand that you dismiss me. And that

Patsy is put back on heavy drugs." "I will deal with him."

Heading back to Patsy's, Patricia was deep in thought.

"Is something wrong?" asked Patsy. "When is Gene

supposed to play the gig?" "Friday night. Why?" "I think

I should see him in action. What time does he start?" "At

around 9:00 p.m. Why?" asked Patsy. "We are going to

the gig." "He doesn't normally invite Mom and me

unless he's messed up." "We will be attending his gig.

Let's see if he's any kind of entertainer. He needs a

challenge. So, keep cool at home. I need to hear from you

twice a day or the police department will be doing

welfare checks." "Got it. He was going to see my

therapist." "I don't believe he will get very far with her.

You don't need to be medicated. You just need to take

out the trash!" Snickering to herself, Patsy now

understood that she had an ally against Gene. As Patsy

came bounding happily through the front door, Marge

met her with a puzzled look. "So?" "Patricia is on our

side. Now I don't feel so alone." "Good. Gene's home

and he brought a bottle." "Jesus Christ! Here we go again!

Let's start dinner." Walking into Gene's den, Patsy asked

"Rough day?" "Well, that bitch therapist seems to feel

that you don't need meds! Talk therapy is best. She feels

you need a sponsor to keep you from self-medicating.

You're more fun when you drink! Sober, you're a prudish anal retentive, tea toddling bitch!" "I thought I should be 'straight' to do your bookings!" "Any moron can do that job. That's why you can do it!" Crushed to the core, Patsy ran out of the den. Gene took a long pull off the bottle with a smile spreading across his face. Talking out loud, he proclaimed, "YOU need to learn your place, Patsy!" While a tearful Patsy called Patricia for her check-in, Marge headed for the den. She told Gene dinner was ready. Before she could finish her sentence, an empty bottle crashed against the wall above her head. "GET OUT!" screamed Gene. Marge came staggering out of the den covered in glass shards! Patsy took a gasping breath when she saw her mother. "Mom, we should take you to the emergency room. Some of those shards look deeply embedded!" Grabbing her keys and purse, Patsy helped her mom to the car. On the way,

Marge explained that she told Gene dinner was ready.

"He exploded with rage!" Once the emergency room

doctor started removing the glass, his nurse went to the

desk to call the on-call Adult Services worker. In an hour,

both an Adult Protective Services caseworker and a

police officer arrived. Terrified, Patsy called Patricia.

"Please come to the hospital! I need your help." "I will

call Dr. Sebastian to let her know what has transpired."

After a meeting between all parties, Dr. Sebastian

announced that Adult Protective Services would be

opening a case. "The cops will be paying Gene a visit.

It's protocol in situations like this. Where is he?" "At

home, in the den" whined Patsy. The police headed out to

interview Gene. Patricia thought it would be best to

accompany Patsy and Marge home. Fear riddled Patsy's

heart and mind. She knew Gene would kill her for the life insurance money. He attacked her mother, an elderly defenseless woman. He was capable of anything. As the drive home came to a close and with her home coming into view, fear gripped Patsy's heart. As she helped her mom to the front door, Patricia closed in behind her. Lights were flashing and Gene was being led out in handcuffs. He screamed obscenities as he walked past them. She knew it was the alcohol and once his head cleared, he wouldn't remember anything. Or so he said. But a night in jail would chill him out. Patsy tucked Marge into bed with a pain pill. Patricia started to clean up the broken glass in the den. After the kitchen was cleaned up, Patsy and Patricia sat down with a cup of tea to discuss the evening's events. Patricia smiled at Patsy, cupping her hand. "This will be over soon and Gene will get what he deserves." "Not until we are all dead, unfortunately!" "Over my dead body is the ONLY way that will happen!" "You can't protect us full time. Eventually he will get a chance and he will take it." "Your therapist has documented everything and made copies of the life insurance policies. If something happens to either of you, they will know to look at him first!" "With an open Adult Protective Services case, he will be on his best behavior" replied Patricia. "I will spend the night and they will notify us if he is released. So, let's get some sleep. Your therapist did give me a sleeping pill for tonight. I will sleep here on the couch. Take this and get some rest." After a hot bath, Patsy sunk onto the cool sheets of her bed and fell fast asleep. Patricia let Patsy sleep and took care of Marge. Breakfast and meds were her first order of the day. Next on the agenda were several phone calls between Patricia, Dr.

Sebastian and the Adult Protective services caseworker.

Patsy emerged from her bedroom at 11am saying, "I

haven't slept like that in years!" "I understand. Your

threat was out of the house. You felt safe. They will let

him out later this afternoon. But there will be a

Temporary Order of Protection so he will behave. The

case will be open for ninety days, which will be our time

table to get him arrested and you guys safely out of his

reach. After this, you both need group today. You need

support" explained Patricia. "I will go to all gigs with

you. So, does he ever do duets?" "Why?" asked Patsy.

"Well, I think I should join him on stage for a duet"

smiled Patricia. "Any suggestions?" "Ha! 'Jackson' by

Johnny and June Carter Cash." "Guess I need to learn

this song then" cackled Patricia. "What will you do if he

goes after you?" "I can handle myself, but thank you for

your concern." "Did you really kill your husband in self-

defense?" "Yes, the district attorney said it was

a justifiable homicide." "Wow" replied Patsy. "This is

why I volunteer as a sponsor. I give back to women who

are survivors of domestic abuse. This is important to me.

I survived. I want all women to survive!" "I guess you

are one of the good ones. Thank you, Patricia." "Your

mom needs counseling too because this is not your first

time in a relationship with an abusive partner. Her hands

have always been tied, so to speak. She didn't know how

to help you. I will assume her relationships with men

were also tumultuous." "You might say that. Dad was

tough, loud and did not believe in showing affection. He

believed in heavy discipline. Women and children were

property. To be seen and never heard from. She was to

cook, clean and perform her wifely duties without question or complaint." "So, there is a family history of abuse. I believe the group can help your mom as well as you. You can't get better or get past it unless you talk about it. You both need to know as women that you deserve better." It was a strange feeling for Patsy to hear how many times her mother had been mistreated because growing up, women were considered property. Many women were married off because of arrangements between parents. They had no vote or say in anything. According to our own laws, women, children and animals were considered property. You were allowed to beat your wife as long as the instrument used was not wider than his thumb. Children were sold off as slave labor. Child brides were common in rural or poor areas. Now we have more rights. But many police officers still feel that women are asking for it. A husband couldn't

rape his wife because he owned her. And protection for

battered wives is a joke, even today. Group is teaching

me so much, thought Patsy. Anxiety filled her as they

pulled into the driveway. She knew that Gene would be

pissed because he had to spend the night in jail. Walking

through the front door, Patsy and Marge were greeted by

the caseworker from Adult Protective Services and an

investigator handing each of them a copy of the order of

protection. Gene looked at Marge with empathy and

sadness. "Oh Marge! I never meant to hurt you. I thought

this was made-up until I was shown the pictures from the

Emergency Room. You are like my own mother. I love

you! I am truly sorry, Marge, honest!" The caseworker,

Ms. Hanoi looked at the investigator with a nod. "So, you

admit that you did this?" "I must have. God, I am so

sorry! I was really hammered." "I feel you should attend

anger management classes and Alcoholics Anonymous is

also a must" "But, Ms. Hanoi, I am an entertainer. My

band plays in bars!" "Yes, I understand this. But they

serve water and soda, so there is no reason for you to

drink alcohol. This case will be open for ninety days if

you follow my strongly worded advice. We will revisit

the need for an order of protection. Here are the lists of

anger management classes and AA meetings. We will

make home visits as well as schedule office visits for you.

I will check with the facilitators to ensure that you attend

and participate in group. You will also be given random

alcohol and drug tests. Do you have any questions for us,

Gene?" "Do Patsy and Marge get to drink?" "They are

the victims. You are the perpetrator of the abuse."

"Neither of us have a problem with sobriety. We won't

drink if it makes things easier for Gene. And we already attend group therapy, so he shouldn't feel persecuted. "Oh, by the way, Gene you need to report to the Department of Labor for a Job Readiness evaluation." "I do black-topping. That work lasts five months of the year! "You need a real job to cover Marge's hospital bill. You will report at 8 a.m. tomorrow morning. We will need to see proof of how much you made on your last tour, with receipts for hotel and any other expenses. Have a nice day, Gene. Ladies." As Ms. Hanoi headed for her car with the investigator in tow, Gene smiled and waved goodbye. Gene closed the door and exploded. "You had BETTER fix this shit, Patsy! If I have to be sober, I will make your life a living hell!" "So, what else is new?!" squawked Patsy. "Look what you did to Ma!" "Guess she'll know better than to tell me dinner's ready to get me to quit drinking, won't she?" "I'm not sure you're going to be able to convince all these people of your angelic demeanor." "You caused this, Patsy!" "No, Gene, you did by throwing that bottle at Mom. The shards of glass they had to pull out of her! You take zero responsibility for your actions!" "Now I have to stay sober and report to the Employment Service! I won't work some two-bit job! EVER! I do not report to a boss! I am a star! I deserve accolades and applause, not this!" "Take advantage of this, like you do everything else. Get some training on the government's dime." "I guess I could see what they have to offer. Anger management counseling couldn't hurt either." "Mom and I go to group therapy. It's not so bad." "Fine! I have to put up with this shit for ninety days. Then we go back to my way of doing things!" As Patsy left the room, a thought popped into

109

her head. "I might have ninety days to live, but as soon as this case closes, Gene will be hell to deal with." "How are you feeling, Ma?" "Better, Patsy. So, how's Gene taking all of this?" "Not well!" It made for a very quiet evening but the tension was thick enough to cut with a knife. Patsy made her evening check-in with Patricia. As she explained the day's events, Patricia snickered. "King Gene is having a bad day, is he?" "Yes. Ninety days isn't much of a safety net. I'm sure he will try something before then. He has no self-control! Plus, his tour receipts will give an idea of how much money he actually made. It will also give a timeline of where he's been. Call me when he leaves for the employment office in the morning. We are still going to his gig this weekend! It will be fun, I promise" said Patricia. The following morning, Patsy was up early to make Gene a good breakfast for his interview at the unemployment office. Gene started bitching. "I cannot believe I have to do this! I work outdoors blacktopping and paving! Real man's work!" Smiling sweetly, Patsy said, "Don't forget, they want the receipts from your tour. "I still do not understand why they need those." "I would guess Gene that it's to prove that you had gigs and how much you were paid. You know taxes. Plus we get food stamps and such." "Well, you get disability. You're entitled to assistance" griped Gene. "But those checks, you were the representative payee." "I'm not hungry. Those people really piss me off!" "I'm sure you're enjoying my misfortune, aren't you?" "No, Gene! I have just as many things to get done as you do. And now, even Mom has to go to therapy." "I suppose you're right. I just feel so singled out in all of this. I'm heading out. See you later." Gene kisses Patsy on the cheek as he walks out the door. Marge appeared in the kitchen doorway. "Is he gone?" "Yes. Let's have some coffee." "Don't forget your call-in to Patricia." Just then, the phone rang. "Hello?" "Did Gene make his appointment?" "Yes, Patricia. He just left." Good! I will be right over. Make sure coffee's on!" "I will." "Guess she's on her way over?" questioned Marge. "Yes, she is." As Patricia sauntered through the front door, "Hello, ladies!" "So," Patsy looked into Patricia's eyes. "What are they really doing having Gene show up at the unemployment office?" "Well, it seems he is well-known for hooking up with women and committing welfare fraud. He's been in jail for it a few times. He also gets paid in cash while he's on tour. He doesn't pay taxes on his gig money." "Seems to me you're looking at him for being more than just an abusive sleaze bag." "Women

112

have accidents around him." "What do you know, Patricia?" "Seems women have disappeared and were found dead. Gene played gigs in all the same towns." "So, what happened to Ma was a happy accident? A way to get the cops involved in our lives?" Patricia looked deep into Patsy's face. "Look, he tried to have you overdosed on psychotropic drugs, took out a life insurance policy so you could have an accident and he could collect the money! He had himself made your payee so he could collect your disability benefits. He needs to go away!" "You're not going to be here twenty-four hours a day, are you?" "I have check-ins with you and therapy. If you aren't there, the cops will be here. We will help you, but you need to keep your head together." "This case will stay open for ninety days. What happens then? He wants us dead so he can collect the life insurance." "Hopefully

113

this will all be over in ninety days." "He is crazy! Check out his military records." "He just acted that way to get out of his four year bid." "Now about his gigs. Does he have a real band?" "He has friends that he performs with, but on his last tour they only played one or two gigs with him and they came home. He stayed out and finished the tour alone." "How long is a set?" "About two or three hours. Does he ever sing with women?" "He has had female backup singers before." "How would he handle a challenge?" "On stage? He would own the stage. Why?" Patricia was slowly learning what made Gene tick. "Please don't give him a hard time at the gig." "Maybe we will have to perform a duet" cackled Patricia. Gene came slamming through the front door. "Those fucking idiots want me to work in the sewer treatment plant! I'm a country star! I'm an International celebrity. People love me and they want me to shovel shit? They say I owe

Uncle Sam money because I am an independent

contractor who was paid in cash. They want records for

the past seven years. They are looking at my exes

receiving welfare. I need a fucking lawyer! This is all

your fault, Patsy! You could have patched your mom up

here! But no, you HAD to take her to the emergency

room! This shit is all on you!" he hissed lunging at her.

Patricia stepped in between Gene and Patsy. "Hello,

Gene. It sounds like you need to go to a group meeting to

vent all that anger" smiled Patricia. Gene growled, "Get

the hell OUT of my house, bitch!" "I believe its Patsy's

name on the rent receipts, Gene." "Patsy, get rid of her,

NOW!" "She is my sponsor, Gene, I can't make her

leave!" "It's not court ordered, you dense broad! You

don't have to put up with her!" "Oh, what's wrong, Gene?

Am I a woman that you can't intimidate?" Gene turned

and grabbed for the nearest bottle. Patsy looked horrified.

She knew exactly what would happen if he were to drink.

"Remember about your drug and alcohol stuff, Gene." "I

don't care! I'm well over twenty-one years of age! I can

drink if I want to!" Gene took his bottle to the den and

slammed the door. Marge looked into her daughter's

panicked face. With a whispered tone she said, "Patricia

is right. He needs to go away. We will never be safe until

he is in jail or dead!" "Patsy!" bellowed Gene from the

den. "Yes?" "Where are my smokes?" Patsy went to help

Gene find his smokes. "What did you do with my bag?"

"It's where it always is." "Get rid of her or you will be

sorry!" he said, shoving Patsy out the door of then den.

Patricia looked at Patsy asking "Are you okay?" "He

wants you to leave." "The only way I will leave is if you

116

and Marge come with me." "But…" "You will not be

safe here alone." "Okay, I'll tell Gene that we're going to

group." After a heated discussion, Patsy emerged from

the den. Tears were streaming down her face and her

clothes were disheveled. "Do I need to call the cops?"

Patricia questioned. "Just get us out of here, please?"

Marge appeared with purses in hand. As they pulled out

of the driveway, Gene stood in the window. His thoughts

of mayhem were coming to light. Thinking out loud,

Gene starts with 'I need to get my hands on that

insurance money. I need to split and start over. But how

can I make Patsy's death an accident? And now, I have to

get rid of that self-righteous bitch, Patricia! This plan has

to be foolproof! I would love to blow their asses sky high,

but that would draw too much attention to me. A slow

poisoning would be nice for Patsy and Marge. But I want

Patricia to feel to feel every bit of pain I can inflict on her! I need to bide my time and get through this bullshit Adult Services case so they will crawl out of my ass. If I have to pay back the IRS, it will come out of Patsy's disability check! This accident needs to give me access to both Patsy and Marge's money!   While Patricia kept Patsy and Marge at group, Dr. Sebastian held a meeting with two investigators in her office. "As we started our investigation into the disappearance of young girls in rural areas, a parallel to dates that correspond with the gig dates of your client's husband has shown up. The unemployment office gave us information that these gigs were paid in cash.   Also, we know that his band only played with him on two gigs. He did the rest of the tour solo." "What is it that I can answer for you?" asked Dr. Sebastian. "We understand that his wife fears for her safety?" "Well, she recently found a life insurance policy he took out on her without her knowledge. He found a doctor that kept her medicated. He had himself designated as the payee for her disability checks after said doctor painted her as incompetent. While he was on tour, there was a hearing to revoke him as her representative payee." "According to our records, women seem to die under strange circumstances around him." "He seems to fancy himself a country music star of International proportions. All women should be honored to serve him!" "Sounds like this investigation has been open for quite a while." "Yes, Doc. It started with one girl, then others. But it crossed state lines. That's how we got involved." "So, you're F.BI, then?" "Yes, ma'am. I'm George Preston and this is John Thomas. This case landed on our desks today. I see that there is an open

Adult Protective Services case." "Yes, we have a copy of the reports and his requirements to satisfy the caseworkers." "We also understand you've assigned a sponsor to help his wife? Patsy, I believe is her name." "Yes, her sponsor's job is to encourage her to follow the program and stay sober. Many women who are in abusive relationships drink to appease their partners. The partner encourages them to drink with him as a show of submission. If the abused partner is under the influence of drugs or alcohol, the abuser feels they are easier to control and dominate." "So, his history has always leaned toward him being a sociopath?" "Yes, he has all the classic indicators according to the DSM-4." "Is there anything you can tell us that could help?" Looking through her files, Dr. Sebastian said, "Pressure will make him unravel. He needs to be in control. He has a need to be adored. When a female makes him feel inadequate, he will snap. Then try to regain control." "Thank you for your help, Dr. Sebastian." "Make sure you have a solid case because if he gets wind of you, he will disappear." "Good to know. We will be looking into his bandmates to see if they can shed any light on their boss's personality. We will show ourselves out, Doc." "Patricia, may I see you for a moment?" "Yes, Dr. Sebastian." "How's it going with Patsy?" "Gene is angry because unemployment has got him a job at the sewer treatment plant. Seems he's been being paid in cash and not paying taxes. It also exposed little welfare fraud from previous relationships because he's too good to work a regular job. He blames Patsy for all of this. Says if she had treated her mom at home instead of taking her to the emergency room, this would not have happened. And he has a serious hate on me!" "Well, two investigators from the F.B.I. were just here. It seems there is an investigation going on involving missing and dead girls. The F.B.I was brought in because the murders crossed state lines. Each girl was taken from an area where Gene played a gig. It seems like a lot of people die or have accidents when they get involved with Gene." "He's unravelling, Doc." "Careful, Patricia, he may decide you are an obstacle coming between him and the life insurance money. You may be in danger" "Patsy and Marge need me to help them. He doesn't intimidate me. I will not let him hurt either of them. This is what I do!" "I thought you should be apprised of the investigation's happenings." "Doc, he was drinking when we left. Is there any way that he could have to take a surprise piss test?" "If he starts his job, he will have to be tested for many things" smiled Patricia.

"Here, get them some dinner…on me. And make sure he is passed out before you leave them at the house for the night." Patricia headed back to group as it ended. "Ladies, let's go out for some dinner before we take you home."

"But, Gene." "He will be passed out by the time you get home." After a big dinner of pasta, salads, bread and desserts the drive home was long and ominous. The tension was so thick it seemed to take their breath away. Gliding into the driveway and silently walking into the house, they could hear the music blaring through the old wooden speakers. Patsy crept into the den to find Gene passed out in his chair. Quietly she turned off the stereo. Creeping back out of the den, she closed the door. Patricia offered to stay the night, but Patsy assured her things were fine. As she pulled out of the driveway, an uneasy feeling filled her throat with bile. Shaking it off,

Patricia headed home. The house was quiet, but to be safe, both Patsy and Marge locked their bedroom doors. At around 5:00 a.m. Gene started smashing dishes in the kitchen and screaming, "Get out of bed, you bitches!" Marge stumbled from her room, looking at the kitchen clock. "Gene, what are you doing up?" "It's my house! I will do whatever I please. You lazy bitches need to be up making me breakfast and tending to my every need, like a good slave should!" "I'll start the coffee, Gene." "Where is that lazy whore daughter of yours?" "She's asleep. Like you should be." Walking down the hall, Gene pushed on the bedroom door. After a few tries, he realizes that the door is locked. "Get out of bed!" demanded Gene. After punching a dent in the door, Gene shuffled back to the kitchen where Marge had eggs and bacon cooking. The smells filled the air. Patsy used the extension in the bedroom to call Patricia. She answered

on the third ring. Whispering into the phone, Patsy told

Patricia what was happening. "I will be there in ten

minutes!" Hanging up the phone, Patricia made a quick

call to Dr. Sebastian's answering machine then called the

caseworker leaving a message for her as well. Throwing

on jeans and a sweatshirt, Patricia grabbed her keys,

purse, and mace and headed for Patsy's home. When

Patsy smelled breakfast, she dressed in a track suit and

grabbing the dog's leash, she dashed out the back door.

Taking the dog out for a quick walk, she entered through

the front door, slightly winded. Letting the dog off of the

leash, Patsy came into the kitchen. After greeting her

mom, she announced "It smells great in here." Strolling

up behind Patsy, Gene raised his hand to hit Patsy in the

back of the head. Feeling a chill run down her spine,

Patsy spun around to face Gene. "You're up early, Gene." "You had the bedroom door locked!" bellowed Gene. "I wasn't in there. I took the dog out!" "You're lying, bitch!" Patsy put her hand up, "Feel. I've been outside." Even the dog went and cowered under the table. Gene's venom filled words came out slurred. "This bullshit case will be over in ninety days and then you will be a dead whore!" Marge looked at Gene and said, "Your breakfast is ready. Your plate is on the table." Grabbing one of the other made plates and leering at Marge, he sneered, "I will eat yours. In case you decided to poison me!" Scarfing down Marge's breakfast, he then picked up Patsy's plate and threw it on the floor. Smiling, Gene said, "Pigs eat off the floor! Patsy, come get your slop!" Laughing, he grabbed Patsy by the back of her neck, shoving her face to the floor and rubbing her face directly in the food. Patricia announced herself by macing Gene directly in his face. After screaming in agony, he ran into the shower and let the cool water soothe his swollen face. Patricia helped Patsy up from the floor. Marge began cleaning up the mess on the floor. Then the bedroom door slammed shut. After several minutes, the sound of Gene snoring came through the bedroom door. Patricia asked, "Does he do this often?" "He woke up still drunk and started this shit. After some sleep, he won't remember any of it." "Maybe we should get you some pepper spray or a Taser. That was a close call. You need something to protect yourself." "He told me that the case will be over in ninety days and after that, he intends to kill me!" "I think we need to let the caseworker know what happened this morning. He starts work when?" "Monday." "I'm sure they will require bloodwork and a urinalysis." Sure enough, the unemployment office called at 9:00 a.m. for Gene. Opening the bedroom door, Patsy called out,"Gene?" "What do you want?" griped Gene. "The unemployment office is on the phone." "Now? Christ!" As Gene lumbered to the phone, he answered, "Hello?" After a few 'yes's', he hung up. "Looks like I have to report to the doctor's office for a work physical. I start at the sewer treatment plant on Monday. Oh, hey, Patricia. What are you doing here? Why do my eyes hurt?" "Guess you got sprayed in the face with bathroom cleanser." "I guess I should take a shower. Don't forget, I have a gig tonight. You girls should come. Bring Patricia so she can see a real performer in action." "Sounds like fun, Gene. I would love to join Patsy and Marge." Gene ran to get in the shower before his physical. Dressed and ready to face the day, Gene headed out. "Oh, Patsy make

128

sure my shirt and jeans are pressed for tonight. You know the blue plaid shirt. I better get going. Okay, bye!"

"Well, he is going to flunk that urine test," cackled Patricia.'' "For him to wake up and still be drunk, he had to have consumed a hell of a lot of whiskey, Patsy." "He has always been able to drink like that." "Does he have memory loss after a night of heavy drinking?" "Yes, he does Patricia." "It sounds like he needs to detox at an in-patient treatment center." "He will never agree to that. He says it's his right to drink." Waiting until Patsy went to change for group Marge told Patricia everything that happened. She also admitted to being afraid of Gene. "He wants to kill us. He's just waiting for the case to close." "There is more than one case open, Marge. There is also a criminal case open. Trust me, he will get his." "I know you're right, but I'm afraid for Patsy." Patsy emerged dressed in a casual, lavender colored pant suit. "Ma, go get ready." "No, I will stay here and clean up Gene's mess. I will press his outfit for tonight." "You need to come to group, Ma." "No, you go. I could use a nap. 4:30 a.m. was too early." "Suit yourself." While Patsy was in group, Patricia was in a meeting with Dr. Sebastian and the caseworker explaining what had transpired that morning. The caseworker wanted to violate him. "Wait until his test results come back. You can use the results to justify violating him." "At the rate that he is unravelling, he will lose it very soon." "He is volatile. He will hurt someone." "According to the F.B.I. he may have already." "I will be attending his gig tonight to see his great performance. I need to take Patsy home so she can get ready." Arriving home, Patsy was almost running to get things ready for Gene's big night. Pushing the door open, Marge greeted her with a smile. "All is done.

Clothes are pressed. Dinner is on the stove." "What kind

of mood is he in?" whined Patsy. "Pleasant, actually. He

is napping before the gig tonight." "We should get a nap

in for tonight too." "I'm too wired to sleep." "What time

is Patricia picking us up?" "I'm thinking we should drive

ourselves" said Patsy. "I'd say we should get there

around 9:00. His set doesn't start until 10p.m." "What's

wrong, Patsy?" asked Marge. "I noticed an influx of guys

in bad polyester suits with side arms in our town."

"Cops?" asked Marge. "B.C.I. or F.B.I. Not sure, but

they are looking for some clown, psycho." "Probably one

of those city guys shot a cow again thinking it was a deer

because they were drunk." City people, anyways!"

cackled Marge. Turning on the TV, Patsy sat down in the

recliner. With her eyelids fluttering, she fell asleep. An

hour passed before Patsy heard "You guys are getting too old to party with the Master." It was followed by a hearty laugh. Patsy got to her feet to warm up Gene's dinner. As she walked into the kitchen, she saw Marge was already serving up Gene's plate. "Thanks, Ma." "You needed the rest, dear." "Are you ladies coming with me?" "No, we are driving ourselves." "No Patricia?" "She is going to meet us there." "Great! I will have them reserve a table for you." "Thank you, Gene." "Where's my suit?" Marge croaked, "It's hanging up on the door in the den so it would stay wrinkle free." "Good girls!" "Don't you mean slaves?" "No" smiled Gene. "Slaves were freed. I own the two of you. I got a two- for-one special!" "Gene, you're terrible!" "Ma, that's why you love me. Because I'm a "bad boy!" Slapping Patsy's ass, Gene headed to get dressed. "He is incorrigible!" cried Patsy. "He was

132

never like this when we first dated." "They never show their true colors until they know you're hooked. If your therapist is correct, Gene shows all the signs of being a Narcissistic Sociopath." "All doctors always think they know everything!" "But in Gene's case, she is correct. Remember his behavior this morning?" "He was still drunk." "That's an excuse, Patsy! You are co-dependent." "Oh? So now you're an expert, huh Ma?" "No, I am the one to blame for this. Because I never stood up for myself! I allowed myself to be treated like I was unworthy of love! We will get through this" cooed Marge. "No, we won't! He intends to kill us! You heard him. He's just waiting for the Adult Services case to close!" "Go get ready, I'll do up the dishes." Patsy headed to her room, closing the door behind her. Patricia walked quietly into the kitchen and placed her hand lightly on Marge's shoulder. Startled, Marge yelled, "Damn! You scared me, Patricia!" "I heard your conversation with Patsy." "She still feels the need to protect him. All he wants is the money from the insurance policies. He only cares about whatever is most beneficial for him!" exclaimed Marge. "That is common for people who are in relationships with sociopaths who have narcissistic features." "This morning's behavior has become the norm, Patricia. I have no idea how to help my daughter. Plus, he informed her that he is waiting for the case to close in ninety days and then he's going to kill her. He is getting more nonchalant about what he does! He feels he's invincible, beyond reproach and untouchable!" "I see" nodded Patricia. Patsy entered the kitchen, greeting Patricia. "Hi!" "Ma, go get dressed." "I need to finish these dishes up." "Later, Ma." "I'll be right back" Marge sighed heavily. "Okay, we should head out soon. We can drive and you can follow us." "No, I will drive" demanded Patricia. "Why?" "It is my job to make sure you follow protocol when you go to a place that serves alcohol! You're doing well with the program. A slip can set you back. "Boy, you take your job as a sponsor seriously!" Laughing, Patricia answered "Yes I do!" Marge joined in. "Are we ready?" "Yes, I believe so." "Patricia is driving?" asked Marge. "Yes, apparently she takes her job as a sponsor seriously." "Let's roll!" "What's the name of this place?" "The Pines, it's kind of a redneck bar." "Oh, this should be fun!" cackled Patricia. Pulling into a filled parking lot, a cold and clammy shiver traveled down Patsy's spine. She knew things could get bad in a hurry. As they approached the door, they were greeted by Bulldog, the bouncer. "Good evening, Miss

Patsy, Miss Marge." "Hello, Bulldog. This is our guest,

Patricia." "Hello, Miss Patricia." "Good evening,

Bulldog." "Your usual table is reserved down front."

Patsy led the ladies to their table. Removing the

"Reserved" sign, they took their seats. Chatty Kathy

came over to take their drink orders. "Oh, Gene didn't tell

us you were coming, Patsy." "Well, who else would he

reserve a table for, Kathy?" "What are you drinking

tonight? Your usual?" "No, we'll have three club sodas

with lemon." "Oh? Back on your medication again?" "I

don't need drugs, I'm naturally happy" smiled Patsy.

Shaking her head, Kathy headed back to the bar. Patricia

assessed where all the exits are. She checked out the

stage. She was secure. She knew how things would work.

After some light chatting, Gene's band took the stage.

The music started playing and Gene walked on singing

"Blue Suede Shoes". His cover was passable. The band started playing some sad ballads that Gene had written. It was music to slice your wrists by. Depressing! People started to boo and threw their drinks at him. Gene was obviously frustrated and began to yell into the microphone. Patsy jumped up and ran for the stage to try and help soothe the situation. "How about a little sing along with your fans tonight?" "Not bad, Patsy!" Gene patted her head. Patsy took the microphone and announced "Gene and the band invite anyone from the audience to come up and join them for a live duet!" As a few brave souls took the stage to sing with Gene, he delighted in showing his musical prowess. No one showed any true talent. Until Gene met his match. Gene had been sipping on several drinks since he arrived. Gene asked "Is there anyone else out there up for the challenge?" Smiling, Patricia said "I'm ready, Gene!"

Taking the stage, Patricia looked at the band and said

"Jackson". Frank snickered as they started to play. The

song had been a duet between Johnny and June Carter

Cash. As Gene began to sing, he took center stage.

Patricia took the microphone and blew Gene off the stage

with her performance. She was a professional! The

audience was clapping and singing along. When they

finished the duet, the audience screamed for more. Gene

was unbelievably pissed off. But she livened up his show.

After five more songs, Patricia waved at the audience and

walked off the stage and joined Patsy and Marge at the

table. "Now I need a large glass of water!" Gene

announced that he was taking a break and joined the

ladies at the table. "Well, aren't you going to thank me

for saving your ass, Gene? I deserve a cut of your pay for

tonight" smiled Patricia. "I don't think so!" growled Gene. "Can we leave?" asked Patsy. "We didn't get much sleep last night." "No problem." Patsy and Marge were already outside when Gene grabbed Patricia by the arm. "You made me look bad on purpose!" "Let go, Gene!" Patricia started to walk away. Gene came up behind her, grabbing for her shoulder. Patricia elbowed Gene in the face, breaking his nose. Blood splattered everywhere. Turning around, Patricia said, "You don't scare me, Gene! You're nothing but an abusive prick!" She walked away, flipping her hair over her right shoulder and joining the ladies for the ride home. Packing his nose in ice to help with the swelling, the band decided to end the show early. Gene immediately headed for the bar to drown his wounded ego. Frank looked at Gene with a smile. "Hey, check it out! We had a video recorded!" As Gene watched the camcorder video, his face turned blood red! "Erase this shit!" "You guys played well together. Maybe we need to hire a female singer!" Frank teased. "Fuck off! I don't need a chick to sing with me!" He refused to pay his band, saying that they hadn't earned it. "Look, we took the stage and played. You're just pissed that a woman showed you up! Go back to your solo act! We don't need your abuse, Gene!" Frank left the bar, livid. Gene stayed at the bar through closing time. Then he left with Chatty Kathy for some more partying. While Patsy was taking the dog out, Patricia called Dr. Sebastian to leave a message about the night's events. Surprised that the doctor answered, Patricia explained how she handled Gene. "He will start to unravel because of the pressure Social Services is putting on him. You just emasculated him in public. He will likely take that rage out on Patsy and Marge. She may need protection from the police." "I feel he will come after me first. I figure he will wait for the Adult Services case to close. Hopefully the criminal investigation will dig up something that will send him to jail!"

Checking on Patsy and Marge before leaving, Patricia headed home. She warned Patsy to lock herself in the bedroom. Gene would be angry when he came home. Patsy stayed up as late as she could, but soon fell asleep. As the sun crept through the bedroom window, the whimpering of the dog stirred Patsy from her sleep. She threw on her bath robe and slippers as she put the dog on his leash to take him out for a walk. Coming in, she started a fire on the stove. Putting on the coffee, she noticed how eerily quiet the house was. Looking outside,

Patsy noticed that Gene's car wasn't parked in its usual spot. "I guess he didn't come home last night. Patricia must have really pissed him off.!" Marge came out of her room, yawning. "Coffee ready yet?" "Just about, Ma." "What's so interesting outside?" "Looks like Gene never came home last night." "Oh, he probably went home with Chatty Kathy. You know what kind of girl she is. Her reputation precedes her as white trash. Seems that's the way Gene likes them when his ego is bruised." "I'm not sure what Patricia did to him, but it had to be a hum dinger. And if she did it at the bar in front of other people, he is going to hurt her, no two ways about it." "I hope she really understands what Gene is capable of." Sitting down to coffee, Marge asked, "What would you like for breakfast? Toast? Maybe an egg? "Are you okay?" "Just concerned that Patricia stirred up trouble with Gene."

Just then, the phone rang. It was the probation office calling for Gene. They needed him to come in for a random drug and alcohol screening. "He never came home last night, Sir." "Do you know where he is?" "I have no idea. There was a problem with Gene and my sponsor, Patricia. Whatever happened, he didn't come home last night." "Please have him contact the police department. They can get in touch with me. I'm on-call this weekend." "Oh, I will tell him whenever he shows up." After Patsy had cleaned up the house, Gene decided to come sliding in around noon. Patsy opened her mouth to tell him about the morning's events. He put his hand up to silence her. "Look, I need a nap before the gig tonight. So, talking to you is not high up on my list of priorities." "Gene, your probation officer called!" "Shit! What did he want?" "You need to call the police station. He's on call.

143

They want you to do a piss test." "It's the weekend. They can't make me. I'm going to bed!" "But, Gene!" "Shut up, bitch! Wake me up at 5 p.m." he demanded slamming the bedroom door.Shaking her head, Patsy looked into her mother's eyes. "Jesus, he is going to end up in jail." "He obviously doesn't care. Let him do what he wants." "He doesn't listen!" cried Patsy. "At least you tried to tell him so that he didn't get in more trouble. So, do we have our grocery list ready?" "Yes" sighed Marge. "We'll go to town and let him sleep off his hangover." Grocery shopping took up a significant part of the day. Checking in with Patricia as usual, Patsy confided about the phone call and Gene's refusal to return their call. Patricia nodded with a smile. "He's just sore about what happened last night. Once he sobers up, what you told him will register. I promise. It will be okay." When Patricia hung up with Patsy, she called the on-call caseworker. As Patsy pulled into the driveway, she saw flashing lights and Gene being led out in handcuffs. Patsy ran up to the officer. "Where are you taking him?" "For his surprise urinalysis. Then, to answer for his non-compliance in an Adult Services case. This may take a while, ma'am." "I will call, Patsy. Bring my clothes for tonight's gig. Be near the phone when I call, okay?" Marge looked at her daughter and said, "He may miss his gig." Hauling bags into the house, Patsy heard a knock on the screen door. "Hello! I see they brought Gene in!" cackled Patricia. "Did you call and tell them he was home in bed?" "I just let them know he had made it home. They contacted the on-call probation officer and he chose to have him brought in. As long as Gene cooperates, he should be out in time for his gig." "Why is he so angry with you?" "He thought he could treat me the way he treats all women. Needless to say, I refused to accept that treatment." "You didn't hit him, did you?" Laughing, Patricia said, "Here, let me show you." Patricia put everyone in their respective places and demonstrated how she broke Gene's nose. "Jesus Christ, Patricia! Do you want him to kill you? And us too?" "He only beats up women that are dumb enough not to stand up for themselves. He treats women like toys that he can dispose of when he is bored with them! If you were half a real woman, you would kill him before he kills you! I got away with self-defense. So can you! Gene saw me at the police station. He knows I have no fear of him, so he won't mess with me." Rolling her eyes, Patsy knew in her heart that Patricia would have an accident at Gene's hands. She didn't understand just how unstable he was. Gene called and demanded that

Patsy bring him his gig attire. "That judge took every

cent I had to get out on bond for my gig! That bitch

Patricia is going to pay for this! I guarantee it!" Hanging

up the phone, Patsy knew life at home would be hell.

Gene would blame all of this on her for sure. As Gene

was getting dressed for his gig, the wheels started turning

in his head about how to get rid of Patricia. Once she's

gone, killing off Patsy and Marge will be a snap. "Now to

arrange a special send-off for Patricia!" cackled Gene. He

relaxed with a few drinks before his set started. The band

took the stage, opening with a few covers before Gene

started singing his ballads. Fortunately, he went back to

taking cover requests. Surprisingly, Gene headed home

when his gig was over. Patsy glanced toward the front

door sleepily. She was surprised to see Gene standing

there. "You're home earlier than normal for a Saturday

night." "Well, I thought we could have a little "quiet"

time." "Gene, are you asking for a little?" "You catch on

fast, darling!" Grabbing Patsy's hand, Gene led her to the

bedroom. Gene being romantic and sweet was a surprise.

Still not trusting Gene, Patsy waited until he was snoring

before she drifted off to sleep. The morning after glow

was grand. Gene was in such a great mood, he made

breakfast for Patsy and Marge. Marge looked at Patsy

quizzically and asked, "Did he hit his head? Is that why

he's being nice?" "I don't believe so" smiled Patsy. Gene

helped with the lawn, went walking with Patsy and the

dog through the woods holding hands. As much as Patsy

was enjoying her time with Gene, in the back of her mind

all she could do was wonder when he was going to turn

back into a jerk. On the walk home, Patsy started to let

her guard down a little bit. Walking through the door, the

smell of biscuits filled the air. Marge had an early dinner waiting.

I need to be up by 5:00 a.m." "Wow, you're taking your new job seriously"

 cracked Patsy. "I might as well put forth my best effort." "It's surprising you're willing to try." "I'm not giving up my gigs! I have star potential! I'm internationally known, after all. I have sold records all over the world. Besides, all the greats had a day job. It keeps us humble." Laughing heartily, Patsy retorted, "You? Humble? I thought your ego equaled your talent?!" "So true, so true" smiled Gene. Heading to bed after watching the news, Gene gave Patsy a kiss on top of her head. While Patsy and Marge played a few hands of Gin Rummy, Gene started planning how he would get rid of Patricia. Thoughts swirled through his head as he fell asleep.

Marge gave her daughter a knowing look. "You know Gene's being too nice, right?" "Of course I do, Ma. Is it wrong of me to enjoy things while he is being nice?" "I understand how much you need tenderness from Gene, but he will kill you without a second thought. He won't even shed a tear while he murders us. You also know that to get to us, he will get rid of Patricia. Do you think she knows that she has a target on her back?" "Patricia?" laughed Patsy "Would kill a dozen men if they got in her way. I feel she can handle any situation." "Think he's asleep yet?" "I think I heard him snoring." "I need to get his dinner pail ready." Laughing, Marge said "I beat ya to it!" "Great! Thanks, Ma!" Slipping into her nightgown, Patsy crept quietly into bed while Gene snored softly in rhythm. Patsy fell asleep, relaxed for the moment. The loud ringing of an old-fashioned alarm clock woke Patsy, but Gene was still sleeping. She placed her hand gently on his shoulder. "Wake up, Gene." His left hand made contact with her chest. "Shit! That hurt." "Huh? What?" "You hit me in your sleep." "Oh man, I'm sorry." "Come on, you have your first day of work today. I'll start your breakfast." "Thanks honey." After twenty minutes in the shower, Gene emerged fresh for the day. He gobbled down his breakfast. "Here's your dinner pail." "I should be home by 5:00 p.m." "Dinner will be ready." "I'm sure I will need a bath ready for me. I'm sure I will stink pretty badly by the end of the day." After Gene left, Patsy tried to go back to bed, but she couldn't sleep. Sitting down with a cup of coffee, she flipped on the morning news. Same stuff, different day. Just as Patsy went for her second cup of coffee, Marge grunted a good morning. After refilling her cup, Patsy took a seat at the kitchen table. Marge spoke softly. "What is going on for today?"

"Group and a trip to the store. We need lunch stuff for Gene's dinner pail." While Patsy and Marge made plans for the day, Investigators Preston and Thomas were discussing the leads that were bringing in answers about the deaths of young girls that crossed state lines. "Looking at this board, it seems that in every place where a girl disappeared, Gene's band played a gig or he performed solo. Now we need to connect him directly to each of the disappearances. Let's start with his best buddy, Frank Snider. I think we should invite him in for a little chat." "Okay, where does this douche bag work?" "I believe he collects disability benefits. Or his wife does." "Where do we find this Prince Charming?" "His favorite hangout is a local dive bar where he plays guitar requests for cash. In other words, he begs when he isn't playing gigs for cash. His wife supports him with her disability checks." "Dirt bags stick together. Shall we introduce ourselves?" Laughing, Preston says, "Let's go scare the shit out of this scum bag!" Opening the bar door, the stench of stale beer and nasty crotch assaulted their senses. Looking around the room, they saw the morning crowd. All were calling in excuses to their employers. The bartender looked up. "Kitchen's not open yet, boys. Got a pot of coffee going though." "Sounds good. We're looking for Frank" The bartender pointed to a disheveled man on the bandstand. "Hello, Frank. We'd like to have a chat with you." "Time is money" cracked Frank, pointing to his tip jar. Smiling, Preston and Thomas flashed their badges. "Shit! What do you guys want? "Well, we'd like to have a chat with you. So, either here or down at the station. Your choice." "Fine, let's do this. Jess, I will be back in a few." Grabbing his guitar, he followed the

investigators to their car. "So, what's this all about,

guys?" "Well, it seems that Gene's band has played gigs

in each town where a girl has disappeared." "That's

convenient, blaming us." "We aren't blaming anyone, but

we are trying to find out who killed those girls. The

murders crossed state lines and coincide with the dates

that Gene played gigs in their towns. So, we need a

timeline from you as to when the band went back home

and Gene continued to play solo gigs." "Not sure I

remember much of that tour." Looking into Frank's eyes,

the cops told him they knew he was involved. "I have no

idea what Gene did after we left." "You were seen at the

first hotel Gene stayed at. On the same night a young girl

disappeared. Look, we know you were at the hotel."

"Maybe we should detain you for a few days. See if it

jogs your memory. Plus, everyone at the bar knows you left with us. Just think it over, Frank. We'll be back in a while. Just a thought, but a phone call to the Social Security office could put a kink in your wife supporting you. You think about that while we're gone." "I need to call my lawyer!" yelled Frank. "You can't afford a free lawyer, and you're not even under arrest! But someone will bring you a phone at some point!" Laughing, Preston and Thomas left the room. Frank's head was spinning.

Going back to the bullpen, Thomas said, "I have an idea. Let's make a phone call to get the exact hotel and gig they played before the band went home. One small push and this guy will fold. Let's see how hard we can push him. He asked for a lawyer! He can't even afford a free one!" "We tell him that in exchange for his testimony, he gets a walk. We just want Gene." "Let Frank sweat a while. He'll sing. He doesn't handle pressure well. Give him a phone." "Let's check the tapes and see if we can physically place him at the gig and the hotel." "They say a picture is worth a thousand words. Let's see if a few pictures can help Frank tell his story." "Let's have a look." Leaving a phone in the interrogation room for Frank, the officer waited behind the glass. Calling Gertie, Frank hypothetically explained that he was being questioned. "I need a lawyer!" "We can't afford a lawyer, Frank. " "Call Legal Aid, the public defender's office. Anyone will do! Now, please? All this bullshit is over Gene. Christ, I'll go to prison because he's a king-sized asshole!" "Don't say anything until I get you a lawyer. Then I will call Patsy to see if she knows what's going on." After the conversation with Gertie, Patsy started to realize what would happen when Gene got wind of this.

156

"He will go into a rage!" yelled Patsy. "This may be what they need to finally put him away. Then we will be safe."

"There is no way he will let any of us survive. Gene will tie up all loose ends. That includes Frank and Patricia.""Should we warn her? We will tell her at the group meeting today."Frank was rejoined by Preston and Thomas. "So, did you make the call to your lawyer? It doesn't seem like you're much of a priority in his or her view. So, let's play a bit of show and tell, shall we?" "We have been viewing some lovely video tapes. Guess who's starring in them? You, Gene and what looks to be a very underage girl. Gene checked in and brought her up the back stairway. Then we see you come in approximately six hours later. Gene signs the guest register the next morning. There is no sign of the young lady." "This young girl was reported missing by her family the

157

following day. She was found days later. Dead. Now, fill in the blanks, Frank!" "I'm waiting for my lawyer!" "Okay. We know the band quit traveling with Gene right after her disappearance. You and the band returned home. Gene went on, solo for the rest of the tour. And, in every place where Gene played a solo gig, a young girl went missing." "See what we're getting at Frank?" "Look, if you can tell us what happened, we can protect you." Laughing hard, Frank looked at them and shook his head. "Accidents happen. Guess I should call my lawyer again. Charge me with something or let me go!" "Sure, we'll give you a ride back to the bar." "No thanks. I'll walk. Cops are bad for my reputation." "We will talk again soon, Frank." As he headed for the front entrance, he walked right into his wife and his lawyer. "Oh, hone! Are you okay?" "I'm fine." "This is your lawyer, Justin

Alexander Esquire." "We should talk at my office, Frank. I will join you in a minute." Walking into the bullpen, he bellowed, "Where do I find Preston and Thomas?" "Right here!" "I am Justin Alexander. I represent Frank Snider. NEVER speak to my client without me being present. Understood, gentlemen?" "Yes, we understand." "I want a copy of the tapes I know you have from talking to my client. He wasn't under arrest. You took him out of his gig at the bar for questioning." Slamming the door, Preston and Thomas looked at each other, breaking into smiles. "We've got him worried." Preston cackled, "A few more visits from us and he'll sing." Frank explained what the investigators had said, including about the tape from the hotel. "Sounds like I need to do some investigating. Remember, I represent you, so anything you tell me is confidential. If there is anything I need to know about this, you need to tell me now." Frank looked

uncomfortable with his wife present. "Let me check into

this hotel tape. Then we'll make an appointment for you

to come to my office alone." "Thanks." Gertie drove

Frank home. "So, what did Patsy say?" "Gene doesn't

know he's being investigated. Not a clue." "It's best not to

mention it to him until it's necessary. His Adult

Protective Services case has put him in a tailspin." "What

happened when you were out there on tour?" "Gene was

just himself." "WHAT do they have, Frank!?"

"Nothing." "Bullshit! What did that dirt bag pull this

time?" "Seems a few girls went missing around the time

of the tour." "Is that why you and the guys came home

early?" "They were young girls, from what the cops said.

Young girls that were found dead." "They are trying to

connect Gene to them." "Frank, I don't care if he is your

friend. If you know anything, have your lawyer get you a deal. I need you." "Look, I don't want to go to jail either!" "Don't take the blame for him. He always convinces you to cover for him." After group, Patsy asked to meet Patricia in Dr. Sebastian's office. With Marge by her side, Patsy explained about the phone call from Gertie. "From what she said, Frank was questioned about missing girls. This will push Gene over the edge. No one will be safe from his wrath." The tears running down her face showed that Patsy was truly in fear for herself, her friends and her family. "Why would you believe he is capable of murder?" "A previous wife died because of a medical issue. Her family believes that he was abusing her, which caused an aneurysm. There are many questions about his past. It looks like we need to check into Gene's past relationships. Let's see what skeletons he's got in his closet." Patricia patted Patsy's hand. "I will protect you. He will never hurt you guys again!" Feeling relieved, Patsy and Marge headed home. Pulling in the driveway, Patsy notices a pile of clothes on the porch. With furrowed eyebrows, Patsy and Marge looked at each other. "Gene's home early." Walking up to the porch, the stench from his clothes was enough to gag a corpse. Stepping into the living room, Patsy began calling out,"Gene!" Walking though the kitchen, she followed a trail of underwear and socks. Fresh steam from the shower proved that he had been there recently. Clothes were strewn from the closet across the floor. Patsy found a scrawled note: Needed a beer. Be home around dinner time. While Patsy picked up the clothes and started the wash, Marge started dinner. Gene walked into his favorite watering hole. "Hey, how was your first day of work?" "Smelly" laughed Gene. "So, what's been going on?" "This morning, two cops hauled Frank outta here with his guitar." "What did "stupid" do this time?" "Not sure, but he didn't come back. He must have fucked up real good." As Gene tossed back several beers, his mind tossed over what the cops could want with Frank. Recalling all his adventures on the road, he reminded himself of how careful he had been. Frank has nothing he can tie me to. It must have been too many parking tickets. Or Gertie bounced checks again. I better head home before the old lady complains to her crazy ass sponsor again. Driving home, Gene got a nagging feeling that he should call on his old buddy, Frank. Strolling through the front door, he announced "Honey, I'm home! Where's dinner?" Marge peeked around the corner as she set the table. "Where's Patsy?" "Trying to get that horrid smell out of your clothes, Gene." "Yeah, I start a new job

tomorrow. Hopefully it will be better." Patsy wiped

sweat from her brow as she walked into the kitchen. "Oh,

Gene. I didn't hear you come in." "Ma said that you were

trying to get the stink out of my clothes. Guess they'll be

my work clothes now, huh?" "The machine stinks, so I

had to do a load of wash with baking soda." "New job

tomorrow. Maybe not as smelly." While she served

dinner, Marge asked about Gene's first day of work. He

talked about some hazing by co-workers but said it

wasn't too hard in the work department. "So, I heard from

the guys at the bar that Frank was hauled off by two

cops." "Yeah, Gertie called, hysterical looking for a

lawyer for him. He wasn't arrested so it couldn't have

been that bad." "He probably forgot to pay some fines or

parking tickets" cackled Gene. The whole time, his mind

was racing to cover anything they might ask him about.

Frank would not dare to say anything about me. He

would be in just as much trouble, thought Gene. In the

eyes of the law, he is just as guilty. Plus, he

worships/fears me. I own him! This brought a smile to

Gene's face. Feeling confident, he watched the news and

slipped into a relaxed sleep in his favorite recliner. Patsy

covered him with his velour Elvis blanket and heard his

rhythmic snoring. She packed his lunch and placed his

work clothes on the table so he could find them easily in

the morning. Slipping into her favorite flannel nightgown,

Patsy joined her mother and they watched T.V. in

Marge's bedroom. "So, what's he hiding, Patsy?" "I'm not

sure, but I think it happened during his last tour. " "Is he

capable of murder?" asked Marge. "If a woman insulted

or challenged his manhood and he was intoxicated, yes!"

165

"Let's invite Gertie over for coffee and muffins so we can gauge what the fallout will be." "Is it possible he could be a serial killer and we didn't know?" asked Marge. Shrugging her shoulders, Patsy let the tears flow. "God, I hope not. I better get to bed. I have to make breakfast before he leaves for work" sighed Patsy. Patsy tossed and turned while horrific dreams danced in her head. Girls dying, with Gene standing over them cooing 'I deserve this! All of your admiration and accolades!' Sitting up in a cold sweat, Patsy saw a silhouette standing in the corner. Gene was watching silently. He knew that she knew too much about him. She would have to go. But first, a special gift for that sponsor of hers. Something she would never forget. Seeing the shadow, Patsy screamed. Gene laughed, "Did I scare you, sweetheart?" "Hell yes!" "I'm sorry. Were you having nightmares?"

"I'm up. Get dressed while I make your breakfast."

Seeing Patsy in such distress brought Gene a feeling of

satisfaction. I will enjoy watching the life drain from her

face. But first, I need to chat with Frank. Meanwhile, at

Frank's house, Gertie was begging him. "Please tell your

lawyer to get you a fucking deal! Because if you don't, I

will be a widow!" The ringing of the phone distracted

Frank for a few minutes. "Hello? Yes, I can come to the

office at 8:00 a.m. Sharp. Thank you." Gertie looked into

her husband's eyes. "I will assume that means you have a

meeting with your lawyer. It being this early isn't a good

thing, Frank." "I better get going then." The phone rang

and Gertie answered. "Hello?" "Hey, come on over for

some muffins and coffee. Gene went to work. I have

been worried about you since you called yesterday." "I

might as well. Frank's lawyer just called saying he needs

to be at his office by 8:00 a.m." This can't be good, Patsy!" "Just calm down. Come over. We'll talk about it over coffee." "I'll be over in twenty minutes. Bye." Marge came up behind Patsy. "Refill?" Yes, thanks, Ma." "Muffins will be done in about ten minutes." "Gertie sounds stressed. Frank got a call from his lawyer to be there now. It doesn't sound good. I better get dressed." "I'll go take the muffins out of the oven." A loud slam startled Marge from staring out the kitchen window. "Where's the coffee?" "Gertie, you're all flushed." "Patsy, I am so worried! I haven't heard from Frank." "So, what happened?" "Well, Frank had a gig set up in the bar, as normal and he was taking requests. Two cops from some big F.B.I office came in. They told Frank they needed to ask him a few questions. But they made a public spectacle out of taking him out to their car. They grilled him and threatened him. It's obvious that

something happened during the last tour. They are

looking into Gene." "What the hell could those foolish

boys have gotten into?" "While they were gone, Gene

took out a life insurance policy on me. That's why he

kept me medicated. To be control me and my money. He

got a surprise when he came home to find out there had

been a hearing and I was deemed mentally fit enough to

be my own payee." "Could he have hurt someone in a bar

fight and killed them?" "Gertie, I have no idea. But the

Adult Protective Services investigation pissed him off

royally. That's how Ma got hurt. They made him show

proof of all his gigs and hotel receipts. Then they made

him go to work in the sewage treatment plant. Sent him

to counseling and submit to random drug and alcohol

tests. I started attending group therapy. They assigned me

a sponsor, which sent Gene over the edge." Meanwhile, Frank was getting an earful. This wasn't a scare tactic. "Frank, I have seen the hotel security tape. They know that you showed up after Gene had been alone in his room for hours with that underage girl. Look, I can get them to cut you a deal. All you have to do is testify against Gene. No jail time. But you have to tell me the truth!" Frank's hands began to shake and the color drained from his weathered face. "Get it in writing. I have to protect Gertie." "Let me see what I can arrange. You start writing down what happened." After making a few phone calls, Justin returned. "We have a meeting with the District Attorney in one hour. Let's see what you've got here." After reading several pages, Justin Alexander looked into Frank's eyes. "This man deserves to be on death row. He is a sociopath with narcissistic features. The District Attorney will give you whatever you want. He just wants to put this sicko away." "I have to protect Gertie. She can't survive without me there to take care of her." "I understand. From what I have learned, there is a string of girls that have gone missing. They have all been found dead a few days later. Each girl is from a town where Gene performed a solo gig." "So, they're thinking that Gene killed all these girls?" "It's looking that way. If you're done with your statement, I will give it to y secretary for her to type up." An attractive woman arrived with coffee. She took Frank's written statement to be typed up. "Just relax and enjoy your coffee. The meeting with the District Attorney should go smoothly." "How long until it goes to trial?" "Once they have enough evidence, they will convene a Grand Jury to determine if there is enough evidence to proceed to trial." "So, when do I testify?" "You will give the Grand Jury your testimony. Then, if they feel that there is enough evidence, they will start preparing for trial. You will be prepped for trial. You will give your testimony. You will be cross-examined by the defense attorneys. Then, after closing arguments a jury will decide if Gene is guilty or innocent." "Will they arrest Gene?" "Yes, but I'm sure his lawyer will try for bail. He's not likely to get it, but they will try." "I have to admit I'm afraid of Gene. I'm also afraid for Gertie." "This will all be discussed with the District Attorney. We'll go in my car. The driver is also there to protect me." "Seriously?" "Yes, sometimes it can get a little dicey with certain clients." Riding in the Lexus, Frank had cold chills climbing up his back. His hands were clammy. As they pulled up to the County Courthouse where the District Attorney's office was, Frank started to feel physically ill. Justin Alexander looked into Frank's face. "As your lawyer, it is my job to protect your interests. They need your testimony, so they are willing to give you what you need." Running up the stairs and walking into those cold marble hallways chilled Frank to his core. Waking into the bustling office, Frank took a seat. He looked almost timid. Pitiful.Smiling, assistant District Attorney Davis Spinney extended his hand to Frank. As they shook hands, he led Frank and Justin to his office. I believe you have already met investigators Preston and Thomas." Looking horrified, Frank glanced at Justin. "What the hell?" "The investigators want to discuss your statement." "I thought you had a deal for me!" Mr. Spinney looked at Frank. With a calm tone, he said "Yes, you do. I know you're concerned about your disabled wife." "Yes, sir." "I'm sure Mr. Alexander has explained your obligations in this agreement." "Yes, he did. "Let's go over your statement. Gene called you to come to the hotel?" "Yes, when I got there, I found this girl. She was unresponsive. Gene said it was an accident. Rough sex." "So, what did he ask of you?""He wanted my help with getting rid of the body. After I took care of that, the band came home. Gene continued on tour solo." Can you tell us if these gigs are in the towns that he performed in?" Reviewing the list, Frank agreed that it looked right. The investigators spread out pictures of the underage girls that were found dead. "Seems like your boy Gene is a psychopath." Frank gasped at the pictures of those young girls. Tears streamed down his face. "My God, I had no idea he could do anything like this! This means.... That the first girl was no accident!" Putting a hand on his shoulder, Justin consoled Frank. "You had no idea what he was capable of." "We will let you know when the Grand Jury is set to convene." "What do I do now?" asked Frank. "Go home. Relax. Nothing has changed. Go about your business." "We will be gathering more evidence. Your lawyer will notify you when we need you." Frank was dropped off to pick up his car and return home. The drive back was agonizing. He knew he couldn't lie to Gertie or Gene. 'I just need to avoid Gene' After Gertie left, Patsy and Marge compared views on how much trouble Gene could be in. Patsy was so lost in her thoughts and the events of the day; she forgot to make her daily call-in to Patricia. Dr. Carla Sebastian took a phone call from investigator Thomas. "We have enough evidence to present to a Grand Jury. We will be making a trip out West to gather more physical evidence.

175

Padding our hand" "How long before they arrest Gene?"

"Soon. Keep your client calm." As Patricia listened to Dr.

Sebastian's end of the conversation, she knew that the

clock was counting down on Gene's fate. Hanging up, Dr.

Sebastian gave Patricia a knowing nod. "Have you heard

from Patsy today?" "No, neither Patsy nor her mother

was at group today." "Drop by and check on them. Once

Gene gets wind of the cops asking questions, his

timetable for killing them will be shortened." Pulling into

Patsy's driveway, Patricia sees a soft light coming from

the kitchen. Then she noticed that Gene's van was parked

in the furthest corner of the driveway. Patricia ran up the

porch steps. As she knocked on the front door, it started

to open. Reaching for her pepper spray, she called out."

Patsy? Marge? Where is everybody?" Making her way to

the kitchen, she felt the pots on the stove. They were hot.

"Is someone here?" Patsy came bustling out of the laundry room. "Where were you? I called out for you and Marge." "Oh, sorry, Patricia. I was trying to get the God awful stench out of Gene's work clothes." "Where were you ladies today? No call-in and you didn't show up for group." "Oh, Gertie stopped by and visited with us for a while. She's upset because of those investigators questioning Frank. She's afraid of losing him. He takes care of her." "Is everyone okay?" "Yes, Patricia." "Where is Gene?" "At his favorite watering hole." "Do not forget to call in, or I will ask the cops to do a welfare check." "Got you. I will call in, I promise." "Where's Marge?" "Taking the clothes off the line." Looking out the back door, Patricia watched Marge struggle to pick up the laundry basket. Patricia just watched silently. Preston and Thomas picked up their plane tickets and flight itineraries from their boss. "We need to build a concrete timeline that connects Gene to the missing girls." "Hopefully other hotels have footage of Gene with these underage girls. Maybe a staff member saw them together." "We need to convene a Grand Jury as soon as possible. No mistakes. We need to lock this man away forever. Remember, he has been doing this for a long time. He is smart and calculating. Our only chance to catch him off guard is to make him feel trapped. Then he will go after Patsy and Marge." "People have accidents around this guy. Usually women. He always gets a financial incentive from these accidents. If there's anything out there, we'll find it. Later, Boss!" "Good speech. Do you actually believe that we'll find what he needs?" "Yes. Idiots like Gene never clean up after themselves." "So, what's the plan?" Preston squinted his eyes, furrowing his brow. "According to the paperwork, he made a state-to-state tour. Here is a list of where he played gigs and which hotels he stayed at. This should give us a basic timeline. We can ask around. With the arrogant attitude he has, someone had to notice something." "Let's try to sleep on the plane. We need to hit the ground running." "Boss is going to want progress reports. How many went missing and were found dead?" "Several." "Well, he's not attractive, so how does he lure these girls?" "They want fame, fortune and money!" "No, it's more than that. He is a sociopath with narcissistic features. He needs praise and accolades. What would send him so far over the edge that he would kill a girl?" Laughing out loud, Thomas said, "I got it! How about if she laughed at how small his Johnson is?" "That might push him over the edge." "Sounds like we have something to go on." "I'd bet lots of people have accidents around him. Let's see how many ex- wives he has that are still alive." "According to the psychiatrist, he had the current wife all doped up so he could be the payee of her disability checks. He even took out life insurance on her. He was setting her up for an accident and a huge payday for himself. Her mom found out about it and told the shrink. The shrink assigned her a sponsor to keep an eye on them." "Think Gene knows we're on to him?" "After we hauled Frank out of the bar, I'm sure he knows we're nosing around." "Think he'll try anything yet?" "I think he will observe and listen to what's being said in town." Once they had boarded the plane, the pilot came over the loudspeaker, welcoming the passengers. Flight attendants asked them if they needed anything. "Yes, pillows please!" As Preston drifted off to sleep,

Thomas started thumbing through the case file, reading the autopsy reports. With a soft whistle, Thomas thought to himself "What a sick and twisted son-of-a-bitch." Putting away the file, he too drifted off to sleep. An announcement came over the PA system. "We are starting our descent. Welcome to Arizona." Shaking his head, Thomas looked out the window to see the airport coming closer into view. "Wake up, Preston. We are in Arizona." "Damn, it seems like I just closed my eyes" The flashing seat belt sign told them it was time to buckle up. The plane came to a halt. As passengers stood up and reached into their overhead compartments, people filled the aisles in a hurried rush to depart the plane. After a stop at baggage claim and the rental car area, Preston and Thomas headed for the Arizona police station as a courtesy to let them know that they had arrived. With each state that had reported a missing girl when Gene played a gig in their town, the stories seemed almost identical. Gene flirted with the local girls.He always zeroed in on the youngest, most vulnerable ones. The desperate ones who wanted to be a star, even if it meant sleeping their way to the top. He would buy them drinks or dinner. They would wait for him to pack up and no one would hear from them again. "According to front desk clerks, he registered alone. He never brought anyone to his room through the front lobby." "Smart boy!" "Guess he never thought about there being cameras in those back stairwells." "So, he WAS seen leading underage girls to his room?" "Now, what happens to set him off once he gets the girls to his room? And how does he move the bodies without being seen?" "They must seriously piss him off" piped up Thomas. "He strangles them. That's extremely personal." "Do any of these rooms have cameras?" "No, sir. That's an invasion of privacy." "True. But it could have saved one of these young girls." "Being alive supersedes privacy. Narcissists need people to tell them how great and special they are. Whenever someone insults or humiliates them, they become unhinged." "So it could be something as small as "where is it?" making fun of his Johnson." "Telling him his singing sucked. Just about anything could set him off" laughed Preston. Thomas had a thought. "He chooses these young girls because of their lack of experience. They have nothing to compare his sex to." "He can't handle a real woman who is immune to his charms. Or someone with more talent than he has." "Yeah, I heard about his wife's sponsor showing him up during one of his gigs. Apparently, Gene did not appreciate Patricia showing him up. Then, he tried to intimidate her and she broke his nose." "Bet he loved that" cracked Preston. "You must remember Patricia Simpson. She killed her husband in self -defense after years of abuse." "And she got off?" "Oh, yeah! She won a big victory for abuse victims and their rights." "No wonder they assigned her to Patsy, Gene's wife." After four days of driving from state to state looking for clues, they arrived at the last place Gene had played a gig. Pueblo was a small town, just far enough away from the bigger cities to draw in a few hopefuls. Preston and Thomas walked into a bar/restaurant that catered to wannabe country stars and cowboys. They had a menu that served BBQ, cornbread, nachos, chili and other favorites. Sitting at the bar, they were given a drink menu. "What will you "boys" have?" "Whatever is on tap. And the House Special chili." "So, why are you boys really here? The polyester suits gave you away." "You're a smart man. We are here investigating the disappearances and murders of young girls." "Really?" "Yes. It seems that whenever this man plays a gig in a small town, girls go missing. Then we find them dead. Preston showed the server a mugshot from Gene's last arrest. "Hey, I know him! Gene played here a few months ago. He wasn't very good by my standards. But he got a decent reception from the patrons." "Was he talking to a certain girl? Well?" Preston slipped a fifty dollar bill under his beer glass and ordered another. "Yeah. He tried picking up our local "good" girl. Marissa. She is going to school and wants to be a doctor." "Where can we find her?" He pointed to the kitchen with his thumb. There, filling orders was a young, dark-haired beauty. "Hey, Rissa, come here." "What do you need?

 The place is starting to fill up." "Casey is on tonight. She can cover your tables. These are Investigators Preston and Thomas. They're asking questions about when Gene played here a few months ago." Preston showed Marissa the pictures of the dead/ missing girls. "These girls went with Gene to his hotel room and never came back." "So did I. When he dumped me, he thought I was dead."

"What happened?" "He chatted me up. We talked about my schooling and me wanting to be a doctor. He dosed my drink with something. I got sick. He expected me to sleep with him and to tell him how great he was. He bounced my head off; I think it was a wall. Did what he wanted and dumped me a few miles outside of town. He left me in a ditch. He thought I was dead!" "You are the only one to survive. We need your testimony." "He hits like a bitch!" laughed Marissa. "I will give you a written statement, but I will only testify if you arrest him." "Our boss will have you testify in front of a Grand Jury. They will decide if there's enough evidence to go to trial." "Let us call our boss." After placing his call using an antiquated phone booth, Preston came back. He was beaming. "You will testify. Then we will hide you away until the trial." "No. I need to be here. My family depends on the money I bring in." "We will only keep you long enough for you to testify before the Grand Jury. Then you can come back here until the trial." "He can't know I survived. He will hurt my family." "No one will know about you until the trial." "My parents are counting on me becoming a doctor. The whole town took up a collection to help with my education. I earned a full ride to Harvard medical school. I have a 4.0 grade point average. My undergraduate schooling has been covered too. I cannot let this town and its people down. I am all they have." "We will make all the necessary arrangements to protect you. Is there anything else about Gene's behavior that we should know about?" Thinking for a minute, Marissa cocked her head to one side and let out a long sigh. "He talked to himself. Answered himself. He said it was a privilege to be with him. Like he was a God or something. I guess "are you done yet" was not the response that he expected." "Okay, so he killed you because HE sucked in bed?" "Yeah. You need a microscope to locate it!" "Okay, thank you for your cantor." Trying to hold in his laughter, Thomas asked if there was anything else about Gene that they needed to be aware of. "The talking to and answering himself was pretty creepy. He also talked about himself in the third person." "Would it be alright if I arranged for us to meet at the Notary's office for you to give your statement?" "How about at our police department at 10 a.m. Tomorrow morning?" "That will be fine."Walking back to the car, Preston looked at Thomas. "If he's nuts, they will put him in a padded cell. Not death row where he belongs." "Let's leave that decision to the shrinks." "Well, between the timeline, Frank and Marissa, Gene will be toast." "Unless he decides to tie up loose ends. Then he will kill anyone who gets in his way." "This will be tricky to pull off before Gene gets wind of it." "Let's hit the rack. I'll call Spinney so he knows what we've found." They headed back home on an afternoon flight. "This will be a snap. If we can keep Gene from killing everyone!" "If he kills any more people, I say we just shoot him and do the world a favor." "The boss wouldn't appreciate that" cracked Preston. "No, but it would save the taxpayers some money." "True" Thomas retorted. "But then we'd be the ones under investigation." "I cannot believe that we found this girl. Seems that Gene has left a trail of bodies." "I'm sure he will leave more if he gets a whiff that we are on to him." "Shouldn't Frank be in protective custody?" "No! It would tip Gene off. If he thinks that Frank said anything, he's a dead man!" "Narcissists like him would kill any and every one to protect themselves." "But seriously, he killed girls because they didn't praise his sexual prowess?" "He needs that in order to function. "Tell me how great I am as a musician and a man! Marissa is very lucky she is still alive. He is one seriously twisted fuck! Imagine a whole town depending on you to come back and be the town doctor. That's some serious pressure!" "No doubt" said Thomas. "How long will it take to get this trial going?" "For the Grand Jury, the ducks have to be in a row in order to arrest Gene." "Think he'll get bail?" "Depends." "On what?" "How many murders we can connect him to." "Spinney has a good reputation as a prosecutor." "Think Gene will end up on death row?" Preston cocked his head and scratched his nose. "His lawyer will plead insanity. They will claim he has a mental defect." "So, what can they do?" "They will put him in a hospital for the criminally insane." "Why?" asked Thomas. Remember in our interview we were told that he has conversations with himself and answers himself. He's not all there in the head!" "So, he's gonna get away with all of this and only serve easy time?" "Probably." "Makes our job mute." "Exactly." "So why do we do this damn job!" screamed Thomas. "For the victims. So they can have closure and maybe some justice, with the help of a decent jury." "Well, it seems like a crapshoot to me!" "That's why if the District Attorney does his job right, the jury will do theirs." "A good defense attorney can poke holes in our case. But in the end, it will be the judge and jury who hold the keys to Gene's fate in their hands." "We will have to make another trip out here to get our star witness for the Grand Jury. Then we'll have to hide her until trial. So keep a bag packed." "I'm looking forward to the Grand Jury indicting Gene!" "It's a long flight home. Get some sleep!" A soft pillow and a dark plane was a comfort. The storm began to brew. Gene had a gnawing feeling in the back of his mind that Frank had betrayed him. "This is getting too close for comfort. I need to cut all my losses and get away clean. But I need to issue some pain on my way out of town. Now, to put my thoughts into action." Gene looked at his watch and thought, 'group should be over soon. I will call Patricia." After several rings, Gene heard a raspy "Hello?" "Patricia? This is Gene, Patsy's husband." "Yes. Gene. I remember you. What can I do for you?" "I have some concerns about Patsy. I think she may be relapsing. Frank and Gertie have noticed Patsy acting erratically. I thought maybe it was just a rough patch in her therapy. I have a gig Saturday night. Frank and the guys will be performing with me. Could you come? Frank can explain to you what he's witnessed. They have really good barbeque." After a blanket of silence, Patricia agreed to the meeting out of concern for Patsy. Hanging up, Patricia then placed a call to Dr. Sebastian. "Have you noticed Patsy acting erratically?" "No. She may be tired at times, but nothing unusual." "I see." "What's going on?" "Gene called. Said his pal Frank noticed a change in Patsy's behavior. He wants to meet and talk after his gig Saturday night." "He is coming after you! Frank was detained for questioning. Gene is tying up loose ends!" "I have this handled, Doc! Later!" Patricia started planning how to survive the meeting."I will need my portable Mace. Make sure people know where I will be. Maybe I should bring a friend. Many different scenarios cruised through Patricia's mind. Survival mode kicked in. If he's tying up loose ends, he must think the cops have a case against him. I should find out what they have on him that makes him this nervous. I hope they crucify that son-of-a-bitch! More thoughts raced through Patricia's mind. I heard they were sending investigators to the areas he played during his tour. I wonder what they found. I need

to relax so I can get some sleep! I'm too jazzed right now.
TV time, I guess. After several sitcoms, Patricia dozed
off in the chair. She awoke to the obnoxious ringing of
her doorbell. She pushed her sweaty, matted hair off her
forehead as she opened the door. A beat cop handed her
an envelope. "Thanks" she said as she slammed the door
in his face. She ripped open the envelope, reading quietly.
Well, I have been summoned to the District Attorney's
office. Smug little prick. I guess my buddy Gene is under
investigation. Maybe they have enough to arrest him and
that's why he wants to meet. Guess I need to go get
dolled up for this meeting with the District Attorney.
After a cup of coffee, Patricia checked the clock. Patsy
hadn't called to check in. "That's not normal for her. I'd
better call her." After several rings, a groggy "Hello?"
came through the phone line. "Are you okay?" Patsy said

that she had the flu and that she had been sick for a few days. "Have you been taking over-the-counter medication?" "Yes, why?" "Be warned. Gene called me saying he was concerned about your behavior. Did he pick up medicine for you?" "No, Gertie did. Why?" "Gene is up to his old tricks. I will stop by to check on you after my meeting. How is Marge feeling? ""She has been taking care of me. But it looks like she may be getting sick too." "I will pick you up some wonton soup. It cures everything. I swear by it", laughed Patricia. "Could you pick up a few double packs of cold medicine? We are completely out. I am so lethargic." "Don't worry. I'll stop by as soon as my meeting's over." Hanging up, Patricia began to go over everything she had been told by Gene and Patsy. She drove to the District Attorney's office. Storming through the lobby, Patricia walked into the office. "Mr. Spinney is in a meeting" said the receptionist as Patricia shoved the summons at her. "Yeah, well, this paper says I'm part of that meeting!" "Just a moment, please?" Patricia walked past the reception area and pushed her way into Spinney's office. "Just in time, Patricia!" "Why was I summoned here?" "You were assigned as a sponsor for Patsy, correct?" "Yes." "We have had her husband, Gene under investigation. Between the witnesses and a perfectly corresponding timeline, it looks as if while Gene was on tour, several young girls disappeared and later turned up dead." "So, he's a serial killer? Well, since we're on the subject, he has asked me to meet him after his gig on Saturday. Seems he and Frank are concerned about Patsy's behavior." "Sounds like he's getting suspicious." "I spoke to his wife earlier. She has the flu, but I think he's putting additives in her over-the-counter medicine. I'm heading over there after this meeting." "We have enough evidence to convene a Grand Jury. We can connect him to the murders and there is a surviving witness." "So, it will be a slam dunk?" "Once he starts to unravel, it will happen quickly, Patricia. He will start tying up any loose ends. I'm sure he will start thinking if he gets rid of Frank, Gertie, you, Patsy, Marge and the psychiatrist that we won't have a case. So, be vigilant. Protect yourself. You should probably advise Patsy and Marge to keep their guard up. Once we convene the Grand Jury we can arrest and charge him. We're pretty sure he knows that we brought Frank in for questioning. So, he's very likely to be in survival mode. Do not go to the meeting without backup, Patricia. He is dangerous! The Grand Jury is set for next Thursday. Once the indictment comes down, we can keep him in jail." "Okay, I will talk to Patsy and Marge." "You may want to tell Dr. Sebastian about this." ""She's already been briefed. I'm heading to check up on Patsy." "Tell her and Marge not to ingest anything he gives them!" "Got you, Boss!" "May I use your phone?" "By all means." After placing an order for two pints of wonton soup, Patricia said,"I need to pick up some cold medicine from the pharmacy and a few other supplies. I think he is dosing their flu medicine. So I'm hoping they might have one dose left that I can have analyzed." "Have it brought to my investigators. They will put a rush on it." "Deal!" As she headed out, Patricia had many thoughts running through her mind. "That fucking prick is trying to poison them!" Calling Dr. Sebastian, Patricia gave her the lowdown. "Is there a doctor who will do a house call?" "Let me see if I can find one." "Let me see if I can figure out what he is

mixing in their flu meds." After a quick phone call to the

pharmacy, Dr. Sebastian was told that Gene had

purchased Flu medicine tea mix and charged it to Patsy's

account. "Okay, what could Gene have dissolved in her

Flu medicine tea?" "What did she say she was feeling?"

"Lethargic. All she wants to do is sleep. And Marge is

getting sick too." "Give her soup and orange juice. No

more of that tea. I will call her house so you can report

how she is doing. I will call an ambulance if necessary."

"I am on my way to pick up soup and juice." Patricia was

apprehensive and very concerned about what she would

find when she arrived at Patsy's. Knocking on the door

and getting no answer only amplified her fear. Turning

the handle, Patricia discovered that the door was

unlocked. As she entered the living room, she noticed

that there were no lights on. Calling out for Patsy and

Marge, the silence was deafening. Turning on the kitchen

light, Patricia headed for the back bedrooms. A dim light

shone through the side of the door. Opening the door,

Patricia rushed over to the bed to check Patsy's pulse.

Then she checked Marge's pulse. Calling the ambulance,

Patricia reported that both women had labored breathing.

Patricia grabbed a cup that contained Flu medicine tea.

Once the ambulance had arrived, paramedics assessed

both women. They attached oxygen masks and started

intravenous fluids. Then both women were transported to

the local hospital. After calling Dr. Sebastian and telling

her to meet her at the hospital, Patricia scoured the house

looking for whatever Gene may have used to poison

Patsy and Marge. Not finding anything obvious, her only

hope was to have the leftover tea analyzed for toxicity.

Arriving at the hospital, Patricia asked at the desk about Patsy and Marge. "They have both been admitted to the Intensive Care Unit."" "Where is their doctor? I need to speak with him. I found this cup of tea on their bedside table. It needs to be analyzed for toxins." "Okay, let me see if I can find the doctor that is treating them." Pacing back and forth, Patricia was afraid that she was too late. "Ma'am, are you the one who came in with the ambulance?" "Yes, I am." "Dr. Sebastian explained to me what your concerns are. So we will have the lab run tests. ""Will they be okay?" "The fluids are to rehydrate them. We are concerned about Marge. With her advanced age, the flu virus and whatever toxin this is, she may not survive. It's touch and go. Time will tell." "Can I see Patsy?" "Just for a few minutes." Patricia looked at Patsy's ashen face. Patsy opened her eyes. "I'm sorry."

She squeezed Patricia's hand and passed out again.

Patricia felt a heavy, crushing feeling in her chest. "Fuck! I should have gotten there sooner!" Dr. Carla Sebastian looked into Patricia's tear-stained face. "This is not your fault." "Dr. Sebastian, I know you're trying to help, but this one is on me!" "No, this is on Gene. We know he did this. But until the lab finishes running tests, all we can do is pray. Let's go to the cafeteria for some coffee. I have my pager on, so we will know if anything changes." "I knew on the drive over there that something wasn't right. I should have called the ambulance before I left." "No, you followed the proper procedure." "I bet you Gene is out drinking beer somewhere. Gloating. He should be getting out of work right about now." "So, maybe the cops should show up to let him know that Patsy and Marge are here." "He will play the part of the concerned

203

husband and son-in-law." "We need to know what he gave them before he shows up here. He cannot have access to them or he will finish the job!" "Well, I think we should notify Spinney at the District Attorney's office. He will send Preston and Thomas here to ensure that Patsy and Marge are safe." As they finished their coffee and Danish, Dr. Sebastian's pager went off. "The lab tests are back. Now we have an answer. Someone got his hands on some homeopathic Belladonna/Nightshade. It can be used to treat earaches and can also be used as a sedative. Two berries can kill a child. Ten to twenty can kill an adult. Health food stores sell the homeopathic version. If it's used over a prolonged period of time, like arsenic it can be fatal. But when combined with the flu medicine, it kept them sedated. The pills are sweet and dissolve almost instantly." "We have given them both the antidote. It will take time to see if it's effective."

Scratching her head, Patricia asked," Where would

someone find this stuff?" "Health food stores, the internet,

stores that sell herbs for practicing magic." "So, the

investigators can arrest him for attempted murder now?"

cried Patricia. "It's a touchy line because homeopathic

medicines are not illegal to use. He would have a valid

excuse if he said they used alternative medicines." "So,

we can't protect them?" "We have to wait until they are

awake to ask them if they gave consent for Gene to give

them that medication. Go home and get some rest. It can

take up to twenty-four hours before we see any results."

Anger and frustration showed across Patricia's face.

Preston and Thomas exchanged knowing smiles. "I

would bet he used the same stuff on the other girls. It

sedated them just enough for Gene to gain the upper

hand." "We will need to ask Frank and our surprise witness a few more questions. This gives us a new lead!" Calling in a security detail for the Intensive Care Unit, Preston and Thomas headed back to brief Spinney on the new developments. With the lab results in hand, Preston filled Spinney in. "Okay, Preston, you talk to Frank. Thomas, you need to go back to Arizona and talk to Marissa!" "Can I call her first, to see if I need to make the trip?" "Make the call." "Preston, you head over to Frank's See what he knows about Gene's preference for alternative medicines." "Will do. Chinese in an hour?" "Circle your choices on the menu. I will call in for delivery when Preston is on his way back." Dr. Sebastian headed back to her office with Patricia. Once inside, with the shades drawn, she pulled a bottle of Jack Daniel's and two glasses from her desk. She poured three fingers of whiskey into each glass. As they started to relax, the phone rang. "Hello?" "Where the hell is my wife and my mother-in-law? What kind of shit are you bitches pulling now?!" "Gene?" "Yes! You know damn well who this is!" "Okay, you should probably sit down." "What's happened now?" "Patricia went over to your house to bring them soup and orange juice. When she got there, they were barely breathing. She called an ambulance. They are both in the Intensive Care Unit at the hospital. We were sent home. You can see them in the morning, or after work." "Thank you for letting me know they are in the hospital." Hanging up, Gene started pacing around the house. Just then, Gene thought 'oh, shit' as he ran to the back bedroom looking for the flu tea. "Shit! The cup is missing. I bet that nosy bitch took it to the hospital. She will be sorry she ever met me. I will enjoy making

207

her death a painful one. Frank will beg me for forgiveness before I kill him! He reached into his pocket and pulled out his bottle of Belladonna. He headed to the cellar; gloving up to check on the Nightshade he had drying. He checked his other herbs and flowers. This will be my best batch yet." "Now to plan Patricia's death. She is not going to willingly eat or drink anything I give her at the gig. So I need to get into the kitchen to give them a "helping hand" with the barbeque. This plan needs to be foolproof. I need to convince Frank he owes me so that he will help with Patricia. Then he will meet his maker. When he doesn't come home, Gertie will call me. Then, I will take care of her. Patsy and Marge will die from complications of the flu. I'll collect the life insurance money and skip town. After asking Frank a few questions, Preston learned that Gene had been "teaching himself about herbs and flowers that can heighten awareness and can be used to control people. He needed to have absolute control of everything and everyone. No one was worthy of his love. Women are only there to support and take care of him financially and spiritually. He has to feel like he can control you to your soul. That's why he couldn't make things work with the band. I was even asked to look into the death of his wife, Agatha. Her family believes that his abuse is what caused her aneurysm." "Will do, Frank. Thanks for the help. Keep cool and don't go anywhere alone with Gene." "Got you. Should I send Gertie out of town?" "No, not yet. We don't want to tip him off. Keep everything as normal as possible." "Okay, I'll try. When is the Grand Jury?" "Thursday. Just a week away." "Okay, later." As he left, Preston had an uneasy feeling. God, I hope he's okay with this." Sitting down in the District Attorney's office chowing down on Chinese food, Preston gave everyone the lowdown on Gene and his interest in alternative medicine. "He's a twisted prick" cracked Thomas. "What did our star witness have to say, Thomas?" "She said that there was a sweet taste to the drink he gave her. She had blurred vision and a headache. She made herself vomit in case he had slipped something in her drink. In truth, that's probably the only reason she survived." "How in the hell has this been going on for so long and no one noticed?" asked Spinney. Going back over his notes, he said "Oh, yeah, Frank says we should look into Gene's past. Seems there are some questionable circumstances in his wife Agatha's death. Her family says he was abusive and caused her aneurysm. She died when it burst. But after a call and a chat with the pretty girl in Records, she is going to have the files overnighted to us. The kicker here

is he also abused his kids. He is quite a dirt bag." "It

sounds like we may have more leads coming at us!" "If it

comes to it, I will send you to interview them." "Is it

possible he's been torturing his family and killing girls?"

Thomas looked at Preston questioningly. "If he didn't get

the love and adoration he felt entitled to, he would

become abusive to get the attention he craved." "So, if

you didn't kiss his ass, he treated you like dirt?" asked

Thomas. "Basically, yes." "So that's why he could never

handle a real job. He needs to have complete control?"

"Yes... you're learning fast, Thomas!" "Wow, he's a real

psycho!" "Close. He's a narcissist with sociopath

tendencies." "The shrinks will have a field day with

him." "He needs the accolades from being an entertainer.

Even though his talent is less than minimal, he feels that

211

he is Elvis. His self-image is grossly exaggerated. He can appear very generous and caring, but it's all an act. His true colors always come through. He just got sloppy. He thinks he's invincible and nothing can touch him." "So, Spinney, think he'll try to use the 'crazy' defense?" "When we interviewed witnesses, they said he talked in the third person and became enraged when people didn't give him the accolades he thought he deserved. He makes people feel guilty, even when he is the problem." "Guess I need a crash course on narcissism." "We will have to guard both Patsy and Marge. He will try to finish them off.Patricia couldn't sleep. A few more drinks? No. A shower? No. A hot bath to relax. "I need to be at the hospital early." Drawing a hot bath, Patricia lowered herself into the bubbles. Closing her eyes, she drifted off to sleep. She awoke just as her head went underwater.

She pushed herself up, spitting out cold water. "Shit! I must have fallen asleep. Damn!" Pulling herself out of the tub, Patricia dragged herself to bed. She dropped onto the bed, rolled into the covers and fell asleep again. Waking up after a bad dream, Patricia ambled toward the kitchen. "God, I need caffeine!" Hitting the brew button, she headed for her closet and dressed in corduroys and a plaid shirt. Looking in the mirror, she noticed bigger crow's feet and a few more gray hairs. "I need a vacation!" she thought out loud. She stood in front of her coffee maker, silently willing it to brew faster. Pouring a large cup of coffee, Patricia inhaled deeply and took a large drink. "Oh, yes. This is better!" After her second cup, she started to feel fully functional. Then the damn phone started ringing. "Hello?" "We were told to call you when there was a change in either of the women you

213

came in with." "Yes, what is it?" "Patsy has woken up and is asking for you." "I will be there shortly." Shutting off the coffee maker, grabbed her keys and headed out the door. As she drove slowly past the sewage treatment plant, Patricia spotted Gene's truck. Relaxing a bit, she drove on to the hospital. Heading directly for the Intensive Care Unit, Patricia put on her best smile. "Hello, sleepy head" chirped Patricia. "I heard you found us." "Yes. I showed up with Wonton soup and orange juice and you were barely breathing. Do you use alternative medicine?" "No. My doctor says it can cause problems with my regular meds. Why?" "Your Flu medicine tea was laced with Belladonna/Nightshade. That's why you were non-functional. Who made the tea?" "Gene did before he left for work. He made some for Ma too because she said she was feeling sick. Ma hasn't woken up yet and I'm scared, Patricia!" "I will check on her for you." "I was truly looking forward to the soup." "Maybe I can bring you some." Patricia left the room to check on Marge and ran into her doctor. He was shaking his head. Patricia could tell the news wasn't good. "Doctor, how is Marge?" "Are you the one who brought Marge and her daughter in last night?" "Yes sir." "Patsy seems to be doing better, but I'm afraid her mother may not survive. If we had known about the toxin sooner, we might have been able to do more for her. Does she have any other family members we should contact?" "Gene is Patsy's husband. He will be coming after work." "According to her medical insurance policy, if there is no hope for recovery, we ask family for consent to discontinue life support." "What about Patsy?" "She has been sedated. She did not take the news well. We contacted Dr.

Sebastian to come and speak with Patsy. "So, Gene gets to make the decision whether or not to keep her on life support?" "Yes, ma'am. Is there any reason why he shouldn't make the decision?" "Just the life insurance policies he has on Patsy and Marge." "We will call Investigator Preston.Once Dr. Sebastian and Investigator Preston arrived, Patricia explained what she had been told by the doctor. "Of course Gene will agree to terminate life support. He wants the money from the life insurance policy! He succeeded in killing off one of them. Who's next? I will assume it's either Patsy or I." "We are looking into the death of one of his previous wives and the mistreatment of his children. This guy has always been an abusive piece of shit." "So, he could have killed before?" Dr. Sebastian became alarmed at how much danger Patsy and Patricia could actually be in! "We will keep you apprised of whatever we find." "You should tell Investigator Preston about your meeting with Gene this weekend." "No. If the cops are sniffing around, he won't follow through with his plans. Right now, we need to concern ourselves with how Patsy is doing." Dr. Sebastian and Patricia checked on Patsy who was still asleep. "I am going to run and get her the soup I promised her. She will need to keep her strength up." Walking outside, Patricia looked into Preston's face. "Is there any way to keep the life insurance policy from paying out?" Preston nodded. "I'm sure they will request an autopsy. That can take a week or more. He didn't receive a payout for Agatha's death. We are still looking into that." Preston whispered, "I firmly believe that Gene is a serial killer. Those girls were done in too easily. He's got experience under his belt!" Patricia returned in fifteen minutes. "Here's your soup. Just like I promised." After a few sips, Patsy started to weep. "I can't kill my mother!" "Discontinuing life support is a hard decision, but your mom will not be in any pain." Patricia did her best to comfort Patsy. Dr. Sebastian listened intently to her through bouts of heavy weeping. Walking through the Intensive Care Unit like he owned the place, Gene announced, "I'm here, honey!" "Oh Gene! I can't kill Ma!" "The machines are all that is keeping her on this Earth. The doctor has assured me she's not in any pain. Let's go say our goodbyes to Mom. I will handle everything." He wheeled Patsy in to say goodbye to Marge. "Mom, I love you and I will miss you so much." Crying inconsolably, Patsy motioned for Patricia to bring her bags into the room. Dr. Sebastian reached for Marge's hand and said a prayer. Gene looked at the doctor with a sadistic smile spreading across his face. "Get out. I need to get this done." As the doctor handed Gene the necessary forms, he turned to the nurse. "Just do it! She has a date with the crematorium!" A few beeps and a flat line and Marge was gone. "I will call the funeral home" snapped Gene. "Because of the circumstances surrounding her death, there needs to be an autopsy. A report will be sent to Medicare and your insurance company." "Okay, no big deal." After checking on Patsy, Gene announced he had to leave to make arrangements. Carla asked Patricia to step outside. "That sick son-of-a-bitch enjoyed pulling the plug on Marge! Patsy won't survive long!" "Grand Jury convenes next week" cooed Patricia. "He is tying up loose ends. I'll bet people he deems a threat are going to start having accidents. We all need around the clock security." "I could see that for

219

Gertie and Patsy. But if things don't look normal at the gig this Saturday, Frank will be put in a bad light. Gene is naturally suspicious. So things need to appear as normal as possible to avoid peaking his attention." I will be glad once the Grand Jury issues their indictment and puts Gene's ass in jail!" "We will be out of town" explained Preston." If you ladies need anything, call Spinney at the District Attorney's office. Gene wanted Marge cremated immediately. Can we say suspicious as fuck?" "No, he just wants the payout from the life insurance policy. The Adult Protective Services case will automatically close now that Marge is gone." "Ah" said Patricia. "But does that mean he's no longer under all the restrictions imposed on him because of the investigation? Random drug tests, employment mandated by the Department of Labor and abstaining from alcohol." "I guess I will have to check into that" quipped Dr.

Sebastian. "Well, getting rid of Marge helped Gene out

on many levels." "I will call Social Services and see how

this affects the ninety-day investigation."While everyone

was showing their concern for Patsy, Gene was enjoying

a beer and gloating to Frank about Marge's untimely

death. "Boy, Frank things sure are turning around for

me!" "Why? Because your mother-in-law passed away?"

"That means no more caseworker bullshit!" "So what?

No more working at the sewage treatment plant?"

"Exactly!" "There is no investigation if there is no

complainant. Now to get rid of Patsy's sponsor. She's a

fucking pain in my ass. So is that crackpot shrink who

runs the women's group!" "What kind of services are you

going to have for Marge?" asked Frank. "Services? What

services? Her fat ass will be cremated and buried! That's

it!" "No memorial service?" "Nah. The old lady will be in the I.C.U for a while longer, so no need." "Damn, you're cold, Gene!" Smiling, Gene announced "I am buying everyone a drink in honor of my mother-in-law's passing! Everyone belly up to the bar!" Shaking his head, Frank swore under his breath. "Asshole!" Walking out, Gene yelled, "Where you going, Frank?" "I need to tell Gertie about Marge's passing. Later, Gene!" Gene enjoyed himself. As he ambled home, he started to think. 'I should finish out the work week. Make it look good. I will tell them Patsy needs me at home. I'll be able to finish her off easily enough. But first, a special surprise for Patricia and Frank.' Laughing out loud, "This will be priceless! I will teach that yellow-bellied pussy what happens when you turn on me! This will be my best work yet! I will check on the release of the body in the morning." Dropping on the bed, Gene turned on the T.V.

Grabbing the VCR remote, he smiled as his favorite

lesbian porn came to life. "Now I miss Patsy. I need a

good blow job! Guess I'll have to do it myself" chuckled

Gene. After a loud scream of release, he passed out. At

7:00 a.m. The phone began screaming in Gene's ear.

"Yeah? Hello?" "Why aren't you at work?!" yelled the

foreman. "Oh, man. My mother-in-law passed away last

night. I need to handle things for my wife. She's in

Intensive Care at the local hospital." "Okay, take the next

three days for bereavement. We'll see you on Thursday.

I'm sorry for your loss, Gene." Click. As Gene headed

back to bed, the phone rang again. It was a condolence

call. Realizing that he wasn't going to get any more sleep,

he grabbed a shower. Then he started the laundry,

washing the sheets from sick beds. Then the doorbell

rang. Opening the door, Gene found a neighbor standing on the porch with a casserole. With a steady stream of family and friends dropping by, there was enough food to last a few weeks. Women were offering to clean the house. Gene was enjoying playing the part of the bereaved son-in-law. Finally, Gene said that he needed to go see Patsy at the hospital. Gertie arrived and told Gene she would clean the house. She knew how Patsy liked her house to look. "Frank can go with you to make arrangements. Gene growled in Gertie's direction. "Let's go, Frank! I guess I'm gonna get stuck having a memorial service." "I have an idea. Have visiting hours so people can pay their respects, then she can be buried." "How much is it gonna cost to have her cremated? Is it cheaper than a casket?" "You need to make this as painless as possible for Patsy. When she comes home, Gertie and I can take turns staying with her. I need to stop at the morgue before we see Patsy." "Alright" Frank offered to visit with Patsy while Gene went to the morgue. "Hello, Patsy" smiled Frank. "Oh, Frank!" cried Patsy. "Honey, I'm sorry about your mom. Gertie and I are here for you." "Where is Gertie?" "She's cleaning up your house. She didn't want Gene to try and clean it. That would be a disaster!" Patsy broke out in a smile. "That's funny." "Gene is trying. But you know he isn't good with emotions, Patsy. He took a few days off from work to handle your mom's arrangements so you wouldn't have to." "Mom didn't have burial insurance. We will have her cremated. Calling hours and then bury her in the family plot." "That sounds fine, Frank." "Did your mom have a will?" "Yeah. She had nothing but a few family heirloom pieces of jewelry and her wedding rings." "So, you would be her beneficiary anyway. Is there anything you know she would have wanted?" "To be buried next to Dad." "Sounds simple enough. Gene will be here shortly." Holding Frank's hand, tears flowed down Patsy's face. She was really feeling the loss of her mother. The wound was fresh, raw and exposed for all to see. Gene came in, giving a hearty laugh. "Geez, can I get in on the action there, Frank? After all, she does belong to me!" "Sure! That's why my old lady is cleaning your house. We share everything!" "Alright, you two let Patsy get some rest." "I just got here" Gene cracked. "It's time for her breathing treatment, gentlemen." "Yes, ma'am." "I will check on you later, honey." With a droopy wave, Patsy was propped up for her treatment. Gene went to the nurse's station and asked when his wife would be able to leave. "You will need to speak with her doctor. His rounds just started. I can attach a note to her chart to let him know you would like to speak with him." "Fine. I will be back.""What did you find out?" asked Frank. "It will be at least three more days before they release the body." "So, calling hours on Thursday?" "I have to go back to work." "I can handle the calling hours for you." "I need to talk to the head boss about getting more time off. I need to go to the funeral home." At Leopold Funeral home, a surly gentleman greeted them and offered his assistance. "The body of my mother-in-law will be released in three days. My wife and I would like to have her cremated and for the calling hours to be on Thursday if possible." "There are no available openings on Thursday. But we do have one available on Friday at 2:00 p.m." "She needs to be buried next to her husband in their family plot." "How about a selection of music?"

"Don't bother. This is a no muss, no fuss funeral. Three hours should be long enough for calling hours."

"Anything else? Do you have a picture of her?" "Yes. I will bring one from home." "Will you be having a gathering at your home after the calling hours?" Frank answered yes. Gene looked at Frank questioningly.

"Gertie and I will handle it. Most people will probably bring a dish. " "Is this really necessary?" "Yes. It's proper funeral etiquette. They don't serve alcohol, Gene." "They do at Irish wakes!" "We'll see about that, Gene." "If I have to pay for this, I should at least be able to have a good time!" "It's a funeral, not an open mic night, Gene!" "Geez, Frank! Loosen up!" "It's a fucking funeral! Not fun. Your wife is devastated and you're a cheap, selfish prick!" "Damn, Frank. You'd think she was your wife." "Marge was like a mom to all of us. This hurts all of us.

228

So, how much did you insure your mother-in-law for?"

Smiling an evil grin, Gene said "100 grand." "So, how

much did you ensure Patsy for?" "$250,000" laughed

Gene. "Wow! Death becomes you!" "Exactly. Okay, let's

get back to the hospital. I want to have a word with that

doctor!" "Gene, have some self-control" counseled Frank.

"Okay, "Dad." I will be on my best behavior."

"Asshole!" bitched Frank. Walking through the hospital

lobby, the staring was obvious. "Got a problem?" As

soon as Gene hit the elevator, the woman from the

information desk called up to the I.C.U to let them know

he was on his way upstairs. As the bell rang and Gene

stepped out onto the floor, he noticed a security guard

slinking about. "Wait here, sir. The doctor will be with

you in just a minute." Gene automatically became

suspicious. Shaking hands, the doctor escorted Gene into

229

a private area to talk. "When can my wife come home?"

"It's hard to say. Your wife's lungs are in bad condition. We need to have our pulmonary team run some tests."

"Her mother's calling hours are this Friday afternoon. Will she be able to attend?" "We'd like to air on the side of caution. Breathing treatments are helping, but she was in bad shape when she arrived. If it wasn't for her sponsor's quick thinking she might have died as well." All Gene could think was that if that meddling bitch hadn't interfered, Patsy would be out of the way too. That bitch Patricia will pay! I'll make it hurt for both her and Frank! The doctor explained that Patsy was going to need oxygen for several months as well as in-home nurses and personal care attendants. 'Christ!' thought Gene. More nosey people floating around my damn house! But if she dies under their care, they can't blame me. This is going to be a challenge, but I'm up for it. Now to set up for this weekend. But first, Marge's funeral.Shit, Frank and Gertie said they would help. I'll just put them in charge.

Frank and Gertie worked on all the arrangements as Gene listened to doctor's drone on about Patsy's health. Gene asked who he needed to call about getting a copy of the autopsy report. "It was sent directly to her insurance company." "Why?" "Well, there was an insurance policy and I will need that report to get those funds to cover Marge's funeral." "You will have to contact them." "What did she die of?" "We cannot discuss our findings." "I am her next of kin." "No, Patsy would be her next of kin." "Fine. I will contact the insurance company." Walking out of the hospital, Gene realized that he may have to dig into his stash of gig money to pay for Marge's funeral. "Damn women! They get my hard earned money, even after they're dead! Christ, I'll have to go back to work at the shit plant!" While Gene planned his attack on Patricia and Frank, the investigators were doing some digging of their own. After reading several pages of case notes from Child Protective Services and Agnes' medical records, Thomas shook his head. His face was red with anger. Preston looked at his fellow investigator and said, "I will assume from your demeanor you have discovered that Gene is truly a dirt bag?" "He's worse. His wife died under questionable circumstances. He physically abused his son. He was sexually abusing his daughter under the guise that some primitive tribes do it. He is so bad; his late wife's family removed her married name and buried her in the family plot. Most of the women Gene was married to either died or ran away and never returned. I have made dozens of phone calls. His own family members fear him. They would hide his son from him when he drank so Gene couldn't beat him. He has been under delusions of stardom since he was a kid. He fancied himself a new version of Elvis. He performs ballads and depressing music. It should be titled music to cut your wrists by." "He sucks so bad, he had to pay a record company to put out his first album. They wouldn't pay for him to tour. He had to cover the cost of promoting and producing his album." "That is pathetic" cracked Preston. "Look at all those long haired rock and roll bands that get signed. They get jets and groupies." "Sounds like that record company saw him coming" said Thomas. "I'm sure Spinney will see this pattern in his behavior. Hell, look at all those bands that wear makeup and dress in drag. They got contracts and record deals. Gene didn't get shit." "I will take a guess and say that's why when those girls didn't praise him the way he thought he deserved, he snapped and killed them. Or maybe when they saw the size of his Johnson, they laughed. Either way, the result was the same." "The narcissist in Gene cannot accept that he has inadequacies as both an entertainer and a man. His work history shows a real issue with authority. He can't handle being told what to do, so he excelled in his blacktopping business where he had no one to answer to." "Did you also notice that he chose women who had jobs or were on some kind of assistance to support him? He considers himself a God-fearing man, but feels that he has never done anything wrong. After looking at all this information, if Spinney can't prove a pattern of behavior, he's a shitty District Attorney!" "I am sure he will know just what to do with all this new information. Here is our copy of

Marge's autopsy report. It looks like Gene will get a payday out of this after all. The toxins were gone by the time they did the autopsy. The cold medicine combined with the daily medications caused a lethal reaction."

"Once he thinks he can't be touched, he will start tying up loose ends. No one will be safe! He will kill off anyone who can tie him to anything. Frank, Patsy, Patricia and the shrink will need protective detail." Thomas interjected "Won't that tip Gene off?" "He will get sloppy. We will get him. The Grand Jury indictment will push him over the edge and he will start making mistakes!"

"Let's get back to the office. Marge's funeral should be happening soon. Let's make our presence known. It may cause just enough paranoia to prevent him from going on a killing spree." " Once they convene a Grand Jury, how long does it take for them to issue a True Bill?" "It really depends on the amount of evidence they have to hash through. Plus, Gene has the right to appear with counsel and testify. They can kick it back to us and say there's not enough evidence. That's why we're going the extra mile. To make sure they hang that prick, Gene! People like him, we should just shoot. Consider it a public service!"

"Unfortunately, we can't." Preston looked at Thomas and explained. "We have to trust in the judicial system and that we have done the best job we could." "Hopefully Gene will shoot at us. I'd love any reason to shoot that fucking prick!" "The worst thing for a man like Gene would be for him to be placed in solitary confinement. So he can't infect others with his twisted thinking." "Let's check in with Frank. He would know when and where Marge's funeral is." "You know, if the insurance company pays out, Gene will be unstoppable!" No, we'll be there to stop him. The drive back is a long one." "We have plane tickets. Spinney sent them this morning." "So, we have time to grab some dinner before we get on the plane? Great! I am starving!" "When we get back, we'll report to Spinney and check in with Frank." After taking a deep breath, Gene called the insurance company. He calmly explained that he is the holder of policy number 968492. "My mother-in-law has passed away. I need to plan her funeral, so when can we expect the payout?" "Just a minute sir. Let me pull up the status report." After several minutes she returned to the line. "We received the autopsy report from the coroner. Her death was ruled accidental due to an interaction between Flu medicine and her normal medication. That reaction caused a lack of oxygen. We are processing your payment. You should have it by next Thursday. Anything else, sir?" "No, ma'am. Thank you." "We are very sorry for your loss."

Click.As Gene hung up, he broke into a sinister smile. "I

am getting a hundred thousand dollars for killing my

mother-in-law! This is fucking great! No one can touch

me! No more working at the shit plant. Now to get rid of

Patsy. Then I can move on down the road. Maybe I'll

move to Nashville, where all the great singers play."

Lighting a cigar and pouring himself a nice drink, Gene

sat in his favorite recliner. Thinking aloud, he said "Well,

I guess I should turn Marge's room into a guest room for

the nurses when they come stay with Patsy." Killing her

will take some planning. Almost makes me sad to have

old Marge cremated. Just then, there was a loud knock.

Walking in, Frank looked at Gene. "We have the funeral

set up for Friday. I put down a payment with the funeral

parlor. The wake will be here, with comfort food. You

will be expected to mingle with the mourners and show

some sadness please?" "Can Patsy come?" "Not sure.

Her doctor says she'll need some in-home health care.

You know, nurses and home health aides. So my house

will be a bit busy" "Why are you so happy?" asked Frank.

"The insurance will be paying out on Marge's death.

They ruled it accidental." "So, you'll be able to reimburse

me and Gertie? We used our savings to cover the cost of

the funeral." "Sure. No problem, Frank. I'll have the

check by next Thursday." "You're one lucky prick!" "It's

not luck! I am truly a God. I never get caught~" "Excuse

me?" "Yeah. I never thanked you for helping me with

that little problem during the tour. I know I can always

count on you. So, we're gonna have an all-out blast at our

gig Saturday night." "Do you really think we should play

a gig so soon after Marge's death?" "Marge loved going

to our gigs. We will even dedicate a song in her honor."

"I guess she would appreciate that. Maybe we can put the song on our next album. Hopefully Patsy will be home on Monday." "Here, this is for Gertie for cleaning the house for me." Gene handed Frank a hundred dollar bill. "Wow! Gertie will love it. She has her eye on a new craft bag, filled with the latest gadgets." "Let's go pick it up for her as a surprise. Maybe we'll even get her a whole case of mixed yarn! You're driving. Let's go, before the store closes." "Boy, Gene, what's with you?" "I will admit that I do have an ulterior motive. I may need her help again with cleaning the house again." "If you're going to be paying her, she'll be at the house daily" cracked Frank.Driving into town, Frank was going a little fast, but he wanted to get to the variety store before it closed. Pulling in, Frank jumped out, hitting the door before the counter girl could turn the sign to closed. Gene lumbered

into the store. "So, where is this craft bag that Gertie has

her eye on?" "Oh, yeah? Who's your wife?" Frank smiled

and flashed a picture of Gertie. "She asked us to set that

bag aside for her." "Well, we came to buy it for her as a

surprise." "I see. Let me go get it for you. It's $ 89.95."

Then Gene asked what was included in the bag. The

counter girl showed him all the listed items. Then Gene

asked, "What do you think Gertie will need to

compliment her new craft items?" Taking Gene and

Frank by the arm, she showed them the latest yarns,

crochet hooks and knitting needles. Frank asked, "Do

they really light up?" "Yes, let me show you." The sales

girl glowed as she turned on the switch. "Wow, they

really glow!" cackled Frank. "Okay, we will take the full

set of light-up hooks and knitting needles. Throw in a

case of mixed yarn and any new patterns you have." "Yes, sir!" "Wrap it all up, nice big bow and all." "Okay. Your total is $289.00. Will that be cash or credit?" Gene whipped out his wallet and pulled out four one hundred dollar bills. Gene smiled as she handed him the change. "The other hundred is for you, doll. For keeping the store open for us." Frank stared at Gene as though he had grown a second head. What the hell? Keep the other hundred for yourself." "Where is Gertie?" "She said earlier that she was going to visit Patsy." "Let's swing by the hospital and see if she's there." As they found Patsy's new room, there sat Gertie and Patricia. "Hello, ladies. Gertie, we brought you a little something for all your help lately." Opening the gift bags, "Oh, Gene! How did you know?" "Frank told me what you had your eye on. Then we picked out accessories to compliment the

242

accessories in the bag, plus yarn and new patterns." "Oh, Gene, thank you! You're so sweet!" Patsy smiled. "Isn't my Gene such a good man?" Patricia looked up and smiled. "Yeah, he's such a peach! So, what put you in such a generous mood, Gene?" "Gertie has been so great, helping me with the house and preparations for the funeral and wake for Marge." "Oh Gertie! Thank you so much for helping him!" exclaimed Patsy. Patricia excused herself so Patsy could get some rest. Gene asked Patricia if they could speak outside. "I hope you will still meet with me at the gig on Saturday night. I still have concerns about Patsy." "Sure. Not a problem, Gene." Frank explained about Marge's funeral plans and the wake. "Oh, that sounds just like what she would have wanted." "It will be on Friday afternoon. Did the doc say when you would be getting out?" "If my stats stay good, it will be Monday morning. We have to get set up with home health care." "Guess I'll start looking for nurses. Any particular company?" "I'm sure the nurses can give you a list." "You get some rest. Frank is driving me home." "Don't forget to eat dinner, honey." "I will. I love you. Patsy" said Gene as he stepped into the hallway. Gene ambled over to the nurse's desk and asked for a list of nurses who did home health care. "We will have one ready for you when you come to visit in the morning." "Will they have a list of what is covered by the insurance and what will be out of pocket expenses?" "Yes." "See you in the morning. I have some errands to run first, but I should be here around 10:30 or 11:00 a.m." "Good, that will give us time to collect the information you need." "Friday will be Marge's calling hours and funeral in case anyone would like to pay their respects. Let's go, Frank."

After dropping Gertie at home, Frank headed out to drive Gene home. "You're awfully quiet, Gene. What's up?" "I'm expected to go to work in the morning. Marge's funeral is tomorrow afternoon." "I would talk to your boss in the morning." "Plus with Patsy coming home on Monday, I need to arrange for her in-home nursing care. I just don't feel I can go back to work yet. With Marge's death, they would have to close the Adult Protective Services case, right?" Scratching his head, Frank admitted "I have no idea." "Social Services is a huge pain in the ass." "It's their job to make sure that children and the elderly are safe from abuse, Gene. They were doing their job. You straightened out and cleaned up your act. It was not a totally bad experience. Do you need me to lay out your black suit? Gertie said she matched your white shirt and striped tie. It's in the front of your closet."

245

"After the funeral, I will need to turn Marge's room into a bedroom for the overnight nurses. Maybe Gertie can work on it Saturday." Walking up to the door, Frank looked into Gene's eyes. "The funeral will be done fast, but we need to prepare food for the wake. We will start bringing food over around 10 a.m. to get set up. Get some sleep." Frank reached out and patted Gene on the back. As Frank drove away, a smile slipped across Gene's lips. "Soon, my friend. Your end will be here soon." While Gene prepared for his busy day, Dr. Carla Sebastian and Patricia were having a warm cup of tea and discussing Gene's behavior. "He knows about the autopsy results He knows they can't pin anything on him. He knows that the insurance company will have to pay out. This is why he was being so generous with Gertie. He has to tie up loose ends." Patricia coughed, and then explained. "If he knows that Frank was questioned, he will get rid of him." The investigators traced Gene's sociopathic behavior clear back to his teenage years."

"When does the Grand Jury convene?" asked Dr. Sebastian. "Next Thursday. I'm fairly sure that my meeting with Frank and Gene at the gig on Saturday night after the gig is so that he can get rid of me" cracked Patricia. "So I am guessing that he is going to try to kill me and Frank." "Preston thinks that from his statement, Gene bullied Frank into helping him dispose of the first girl he killed. It was after that Frank decided to return home with the rest of the band while Gene continued on tour." "Do not underestimate Gene. He can convince Frank to do his bidding and Frank will because Gene has him convinced that he owes him. So Frank will do whatever Gene says." "Can they use Frank's statement if he is killed?" "Yes, under certain circumstances." "Wow! What do you know about the witnesses they found, Carla?" "Nothing. District Attorney Spinney is keeping tight-lipped about her. They will present her to the Grand Jury to give her testimony. Then she will go back into protective custody." "Will they arrest him immediately?" "Yes, but he will get a lawyer and very likely be released on bail." "That's if he doesn't skip town after getting the insurance check." "Well Patsy will have in-home nursing care that should help keep her safe." "I will head home. Marge's funeral is tomorrow afternoon." "I will be bringing members from group to say their goodbyes to Marge." "With that many people around, Gene will be charming and on his best behavior." "With that insurance payout, Gene won't need to keep his job at the sewage treatment plant. He will have plenty of time to complete his plans." "Be careful. I will see you with the group at Marge's funeral." "Later!" cracked Patricia. Heading home, thoughts swirled around in her head. How she should prepare for Saturday night. Notify Preston and Thomas of her meeting with Frank and Gene. Opening the front door, Patricia did a cursory security check. She locked the door. Pouring a drink, she listed all the things she needed in preparation for her meeting. Opening a long metal box, Patricia pulled out a can of mace and pepper spray, a small boot knife and a small purse gun. This should help even the odds a little bit. Pulling out a Taser, Patricia smiled. The last item was a pair of brass knuckles. Talking out loud Patricia screamed "Let's party, Gene! I will fuck you up!" Gulping down her Scotch, she said, "This will be almost as much fun as killing my old man!" Thinking for a moment, she said "Well, maybe I'll just hurt him good. He needs to make it to Death Row!"

After another Scotch, Patricia headed to bed. Spinney sat

in his office going through all the paper files that Preston

and Thomas had brought back. Gene has been a busy boy.

Even the military couldn't control him. If we can put

together a time line, I will be able to prove that he is a

sociopath with narcissistic features. The worst

punishment for him would be isolation from his fans! I

can see solitary confinement in his future. Without

adoration from his fans, he will wilt away or do the

Thorazine shuffle. Either outcome is fine with me as long

as we get him of the street. He smiled as he shut the file.

He turned out the light and headed home. The next week

will be busy, but it will be worth it to see Gene in

handcuffs. There were many people who wanted to see

Gene in jail, but Spinney had other plans! Gene's phone

had started ringing by 6:00 a.m. People called asking about Marge's funeral. Many asked what they could do to help with the wake. Food, flowers or donations to help cover costs. Once Gertie arrived to prepare the house for the wake, Gene handed Frank a wad of cash to take to the funeral director. "Where did you get this much cash, Gene?" "Gig money I'd been saving up to buy a tour bus!" "Oh, okay. You should have told me before we took out our savings to help you with Marge's funeral!" "How much am I into you for?" "Ten thousand. It took all of our savings to cover the funeral." "Well then, I guess that money belongs to you then, Frank!" "Thank you, Gene." "Where do you need to go?" "I need to get to work. Then to the hospital." "I will help Gertie set up. Then I'll head to the bank to deposit this into our retirement account." Gene jumped into his pickup and

251

headed toward the sewage treatment plant. Pulling into a full parking lot Gene headed straight for his bosses office. Knocking on the door Gene let himself in. "Hey! You're not dressed for work!" "The funeral is this afternoon, with the wake to follow. Patsy comes home from the hospital on Monday, but she'll still need in-home health care." "I told you to be back to work today!" "No can do, Don!" "I'll dock your pay from the days you did work! Insubordination!" "Fuck you, Don!" "You're fired!" "Fuck you! I quit!" "We'll see what the county has to say about that! We took you on as a favor to them! Seems you aren't very trustworthy, Gene!" "I will walk away because today I am burying my mother-in-law! But if I ever catch you out at the bar, I'll clean your clock!" Gene slammed the door on his way out. "Fucking little prick! Let me catch him off company property!" Heading to the hospital, Gene knew that he had to calm down before dealing with Patsy and the hospital staff. Stopping at the coffee shop, Gene sat down in a booth. "What'cha need, Sugar?" "Give me one of those strong, fancy latte things and a sticky bun." "Sure thing. Sorry about Marge. She was such a nice lady." "Thank you. Her funeral is today and the wake will be at my house afterward." "Okay. The boss has a pecan pie to drop off. Be right back" she said as she patted Gene's hand. Gene smiled as he stared at Ginger's ass as she walked away. Letting out a long breath, Ginger returned with the latte and sticky bun. Gene relaxed and enjoyed his breakfast. As he wiped his mouth, he winked at Ginger and left her a ten dollar tip with a pat on her ass as he walked out the door. Jumping in the truck, he headed for the hospital feeling much more relaxed. As he headed directly for Patsy's room, he was called to the nurse's desk. "Here's a list of Registered Nurses who do home health care, along with the Certified Nurse Aides who cover personal care and housework. There are both private nurses and nursing agencies." "Thank you very much." "Hello, sweetheart! How are you feeling?" "They won't let me attend Ma's funeral!" "If you are doing well, you will get to come home on Monday. Don't push yourself, sweetie." "She is MY mother! I need to be at the funeral!" "If the doctor says no, that means you are not ready to leave the hospital. Gertie and Frank did a wonderful job arranging everything. She will be cremated and put in the nicest urn. She will be buried next to your dad. It's just the way Marge would have wanted it." "Oh Gene! I am so sorry I was not there to handle this for you. I know this isn't your thing." "No worries, sweetheart. I have it handled."

"What is that in your hand?" "A list of nurses and nurse's aides for home health care." "I don't need a damn nurse!" "Well, for a little while you will need breathing treatments and help with the housework until you get your strength back. I need to go get ready for the funeral. I will come see you after everyone leaves the wake." "What about your job?" "We had a disagreement. Don felt my job was more important than Marge's funeral and you coming home on Monday, so I quit. You are the most important thing in my world, Patsy!" Patsy had trouble catching her breath. Gene yelled for a nurse. "Okay, Patsy. Let's give you a breathing treatment. Sir, you need to leave now." "Tell her I will be back this evening to see her." Leaving the hospital, Gene headed to the house. It took several minutes for Patsy to breathe easy. The nurses were whispering in the hall. "Doctor I know this isn't my place. But is it safe to let her go home if just his talking to her upsets her so badly that she can't breathe?" "You are absolutely right! It is my call, not yours. I am her doctor. You are just a nurse!"Patricia arrived to help Dr. Sebastian with the women from group. "How many of you would like to attend Marge's funeral and wake?" All the women raised their hands. "Can we donate?" "I believe we can do that!" "What about flowers?" "Patricia has already taken care of that." "Is 'he' going to be there?" "Yes, I am sure he will be." "It will be difficult to see him there, knowing what he did to them." "Remember, what we say in group stays in group. If you do not feel you can handle this, please say so." There were several hushed whispers among the group members. "We will do this to honor Marge and show support for Patsy."Patricia dressed in a black pin striped pant suit with a silk white shirt and a gold cross. Dr. Sebastian dressed in a navy blue dress for the day's business. Patricia brought the van around to the front of the building. While Dr. Sebastian prepared the group for the events of the day, Patricia checked in with Investigators Preston and Thomas. "Hey, will you guys be attending the funeral?" "We will make our presence known." "Good! I thought I should tell you I have a meeting with Gene and Frank Saturday night after the gig." "You need our help?" "No. I'm just letting you know so if no one hears from me, go see Gene." "Will do." "See you later." Gene was dressed all in black and ready for his job as the bereaved son-in-law. There was plenty of food, soda, coffee and alcohol. Frank showed up in a black sedan. He and Gertie had arranged for a driver in case Gene hit the booze early. Gene walked to the car. He was somber but polite when spoken to. He had practiced sounding empathetic in the mirror. Can't wait for this shit to be done and over with so I can have a drink tonight, thought Gene. As they pulled up to the funeral home, Frank and Gertie hurried for the door as people would be arriving soon. Gene stepped out of the car and stretched his legs. Looking at Frank, a single thought came to his mind… its show time! Frank and Gene greeted guests as they came through the doors while Gertie went person to person checking on everyone's well-being. The gallery was filled to capacity. Gene looked out at the crowd of mourners and thought, "The old broad was popular!"As the pastor stepped to the pulpit, the gallery quieted. "Quote the Good Book to help ease the hearts of Gene and friends." Both Frank and Gertie took turns talking about Marge's generosity and her willingness to help anyone. Then Gene was asked to say a few words. "Marge was the light that made my world bright. She encouraged my music. She told me to go on tour. That she would take care of our home. Having her in my life made the loss of my own mother bearable. Our heart-to-heart talks were what kept me going. I trusted her with all my secrets. Marge was the only woman to see me cry, except for my mother. I will miss her so much!" With tears filling his eyes, he walked back to his seat. Preston and Thomas shook their heads in unison. They knew he was lying through his teeth. He had no feelings. Sociopaths don't care about anyone. This was just a façade to gain sympathy. Preston whispered, "I'll be happy when we nail his ass!"The pastor started the service with the first Psalm. "The Lord is my Shepherd, I shall not want. There will be a wake after the graveside prayers at Gene's home."The crowd walked single-file toward the cemetery. When people arrived for the wake, so did donations of flowers, food and cash. Gene, being ever the showman brought out his guitar and sang a song that he dedicated to Marge. Taking a few requests he turned Marge's wake into his own private party. Soon after the music started, so did Gene's drinking. Friends just shook their heads as they watched Gene show his true colors. Preston and Thomas took many notes regarding his behavior. His jovial party personality made the women from Marge and Patsy's domestic violence support group cringe in horror. "Please take us back to the office Dr. Sebastian. We have witnessed so much blatant disrespect." "I understand completely." "Patricia, shall we?" "It's like a train wreck you can't take your eyes off of. Can you believe this?"

asked Patricia. "No, but let's get these ladies back to the office."Once Patricia started the drive back, Dr. Sebastian did her best to console the group. "We will never understand his level of disrespect for Marge's life." "Narcissists always make everything about themselves." "Did you notice that his eulogy was about his feelings and the loss of his own mother?" "When you arrive home write how this behavior has affected you. We will discuss this next group meeting." Patricia wheeled into the office parking lot. Turning off the engine, she turned to address the group. "We all loved Marge. Do not allow him to rob you of the right to mourn your friend. I, too hurt for the loss of Marge." "How is Patsy doing?" shouted a member of the group. "She is getting better. They may release her on Monday, but she will need some in-home care for a while." "Wil she be able to come back to group?" "Yes, when the doctor clears her." "Can we go

visit her?" "That's up to her doctors. You should head

home. It has been an emotionally draining day."

Watching the group disperse, Carla shook her head. "I

think our next session is going to be brutal." "I agree"

said Patricia. "Let's go to my office and talk about your

meeting with Gene and Frank tomorrow night." "I have

all I need to protect myself. I also mentioned my meeting

to Investigators Preston and Thomas. So if no one hears

from me, their first stop will be to visit Gene. I will check

in on Patsy before I head home." "So, have you thought

about the possibility that he may come after you, Doc?"

"Yes. I have a guard that checks my car and follows me

home. Just to be cautious." "Sounds like you have

common sense to go along with all those brains." "I think

he will try to get rid of Frank, Gertie, you and Patsy once

the Grand Jury indicts him. Then, his lawyer will ask for a list of potential witnesses. This includes the one they found. She will have to be hidden in a safe house until he is sentenced." "That's our job" croaked Thomas. "I'm happy for your input, gentlemen." "We know he is a dirt bag." "So, how did the hunt go?" "Here's our file. Take a look, Doc." "I can't. Patsy is my patient." "First, check out his top ten listed offenses. Child abuse in all forms. His wife's mysterious death. The interviews with Agatha's family." Looking through the papers, Carla nodded. "I see he's been at this since he was a kid." "Can you give us some insight, Doc? Is he twisted, like sick?" "Yes, from what I have read, I would say he suffers from a personality disorder. He is a sociopath with narcissistic features. He has no empathy. He does not feel love like everyone else. He is charming, but he can turn on you in a minute. He feels no remorse. If you can put him away, and they put him in with the general population, he will be running the prison in short order. He will convince the other inmates to do his bidding and even kill for his personal enjoyment. He cannot have that kind of control. I would strongly suggest he be placed in solitary confinement so he has no access to other prisoners." "Do you think he has always been this way?" asked Thomas. "If I had to guess I would say yes because children that are sociopaths cannot be properly diagnosed until they are eighteen. That's why he had no self-control. The military was a disaster for him because he cannot take orders. He needs to be in charge. He has always been a leader not a follower. Anything he ever did wrong was someone else's fault. "Okay, thanks, Doc. What about his music 'career'?" "He is a star only in his own mind.

When women turn him down or emasculate him, he flies
into a rage and kills them. He needs the accolades and
applause. When his worth is challenged, he loses it."
"Anything else?" "He will not go quietly when you arrest
him." "This helps open a window into his psychopathy."
"Keep an eye on Patricia. She thinks she can handle Gene,
but this is personal for her. She killed her husband in
self-defense, but not before he did irreparable damage to
her physically. She identifies with Patsy on a level that
I'm not sure we will ever understand. If Gene feels that
he is losing control, he will kill all those that he thinks
are a threat to him. He will manipulate Frank and Gertie.
I fear that this will get really bloody because he has no
remorse." "You be careful too, Doc." "I have a guard.
But killing me would not suit his needs. He needs me to
be involved with Patsy's case." "He's a fruit basket, so

265

we will advise our guard to check your house as well as your car and office." "Patricia is on her way to see Patsy. Gene may show up there too, so you may want to check in with her doctor." "Good idea. We will stand by while you lock up your office, ma'am." After a thorough search of the car Melvin followed Carla home and followed the same procedure inside her house. "All secure, Doc!" "Thank you, Melvin. Let me give you some coffee at least." "I'll be fine, ma'am. The wife packed me a lunch and filled my thermos with really strong coffee. Shift change is at midnight. Never open the door unless it's me or Jack." "Not a problem. Good night, Melvin." "Good night, ma'am." Patricia stopped in to see Patsy. "How are you feeling?" "Tired" whispered Patsy. "How was the wake?" Thinking for a moment, Patricia smiled and told her that members from group had come to say goodbye to Marge. "Oh, she would have liked that. How is Gene holding up?" Pausing in thought for a moment, "Gene turned the wake into a happy party send off. He even played a song that he dedicated to Marge." "That's nice. Ma would have liked that." "It had an Irish wake feel to it." "You get some rest." The doctor motioned for Patricia to come outside. "We are having trouble keeping her O2 stats up. It looks like there was more damage to her lungs than we realized. She will need oxygen at home as well as nebulizer treatments. There cannot be any smoking in her home at all. I'm afraid she will need around the clock care."Patricia cocked her head to one side looking at the doctor. "I thought she was doing better." "During a visit earlier today with her husband, her breathing became erratic. Her lungs are not expanding to full capacity. A breathing treatment helped.

After he left, she seemed to relax. She will not survive any more abuse at his hand. No more being his servant. I have discussed this with the director of Adult Services. She needs to be in a convalescent home. She is no longer capable of caring for herself without help. It may take a while for the social worker to find a placement for her. I feel she should stay here and not return home. I have notified Dr. Sebastian of this, as well as the investigators." "I would like it if you could stay when it's explained to Gene. Does Patsy know?" "Yes, I explained everything to her while her friend Gertie was with her. I tried to contact her husband but he was pretty inebriated and refused to listen." "I see" cracked Patricia. "He was counting on her going home. This put a kink in his plans. Now he will have to use the insurance money to cover the costs that her insurance does not. He won't be able to spend the money on himself. I would up security around here he's gonna be looking for another insurance payout. Thank you, Doctor." Heading home Patricia's thoughts began to race. Gene won't have as easy of a time getting rid of Patsy while she's in a convalescent home with staff and visitors. So he will have to make his move sooner than he planned. Speeding up his time table will cause him to devolve. Frank and Gertie will be at risk too. This will go south real fast. I must revise my plan for Saturday night at the gig. The news about Patsy not coming home will make Gene more dangerous. Maybe Spinney will be able to move up the convening of the Grand Jury. Pulling up to her house, Patricia left her headlights on as she checked all the doors. Turning on her porch light, she turned off the car's ignition. Locking her car doors, she used a flashlight to illuminate the walkway. She then walked through the house flipping on all the light

switches. Feeling secure, she locked the front door. Then

she walked briskly to the back and the cellar door .She

was satisfied now that her house was secure.She poured

herself three fingers of Scotch. Flipping on the T.V. she

had an uneasy feeling. Sitting up in her recliner, Patricia

kept her gun in her lap. She caressed her .38 special,

knowing that she could handle anything that dared to

come through her door. Her eyes began to flutter. Her

glass slipped from her grip, smashing against the floor

and jarring her awake. "Shit!" Shaking her head, Patricia

gathered a broom and dust pan to clean up the mess.

"Christ, I'll be stepping on glass shards for weeks after

this!" She flopped into bed, wrapping herself in the

flannel afghan. Her .38 was still within reach on the night

stand.The afghan was the only thing she had inherited

from her 'mouse' of a mother. With animosity, Patricia

had vivid memories of her stepfather beating her while

her terrified mother made excuses for his behavior. One

night, after a major fight, her stepfather came into her

room. He was drunk and felt that he was owed what he

could no longer get from her mother.Patricia slept with a

hunting knife under her pillow. He crawled on top of her.

His breath reeked of stale beer and cheap sour mash.

Pulling her hands over her head, she reached for her knife.

With a thrust of anger and pain, Patricia brought the knife

down on his back. Screaming in agony, Patricia wriggled

out from under him and ran for the rifle that was kept in

the corner of the parlor. Grabbing the rifle and pulling it

up level with her shoulder, she screamed. "Mom! Call the

cops and an ambulance!" Staggering from Patricia's

bedroom, he lunged for her. "You bitch! You will pay for

271

this! I'll fuck you and your baby sister!" At that moment, Patricia loaded a special shell. "If you hurt my mom and sister, I'll kill you!" "You don't have what it takes! So just assume the position, you little bitch!" As he lunged at her again, a shot rang out. But it wasn't from the rifle. Her baby sister had fired their Papa's handgun. As he fell forward, the cops came charging through the front door. Taking the guns from the girls, they asked, "What happened?" "He hurts us and Mommy too." They arrested baby Suzy for killing her stepfather. At the age of eight, she was sent to a girl's reformatory. After reviewing all the evidence, a judge decided that she was trying to prevent him from hurting her family. Sadly, by the time this ruling was made, Suzy had killed herself by hanging. Patricia's mother had been committed to an asylum and Patricia was sent to a reformatory for juvenile offenders. Dr. Carla Sebastian had rallied for her release.It seemed so long ago, but I remember like it was yesterday. My reason for helping abused women like Patsy. I see myself in her. As her eyes closed again, Patricia thought how this old house hadn't changed. There had been some minor cosmetic changes, but the ghosts of the past still remained. As Patricia awoke, she looked at the alarm clock. It was ten a.m. "Shit! I slept late. Big night tonight. I must get ready for the biggest battle of my life. While making coffee, Patricia started to think out loud. Gene will try to kill me. I must kill him to protect Patsy, Gertie and Frank. Okay, I know how this needs to go down. As Patricia sipped her large cup of dark roasted coffee, the phone rang. Dr. Sebastian was telling her about the discussion with Patsy's doctor. "Yes. He spoke with me last night." "You know Gene will not handle this news well." "Agreed. I have called the District Attorney at home. I have a bad feeling they will need to convene the Grand Jury sooner than Thursday. I'm hoping he will return my call. Are you still going through with the meeting with Gene and Frank?" "Yes! Hopefully I can slow his momentum of acceleration down a bit." "Please be careful! Gene is dangerous. He is not your stepfather or your ex-husband. He has left a trail of bodies and has never been caught." "I know what I'm doing, Carla!" "What time does the gig start?" "Ten p.m. They play until one a.m. I have everything I need to handle this situation. I need to check on Patsy today! I'll call you later!" Hanging up, Patricia went back to her coffee and her mental preparations for the evening's events. After a few more cups of coffee and some biscuits and gravy, Patricia was ready to start her day.

She dressed in jeans and a t-shirt for her visit to the hospital. After securing the house, she headed for the hospital. Meanwhile, Frank was pounding on Gene's front door. Walking in, he asked, "Are you dead?" "Fuck you, asshole!" "I guess that means you survived the wake." Gertie came in behind Frank. "What the hell happened in here?" "The party went on for a long time after you all left." "I see that" snarled Gertie. "Did I talk to Patsy's doctor last night?" "I'm sure you did! Her lungs are worse than they first thought. They want her to go to a convalescent home!" exclaimed Gertie. "Those places are expensive" quipped Frank. "It will take all of her disability payment to cover the balance, Gene." "WHAT!?" "Here. Frank, clear me a path to the kitchen. I'll make Gene some breakfast. He'll feel better after he eats something." "Coffee too, ma'am" cracked Frank.

"You brat, Frank!" "Start picking up, Frank! You boys have a gig tonight, right?" asked Gertie. "Yes we do" smiled Gene. "Guess I will be on clean up duty" complained Gertie. "I'll make you a deal, sugar. You clean the place up the way Patsy likes it, and I'll pay you this." Gene pulled out a crisp one hundred dollar bill. "Plus, any money you find while cleaning is yours. Fair, Gertie?" "I guess so." "That's my girl!" smiled Gene as he patted her large ass. "Watch it, Gene! I know how to use this cast-iron skillet for more than cooking! You remember that, boy!" With a hearty laugh, Gene said "Yes ma'am!" "After I get my head straight, I guess I need to have a word with Patsy's doctor. I bet that damn shrink of hers is behind all this bullshit! She belongs here at home with me where I can take care of her. That's my job as her husband! Right, Frank?" "Yes, Gene, but if she

276

is having trouble breathing, she will need constant

oxygen. No more cigars in the house." "That's a small

price to pay to have my girl back home with me." "Here,

start eating!" snarled Gertie. "Where's mine?" whined

Frank. "Do I look like your maid, Frank Lee Snider?"

"No ma'am" snickered Frank. "Guess she's got your

number, Frank!" cackled Gene. "Shut up, Gene!" Gertie

handed Frank his plate. "Have a seat, Gertie." "Oh, thank

you, master Gene!" "Now that's the way ALL women

should address me!" Heading for the shower, Gertie

yelled "Asshole!" "That's Master to you, Gertie!" "Oh

Frank! You better get his smug ass out of here before I

hurt him! Master my foot!" "He's not worth it, Gertie.

Don't get yourself worked up." "I guess I better go

through Marge's things, since Patsy won't be home for a

while." "Yeah, I'm sure Patsy is going to want some

things from home for her new room. "I got the idea from the doctor last night that she will be in a rehabilitation unit first, and then moved to the assisted living floor. She needs therapy for her lungs. She needs to build up her strength for walking. To walk, she needs to be able to get enough air moving through her lungs." "Sounds like she's in for a long fight to get healthy again." "She don't need any nursing home!" yelled Gene. "We will just see about what she needs!" "Hey, we have rehearsal for tonight. Let's go! We can visit Patsy afterwards." "Can you press my outfit for tonight, Doll?" "I am not your wife, Gene!" "Frank doesn't mind sharing you with me, right, Frank?"Steam poured out of Gertie's ears. "I AM NOT YOUR ENDENTURED SERVANT, GENE!" "Thanks honey!" smiled Gene. "Have dinner ready when I get back." "You have two tons of food here from the wake. Warm something up, Gene!" "Now, Gertie, you know you love to take care of a man!" "Come on, Gene. Before she starts throwing shit! cracked Frank. "Let's take my truck", smiled Gene. Heading to rehearsal, Gene still looked like he was drunk. After an hour run through, Gene headed to the bar to get a drink. "Shit, already?" "No, I ordered a Coke. Still have to visit Patsy. So, Frank that chick Patricia will be at the gig tonight. I may need your backup." "Why, Gene?" "She pushes my buttons." "Oh, she's the one who pepper sprayed you and broke your nose, right?" "Yeah, she's Patsy's sponsor. She's a real man-hater. You know, a ball buster." "I see." "Just help me out when I ask, okay?" "Depends on what you want me to do." "You know", said Gene. "No, I don't, but I'm sure I will not like this." "You're my best friend, Frank." "No, I'm your only real friend. I have always had your back, Gene." "Hey, why did those cops take you in?" "Unpaid tickets from the tour. I covered it for you. The hotel bill, too" "Thanks, buddy. You know Patsy wouldn't understand." "Probably not, Gene." Driving to the hospital, Frank had a nagging feeling in his head. Something's up! I need to be on guard tonight. He knows something! If he knows about my turning state's evidence, it will be the end of me! They will find pieces of me across ten states! Patricia sat at Patsy's bedside when Gene arrived. "Hey, Doll! I see you've had some company." "Yes, she's been telling me about topics from group. Where's Gertie?" "Oh, she stayed at the house. She's cleaning it up after the wake." "I heard it turned into a party, Gene" scowled Patsy. "Nothing to worry about. We gave Marge a great send off." "It seems the doctor isn't ready to send you home just yet." "Yes, he says I need to be transferred to a rehabilitation unit for therapy." Annoyed, but keeping a smile, Gene said, "Gotta get your wind back. So my girl can cheer for me from the front row of our gigs." "Thank you for understanding, Gene." Patsy said with a weak smile. He knew not to upset her. "But who will take care of you now that Ma is gone and I am here?" Frank chirped, "No worries, Patsy. Gertie and I have it covered. He will be just fine." "Are you sure, Frank?" "Oh, sure. No problem."Squeezing Frank's hand, Patsy whispered "Thank you, Sweetheart." "Always here for you, Patsy." Patricia watched the scene unfold knowing full well that someone would die tonight. But it has to happen. I only hope that she will forgive me for what I must do to protect the world from Gene. "Oh, I am sorry Patsy, but I have a list of things to get done tonight. Weekends are too short." "Go ahead. We will be fine", chimed Gene.

"Frank, come here for a minute. Don't let him upset her.

She has trouble breathing and it takes at least an hour for

her O2 stats to come up after a treatment." "Got you. I

will keep him in line." "Thanks." Leaving in almost a

sprint, Patricia headed home to prepare for the evening.

Investigator Preston stopped Patricia at the entrance of

the hospital. "Why are you running? What happened?"

"Nothing. I have errands to run." As she jumped in her

car, her thoughts ran rampant. How she must kill Gene to

protect them all. After checking her supplies and going

over her checklist, she snuggled in for a nap. I need to be

wide awake and refreshed for tonight! Setting her alarm

for 7:00 p.m. Patricia pulled down all the shades and

crawled under the flannel afghan that had been her

mother's. Closing her eyes, she was asleep before the

count of ten. Her sleep was hard and without dreams. As the sun went down and Gene put his plans in motion, Patricia got up, showered and had dinner. Now to get ready. She pulled out her favorite plunging V-neck sweater and a push up bra. Black jeans and her favorite pair of cowboy boots. These were custom made with a built in sheath to hold her knife. Her purse had a concealed carry compartment for her .38 special. The inner lining had pockets that held her brass knuckles, mace and pepper spray. She was ready. She applied her makeup/war paint and teased her hair to complete her look. Checklist:

Full stomach. Armed. Dressed to kill. Carla and the investigators knew about the meeting with Gene. Ready. Locked and loaded! Across town, Gene was preparing for his gig. Boots, jeans, string tie, rhinestone jacket and cowboy hat. Reaching into his closet, way in the back behind some shoe boxes was a wooden box. Smiling, Gene opened the box and pulled out a vial. "This should work nicely. Colorless, odorless, tasteless and could sedate a rhino. This should help me control that uppity bitch, Patricia" he said as he slipped the vial into his inner jacket pocket. Smiling, he announced,"It's party time!"He headed to his truck with his guitar in hand. The drive to the gig had Gene all aflutter, exhilarated at the prospects. Gene arrived to find his band mates waiting. Everyone was ready. "I'll be with you in just a minute." He had reserved a table in the front row for Patricia. Upon her arrival, Patricia was escorted to her front row table. The appearance of a waitress made Patricia jump. "What would you like?" "Club soda with a twist of lime, please?" After the show started, Patricia tried to enjoy it.

After hearing several songs, she was ready for ear plugs.

He sounded horrible. The waitress came over with an

order of deep fried catfish fillets with a spicy dipping

sauce. "What's this?" "Frank ordered it. He said you

might enjoy it." Since both Frank and Gene were up on

stage, Patricia figured it was safe to eat. The smell of the

catfish made her mouth water. She dipped a fillet into the

sauce and took a huge bite. Wow! That sauce was spicy!

"Looks like you will be needing another club soda,

ma'am." "Yes, please." "Normally, people order the

cheesy bread to help curb the spiciness." "Maybe I need

an order of bread too." Kathy returned with the cheese

bread and another club soda. The sauce was addicting!

Frank and Gene came off the stage on break and joined

Patricia at her table as she grabbed another fillet and

dunking it in the sauce. "I love these things!" Gene quietly sipped a soda. "So, what do you think of the show?" "This is what they refer to as classic country, right?" "Yes, it is." "I prefer classic rock, myself. How about you play something perky?" "I will see what I can do", smiled Gene. "Oh, man! I ate all your catfish! I'll order you another" said Frank. "Hey, Kathy?" "Yeah, Frank?"" "I need another order of catfish over here. I ate hers." "Okay." "That sauce seemed extra hot tonight" Frank said. Shaking his head, he managed to finish the set. Patricia finished the sauce with her cheese bread. When the band finished their last set, the bar started to clear out. "It's awfully hot in here. I need some air" smiled Patricia. "I'll go with you. I'm feeling a bit overheated as well." As they headed out to the empty parking lot, Gene asked, "Looking for this? Boy, you women carry around a lot of junk." Leaning against his

truck, Gene gave an evil smile. "Let's see what we have

here. Mace, pepper spray and brass knuckles." "Give me

my purse! I thought we were going to talk." "I guess you

thought you needed to be prepared for a fight. That's not

lady like. You seem to be feeling dizzy and hot. What

else do we have here? Looks like a concealed carry

pocket. A .38 special. Nice choice!" "You are such a

pussy! You have to dose me to kick my ass! Pathetic!"

With that, Gene gave her a right cross. "Mind your

manners, little girl!" "Gene, what is your problem?"

slurred Frank. "Help me get her in the back of the truck."

Once she was secured, Gene threw a tarp over her. "Get

in the cab, Frank!" Driving to Patricia's house, Frank

noticed his truck was parked in her driveway. "How did

my truck get here?" slurred Frank. Gene took Patricia's

287

house keys and opened the front door. With what little help Frank was, they carried Patricia into her home. Neither Patricia nor Frank could move. Gene didn't even bother to secure them. He took his truck back to the bar. After asking Kathy for a ride to town, he walked back to Patricia's. Opening the door, he announced, "I'm back! Did you miss me? Now, let's have that talk, shall we? Dumping ice water on Patricia's head, Gene yelled. "Wakey, wakey! Now, I bet you'd like to hit me, right? Here, pick up your fist. Oops, your arm feels like lead! That's the poison I put in the dipping sauce! You can't do anything. Here, would you like your gun? Oh, shit! Your hand doesn't work. You have no muscle control. Come on, you're normally such a mouthy cunt. Nothing to say? How about you, Frank? Let's start with you turning state's evidence! "But-I" "Can't speak, can you? Just so you know, you will die for your betrayal!"Struggling into

an upright position, Frank breathed, "I ne-ver betrayed

you." "What about you, miss sponsor? Got anything to

say? Oh, that's right! The poison is messing with your

speech. So, I will fill you in on what's about to happen

and why. Why is because you interfered with my plans to

remove Patsy and Marge so I could have the insurance

money. I had everything all set up. I was having Patsy's

disability checks sent to me. She was nicely medicated

and did as she was told. But Marge and that drunken

bitch Dr. Carla Sebastian had all my great work undone!

Then, to top it all off, because of nosey Adult Services

workers, I had to prove what I did on tour and show them

receipts. While they were investigating me, they turned

up some of my small indiscretions." "Murder is an

indiscretion?" slurred Patricia. "Yes, that was truly

unfortunate. Now I need to tie up loose ends. Now you know the why. Let's discuss how you will die. It will be a murder-suicide. Frank will kill you because you threatened his family by telling Gertie about your affair. He will use your gun. Nice and neat, right? I thought so. Now I am truly bored, so let's finish this!""Can't fight like a man, Gene? Laughing at Patricia, Gene shook his head. "Any last words before Frank kills you?" "Yeah." He bent down to hear her final words. "You suck as a singer! You're no entertainer!"Gene's face turned scarlet red. Picking up his fists, he pummeled Patricia's face. "Here, let's make use of that fuck hole you call your mouth!" Unzipping his pants, Gene pulled out his penis and shoved it into Patricia's mouth. "Anything to say before I fuck your face?"He leaned in to hear her breathy last words. "No wonder all those little girls laughed at you! You aren't a man! You have no dick!" Gene

grabbed the .38 and shot Patricia in the face. "How do

you like me now, bitch?" Turning to Frank, Any last

words?" "Yeah. Fuck you!" Three more shots rang out.

"Bye, friend!" Throwing the gun on the floor, Gene left.

Peeling of his gloves, he walked through the woods to

cover his tracks. He burned the gloves with the rest of his

garbage. A shower and some sleep were in order.At

around noon, the phone rang. Gertie asked if Frank had

stayed the night at Gene's. "I thought he caught a ride

home." "He never came home. I figured you boys were

hitting the whiskey, so he couldn't drive home." "Honest,

Gertie. This time it wasn't me feeding him booze." "Well,

if he doesn't show up or call me soon, I will ask the cops

to help me find him." "I will be at the hospital. If you

need my help, you know where I will be." "Thanks,

Gene." Guess I need to go see Patsy's doctor, find out where the want to send her. But I will have to deal with one of those self-absorbed Adult Services workers. This is gonna be a nightmare! She should just come home to my care! No one can take care of Patsy better than me, cackled Gene. Looking in his closet, Gene decided to go with a nice denim shirt with a deep blue short sleeved shirt underneath. Faded jeans and a black cowboy hat. Looking at himself in the full-length mirror, he said "Yes, I look the part of the caring husband." Gene then slipped on his wedding ring for good measure. "Now I'm ready!" He smiled smugly into the mirror. Grabbing his keys, Gene headed for his truck. Driving to the hospital, Gene felt relaxed and calm. You would never know by his demeanor that he committed double murder last night. Pulling into the parking lot, Gene made a small detour. A nice bouquet will cheer Patsy up. With a cuddly stuffed Husky or a Rottie, depending on what they have to choose from. Walking through the gift shop, Gene looked for the perfect gift. Then he found a glass doll that looked so real he had to touch it. "May I help you, Sir?" "Tell me about this doll." "She was designed to look and feel like a real baby. She cries and coos. We encourage patients that bring a new baby home to get one of these for their little girls to help take care of." Gene paused for a moment. He thought back to when Patsy had wanted to be a mother so badly that her body produced pregnancy symptoms. This should help me out. Looking at the toys, Gene grumbled at the price tags. But getting in Patsy's head for his ultimate plan to work was essential. "Are there boy dolls too?" "Yes. We also have twins." Smiling, Gene took the boy and girl twins, a wicker baby carrier

293

and a dozen roses. Two hundred dollars later, he had the perfect gifts to make Patsy happy. Gene remembered how Patsy thought she heard babies crying and how that was a factor of her being put on antipsychotics. Her past issues with attempting suicide will be what pushed her over the edge. That was how Gene could kill her without suspicion.Peeking into Patsy's room, she looked so sad and lost. This was the perfect time to start causing Patsy's psychotic break. While her eyes were closed, Gene snuck in, holding the dolls in his arms. Patsy opened her eyes slowly. Gene smiled. "I brought something to keep you company. Hold out your arms." She squinted as Gene put the twin dolls in her arms. "Oh Gene! They look so real!" "They are as close as you can get without childbirth. There's an old-fashioned wicker carrier for them to sleep in and roses for the new mommy." Looking them over, he explained, "They are anatomically correct. They cry and wet, just like real babies. I know you have to go to a convalescent home. I thought they would be a nice addition to your room." Smiling with tears of joy, Patsy said "You're the most wonderful husband, Gene!" "Yes, I know", cackled Gene.Standing in the doorway, Dr. Sebastian watched how Gene preyed upon Patsy's wish for the children she could never have. "Hello, Patsy!" "Hi, Dr. Sebastian! Aren't these babies beautiful?" "Yes, they are. Twins I see." "Look at this old-fashioned carriage!" "It's beautifully crafted." "Ma would have loved these dolls!" "I'm sure she would have." "I will have to make an afghan for the carriage." "Crocheting is a good thing" smiled Gene. "I even got roses as a 'new' mom." "Oh, they are beautiful! Let me see if we can get them put in water. Gene, join me" smiled Dr. Sebastian. Handing the nurse Patsy's roses, she turned on one heel. Grabbing Gene by the elbow, she marched him into a private waiting area. "What the hell do you think you're doing?" "Look, her mom is gone. She will be moved into a convalescent home. The dolls are to keep her company. Those places can be very lonely. I'm still playing gigs and I have work. I just thought it would be a nice gift for her." "They look real, Gene." "Yeah, I thought that was pretty cool. Hell, she can keep herself busy making clothes for them. "She had a very hard time with not being able to have children because of the abuse she endured." "Lighten up, Carla! She is my wife. I know what's best for her! So, back off, or I'll have you removed from her case!"Fuming, Carla tried to call Patricia to tell her about Gene's new mind fuck. After several unanswered calls, Dr. Sebastian became concerned. She called investigators Preston and Thomas and expressed her concern to them. "Patricia isn't the only person that has not been heard from since last night's gig. Frank never made it home last night. His wife was extremely upset when we explained that Frank would need to be missing for at least forty-eight hours before she could file a Missing Person report. We are headed to the bar to find out when they left and with whom. We will let you know if we find anything."

Preston started questioning Kathy. "So, where did Frank and Patricia sit last night?" She pointed to the front row table. "Okay, do you remember what they ordered?"

"Yes. The lady had two club sodas with lime. Frank ordered her deep-fried catfish with spicy dipping sauce. After the first set, he and Gene joined her. Frank must

297

have been hungry because he ate the whole order. So, he ordered her another. She got an order of cheese bread too because the sauce was so spicy and addictive." "What about Gene?" "He had a soda, no food." "Anything else?" "Must be the sauce got to them because they had to go outside to cool down." "Who?" ""Frank and the lady." "What about Gene?" "He left after we closed. "Okay, thanks, Kathy." "Let's head over to Patricia's and see what we find." "Sounds good. Where's Gene?" "The doc said he's at the hospital with his wife." "Frank's wife called his house this morning. He'd been there all night. Supposedly" cracked Thomas. "I guess we shall see what we find. Heading to Patricia's, Preston slowed down at the top of her driveway. As they pulled in, they ran a check on the license plates of both vehicles. One belonged to Patricia, the other was Frank's. Having an uneasy feeling, Preston requested backup. They walked up to the front door and knocked four times. Drawing their weapons, Thomas kicked in the door. The stench of death assaulted their noses. On the right side of the couch, they found Frank. He had been shot several times in the head. On the opposite side, was who they could only assume was Patricia. There was nothing left of her face. "We need to call the State Troopers and have them send a Crime Scene Investigation team." As their backup arrived, they secured the rest of the house. After the coroner removed the bodies, the crime scene team announced there were more than two sets of footprints. "This means it wasn't a murder-suicide. It was a straight up murder." "While you guys look around the house and property, we will notify his wife." "This will hit Gertie hard. She depended on Frank for everything." A check on

Frank's truck showed that it hadn't moved in twelve hours. Patricia's car had not moved in over twenty-four hours. Preston called the garage to have both vehicles towed to the impound lot. "I dread this, but it has to be done. We need to notify Gertie." As they pulled up to the driveway, Gertie opened the front door. "Did you find Frank?" "Let's sit down, Gertie." "Stop stalling! Where is he? Is he in jail? Another DWI? What?" "I'm sorry, Gertie, but Frank is dead." "WHAT!? No! Was he with a woman?" "We found both Frank and Patricia deceased at her house." "Oh my God! Who could have done this? Everyone loved Frank. He treated everyone like they were family. Does Gene know? "We haven't notified anyone else. Gene is at the hospital with Patsy." Preston hugged Gertie while she sobbed inconsolably. "You don't understand. Without Frank, I will have to live in an old age home. I use a walker and need help doing things. The doctors have been telling me for years that I should live in an apartment made for people with disabilities but Frank was healthy, so we didn't qualify. What do I do now?" "I'm sure Social Services can help you figure things out." "I loved him so much, you know." "We understand. Is there anyone we can call for you?" "No, Gene and Patsy were our best friends. I need Patsy!" cried Gertie. "Would you like us to take you to the hospital?" "Yes, please. Let me wash my face." Taking her purse, she walked with Preston. Thomas opened the back door of the sedan to help Gertie inside. Heading to the hospital, the silence was deafening. "Let us tell Gene, okay Gertie? We need to contact Patricia's next of kin as well." As the tears started to trickle down Gertie's cheek, she said "I don't know if I can handle another funeral.

301

Frank kept track of our finances. I am not good at those things." "We understand, Gertie. That's why I suggested that Social Services could help. Adult Services caseworkers are there to help with things like this." As they escorted Gertie into the hospital, she headed immediately for Patsy's room. Thomas was hot on her heels trying to prevent her from bursting into Patsy's room.Preston asked Gene and Dr. Sebastian to meet them in the chapel along with Patsy's doctor. Once everyone had arrived, Preston and Thomas looked at each other and Preston got right to the point. "This afternoon we started to investigate that Frank didn't come home last night and that no one could make contact with Patricia. After speaking with a waitress from the bar, we went to Patricia's home. In the driveway, we found both Frank and Patricia's vehicles. Once we entered the domicile, we discovered both Frank and Patricia dead. Frank was shot in the head and Patricia in the face. There was a third party there. This was a double murder. Gertie is having a hard time with all of this. She cannot live on her own at home." "I will need to be there when Patsy is told all of this" explained the doctor. Staring, open-mouthed, Dr. Sebastian was in full shock. Taking a large breath, Gene began to speak. "I will take care of Gertie and handle Frank's funeral. Gertie can stay with me until she can get into one of those places for the disabled." Carla said she would handle Patricia's arrangements. "This will be investigated" growled Thomas. Gene announced, "I need to be there for Patsy and Gertie. If you'll excuse me." Once Gene was out of sight, Dr. Sebastian said, "That son-of-a-bitch killed them! He knows we were on to him. He knew Frank was questioned. He knew Patricia was on to his bullshit! That meeting was supposed to be about Patsy relapsing! He killed Marge. Now he needs to get rid of Patsy to get the life insurance money. You already know those girls went missing while he was on tour. This sounds like a slam dunk to me!" "I understand, but during the trial, we will hear testimony from a witness that will tie all of this together." "So, in the meantime, he just kills off the rest of us!?" "The Grand Jury convenes on Thursday. We will get a True Bill and arrest him." "Not before someone else dies!" "I now have to explain to our women's group that Patricia is dead too!" "I left a message with Spinney to see if we can move up the Grand Jury. We need to head back to the office and see if the coroner has any more information for us. You should have Melvin step up the patrol of the perimeter. Gene may try to make you nervous. "Me, nervous? Never!" Dr.

Sebastian said, her voice dripping with sarcasm. "You will be safe. We will add another guard so that you're covered at home and at the office. We'll call you later, Doc." Jesus Christ! Gene is tying up loose ends and these cops are idiots!" As Dr. Sebastian made it back to her office, she mentally prepared herself for breaking the news of Patricia's death to the women's group. "It's Sunday. I should be relaxing at home. But since I'm here, I should go through Patsy's file. As she sat down, Carla decided she needed some strong coffee. Calling the coffee shop, she put in a large order to go. "Can it be delivered?" "No delivery on Sundays." "Okay, I'll be there in ten minutes." Locking the file away in her desk, she headed out. Melvin smiled at her. "I could have run out for you, ma'am." "We need to talk when I get back." "Yes, ma'am." She ran into the coffee shop. "Here you go. I included a sandwich, cream of broccoli soup and dessert.""Thanks. " "You're working on a Sunday? Someone must be really sick." "There's always someone in need of my assistance." Gene stood looking out the window. He watched Dr. Sebastian pull into the parking lot with her food in hand. He was thinking of what he could do to remove her from his life. 'She has all the stuff that Patsy and Marge told her in a file, locked away from sight. Killing her could be gratifying in this situation, but the file is more important' thought Gene. 'That file has enough to seal my fate. I know those bitches talked shit about me. Intimidation or do I just steal the file? Which shall it be? Hell, I'm up for some fun! Let's do both! Seems she's got herself some company. A guard. Good to know. Guess I will be doing some surveillance, to find out what the doctor does in her free time." "Are you done with your treatment?" "Yes."

"What do you need?" "Maybe you can order Gertie and I

some wonton soup and a puu puu platter?" "I would be

honored to have lunch with you ladies. I will go to the

nurse's station and order it for you. Heading to the

nurse's desk, "Ahem" "Yes? What can I do for you?"

"My girls would like me to order some Chinese food for

them. Can they deliver it here?" "Yes, our nurses order

food often. So, let me call them." "Just a minute. I need

two large wonton soups and three puu puu platters and

two orders of crab Rangoon's." He threw three fifty

dollar bills on the desk. "Order something for the nurses

too." "Well, thank you, Gene. I will call in that order for

you." "No problem. You ladies have been good to my

girl." As Gene strolled back into Patsy's room, the

nurses gathered around the desk whispering. "What's up

with him? Buying us dinner?" "At least we know it won't be poisoned! It's take-out!" cackled Nurse Rachel. "Yeah, I wouldn't trust that man to make me coffee!" "Agreed!" "What's with him? He's up to something!" "Did you see those dolls?" "Yes, they are so life-like." "I think that's the point. I bet Gene is trying to push that poor woman over the edge. Psychology101." "He's a sick one!" cried Nurse Williams. "I checked out her files. He has a life insurance policy on her, just like he did on Marge. May she rest in peace. That's why her doctor is sending her for rehabilitation in a convalescent home. For the therapy she needs and to keep her safe." "What about him saying Gertie can come and stay with him?" "He is most definitely up to something." "Great! He's gonna kill her off too!" "Ladies, do you need more work to do? If you have too much time on your hands, you can restock supplies. I'm sure there are bed pans that need to be emptied!" "Yes, ma'am." "What have you been told about gossiping at the nurse's station?" "We don't trust Gene, that's all." "No one does! Get back to work!" "Here's the money for the food delivery along with what Gene ordered. The rest is for the nurses." "I see."Sitting in the chapel, Gene was planning what he could say to Gertie to get her to accept cremating Frank. 'She'll be with me for a while, so I should get her to sign on the dotted line so that I can control their money too. Just in case Gertie has any problems! I don't think the caseworker will be able to find her a placement that quickly. Patsy will be moved in the next few days. I will arrange for Gertie's house to be sold and have the money transferred to my bank account. This will be as easy as pie! Gertie loves and trusts me! Now to plan Patsy's accident/suicide. Patsy has to have an accident! I have a few days to put my plan into action!' Thinking out loud, "With Frank out of the way, anything he gave the cops will be moot because he's not alive to testify. Neither is that fucking bitch Patricia! Once Patsy is gone, I will be home free and rich. None of those other whores are alive. I'm home free! Besides, if there was any real evidence, that idiot District Attorney would have already convened a Grand Jury! Once I get rid of Patsy and Gertie there's no one else to put on the stand!'Smiling, Gene headed back to Patsy's room. "Hello, ladies! How are my girls doing?" "Fine, Gene. The food should be arriving soon." "After lunch, you get some rest. I will bring Gertie home with me." "Oh, Gene, we will need to stop by my house so I can pack a bag, okay?" "No problem, honey." "Yeah, I need to speak with you about something." "Go ahead."

"In order for me to handle Frank's funeral and the sale of the house, you'll need to sign some forms that give me the authority to do those things on your behalf."Gertie looked stunned as the realization of Frank's death hit her like a ton of bricks. "Yes, I guess I should let you handle everything .Frank handled all of our finances, so I have no idea where to begin." Tears filled Gertie's eyes and streamed down her cheeks. "He's really gone, isn't he?" Gene wrapped his arms around Gertie, hugging her tight. "Yes, he is. He was my best friend, too Gertie. I know he would have wanted me to handle things for you." "You're probably right, Gene." "He would have wanted to be cremated and put into an urn shaped like his favorite guitar. I will take care of his funeral arrangements. The wake will be at our favorite dive bar. We were like royalty there." "We have no family to invite!" Gertie sobbed. "Frank had many friends and fans of the band. It will be a great turn out. I'll get the band to play." "I will have our lawyer draw up the paperwork so I can deal with all of this and you can rest." "Thank you, Gene."Dr. Sebastian stood in the doorway listening to Gene working his magic convincing Gertie to trust him. She knew that Gene was setting himself up to have total control of Gertie's finances. She would never know what hit her! He was good! "Oh, hi, Dr. Sebastian!" "Hello, Gertie. I came by to see if you'd like to talk for a while?" Looking into Dr. Sebastian's face with a cold stare, Gene said "The girls have Chinese coming." "Well, she can bring hers to my office. You and Patsy could be alone together." "It has been a while" smiled Patsy as she patted Gene's left hand. "Okay, sweetheart" smiled Gene. A nurse's aide announced abruptly, "Your takeout has arrived" as she dropped the bags of food on Patsy's bedside table. "Boy, she was rude!" commented Gene. "Looks like someone's having a bad shift." Pulling out Gertie's soup and patter, Gene smiled. "Just what you ordered." "Oh, no tea?" "I have tea in my office, Gertie. Let's go." "I'll be back in a while, Patsy." As they left down the hall, Gene turned his attention to Patsy. "Anything else I can get you?" "A grape soda would be good." "Let me see what the machine has." Walking out, Gene headed for the vending machines. No grape. But they did have orange. That should pacify her. That doctor is getting a little too nosey. Wonder what she's up to? Maybe a warning is in order. As Dr. Sebastian got Gertie settled, she asked "How are you doing?" "Not sure" cooed Gertie. "It doesn't seem possible that Frank is gone." "Did you have any arrangements in place should one of you pass?" "I am the one in bad health. We always assumed I would go first, to tell you the truth." "I understand" smiled Dr. Sebastian. "Tea?" "Yes, please" nodded Gertie. "I understand you will be staying with Gene." "Yes, Dr. Sebastian." "Why don't you call me Carla since we are friends?" "Thank you" said Gertie. In a soothing tone, Carla pressed. "Gertie, do you know why Frank was questioned by the investigators?" "Just tickets from the tour that Gene never paid." "I see. Did you know that Patsy and Marge had issues with Gene's behavior?" "I know that for a while, Gene was the payee for Patsy's benefits. She was put on lots of medication and wasn't well." "Did Marge ever mention that Gene had taken out life insurance policies on them?" "I thought everyone had life insurance" joked Gertie. "But with Gene as the beneficiary, if they have accidents, he gets

314

paid." "Oh. That is kind of creepy" Gertie said with a shudder. "It's also odd that both Patsy and Marge got sick under Gene's care. The flu medicine caused a bad reaction with Marge's other medicines." "Has Gene asked you to sign anything putting him in charge of your finances?" "He did say it would make it easier for me if I were to let him handle things. Frank handled all our finances. I wouldn't even know where to begin." "Well, I would be happy to help you." "Is there something I should know about Gene? Why was Frank really questioned?" "From what I understand, something happened during the last tour." "Well, I know the band came home early. When I asked questions, Frank shut down and would not discuss it. I figured the band had another fight with Gene." "I see." "The investigators said that since I can't live on my own, the county workers would find a placement for me." "Yes, they can do that. They have apartments that are designed for people with disabilities. A nurse or home health care worker comes in daily to help with medications and things like that." "It would be nice if Patsy and I could live together with a nurse to help us instead of living in a convalescent home." "I would agree with that, Gertie. The facility is divided up into a full nursing home and assisted living apartments for those who are disabled but don't need the care of a nursing home. You are allowed to bring your own furniture and personal items from your own homes" smiled Carla. "Could you help us talk to the caseworkers about this option? I will have to sell my house to cover the costs, so it should be some place I would like to live." "I would be happy to help you. But Patsy has to have oxygen and breathing treatments. That's what the nursing care is for. There is a call button intercom system that is connected to the nurse's station so you're never alone. The county has their own lawyers to handle the sale of your home too." "But Gene?" "I am sure Gene would want the best for you and Patsy." "I am concerned that he will be angry about this." "You are too active to live in a nursing home, Gertie. I'm sure Gene will agree with that." "I will contact my friend, who works in Adult Services. The facility offers activities and classes to keep you busy. I think Frank would approve of this for you." "Now I know why Marge and Patsy raved about how nice you are." How about we talk about Frank?" "What do you mean?" "How do you feel?" "I was raised believing that you don't cry in public. Gene says Frank would want to be cremated. But I'm not sure about that. How will I mourn my husband?" "Mourning is a very personal process. It can be as long or as short as you need it to be." Gene wants to have the wake in the dive bar that they hung out in. I truly don't think that is right."

"What do you think?" asked Carla. "I'm not sure." "What does your gut tell you?" "I think Frank would want a real funeral and a service performed at our local church."

"What else?" asked Carla. "Well, Gene should be singing hymns at his wake." "What else, Gertie?" "No dive bar. I want him buried in his best suit. With our friends there showing their love for the great man that Frank was." Gertie was sobbing deeply. Carla gave her a big hug. "Gertie, this needs to happen. You are so busy being strong, you haven't had time to mourn Frank or say goodbye. Grieving is a process. You need to go through all the steps. If you don't mourn, you can't start to heal."Standing outside the office door, Gene listened. He was bitter that his plan was being derailed. 'I guess I can allow Gertie a church funeral for Frank. It has been a while since I sang a church hymn. And if she can get Patsy and Gertie into an assisted living apartment, killing them will be a piece of cake!'Feeling almost sad, Gene decided to let Carla think she had the upper hand. Taking a breath, Gene knocked on the office door. Nodding to Gertie, Carla stood and answered the door. "Are you ready, Gertie? We have to stop at your place so you can pack a bag." Taking in a ragged breath, Gertie said, "Gene, about Frank's services." "I heard. You would like a church service." "Yes, I would. With Frank wearing his good suit. Maybe you could sing a few hymns?" I would be honored to, Gertie." "And I'd like the wake at our church rectory." "I'll see what we can arrange. I know you need to say a proper goodbye to Frank. You knew him longer than you lived with your parents. You want

him buried next to your parents, too. Am I right? "Yes,

Gene." Looking into Carla's eyes, he asked, "How are

the preparations for Patricia going?" "She didn't have

any family, so it will be a small memorial service." "We

could do a church service for her too!" cried Gertie. Gene

smiled. "I would be happy to sing a few hymns." "No.

It's just me and the ladies from our group." "The church

will be reserved for the day. We could give her a special

goodbye too" cracked Gene.Fighting the urge to smack

Gene right in the face, Carla said, "I don't know." "We

would be more than happy to help" offered Gene. "I

believe there needs to be an autopsy performed before

they will release the bodies!" sniped Carla. "No problem.

Let us know. We'll talk later. Let's go, Gertie." Holding

Gertie's hand, Gene headed out. A voice in Carla's head

screamed 'You fucking murdering prick! I will make sure you pay for this!' She fought the tears that stung her eyes. After a few composing breaths, Carla picked up the phone and called Spinney at home. She covered her conversation with Gertie. "I need you to use some of your clout to help the Adult Services caseworker place Patsy and Gertie in an assisted living apartment that s connected to the nursing home." After some pleading, cajoling and intimidating, Spinney agreed. "But only if Patsy's doctor will sign off on her living there." "Thanks, Spinney! So, what about the Grand Jury?" "We have to postpone it a week or two." "Why?" "We need the autopsy reports. I have to be able to prove it was murder and tie it to Gene.""The nurses saw Gene having a conversation with himself in the chapel. Obviously he is starting to unravel. I would like to see if our witness'

Grand Jury testimony can be done without Gene knowing immediately." "I'm sure his lawyer will demand to know of all witnesses so he can depose her." "Can't you do it like if someone were testifying against a mobster?" ""Leave the law to me, Carla. I don't tell you how to shrink heads, do I?" "Fine! Gene is a narcissist, but he's not very smart. I have this under control." "I would get some protection for yourself." "I have a guard." "Yes, Melvin is good. But the minute Gene feels you're a threat to him, you will be on his 'hit list.'"He figures he is safe now with Frank and Patricia out of the way. That's why if they are together it would be easier to protect them." "I got the message, Carla. I will see what we can do." Locking up, Carla was preparing to leave. A knock on the door slowed her pace. "Yes?" "It's Melvin, Dr. Sebastian. We need to chat about something." "Come on

322

in." "Did I do something wrong, ma'am?" No, I was just wondering if you heard about the two deaths." "Yes. Word is it was a double murder." "Well, it's possible that the guy you're protecting me from may be involved. We need to be extra cautious. Maybe there needs to be more shifts." "Are you worried, ma'am?" "It's Carla." "Yes, I am concerned. Maybe you could check my car a few times a day. Check any and all packages that come to my home and office.""Will do, ma'am." "And if you see Gene anywhere near my car, office or home, I need to know." "Should I relay all of this information to the night shift?" "Yes. If you see anything suspicious, call Investigator Thomas or Preston." "I understand, ma'am." "Thank you, Melvin. Let's go." Heading for the parking garage, Melvin had Carla stand in the well-lit area while he checked the car. He was turning the key in the ignition when he heard a funny click. "Call Preston and Thomas, now!" "What is it?" "Just do as I say! Tell them to bring the dog!" "Is it a bomb?" "I'm not qualified to say, ma'am. But I think so." "Silent ride on this call, boys. Melvin is only a security guard. Could he be wrong?" I don't think so." "We don't want to alarm the Doc unless we have to." "Got you!" Pulling in, Preston and Thomas smile and nod to Dr. Sebastian. "So, what do we got, Melvin?" "The click when I tried to start the car concerned me, so I peeked around. I'm no expert, but that looks like a bomb to me." The K-9 unit arrived, along with a bomb technician. After everyone including the K-9 had checked out the car, the technician announced, "Yep, it's a bomb. She would have started the car, gotten a few miles down the road, and boom! Melvin, take her home and stay with her!" Melvin drove Carla home. "I need to call my wife." "No problem, Melvin." After a few hours, Preston drove Carla's car back to her house. "Well?" "It was a crudely made bomb. More to scare you than anything else." "Could I have died?" "That thing would have probably maimed, but not killed you. That doesn't mean his next toy won't be a better device. What did you do to piss him off?""I talked to Gertie. I ruined his plans to have her put him in charge of their finances. I talked her into giving Frank a real funeral. Not a bullshit Gene style party." "I see" smiled Preston. "Do you believe that son-of-a-bitch had the balls to offer to help me with Patricia's funeral and offered to sing hymns? It took every ounce of self-control I had not to smack his face off!" "He was trying to get into your head. Guess it worked!""I have no idea how long he stood outside my office door. We discussed her and Patsy sharing an assisted living apartment." "Let's see how he acts. Remember, the game of cat and mouse is a long one." "He is devolving, so he won't be able to wait out his timetable." "Exactly!" "Just be careful, Doc. Goodnight" "Well, Melvin, it's back to surveillance. Do you need a refill of coffee for that thermos?" ""Yes, thank you, ma'am." "It's CARLA, Melvin!" "I personally need a drink. Three fingers of Scotch, neat. The pot is full, give yourself a refill, Melvin." "Aren't you afraid, Doc?" "Yes, but I will never let that narcissistic prick control me!" "I'm sorry about your friend Patricia." "Thank you." "Did you know her a long time?" "Yes, since she was a young girl." "Oh, wow." "I'm all she had left." "Will there be a funeral?" "I'm not sure." "I better get out to my car so you can get some sleep. Goodnight. Lock the door!" "Goodnight, Melvin."Carla headed for a hot bath to help her relax. After finishing her Scotch, her

eyes began to close as she sank into a bubbly bliss.

Thoughts of dead girls slid through her mind in a slow

motion picture show. She could hear Gene laughing

'You'll never prove a damn thing!' Startled awake with a

cold chill, Carla climbed out of the tub and into bed.

Pounding on the front door woke Carla from her heavy

sleep. Outside her window stood Melvin's replacement.

"Rise and shine, ma'am!" Nodding, she headed for the

coffee pot. The brew of life was calling her. "Jesus, it's

going to be a long day. Group is meeting today. I'm

going to be bombarded with questions about who did this.

Hopefully there will be better news for Gertie and Patsy."

Dressing for the day in her best suit, she headed out.

With the parking lot full, Carla felt more secure.

Unlocking the office, Carla took her place behind her

desk. Bursting through the door, Carla's secretary Charlie

announced that she had several messages and an

economy sized coffee. "I have heard from all the

members of your Survivors group. They are all

concerned about you and they have safety concerns.

"How's my schedule look?" "I cleared your day. I

figured you would need to be free to make arrangements

for Patricia's funeral. Spinney called. So did the coroner.

The autopsies have been completed. I called Leon

Brothers funeral parlor to arrange for Patricia's cremation.

Will there be calling hours?" "No. She had no family."

"What should they do with her ashes?" "I will pick them

up myself. I know where she would want her ashes

scattered." "I heard about the gift that someone left

attached to your car." "It was just a scare tactic. I am

fine." "I will be heading to the morgue in a few minutes."

"I will have Preston and Thomas meet you there."Charlie left to call Preston. As the door closed behind her, Carla put her head in her hands. It was going to be a very bad day. Pulling herself together, she headed for the morgue. The walk was so frigid, the morgue seemed almost warm.Expecting silence, Carla was surprised at all the movement happening in a place laden with death. "Hello?" "Oh, hello Dr. Sebastian. You are here for whom?" "Patricia Simpson." "Yes, here are the findings." He handed the report to Carla. "Did you run a tox screen?" "Yes, the food she ate was poisoned. She was beaten and orally sodomized. We found traces of DNA in her cheeks. Neither she nor Frank Snider could have fought back. It paralyzed their muscles." "So, they were defenseless but they were aware of everything that was happening to them? Then this was murder?" "Yes, there is no doubt in my mind." Tears filled Carla's eyes

for the first time since she was notified of Patricia's death.

"Would you like to see her?" "Yes, just for a minute."

Pulling open the drawer, Carla looked at Patricia's gray

skin. It was frigid to the touch. "Damn it! I told you to be

careful and not to trust him! You were my right hand in

group. Who will be there to protect our girls? Damn you

for dying on me! I loved you ever since I found you in

that horrible place!"Carla's tears flowed freely, landing

on Patricia's face. Preston placed a firm but gentle hand

on Carla's shoulder. "We will get him. I promise. Gertie

is here to see Frank. She will need your strength."

Wiping her eyes, Carla gave Patricia a kiss goodbye

before closing the drawer. The coroner then brought in

Gertie and explained Frank's death to her. Gertie

collapsed in a heap on the floor. Gene helped her to her

feet. "I'm right here, Gertie. Would you prefer to wait to see Frank at the funeral parlor?" "I need to see him. I need to say goodbye." "I think you should wait. You can see him after he's fixed up. You don't want to see him this way" soothed Dr. Sebastian. Gene looked into Gertie's eyes with a gentle smile and said, "I agree with Dr. Sebastian. You do not want to see him this way." With arms around each other, Carla walked Gertie to the lobby. Gene asked if he could have a moment alone with Frank. Nodding, the assistant opened the drawer that held Frank's corpse. Gene stared blankly at Frank's face. Bending down, he whispered, "This is what you get for crossing me. Goodbye, Frank!" He slammed the drawer closed and headed for the lobby. He felt completely justified in what he had done. Now to grab Gertie and make an appearance at the hospital. Upon their arrival at the hospital, Nurse Rachel looked at Gene as she informed him that he was to join the meeting. "What meeting?" "Your wife's doctor and a social worker for both Patsy and Gertie." Gene walked into the doctor's office like he owned the place. "So, there's a meeting being held about Gertie and Patsy's welfare without me?" "No, we wanted you to join us, Gene." "Well, what's going on?" "After speaking with both Patsy and Gertie's physicians, we feel that an assisted living apartment is the best solution for meeting their needs. It is connected to the nursing home. The nurse's aides will be available to give Patsy her breathing treatments and physical therapy. Since Gertie cannot live alone, this placement is an ideal fit. Also, with them being as close as they are, it should help with adjusting to the new environment. They are allowed to have personal belongings brought in so that it will feel more like home." "Sounds nice. What's the cost of this apartment?""That's another issue, Gene. Mrs. Gibson and I will need to go over their financial records to see if they can afford it on their Social Security benefits alone or if the will need some public assistance to fill in the gaps." "We have accessed the bank records, as Gertie receives Medicare and Medicaid. As soon as the house is sold, Gertie should be set for a while." "As for Patsy, we've accessed her file as well. She will be short about six hundred dollars a month, so you will be expected to pay the remaining balance." What the hell do you mean, pay the difference!" screamed Gene. "She is your wife. You are legally responsible for her care. It shouldn't be an issue for you. Didn't you receive a life insurance benefit as Marge's beneficiary?" "Not yet, I haven't!"

"We also need to see the bills for Frank's funeral." "I haven't made the arrangements yet. His autopsy was just finished!" "We can help you with making his arrangements so you don't have so much to do." "Thank you for the offer, but Frank was my best friend. I think I should handle it." "Well, Gertie has signed he forms allowing us to handle her affairs. She won't be needing your help." "I see" grumbled Gene. "When will they be moving into their apartment?" "We would like to move them in the next few days. We need to arrange for the nursing care." "Do I at least get to move 'my wife' into this place?" "Sure. I would expect that you would know what personal items she would want to bring to her new place.""Christ, this will be so hard on me!" "Why? This will free up your time for performances. You should be secure in the knowledge that both women will be safe and well taken care of." "Yes, that is comforting. This

may sound selfish, but I will miss my Patsy not being

with me." "You can visit as often as you'd like." "This is

the best solution for both women" chimed Mrs. Gibson.

"Mrs. Lacy, do you agree?" "Yes. I am positive that this

is best for both of them." Looking at Patsy's doctor,

Gene nodded in agreement. "I will assume that since you

ladies are professionals you know what you're doing"

Gene said, his tone dripping with sarcasm. Slamming the

door as he left, Gene was fuming. On the walk to Patsy's

room, he knew that he had to compose himself. Closing

the chapel door, Gene was bitching out loud. "I know

that nosey bitch, Dr. Sebastian is behind this! Well, at

least I can help Patsy move in. I can see the layout of the

place. With both women in one place, killing them will

be easier!" The nurses stood outside the chapel door

listening to Gene's conversations with himself. The nurse's aides were cackling. "Check this out. He's answering himself. This guy's a fruit cake!" "Get away from there!" yelled nurse Rachel. "But he's talking to himself. And he answers himself in the third person. I heard him." "That will be enough. Go answer those call lights, NOW!" The nurses shook their heads and snickered as they disappeared down the hallway. Pulling himself together, Gene hustled through the chapel doors and headed for Patsy's room.He burst into Patsy's room. "Hello, ladies! I hear you girls are getting an assisted living apartment together." "My doctor says I can still get my breathing treatments and some physical therapy to get my strength back." "How do you feel about it, Gertie?" "Well, I can't live by myself. I will be there with Patsy and there will be nurses checking up on us. It sounds perfect!" "I guess you won't be needing MY help anymore!" "No, that's not true, Gene. There will be activities for us to do and you won't be stuck trying to care for two disabled women.""Gertie, do you not trust me with your and Frank's money? We are like family! This cuts me to the bone!" "Mrs. Gibson was very nice to help us." "I guess I could pack up your things for the new apartment. Make a list of what you want me to pack up for you." "Well, we have to ask what we're allowed to have." "Mrs. Gibson gave us a small list. She said that she will check on other items we are allowed to have." Gene looked at the list. "Okay. Pots, pans, dishes and bath towels. What about furniture?" As Mrs. Gibson listened in, she spoke. "The doctors have asked for hospital beds and recliners that are remote controlled and can raise the patient to a standing position." "So, a love seat, dining room table and chairs. Blankets." "All blankets, towels and clothing needs to be sanitized before it is brought into the facility. Smoking is not permitted, as Patsy will have oxygen in use." Glancing over at the antique wicker carriage, Mrs. Gibson asked, "Is that a collector's item?" "Yes and the beautiful dolls that Gene got for me." "They are lovely." "Gertie is making them matching sweater sets and blankets." Smiling, Mrs. Gibson said, "They are very life-like." Patsy proudly announced, "They sound real, too!" Nodding, Mrs. Gibson smiled. "They are beautifully crafted. I have seen some lovely doll collections. Did you know there's a museum dedicated entirely to dolls?" "No." "Oh, Gertie, wouldn't that be a great day trip?" "Yes, it would." Gertie asked about curtains in the apartment. "We have standard curtains that are in every unit. Apartments are cleaned daily and inspected once a month. Nurses make rounds two or three times a day. There will be a home aid to help with the housekeeping. They use cleaning supplies that are approved by our medical team." "It sounds like you have everything under control, so I won't be needed" pouted Gene. "Oh, you will have the most important job, Gene. Decorating the apartment so that it feels like home for these ladies." "I have arranged calling hours and a burial service for Frank tomorrow at eleven a.m." "Gene, would you mind bringing Frank's good suit?" "No problem, Mrs. Gibson. I will start gathering up stuff for the apartment." "Mrs. Lacy and I will help you go through everything to determine which items are appropriate." "I will go with Gene" smiled Gertie. "Honey, don't forget our wedding quilt that Ma made for us. I want it for my bed." "We need to purchase a love seat from a furniture store and it will need to be steam cleaned." Gene had a confused look on his face. Mrs. Lacy clarified that it was a precaution to keep out bed bugs and roaches. "Oh, I understand" cracked Gene. "Guess I'd better go and get this started. I will come get you when I'm ready for you, Gertie." "Here's the house key so you can pick up Frank's suit and his pictures." After taking a call at the nurse's desk, Mrs. Lacy returned. "I was just speaking with the mortician." Taking a deep breath, she said, "Frank will need to have a closed casket ceremony or to be cremated. There was too much damage to his face." As Gertie's tears started to fall, Gene took the cue. "We can have him cremated and get him an urn shaped like a cowboy boot and we'll use his band picture." "It is Gertie's decision." With a quivering lip and a child- like voice, she whispered, "Gene's right." "I will meet you at the funeral parlor in an hour" said Mrs.

Gibson. "That will be fine. I authorized the body to be

brought there. We need to get this taken care of. Then

you and I can go to a furniture store to choose a love seat

or a small couch. The doctors have requested the

recliners and hospital beds .Everything you have will be

sanitized and the apartment will be set up for your

oxygen. The stove is electric. We should have their

apartment setup by Thursday. This will give Patsy a bit

more time in physical therapy before she will need to

handle walking independently. She will have a walker to

help her get around the apartment. I need to stop in at the

office. We will meet Mrs. Lacey at the funeral parlor.

"Yes, ma'am." As Mrs. Gibson walked away Gene was

fuming. Who the hell did she think she was? I don't take

orders from anyone! Especially not a snooty bitch

caseworker! Why do I have to pay for new furniture? That money is mine! I earned it fair and square. Marge is gone! I made that happen. That insurance money is mine!" Walking to his truck, Gene started thinking about the file in Dr. Sebastian's office. The bomb didn't do the trick. Back at Spinney's office, Preston and Thomas had arrived to discuss what had transpired and the autopsy reports. "So, I hear the good doctor had a bit of a scare?" "Yes. Gene was sending her a message. The message is 'back the fuck off'. "Why?" "The doc has been talking to Gertie and it put a kink into Gene gaining control of their finances. Social workers got Patsy and Gertie into an assisted living apartment. It will be a little harder for them to have accidents with staff around." There was a long sigh as Spinney flipped through the autopsy reports. "There was DNA left on Patricia. The oral sodomy left us a trace amount. The killer was smart. He used a toxin known as Devil's Breath or Scopolamine. It's colorless and odorless so mixing it into the catfish dipping sauce didn't change the taste. It takes effect almost instantly. Depressing the central nervous system, wipes out memory but they are fully aware of what's happening. It causes a zombie-like effect. Under the influence of this, you have no muscle control. Speech is affected as well as coordination. Dr. Sebastian announced her presence by saying "Patricia brought mace, pepper spray, brass knuckles, a knife and a hand gun. She was prepared for a physical altercation. She drank club soda that night. No alcohol." "So, he planned this. He knew that Frank would not allow her to be killed, so he killed both of them. And because he used a paralytic, people would have just assumed they were drunk." "Doc, any thoughts on this?"

"These are my files on Marge and Patsy. The life insurance policy and everything Gene did to become the payee for Patsy's benefits. He made Social Security think that she was depressed and suicidal. He will try to break into my office to get this file." "I will have my secretary make copies and I will keep your originals. Let him think he got your original documents.""About the funeral, Frank's face was so messed up it will have to be a closed casket or a cremation." "You know if you convict him, jail in general population just gives him another platform for his bullshit and more people to prey on." "He truly is mentally disturbed. The proper and ideal situation would be for him to serve out his sentence in the wing of the hospital for the criminally insane. Because of his magnetic personality, he would need to be put in solitary or complete isolation." "It is possible to get a judge to go along with that. We have plenty of past behavior to show

a pattern of behavior. The sight of the girl he left for dead

will set him off, but to set him off, she needs to say

something that his ego will not be able to

handle."Smiling, Preston and Thomas looked at each

other. "You hit like a bitch" is what Marissa said. "That

would do the trick" smiled Dr. Sebastian. "You know

that's why he killed those girls during his tour. They

didn't praise his prowess as a man" cracked Spinney.

"That's what got them killed?" "Yes. He is a true

Sociopath with Narcissistic features. He has no empathy.

He does not feel love. He isn't capable. But he is a

fantastic manipulator." "What is with the talking to

himself and answering himself in the third person, Doc?"

"There are many possibilities. Schizophrenia. Bipolar

disorder and others." "How will he respond to jail, Doc?"

345

"He has issues with authority. He needs to be in charge. That's why the military would not have been a good fit for him. If I were his lawyer, I would ask for a psychiatric evaluation. He has no impulse control and he shows signs of Anti-Social personality disorder." "I have been cleared to request the death penalty. "When we get the true bill from the Grand Jury, he will be arrested and arraigned. We can discuss the option of him accepting a plea bargain based on mental illness or we will push for the death penalty." "I have to be honest. I do not feel sorry for him. But I would be remiss in not telling you that he should have scans done of his brain." "What are you expecting to see in the scans?" "Well, this term doesn't appear in the DSM-4 guide, but it has been used since the 1960's to describe someone who is just plain evil. Malignant narcissism as a syndrome is characterized by Narcissistic Personality Disorder, antisocial features,

paranoid traits and egocentric aggression. Other

symptoms may include a lack of conscience,

psychological need for power and an exaggerated sense

of importance or grandiosity. Many serial killers brain

scans show different things that are lit up in comparison

to a normal brain. He thinks there is nothing wrong with

his behavior. Basically, his brain is wired wrong. So

prison isn't the answer. He is sick and if he were put in

general population, he would be running the place. ""Is

he criminally insane?" "That isn't listed in the DSM-4

guide but he should be in a hospital for the criminally

insane. No psychiatrist would ever let him be released.

Gene would consider him or her a threat." "So, we will

be asking for the death penalty" smiled Spinney. "He

needs to be in a padded room!" cried Dr. Sebastian. "I

understand that. But no decent lawyer will allow their client to get the death penalty if they can be institutionalized in a hospital for the criminally insane. It would be career suicide." "So you're willing to play the odds?" "Yes. I am sure that his lawyer will get him to go along with this." "This is not a hand of poker. This is a sick man." ""But he deserves to be punished severely" complained Thomas. "Agreed. But imagine being in a five-by-nine cell with zero human contact. Solitary confinement can drive a sane man off his rocker." ""He deserves to die! Like all those women he killed!" shouted Thomas. "A hospital for the criminally insane makes prison seem like a picnic" replied Preston. "I am leaving you my file, Spinney. I trust you will utilize it to the best of your ability. I have to pick up Patricia's ashes at the mortuary and spread them in the garden at the juvenile facility. ""Would you like one of us to go with you?"

"No thanks. I need to do this alone" smiled Dr. Sebastian.

"Before I go, Gene is supposed to set up funeral services

for Frank. You may want to make your presence known.

Patsy and Gertie will be moving into the assisted living

section of the nursing home. Gene will be chomping at

the bit to cash in on Patsy's life insurance policy." "So

they will be his next targets?" asked Preston. "Exactly!

He needs to feel important. He will be on edge because

the social workers have been giving him orders about

furniture and other things for the apartment. They are

also taking possession of Frank and Gertie's house and

selling it to cover the costs of living in the apartment.

Gene is not going to be in charge of Frank's finances like

he thought he should be. He has already received the

insurance money for Marge's death. The social worker

also informed him that he will have to relinquish Patsy's benefits as well as cover the remaining balance that her benefits and insurance don't. He is livid and it's been slowly brewing just below the surface. He will try to kill Patsy and Gertie very soon. He won't be able to control the urge" explained Dr. Sebastian. "I really need to go take care of Patricia!"Heading toward the mortuary, Carla knew what Patricia would want. Her final resting place would be in the flowers where she spent her free time as a child. The detention center had been remodeled but the garden was still the same. Pulling into the mortuary parking lot, Carla headed inside. Taking a deep breath, she pulled open the door. Antiseptic filled the air. It was almost an assault on her senses. "Hello, Dr. Sebastian. Patricia is ready. I put her in a lovely urn." "Thank you." "Did you want a service?" "No, she wanted to be put in a garden." "I see." Paying with her credit card, she carried Patricia to her car. Pulling out of the parking lot, she began talking aloud. "Patricia, I will miss you and our talks. Damn it! I warned you how dangerous Gene was!" She cried as she drove. She pulled into the parking lot of the detention center and opened the door. She carried Patricia down the path to the garden. It was just starting to bloom. She sat down on the bench where Patricia had spent many an afternoon. "I have loved you since you were a child. I worked with you to help free your heart from all of its tragedy. I now will set you completely free." Opening the urn, Carla gently sprinkled ashes around each plant as she said her final goodbye to her friend Patricia. The drive back to her office was full of hurt and anger. She knew that the ladies from group would need to talk about Patricia and to say their goodbyes.Meanwhile Gene was arranging a service for Frank. Talking to the mortician, he said that Frank needed to be cremated because of the damage to what used to be his face. "Here's a picture to be enlarged for the service." Gene was wearing one of his gig outfits. "This will be hard on his wife, so a short service and reception at The Little Woods Church. He will be buried with his family in their mausoleum. Can you have him ready by tomorrow?" "Yes, at one p.m." "Fine." "Now to meet with those damn caseworkers!" Gene pulled into the parking lot of the furniture store and stepped out of his truck. He was greeted by a shrill "You are late, sir." "I was arranging Frank's funeral. It's set for tomorrow at one p.m. at the Little Woods Church. The reception will follow in the rectory." "Well, we are on a schedule, but since you were making arrangements for Gertie, I guess that's acceptable." "Do you have a list of what you found

for our ladies?" "Yes. I took all the personal items to the

assisted living facility because it has to be sterilized."

"Yes, it keeps people from bringing in bed bugs and

lice." "All of Gertie's personal possessions from her

house will go into storage and the house will be sold at

auction. She did mention that she would like you to have

all the musical instruments. We feel that would be

acceptable. Now that you've been brought up to speed,

let's find some suitable furniture for the apartment. We

have arranged for their beds and recliners. They need a

couch or a love seat and household items. I have brought

the specifications for size and colors of furniture that is

allowed." Scratching his head, Gene smiled. "Guess

there's no room for personality in that place. "We do

allow for personal touches, but furniture needs to be

universally accepted. Wall colors are shades of white or beige. There are pastel colors in the bedrooms and bathrooms." "Christ! The military had a better color scheme!" "We need to get this done, Gene. We have other clients." Okay, let's go in" cracked Gene. With notebook in hand, Mrs. Gibson and Mrs. Lacey entered the showroom. The sales personnel recognized the social workers immediately. "How can I help you?" Smiling, Mrs. Gibson handed the sales girl her list. "Furniture this size is kept in the efficiency apartment section." Gene looked at the boring colors and fabrics shaking his head. "What color are their recliners?" "A nice blue suede. Here is the material." She pulled a swatch of fabric from her portfolio and handed it to Gene and then the sales girl. Looking disappointed with the options, Gene sat down on a few love seats. They were not very comfortable. Gene

then spotted a blue flowered bouquet printed love seat.
"Now this is something the girls will like. And the
recliners will match" smiled Gene. Mrs. Gibson ran her
hand across the material, admitting it was soft. "It has
just been re upholstered. I can give you a great deal. Let
me talk to my boss." She returned with her boss in tow.
"What can I help you with?" "According to this young
lady this love seat has just been reupholstered." "Yes, it
has been refreshed." Smiling, Gene asked, "How much?"
"One thousand." "WHAT? It was reupholstered, which
means it's old." "How about I include a small dinette
set?" "Done!" smiled Gene. "Now, what else is on our
list?" "Dishes, pots pans and a microwave." Gene spent
three thousand dollars and everything was new. "So, does
this mean I get a break on the remaining balance for the
apartment?" "Let me call our boss." "For them to move

in, it's fifteen hundred dollars and six hundred a month after that. Since you generously covered all the items needed for the apartment, the rent is reduced to six hundred per month." "Acceptable" announced Gene. "Maybe I can even do a solo gig once a week for the folks at the facility." Smiling, Mrs. Gibson said, "I'm sure they would enjoy that, Gene. Also, we need you to bring the rent money to our office tomorrow so they can move in." "Frank's funeral is tomorrow." "Everything is already set up and waiting. They just need to be brought over." Whipping out his wallet, Gene handed over two months' rent on the new apartment. "We will bring Gertie to the funeral and they will be ready for move in by 9:00 a.m. tomorrow morning." "Oh, don't forget Patsy's dolls. She loves them. Can I have a look at the place in the morning once everything is moved in?"

"Sure. I don't see why not, Gene. How about at 10:00a.m?" "Sure, no problem" smiled Gene. "I'm going to shoot over to Gertie's old house to pick up Frank's instruments." "We have a crew over there right now, so just make sure they write down everything you take." "No problem" said Gene. Heading in opposite directions, Gene started thinking about how to eliminate Patsy. The drive to Gertie's was full of scattered thoughts. Pulling into Gertie's driveway, Gene saw a crew of at least ten people going through the house. Heading to the front door, the head of the work crew greeted Gene. "I'm here to pick up the musical instruments." "Yes, Mrs. Gibson contacted me to let me know you would be coming out. This is what we have found so far." He led Gene into the parlor where all the musical instruments sat. Gene carefully carried the guitars to his truck. Returning, he grabbed the mandolin and violin. "What about this baby grand piano?" "Wow! I'm not sure." After a moment, Gene smiled. "Maybe it should be donated to the nursing home." "Hey, wait Gene. Mrs. Gibson wants to speak with you." He handed Gene the phone and overheard, "Anything you cannot take will be put through the auction and sold." "I see" frowned Gene. "FUCK!" cried Gene. Those county bitches just want to make a buck off Gertie's stuff! "I will have to come back with a moving truck." "We have one that we could lend you after hours." "Sounds great" said Gene. "Gertie just said to take the instruments. She never said what I could do with them. We will bring the piano to the nursing home. Those folks deserve a little music in their lives. See you in a few hours, okay?" Smiling as he drove away, Gene cackled "Two can play that game, you psycho bitches!"

Gertie and Frank would agree with my decision to donate it. No bitch tells me what to do! As he unloaded the instruments, Gene decided he should turn Marge's bedroom into a music room. "What do I do with all the shit in the closet? I can use the dresser in my room. It will be a nice place to write music. Looks like I can finally have the house the way I deserve! No more girly shit. I can display my rifle collection. This will be good. Now to see what food the neighbors left for me."

Warming up lasagna, Gene relaxed with three fingers of bourbon as he laid out plans to rearrange the house to his liking. Checking the clock, Gene thought I have an hour until the crew arrives. Guess I'll move the dresser and dressing screen from Marge's room into mine. Then I can set up the music room and the band can practice there whenever we want. As loud as I want! The single life is going to be so good for me! Once Patsy is gone, I will have the energy to be on tour as much as I want. I smell dinner. Better move this stuff before I eat. I'm gonna need a dishwasher for my dirty dishes too. Bringing his thoughts back into focus was the sound of a horn honking out in the driveway. Hustling out the front door, Gene greeted the guys. "We delivered the piano to the nursing home. It's in the day room. The Director of Nursing was thrilled." "So, how much do I owe you boys?" "We are working off our old ladies' public assistance grants." "That sucks. How about I slip you all some cash? Want some supper? I got lasagna warming up in the oven." "I dropped the guys off a while ago. It's just me and Hank here." "Come on in" Gene said, leading them into the kitchen. Gene opened the fridge. "Want a beer?" "Sure thing." "Let me throw the garlic bread in the oven. We'll eat in ten minutes or so. So, how much do I owe you boys?" "Anything would be appreciated." "Well, I have a small job that needs done if you're interested." "Sure! What is it?" "We'll discuss it during dinner." Pulling out place settings, Gene set the table to accommodate his guests. Pulling the lasagna and bread from the oven, he announced "It's ready. Grab your plates and help yourselves!" Chowing down, the men ate in silence "So, what's the job?" asked Hank. "My mother-in-law passed away and my wife is in a nursing home so I need to get rid of all these boxes of stuff. You can go through them and keep whatever you want. Donate the rest to the thrift store." "Let's see how much stuff you got there." After a cursory inspection, the men looked at each other. "Will you pay us a hundred bucks a piece for this job?" "Sounds fair. And I'll give you each another hundred for the piano delivery." "Great! Let's get this out to the truck." "Here, let me pay you boys." "Boy, our old ladies will love going through this stuff. Thanks for dinner, Gene." "I may have more work for you boys later on, so check in with me. Here's my number. My band plays a lot of local gigs, so I'm always around. My buddy's funeral is tomorrow afternoon. After that, I will be checking up on my wife. After that, I'll be around. How are your carpentry skills? I may need to sound proof my music room. The tiles for that are sold at the hardware store." Waving goodbye, Gene headed back into the house, smiling at all that he had accomplished for the day. Looking at the dishes, Gene was less than impressed until he realized that the lasagna pan was a foil one that could be thrown away along with the plates and silverware. Throwing everything in the garbage can and calling it a day, Gene headed for his bedroom. Dr. Sebastian closed

up the group meeting and packed up to head home early.

"Ma'am, you may not enter the vehicle until we have

checked it. Please move back." "Okay, do your thing,

Melvin." After checking her car over completely, he

signaled that all was clear. "I know you put Miss Patricia

to rest today. I am very sorry for your loss. She was a

nice lady." "Thank you, Melvin." "Are you going to Mr.

Frank's funeral tomorrow? It's at 1:00 p.m. At the

country church." "Yes, I know. One of my clients will be

moved into an assisted living facility in the morning and

after that, I will attend the funeral with Gertie. Because

of the way he died, there will be police officers in

attendance." "Would you like me to accompany you,

ma'am?" No. I will be fine. You need your rest to keep

guard over me at night." "Let's get you home, ma'am."

"Fine, Melvin." As Melvin followed Dr. Sebastian home, he realized that she could be a target. He thought to himself 'We need to put more guards on her.' Melvin pulled into the darkened driveway and got out of his car. With flashlight in hand, he checked the grounds. As he unlocked the front door, he checked the interior of the house before giving Carla the all clear sign. Carla jogged through the front entrance, dropping her keys and briefcase on the stand in the hallway. She then removed her shoes and headed to the kitchen to pour herself a drink. "Okay, ma'am. Come lock your door, please?" "Yes, Melvin. Goodnight." "I will see you in the morning, ma'am." "Please, call me Carla." "Okay, Miss Carla." "Goodnight, Melvin." After locking the door, Carla went and ran a bubble bath to help relax the day away. After two glasses of wine and her bath, Carla was ready for bed, but sleep came hard. Patricia's voice was loud, warning

Carla through her dreams that she was in danger. To

protect herself, Carla had given Patsy's file to A D.A

Spinney. She no longer posed any threat to Gene. Carla

was startled awake by visions of Gene killing Patsy.

Unable to get back to sleep, she decided to catch up on

her paperwork and dictation. After having a shower to

wake up and a pot of coffee, Carla was ready to work.

She was still a bit on edge so she decided to make sticky

buns. About halfway through the cooking process, Carla

heard a knock on the door. Grabbing her handgun, she

walked toward the door. Peeking out of the peephole,

Carla saw the sun rising over the top of Melvin's head.

"Miss Carla, are you okay?" "Yes, Melvin. Come in and

have some sticky buns and fresh coffee." "Thank you,

Miss Carla. May I use your restroom?" "Down the hall.

Second door on the left." "Ma'am?" "What did I tell you about calling me that, Melvin?" "Are they ever gonna arrest that man who hurt all these people?" "Soon they will be able to." "It seems like that District Attorney wants to be popular more than he wants to do his job." "I have faith in our D.A. to do what it takes to put that monster away for good." Spinney was getting his files prepared for the Grand Jury. They were set to convene in two days. Between what my investigators found and testimony from the only surviving witness, there's no doubt in my mind that the true bill will be issued. Then I will have Gene's arrest warrant in hand. That will get me a shot at becoming the Attorney General. I cannot afford to fuck this up! Putting Gene away will make my career jump ahead. Going through the file, he arranged the papers into sections. A-1 was proof of prior behaviors including the abuses of his children, wives and lovers. B-1 was the paper trail proving that he was in each town at the time that each girl disappeared and was found dead. C-1 was financial expenditures during his supposed tour. Very few of these were actually tour related. D-1 detailed his meeting with Patricia. The autopsy reports showed that both Patricia and Frank were shot in the face. Frank signed a statement because he was present at the crime scene and he helped Gene dispose of the first girl's body. E-1 was the life insurance policies he took out on both Patsy and Marge. He made Patsy look crazy so that he would be made her representative payee for her disability checks. She was re-evaluated while he was on tour. The board decided she was fully competent to handle her own money. F-1 was the Adult Protective Services abuse case that was opened over Marge. G-1 military discharge records. He was deemed unfit for service and could not be stationed overseas. He had drug and alcohol issues as well as problems with authority. H-1 In interviews from witnesses, he talks in the third person and answers himself. This illustrates a pattern of issues. Both mental and otherwise that feed his narcissistic personality. I am requesting a true bill to bring this man to trial for his crimes. Spinney smiled. "I will have that prick tried for the deaths of ever one of those young girls!" Could it be that Dr. Sebastian is right? Is he truly ill? Either way, I will have him tucked securely away so that he can never hurt anyone else. Patsy and Gertie will be safe in the assisted living facility. I am fully prepared for the Grand Jury on Thursday morning. Putting his file back in order, Spinney locked it away in a double locking steel cabinet. Heading out, he was confident in his skills as an attorney to get the right decision from the Grand Jury. While Spinney planned for Gene's incarceration, Gene had plans of his own. Gene poured himself a drink as he sorted through his sound effect tapes listening for just the right sound. "Ahh, here it is. This will send Patsy right over the edge. She will think her dolls are live babies. I will set this up in Patsy's room so that when she goes to sleep, she will hear babies crying "Mama". Laughing heartily, "She will be medicated and ripe for an accident. The money will be all mine!" Gene spliced several tapes together to get the desired effect. Turning off the lights, Gene listened intently. "Yes! This is perfect. She will be as crazy as a fruit basket! The accident will be simple but effective. The tape will send her into an attack. She won't be able to breathe and she will die! I will collect the insurance money and then be able to go on a lengthy

369

tour." Thinking about Frank, Gene again started talking aloud. "Well, you son-of-a-bitch! It did you no good to sign a statement against me. You are dead, so you can't testify and no one else knew! I will continue being an international star and now you're nothing but fucking ash! That will teach you to betray me! Gertie will have a nice, quiet goodbye and then we won't think about you ever again! I will be rich and you're history!"As Gene got ready for the morning's events, he smiled at a job well done. Preparing for his trip to Patsy's apartment, he even planned out the story he would tell Mrs. Gibson and Mrs. Lacey. Then he would dress to take Gertie to Frank's funeral. It would be a full day's work. Gene's black brew wafted upward toward his nose. He pulled out the new stereo system for Patsy's room along with a few of her favorite tapes of his concerts. Carrying the box to his truck he was prepared for the trip. As Gene pulled into

the facility parking lot, he noticed both caseworkers out

front with a moving crew bringing in the new furniture.

Hopping out of the truck, Gene reached for the box that

held the stereo. "Hello, ladies!" smiled Gene. "What's in

the box?" "I got my girl a new stereo system so when

she's missing me, she can listen to my music. Frank is

also playing on these cassettes. There are speakers so the

ladies can listen to them in stereo." "I see"" cracked Mrs.

Lacey. "Let's have a look at the place." Going from room

to room, Gene gave a nod of approval. "Where shall I set

up the system?" "In the entertainment center in the living

room." "I have extra speakers so my girls can enjoy the

music in their bedrooms too." "How long will it take you

to set it up?" "Give me thirty minutes." "Okay, Gene. We

are trusting you to have this done in the time you

requested. We are going to pick them up from the hospital. Once we have them settled in, we will take Gertie to the church for the funeral.""Oh, I had planned on doing that. I arranged a really nice service for Frank." "Get busy and we will see." Gene started working on the stereo setup. He ran the loop of sound effects to start at 10 p.m. while they would be sleeping so that it would be playing subliminally in Patsy's mind.Once he had that in place, Gene went to dress for the funeral. Upon his return to the apartment, he watched Patsy and Gertie looking around in dismay. "It's nice and clean" said Patsy. "Almost antiseptic!" whined Gertie. "I hope you like the stereo system, ladies!" "Gene!" smiled Patsy. "I figured you would like some of our gig tapes in case you girls missed me." "Oh Gene! You know what I like" laughed Patsy. "Here, let's have a look at your bedroom." "Where are my babies?" "Oh, the carriage is by the window."

"Good." "Ma'am, we need to set up your breathing

treatment machine and wall oxygen." "By all means, go

ahead" said Patsy. "The nurse will come in three times

per day for your breathing treatments. They will also help

with the household chores and getting you to any

appointments. Otherwise, this is your home. So relax and

enjoy it" smiled Mrs. Lacey. "Who will hang our

pictures?" "We have a crew of men that will help get

things organized for you in the morning. Once you get

settled in, we can look at all the events happening at the

nursing home. Holiday parties, holiday leaf bus tours,

and many other events. Crowing, Gene announced that

he would do solo performances on Country music day,

which was every Wednesday. "That sounds wonderful!"

smiled Gertie. "I brought quilts and things to help you

feel more at home" smiled Gene. "I will take Gertie to the funeral service" announced Gene. "It will free up your schedules. Patsy, you make me a list of what needs doing and I will get to it after the service." "They have rules and hours for visitation, Gene." "My wife lives here. She is not a prisoner. I will visit her any time I please! Now Gertie needs to get ready for Frank's service. You ladies are excused!" snapped Gene. Patsy helped her to fasten her best pearls. "Oh, but I have gained too much weight to wear my black dress." "I thought you would say that" sighed Gene. "So I picked you up a nice navy blue dress. It matches perfectly with your pretty blue eyes, Gertie. Plus, you can wear it for other dressy occasions." "Oh, thank you, Gene! You think of everything." "Patsy, don't you touch a thing until I get back here. When I do, I will start putting things away."

Gertie reappeared in the doorway dressed for Frank's service. "You look lovely! Frank would be honored to be seen with you. Let's be leaving." As they got into the limousine, the nurse arrived to settle Patsy in with her new medication schedule. "Let's review your medication list. You are administered eight medicines three times daily along with three breathing treatments plus oxygen. You have wall oxygen in your bedroom plus portable tanks for when you are moving around the apartment." "Why do I need all of that?" asked Patsy. "It looks like you will also be doing physical therapy to get you mobile again. Once you get into a routine, it will be easy. There is an intercom system. If you aren't well, press the call button and a nurse will come see you. Staff is always on-call. You will never be alone here. Your roommate gets medicine twice a day and will also be attending physical therapy. Here is your temperature control. You will also have a home health aide that will come and help you with cooking and cleaning. If needed, we can arrange for one to stay o0vernights with you as well. You need some grocery shopping done. Both of you are on a 1500 calorie, low sodium diet. Our staff has experience in shopping for residents here. We have a farmer's market on Saturdays for fresh fruits and vegetables. Any questions?" "We have visiting hours?" "Yes. Usually from 10 a.m. to 8 p.m. so our residents can get to sleep early. Plus, it gives residents time to complete therapy." "It sounds like we are in prison here." "No, you're not. But sticking to a regimen helps residents remember things. It becomes second nature." "Did we join the military and they didn't tell us?" Laughing hard, Nurse Willets said, "No, but having a daily schedule of things to accomplish keeps our residents alert and oriented." "I will trust your judgment" giggled Patsy. "Do you have male nurses?" "Yes, we have both male and female nursing staff. Would you like to join the other residents for lunch? Or would you like to eat here?" "I'll have lunch here. There's so much to do here." "Let's start by displaying these beautiful quilts and pretty dishes." "You don't have to help me with that, Miss Willets." "It's fine. I am here with you for the day. I will get you some lunch and we will start decorating." As the church filled with mourners, Gene smiled to himself. "This will be a good service." Gertie greeted the guests as they took their seats. Dr. Sebastian sat beside Gertie for support. Gene noticed the investigators standing against the back wall making their presence known. Scowling, Gene wondered what those cops were doing at Frank's funeral. There was no time for thinking. He had to prepare to give a eulogy to honor Frank. After the minister gave a beautiful sermon, Gene stepped up to the microphone. He told everyone how Frank had been his best friend, a wonderful husband, good son and a talented musician. The portrait of Frank smiling in his gig uniform was a great touch. The announcement of the reception in the rectory following the service brought relief to a sullen audience. Gene walked Gertie out to the rectory. Then, he turned to Dr. Sebastian and sniped, "What did you do for Patricia?" "Her ashes were sprinkled in her favorite garden." "Oh, is that all?" "It's what she would have wanted." Smiling, Gene returned to his role as the host of Frank's funeral. The reception was small, but filled with an outpouring of love. Gertie held up well, but by the end she started crying inconsolably. "I loved him so much!" "I know" whispered Gene.As they headed back to the apartment, Gertie was quiet. "When we get you home, you should rest" Gene said, patting Gertie's knee. "We still have all of our belongings to put away. I need to stay busy, Gene." "I know you do, Gertie. Patsy won't admit it, but she needs you to take care of her. Even with all the snotty nurses and caseworkers, she will not tell them if she does not feel well. She trusts you, Gertie. I get the feeling they will not let me stay the night. They have 'visiting hours'." "This place reminds me of jail!" "I will work on getting you girls out of there. Admit it, Gertie, even if you were my housekeeper, you would have more freedom than you do right now." "Yes you're right, Gene." Smiling, Gene replied, "I am always right, Gertie." Anytime he was told he was right about something, it fed his ego and the delusions of how important he thought he was. As they arrived in the parking lot, Gene parked the truck in a shaded spot and stepped out to open the door for Gertie. Abruptly turning to face Gene, Nurse Willetts announced, "This is a private residence!" Gertie smiled, patting Nurse Willetts' hand. "Honey, I live here. I was just at my husband Frank's funeral services." "Oh, I see" said Nurse Willetts, looking over Gertie's chart. "I need to review your medications and physical therapy schedule with you." Gene gruffly replied, "Can't this wait? We just buried her husband!" Turning on her heel, Nurse Willetts looked Gene square in the eye. "And you would be whom?" Patsy spoke softly, "This is my husband, Gene." "Ah, yes. I have notes here about him as well. You should know my nurses and I run a tight ship and the health and welfare of these ladies is my only concern. Feeding your fragile ego is not in my job description!" "I see" grunted

Gene. "Just so we understand each other, I answer only to the doctors in charge of their care. If I feel you or the caseworkers are a detriment to the care of my patients, I will have you removed. Do we understand each other?" "Yes, ma'am. You sound like a drill sergeant I had back in the Army." "Well, I did serve in the Marine Corps as a medic" smiled Nurse Willetts. "I served my country in third-world areas. Then in the Veteran's Hospital." "I am now fully assured that my wife and Gertie will be receiving outstanding care!" "Now why are you here?" "I need to make sure the wiring for the stereo and speakers is good to go. Patsy likes to listen to my music when she's feeling blue and missing me." "As long as the music doesn't interfere with their therapy, I see no issue with it" said Nurse Willetts. "Here, let me give you one of my CD's. How about I put one in the stereo so you all can listen?" "As you wish!" cracked Nurse Willetts.

"Patsy, I will help you hang those pictures in just a

minute." Gene started the CD and set the timer for the

loop of crying babies to play while Patsy slept. Patsy

gave Gene instructions as to which pictures should go

where. Then they put the remaining dishes away. Nurse

Willetts announced that there were no loud noises

permitted after nine p.m. so they needed to finish up the

tasks quickly. "I see" grumbled Gene. In an effort to get

Nurse Willetts to lighten her mood, Gene asked, "So,

what did you think of my music?" Nurse Willetts thought

for a moment. She was trying to compose her thoughts.

After exhaling a deep breath, she began. "This music is

not something I prefer to listen to. It is extremely

depressing. It is not musically written correctly. A

squawking chicken has a better melody! Did anyone in

your band ever take music lessons? Kindergarteners have better grasp of lyrics! This is music to slit your wrists by. Point blank, it is horrible! Did you actually make a living performing that garbage? No wonder your wife has issues with depression!" "Well, hell girl. Don't hold back on my account!" Gene said sarcastically. "A Marine always tells the truth no matter the cost." Gene glowered. "How would you feel if I were to critique your nursing skills?" Smiling, Nurse Willetts said, "I would welcome the criticism of my nursing skills because I was trained by the best the Marine Corps had to offer. I did my job or people died. I performed my job and I challenge anyone to prove that I lacked in any capacity! The Marines do not produce inferior soldiers. The Army cannot make that claim. I will put my service record against yours any time. I guarantee mine shines in comparison to yours. Got any

383

other issues?" "No, ma'am!" "I am a retired Major, so I demand respect. You may call me Nurse Willetts." Patsy and Gertie cackled in the corner while Nurse Willetts ripped Gene a new one. "Gene, if you would care to be helpful to these ladies, I will give you a grocery list that is to last them until they are assigned a Home Health Aide." "Sure, Nurse Willetts. Let me finish this stuff for the girls." "You need to hurry because you cannot come back into the facility after eight p.m." "Alright, I will go now. This list doesn't have anything on it that Patsy or Gertie likes." "Likes are irrelevant. They are both on a 1500 calorie diet. Lots of fresh vegetables and no sugar. They are both overweight. No more than two cups of coffee per day. Fruit juice, green tea and water to drink starting now. No soda. Skim milk." "Oh boy!" complained Gene. Shaking his head, he headed for his truck with the list in hand. As he drove to the store, Gene complained. "Son of a bitch, that nurse will be a problem. I don't think I can kill that bitch. She probably sleeps with her service revolver! Christ, she probably has bigger balls than me and they're steel, not brass! It's not fair to put those girls on a diet. They will be healthy and live forever!" Gene walked into the produce section of the grocery store looking confused. A young lady came up and asked, "May I help you?" "I was asked to fil this list." Smiling, she said, "You're going to need a cart." "Miss, can you help me with this? I am not normally the one who does this sort of thing." "I will fill your list if you'll take me out for a coffee." "How about you come see my band play?" "That sounds wonderful! But let's have coffee first." "I haven't seen you here before" smiled Gene. "This is my first real job." "How old are you?" "Sixteen." "Here, let me help you with the rest of your list." Looking at the girl, all Gene could think was "she's perfect as my next conquest."After filling Gene's cart and leading him through the store, she said,"You're ready to check out. I will call someone up to the front." Keying up the mic, it came to life with a squelch. "Customer service, please come to register five!" Huffing up to the register was a man in his fifties. "Are you ready to check out?" "Yes, I am." "Did you find everything okay?" "Yes. Jenny here was very helpful" Gene said, giving her a wink. The older man turned to Jenny. "Get to work stocking the toiletries on aisle three!" he barked. "Yes, sir" Jenny answered as she turned to walk away. Returning to Patsy's apartment, Gene went to open the door with his arms full of the groceries, but the door was locked. As he banged on the glass doors, Nurse Willetts appeared and let him in. Gene loudly asked, "Why was I locked out?" "It's after eight o'clock. The doors are locked." "Jesus Christ! This place is like prison!" "No, it's for safety. Visitors are not allowed after eight p.m. It is now eight fifteen p.m." Growling, Gene carried the groceries to Patsy's apartment. "Say goodnight to your wife. It's time for you to leave!" Heading into Patsy's room, Gene smiled. "The warden here says I have to leave. Goodnight, sweetheart. I'll see you in the morning." "I have therapy, so you need to check with Nurse Willetts to find out when I will be able to have visitors." "I am not a visitor, I am your husband!" "Those are the rules." Kissing Patsy on the forehead, Gene smiled. "Sweet dreams!" Sticking his head around Gertie's door, Gene said goodnight. "Thank you for handling Frank's funeral for me, Gene." "No problem,

Gertie. You're my girl too. See you tomorrow." As Gene

headed for the kitchen, Nurse Willetts was standing near

the door. "When can I stop by tomorrow?" She glanced

over Patsy's chart. "At lunch time. The ladies have

therapy and they need to get adjusted to our schedule." "I

see" growled Gene. "Good night, Nurse Willetts." As

Gene exited the building, he heard the various locks

clicking and sliding into place. Gene was pissed as he

headed home to his bottle of bourbon "I take orders from

no one!" screamed Gene. Pulling into his driveway, Gene

stomped up the front steps and punched the door. It

popped open. He headed directly for the kitchen,

cracking open a bottle of Kentucky Bourbon as he went.

He took a long pull from the bottle. "That bitch nurse has

got to go!" After drinking half the bottle, Gene went to

bed. As he turned out the light, he smiled, "Sweet dreams,

Patsy!" While sleeping, Patsy thought she heard a baby

crying. She woke up shaking her head and chalked it up

to a bad dream. Gertie also heard crying, but she thought

it was from her dreaming about Frank. They heard the

same crying baby at around three a.m. Disturbed, Gertie

got up and went to check on Patsy. Peeking around the

doorway, she realized that Patsy was awake. Coming to

her bed side, Gertie asks, "What's wrong?" "I keep

dreaming that I hear a baby crying." "That is odd. I heard

crying too, but I thought it was just me. I had a dream

about Frank. I'll make us some warm milk with a shot of

chocolate?" "Sounds good!" "You stay put. I'll bring you

a cup." After the warm milk, Patsy drifted off to sleep

again. Gertie turned on the TV in her room to drown out

the quiet. At seven a.m. Gertie heard the locks slide.

Getting up and pulling on her robe, she headed towards

the kitchen to put the coffee on. Nurse Willetts had another nurse and a home health aide with her. "Company?" Gertie questioned. "This is Nurse Hatch and your home health aide, Nancy. She will help you clean the apartment and help you run your errands from 7:00 to 3:00 and Susan will be your home health aide from 3:00 to 8:00 p.m. five days per week. Nurse Hatch will give you your afternoon and evening meds. I will be your med nurse from 7:00 a.m. to 7:00 p.m. I will be at the nurse's desk when I am not giving meds. Your aides will help you get to the main building for therapy. Nurse Hatch and I will give Patsy her breathing treatment."Gertie scowled at them. "I have been cooking and cleaning for over sixty years! I don't need a health aide to clean my house!" "That's why we are here" replied Nancy. "So you don't have to work so hard anymore." Shaking her head, Gertie agreed to try having an aide to help her with the household chores. "What else do you do?" "Take you shopping. They have craft classes, country music on Thursday nights and lots of other things for you to do."Patsy peered around the corner at them after listening to Nurse Willetts explaining things. We are capable, you know!" cracked Patsy. Nurse Willetts turned her attention to Patsy. "This is Nurse Hatch. She will be doing your afternoon and evening meds and breathing treatments. Let's get your first treatment done before coffee." "If you say so Nurse Willetts." While starting the treatment Patsy asked, "Nurse Willetts? Are there side effects to any of the medicines I am taking?" "Yes, why? Did you have an issue last night? Here, let me grab your chart. What was the issue?" "I had dreams of a baby crying." "Sometimes the sleep medicines can

391

cause vivid dreams." "Even Gertie thought she heard something." "Sometimes the combination of medication and the quiet of being in a new place plays tricks on the mind. If you have any more issues, we will talk to your doctor about adjusting the dosage, okay?" "That sounds reasonable to me" said Patsy. "You do know there is an intercom system. You can always call the nurse's desk and we will check on you if you need us." "Oh, I forgot about that." "We will give you a lesson on how to call and answer the intercom system." "Thank you. That's a relief." While Patsy and Gertie started their day, District Attorney Spinney was getting his files together to the Grand Jury. After three cups of coffee, Spinney was chomping at the bit to get a True Bill TO PUT Gene in jail where he belonged. The office was eerily quiet at that time of morning. A knock on the door caused Spinney to jump. His boss smiled. "You're here early this morning."

"Yes. I'm preparing for the Grand Jury this morning. I don't foresee not getting the True Bill." "I have been authorized to tell you that considering Gene's path of destruction we will be seeking the death penalty against him. We may not be able to use Frank's signed statement since he's dead. I know that whoever his defense attorney is will argue that Frank cannot be cross examined." With a smile, Spinney listened intently as his boss reminded him how to get around that obstacle. "Did your investigators go get Marissa?" "Yes, but considering that Gene tried to kill her, we are doing everything possible to keep her identity under wraps." "Bring her in through the side entrance of the courthouse so she isn't seen." As he headed for court, Spinney was confident that he had his case ready to be presented. As the docket number was called, he clutched his case file as though it were made of gold. Walking into the courtroom, Spinney took a look around. He knew he was ready. He would get the True Bill and Gene would pay for everything he had done. Judge Smith presided as Spinney laid out his case with enthusiasm. He painted a vivid picture of a narcissistic serial killer. Then Spinney announced that he had a witness. Preston and Thomas led Marissa into the courtroom. The jury looked aghast at this small, emaciated looking girl. Spinney began by asking her to describe what happened on the night that Gene attempted to end her life. She told them exactly what had happened. How he had made small talk with her at his gig. How he had brought her up to his hotel room, plied her with alcohol, and raped her before choking her unconscious, throwing her against the wall and later dumped her in a ditch on the side of the road. At the conclusion of her testimony, the jury was excused to a separate room. Spinney, Preston and Thomas were discussing Marissa's testimony and what a phenomenal witness she had been when the bailiff appeared and handed Spinney a piece of paper. "Damn! That took less than fifteen minutes!" Unfolding the paper, Spinney was smiling from ear to ear. It was a True Bill. "Put Marissa on the next flight home and go arrest that prick!" he shouted to Preston and Thomas. "I'll have your arrest warrant in an hour." "Give us two hours. We need to get her some lunch before we send her back." Back at his office, Spinney had arrest and search warrants in hand. "I am going to crucify that prick!" Barging through the door to Spinney's office, Thomas announced, "She's on her way home." With an evil grin, Spinney handed them Gene's arrest warrant and the search warrants. "Let the State boys handle the search warrants. They need to search his house, vehicles and Gertie's house too. Go get that prick!" "On it, Boss." "Try his house first. Avoid arresting him in front of Patsy. Her health is bad." "He is supposed to show up at her new apartment around noon. I checked with the on-call nurse at the front desk of the assisted living facility." Thomas cracked, "I am gonna enjoy this!" Preston looked at Thomas with a sigh. ""He will probably get bail." "WHAT?!" "He's smart, so he doesn't actually have a criminal record. With a decent lawyer, he will get bail. So don't get too excited. For him to collect the rest of the insurance money, Patsy will have to die. We'll be waiting for him!" "How does that work?" asked Thomas. "When he files the insurance claim, he will "need" to personally pick up that check. We will be waiting." "I am not sure I understand" exclaimed Thomas. "You will"

smiled Preston.Pulling into Gene's driveway, they parked

the car behind his truck. Preston and Thomas walked to

the front door and gave it a light knock. Gene appeared at

the door. "Is Patsy okay? What are you boys doing

here?" "We need to speak with you." "I'd love to, boys.

But I'm on my way to see my girls." Pulling the door

closed, Gene attempted to walk past the

investigators.Turning to face Gene, Thomas announced,

"Gene Allen, SR, you are under arrest!" Cuffing him

brought a sense of satisfaction to Thomas that he could

not hide. Gene said, "There must be some mistake." As

Thomas read Gene his Miranda Rights, he asked, "Do

you understand these rights?" "Yeah, call my lawyer!"

"You'll get your phone call once you've been booked

into the jail." The State police were smiling as they

397

pulled into the drive. They walked up to Gene and placed copies of the search warrants in his shirt pocket. "Here you go." "What the fuck is this shit?" "Getting a little worried, Gene?" "This warrant gives us permission to search your house, all outer buildings, all vehicles and Gertie's home." "I have done nothing except take care of Gertie! This is bullshit!" screamed Gene. "Let's go, country star!" laughed Thomas. As they drove down Main Street, the townspeople stared, mouths open. Preston smiled. "We will make sure you get a four-star perp walk for your arraignment." Gene said nothing, but a low growl came from the back seat. They walked Gene through the police station like the star he thought he was. "My phone call, boys!" "You need to be processed, so we'll put you in here with your peers in holding. Once you are processed, you will be transferred to county jail to await arraignment." "So kind of you to break down the process for me." "Here you go, Gene. The star suite in your honor." A firm push into the cell put Gene in his place. "What did they get you for?" "Damned if I know. These officers just showed up at my house and arrested me." "They didn't tell you what you're charged with?" No, man. I have no clue." "They didn't question you?" "No." "That means they have you on something big. I bet they have been working on it for a while. You better start thinking real hard about who you've pissed off lately!" "Let's go, Star! Mugshot first. No smiling, asshole! Fingerprints next." "Okay. Now can I call my lawyer?" "Here's the phone. Make your call." "Sam, it's me, Gene. I have been arrested." "What are they charging you with?" "They didn't tell me shit!" "I'm on my way down there. They have seventy-two hours to arraign you."

Click. "You had your three minutes. Let's go. You boys
will be moved to county. Your lawyers can find you
there." The guards put him back in his suite. "So, what
do you do for a living?" "I'm an internatio9naly known
country music star. I'm in a band. We play country and
rockabilly. I write my own songs. I have a major
following." "I don't remember ever hearing your music."
"I have CD's out."

"I'll have to see if I can find it. You been on tour and
all that?" "Yep." "I bet you had yourself some tasty
young morsels." "You know it!" smiled Gene. "I had a
lot more fun after my band went home on the last tour. I
had a new beauty every night of the week!" "How did
you keep that from your wife? My skills aren't that great.

My old lady always catches me!" "Ha! I had my old lady's doctor convinced that she was nuts. She was kept heavily medicated. I had control of her money. It was great! Then some nosey, women's lib shrink stuck her nose in my business. But when people stick their nose in my business, they end up having accidents. No one fucks me over and gets away with it! I am a God and should be treated as such by all women!""Damn! Sounds like you have your shit wired tight." "I have done alright for myself." "Got room in your band for me?" "Gene snarled, "Can you play guitar?" "Sure can." "Well, we have a gig this weekend. Ready to try out?" "Sure, no problem." "Do you read music?" "Yes. I took lessons from sixth grade to my senior year. I got thrown out of school for punching out the band teacher. We had a disagreement. He wanted us to play classical music but we wanted to play more current stuff. I was not allowed to graduate!"

"We'll be moved to county before nightfall." "So, is the Assistant District Attorney reasonable?""No, he's a prick who's trying to make his bones." "I see" replied Gene. "I called my lawyer so he can figure out all this bullshit. What's your name, anyway?" "John J. Jameson." "Like the booze" cracked Gene. "Yep, but I'm more partial to bourbon, scotch and beer." "In other words, you'll drink anything as long as it's free" smiled Gene. "Pretty much!" cracked John J. "Just call me JJ." "Sounds good. I'm Gene, but you can call me God!" "You bragging, Gene?" "No, JJ. Just telling it like it is!" "I bet you have kicked some ass in your day, huh?" "Oh, yeah! But I have a perfectly spotless record. Never been caught! So whatever they think they have on me won't stick. I'm Teflon!" "Wow! I always get busted. Domestic violence,

DWI, fighting. Petty stuff" whined JJ. "Sounds to me like you need to train your old lady. You need to be in control of everything so she knows her place. Asshole bitches like that Dr. Sebastian going around making women think they have rights! Women need to be shown their place!" "Agreed!" piped JJ. There was a loud crash against the bars. "You have an issue with women, Gene?" "No, ma'am!" "Around this block, I'm in charge of your world!" "Of course you are, ma'am" Gene said smiling. "Just remember, in county, you will be MY bitch!" Unable to contain his rage, Gene raised his voice a few octaves. "I AM NO ONE'S BITCH, male or female!" Laughing, Guard Lewis said, "We shall see about that. After lunch, you boys will be moved to county. I expect you to behave yourselves, gentlemen." "Yes ma'am." "Good boys" sniped Guard Lewis.As she walked back to the front desk, Gene grimaced. "She needs to be bent over a desk and taught some respect!" JJ sneered, "I'd like to be the one to give her a lesson!" "Bitches like that make me appreciate my Patsy. She's a good woman who knows that her place is to please me!" Overhearing their conversation, Guard Lewis cackled, "I bet she laughs when you drop your pants!" Growling, Gene offered to show her. "I know it's not my place, but I have to ask. Have you ever thought about getting a penile implant?" Guard Lewis had everyone in the holding area laughing uncontrollably. A male guard came over and joined the conversation. "From what I've heard, Gene has to date little girls because they have nothing else to compare him to! You like them, what, about ten?" Gene shook the bars angrily. "Now, now. Behave yourself. It's a long ride over to county. You could have

404

a nasty accident along the way!" JJ whispered, "Don't let them get to you, Gene. Guard Jackson is a sadistic prick. Cool down, brother. After lunch, they will bring the van to take us to county. The sheriffs are easier to deal with. Just keep your head down and don't mouth off and you'll be fine. They are trying to piss you off so they can justify giving you a beating. It's an old military ploy to try and break you down." "I was in the service. Basic was horrible! But I beat them at their own game," "Sounds like lunch is coming. Step back while they are passing trays."Keeping in mind all that JJ had told him, Gene plotted his revenge. After lunch Guard Lewis announced, "Transport to county is here!" Handcuffing Gene, she smiled. "Single file, boys!" Guard Jackson walked in front and Lewis brought up the rear. Sheriffs awaited them, looking over the new prospects. "Okay, boys. One at a time. Nice and easy!" The inmates were placed in leg cuffs, which were attached to the floor. "This ride will be silent. If you need to speak, I will inform you. Otherwise, silence!" As the drive started, Sheriff Browne smiled. "I see we have a few frequent flyers. Mr. Jameson, your usual suite is ready. I see a few of you are scheduled for arraignment. And what is this? We have a country music legend! Maybe you can sing for us at county, Gene! How did we earn such an honor? I'm sure we will get to know each other real well. Right, Gene? You may answer!" "Yes, sir!" "Sounds like you catch on quick! That's good! Do you perform just cover songs or do you write your own? Go ahead." "We do perform cover songs, but I write three-quarters of all the songs that my band performs." "Do you feel like you are an accomplished musician?" "Yes, sir." "Well at least you will have something to occupy your time with us. Maybe I will even inspire a song or two." "Yes, sir." "JJ, what brings you back to see us? Oh, I see. Domestic violence and DWI. I thought you were in treatment?" "I went to Alcoholics Anonymous. Everyone shared their stories. I needed a drink, Boss!" The sheriff gave a belly laugh. "You need to dry out. Lock down for six months should do the trick."JJ decided it would be better not to answer that one. "Looks like you boys won't be arraigned for a couple of days. We can spend that time getting to know each other." Gene did not like the sound of that. His lawyer needed to take care of this. NOW! Shit, I bet that pussy Frank wrote a statement against me. But they don't have a case if their 'star' witness is dead! Patricia is gone. They have no one. Patsy is too dumb to see what's going on around her. Hell, she never realized that Marge had

407

more health problems than just the flu. Damn, I'm good! The smile that crept across his face showed he was deep in thought. "Are you talking to yourself?" "It's better than talking to you!" Arriving at the county jail, JJ says, "Remember, keep your mouth shut. They will rag on you. Do not respond!" Being led into the jail, they were given a list of commands. "Okay, boys! Time for you to have a 'lice' shower!" Gene glared at the guard with disdain.

1)   You will use this shampoo on your hair, under arms and pubic areas

2)   Your clothes will be put in a plastic bag and you will be given your orange jumpsuit. You will be given a pillow, blanket and your personal items.

"Any questions, gentlemen?" "How will my lawyer know where I am?" "Oh, a newbie! The precinct will tell him where you have been sent." Looking at the clipboard, he smiled. "Seems you and JJ have been awarded our best suite." "Guess it pays to be a frequent flyer" cracked Gene. JJ smiled. "We will just say I've got the goods on most of the guards and their habits and perversions." "I see" smiled Gene. After they made their bunks and were getting comfortable in their new environment, JJ asked, "So, what could they have on a guy like you?" they possibly have on a great guy like you?" Thinking for a moment, Gene said, "I never knew that breaking young girls' hearts was a crime. Hypothetically, if a guy wrote a statement against you and he died, is there still a case?" "No. If there is a witness, the defense attorney has the right to depose and question him or her. You have the right to face your accuser. They have a law library here. When you've had as many public defenders as I have, it pays to do your own leg work." "I may have to check it out" laughed Gene. "Also, if you don't feel your lawyer is representing you to the best of his abilities, you can fire him. You also have the right to represent yourself."

"Interesting. I'll keep that in mind." "Hell, I have friends that earned their Juris doctorate in prison. They had life sentences. The learned how to file their own appeals. It's amazing what you can learn with time on your hands. Because of your musical talents, you could offer lessons in exchange for other favors." "You are smarter than my last road manager." "Thanks, Gene. It's nice to be appreciated for my entrepreneurial skills." "When do you get visits with your lawyer?" "They usually happen between nine and five, but in emergencies they can happen until lights out." "I see." "How's the old lady?" asked JJ. "The doctors would not let her or Gertie come home. They are in an assisted living facility that is connected to a nursing home." "An old age home?" questioned JJ. "Yeah, her doc says she needs breathing treatments, special diets and physical therapy. My buddy Frank died. He took care of Gertie. Those damn social workers said that they needed supervision. It's costing me an arm and a leg!" "Geez! Doesn't Social Security and Medicaid cover it?" "Partially, and I'm stuck paying the difference. They don't even get to eat what they like. They are on a 1500 calorie diet. Their nurse is an ex Major and a retired Marine. She's a big bitch that could probably kick my ass, and I'm no pansy!"Laughing, JJ said, "I bet if she wanted it, she'd just take it!" "Oh yeah! You wouldn't be able to tell her no. Just yes ma'am!" "Ha." "She sounds like a real badass!" "Yeah." "So, what are your charges?" asked JJ. "Truthfully, I have no idea. Guess I'll find out when I'm arraigned." "If they don't have charges in seventy-two hours, you walk" cracked JJ. "They are just whiny bitches!

412

Especially Dr. Sebastian. It would take a blast furnace to warm her up!" Maybe she just needs a real man!" "I think she is into women. She ran the women's group that my wife and mother-in-law were in. All man haters. They just need a good stiff dick to change their minds!" cracked Gene. "I had shit set up perfectly. I was on tour and my old lady's Social Security benefits were direct deposited into my bank account. I had the doctors convinced that she had 'mental issues'. I had life insurance policies on her and my mother-in-law. That bitch Dr. Sebastian got involved and fucked everything up so Patsy got to be her own payee again. Then Ma got sick. Flu medicine reacted badly with her other medicines. Patsy got sick too. Her mother died and they tried to blame it on me but the life insurance paid out on the policy." "I see" smiled JJ. "So they couldn't pin it on you." "Yeah." "Bet you're sitting pretty." "I'm comfortable. But if Patsy dies, I can afford to stay on tour for at least a year!" Sounds like you have a plan!" snickered JJ. "Always!" smiled Gene. "Would you be able to tour for a year, JJ?" "I got no ties. It'll take me about a month to learn your catalogue." "That's reasonable. When do they feed us in this shit hole?" "Dinner should be shortly." "Is the food bad?" "It's almost equivalent to Army food. But on the weekends, there is a sweet Christian lady who cooks for us. We get cookies and other desserts. She also cooks the holiday meals,

so it's good on days like Thanksgiving and
Christmas. She even makes BBQ in the
summer.""" "I do miss cracking open a cold
one." "Bet your mouth piece will have you out
for the weekend!" "What in the hell is that
clanking sound!?" "Dinner is coming." "Okay,
great!" said Gene.ADA Spinney dropped in to
county. "So, how is our canary?" "He's singing
to JJ." "Are you recording all of it?" "Just like
you wanted. From what we've heard so far, it
sounds like he has some serious issues with
women. After two days with JJ, he will be
telling all." "Good." "Will JJ be testifying?"
"No. We just need to get inside Gene's head.
We searched his house. Here's his guitar. Offer
to let him play." "I thought he was some big

star." "He is. In his own mind. He plays a lot of local gigs in dive bars. The caliber of star he thinks he is does not equal his lack of talent. In other words, he stinks. He's mediocre at best. Most recording contracts cover all expenses and send you out on tour to promote your music. He had to pay them to produce his record. He pays for his own tours. He's nothing but a wannabe star!" "Ha ha! This should be entertaining!" laughed the corrections officer. "Gene will not be able to turn down a chance to be in the spotlight." "Oh, I get it." "I want him comfortable and completely off guard. Library time, the works. He will be arraigned just under the seventy-two hour mark." "Will he get bail?" "To collect on the other life insurance policy, he has to get rid of his wife." "I see. "Just keep him talking." "Got you." "His lawyer has already been asking about charges. Did they find anything in the search?" "Some medications that may have been used in combination with Marge's flu medicine to cause her death. We might have found the gun used in Frank and Patricia's deaths. The lab has been authorized for overtime on this. We have a timeline of his life of accidents, death and abuse. He is a serial killer! There's no two ways about it." "You wouldn't be smiling that much if you didn't have an ace in the hole, Hoss!" Spinney cackled loudly. "I don't want to spoil the surprise now, do I?" C.O. Banes looked at Spinney with a raised eyebrow. "I may have to

417

come down and personally watch this trial."

"Banes, I'll call you later" smiled Spinney. As
Spinney drove back to the office, he began
going over the new evidence in his mind. 'I
hope that stupid son-of-a-bitch turns down my
offer!' he thought aloud. 'I want to watch him
die by lethal injection! But if the doc is right,
they will put him in a hospital for the criminally
insane. Either way, that prick goes away. I need
to talk to the doctor. There must be a way for
Patsy to survive this. Maybe we can make it
look like she died. Maybe Witness Protection is
an option. That would make it fraud for him to
collect the life insurance money. If Patsy is in
Witness Protection, she is safe.' As Spinney
mulled all this over, he grew more and more

concerned for Patsy and Gertie's safety.He made a mental note to check in with his boss. As he headed into his office, Carla was on a social call. "Oh, Patsy this is a lovely apartment. The ladies miss you at group." "I miss them too." "You seem under the weather. How can I help?" "Can I tell you something private?" asked Patsy. "Here, let's sit. I'll put on the kettle." "Our home health aide took Gertie shopping for some real food. This 1500 calorie diet stinks." "Herbal tea, I see" smiled Dr. Sebastian. "Honey. No sugar." "Nurse Willetts is worse than a drill sergeant." Carla laughed. "But you look like you've lost some weight." "Yes, both Gertie and I have. I'm sorry about Patricia. She was a great lady and a good sponsor. She kept me on my toes." Carla brought in the tea with a plate of butter cookies. "Now, Patsy, what's bothering you?" "Well, I haven't been getting much sleep. I know Gene was being sweet when he gave me those life-like glass dolls. But when I go to sleep, I hear a baby crying. Then a baby laughing and saying 'Mama'. It happens a few times a night. I thought it was my mind playing tricks on me. But Gertie has heard it too! Nurse Willetts says the doctor may have to increase my meds. I don't want that. I take so many already.""It is unusual for two people to have the same auditory hallucination. Let's go over what time you're hearing this." "About 10:30 p.m. and again at one a.m. and at three a.m. It's almost as if it's on a timer!" cried Patsy. "When was the last time you saw Gene?" "He was supposed to be here yesterday, but he never showed up! I'm concerned!" Patsy wailed. "I'm sure he just got carried away with rehearsals. Did he help with moving you in here?" asked Carla. "Oh, yes! He hooked up this wonderful stereo system so we could listen to his recorded gigs and other music we liked." "I see" smiled Carla. "Am I crazy, Dr. Sebastian?" "No. And I don't want to see you put on any more medication. Let me speak with Nurse Willetts." A key turning caused Patsy to look toward the door. Gertie along with the aide had their arms full of groceries. "Hi, Dr. Sebastian!" "Hello, Gertie! Come and sit with us. I will make you a cup of tea so we can catch up." The aide said, "I'll put away the groceries. You relax, Gertie." After retrieving a cup from the kitchen cupboard, Dr. Sebastian poured the tea. "Patsy has explained what she's been hearing at night. What do you hear, Gertie?" "I hear a baby crying. It starts out low and gets louder each time. It wakes me up from a dead sound sleep!" "Okay. When do you expect Nurse Willetts?" "Soon. She does my breathing treatments." "Do you mind if I wait?" "Not at all. You are our first visitor that isn't here to give a treatment." Gertie showed off the bedrooms. Noticing the speakers in each bedroom, Carla asked, "Did Gene install the speakers in the bedrooms?" "Yes! Now we watch TV in stereo!" chimed Gertie. Walking

422

through the door, Nurse Willetts announced herself with the all the authority she demanded on any given day. "Patsy, head to your room so we can get your treatment started. Who might you be?" "I am Dr. Carla Sebastian. I dropped in to see Patsy. She is a member of my women's group. I would like to speak with you." "Let me get Patsy's treatment going. The aide can sit with her." Looking in the refrigerator, Nurse Willets said, "I see we have been shopping!" Gertie snapped, "We followed the guide you left!" "I see this. There are fresh fruits and vegetables, fish and lean meats. You did well." "Just don't ask us to go vegan!" Smiling, Nurse Willets said, "We will not go that far unless it's warranted. The scale doesn't lie. My diet plan is working." "We have water aerobics tomorrow. It's a lot of fun, Gertie." 'I like aqua therapy" smiled Gertie. "There's arts and crafts tonight, ladies!" "Shall, we, Doctor Sebastian?" "I will assume Patsy has told you what she's been hearing at night?" "Yes. Auditory hallucinations are not usually shared. Increasing Patsy's medication will not resolve this." "I think we need to stay overnight in their apartment and listen for ourselves. I have reviewed my files concerning Gene. Patsy had a hysterical pregnancy due to abuse. She has always wanted to have children. Gene had arranged it so that he was the payee of her disability benefits. He had her declared incompetent. I was instrumental in getting her restored as her own payee. Accidents happen around Gene. I would not be surprised if he set up a timed loop of crying babies to push Patsy over the edge. He probably deduced that it would cause her to need more medication. When her doctors said that she needed to live here, Gene was livid. It's a bit harder for her to have accidents if she is under constant supervision." "Not on my watch!" yelled Nurse Willetts. "We need to spend the night in the apartment and figure out where that tape is. It will prove that Gene is trying to cause Patsy to have a psychological breakdown." Okay. Let me change the schedule." "If you don't mind, I'd like to arrange for Investigators Preston and Thomas to be present on the night we stay in

425

the apartment. Gene is being arraigned in two days. Whatever we find in the apartment would help Spinney's case. The safety of these ladies is paramount. Gene has a life insurance policy on Patsy. He had one on Marge. She's dead."

"Okay. Let me call the doctor and have the schedule changed." After a few phone calls, everyone was set for the overnight shift. "Is Nancy coming?" asked Gertie. "No. I will be your overnight nurse." "After dinner, it's arts and crafts." Dr. Sebastian said her goodbyes and headed for Spinney's office. As she burst through his office door, Carla began explaining her visit with Patsy and Gertie. "It seems Gene has plans. Can Preston and Thomas join us? We are staying overnight in their apartment to find out what it is that they have been hearing."

"That sounds reasonable" smiled Spinney.

"How is Gene doing in jail?" "He's got a

captive audience and a new friend. Right about

now, he should be giving a command

performance." Will we need a warrant to collect

evidence?" "You have the resident's permission

to be there. But I will get one just to protect the

chain of evidence. You need them there at

what time? Around ten?" Spinney grinned like

a Cheshire cat. "This is the icing on top of the

cake! My case is a slam dunk! Gene will never

see daylight again!"Corrections Officer Banes

brought Gene his guitar. "I figured you'd be

missing this. Would you perform for us? I hear

you're great." "Yes sir. I am." "Give me a few

minutes to set up the Visitor's Room." After setting up the chairs, the C.O.'s were all in place as the inmates were lead single file into the visiting room. "What's this about?" "You are going to have the honor of seeing a country star perform." Once everyone was seated, Gene was brought in. "This will be an acoustic concert." There were a few guards setting up the sound system for Gene's debut performance. Removing his handcuffs, Officer Banes gave Gene a warm introduction. Gene played his standard set and took requests. The inmates were just happy to be out of their cells. "How about Prison Blues, Gene?" "The C.O is coming around with pen and paper. Give him your requests. Everyone gets a request!" After two hours, C.O. Banes called an end to the concert. Gene flashed the audience a big smile. "Let's give C.O. Banes a big hand for allowing me to perform for all of you!" The inmates voluntarily folded and stacked the chairs before returning to their cells. As his cell door was opened, Gene turned and handed Banes his guitar. "Rules, right?" "Yes. Thank you for sharing your talents with us. Lights out!" JJ said," Hey, I made a list of all the guys who are into you. Time to barter some goods and services. Smiling in the dark, Gene said, "I knew you would come in handy. Goodnight, buddy."Meanwhile, Patsy and Gertie were just returning from the arts and crafts activities. Nancy helped them with turning down their beds and settling in to watch some TV. They sat in the living room and had a snack of graham crackers and milk. There was a soft knock on the door. Nancy shuffled to the door and looked out the peephole. "Dr. Sebastian. It's a bit late for a visit." "I have come to stay overnight with Patsy. She is having trouble sleeping." "I see" replied Nancy. "Nurse Willetts will be here shortly to administer Patsy's breathing treatment." "Hello, ladies!" "Hi, Doc!" "I thought you might feel better if I was here." "Maybe you'll hear it too!" cried Patsy. "That's exactly what I was thinking" replied Doctor Sebastian. "Then you'll know I'm not crazy!" "I don't believe either of you are crazy." "Patsy, let's get you set up for your breathing

430

treatment." "Alright, Nancy." "I will bring in your evening medications." Dr. Sebastian studied the chart Nancy had been looking over. "Excuse me, I am also a doctor. I am qualified to read those charts." After double checking all the dosages, Carla handed the chart back to Nancy.Nancy laid out Gertie's pills beside a glass of water. After ensuring that Gertie had taken all of the medicines, Nancy sent her to her room. She then repeated the process with Patsy's medications. "Would you like your pills or your treatment first?" Nurse Willetts asked. "Pills first" replied Patsy. As Nurse Willetts doled out the pills, she started the breathing treatment. "Nancy, head on over to the nurse's desk and do your paperwork. I'm the overnight nurse for tonight" Nurse Willetts instructed.

"Yes, ma'am" replied Nancy. "Shall we get comfortable? I'll put the kettle on." "What time do you expect the investigators to get here?" "Around ten." "Dr. Carla?" "Yes, Patsy?" "Will you be here all night?" "I brought my pajamas." "Thank you." "No problem. Get some sleep." Nurse Willetts asked, "Is Patsy okay?" "She's afraid to fall asleep. Tonight's sleepover should alleviate her fears. I gave Patsy's doctor a brief explanation of our suspicions. He agreed that her lack of sleep and heightened anxieties would make her more prone to accidents. At ten o'clock, Preston stood at Patsy's door waving a warrant for any evidence that would be collected. "Where's Thomas?" "I'm flying solo tonight. He needs his beauty rest. I hear Gene is trying to push his wife's crazy card." "I am afraid so. The ladies are hearing a baby crying at ten p.m. one a.m. and three a.m." "That would have to be a timed loop set to play at those specific times." "The loop has highs and lows, which means it has to be homemade. Gene has all the tools necessary to set something like that up. He is playing on Patsy's emotional trigger. If she has an accident, he will collect on her life insurance policy." At 10:33, they heard a soft sound coming from the speakers. It got louder, just as Patsy had described to Dr. Sebastian. It was a baby crying, then a baby laughing and finally a baby crying "Momma". After fifteen minutes, the apartment was quiet again. The loop repeated at 1:00 a.m. Preston set about searching for the tape. The sound was amplified in Patsy's room, so logic dictated that there must be a tape in each room. Preston pulled out a device that looked like some sort of meter. The closer he got to the sound, the more the device's gauge moved. As the needle hit red level, Preston asked Carla to run her hand under the top of Patsy's nightstand. Carla found what she believed to be a micro cassette player. Removing it, Preston made his way into Gertie's bedroom. Sure enough, he found an identical cassette player in the top of Gertie's nightstand. Preston was elated. He thought they had located all of Gene's hidden devices. He was surprised to hear the same sounds at 3:00 a.m. He was perplexed as he

again went from room to room. He noticed a

light shining over the carriage that held Patsy's

glass dolls. Feeling along the walls, Patsy

screamed, "My dolls are alive!" "No, it's a

cruel joke" explained Carla. With all the

commotion, Gertie was now also awake.

Preston asked, "Do you ladies mind if I check

behind that panel in the wall?" "Not at all. After

moving the bed in Patsy's room, Preston

discovered a projector hidden behind the wall.

It was positioned just above Patsy's headboard.

Once it had been retrieved, Carla told Patsy and

Gertie they could go back to sleep. They

wouldn't be hearing babies crying anymore.

After checking vitals, Nurse Willetts said that

she needed to go chart at the nurse's station.

Preston suggested that the ladies go out for the

day so that he could bring a team in to go

through the apartment. "I agree. They have an

aqua therapy session tomorrow. Maybe they

can come to the women's group for the day." "I

have checked tomorrow's schedule. They don't

have anything else scheduled for the day." "I

will call Spinney at 7:00 a.m. I want to get the

stuff we found to the lab. Thomas said he

would be here at six. Gene is one seriously

twisted bastard! We need to know what his

plans were with that projector. Unless we find

something incriminating on the tapes, it's not

illegal." "Okay, let's have the C.O ask him. Tell

him that the staff found it and it wasn't

approved." "Have his lawyer meet me at county.

That audio loop is a whole different ball game.

The crying baby is connected to his wife's

mental stability." "If he is granted bail at his

arraignment, will he come after Patsy?" "Yeah.

She will be a sitting duck." "Thomas is gonna

love this shit." "Well, he wanted to cause

mental anguish to induce a mental breakdown."

"That is some seriously twisted shit!""I'll take a

guess that if Patsy had a breakdown, the doctors

would heavily medicate her. That would make

it easier for her to have an accident." "Isn't

there any way to protect Patsy?" Carla snarled.

Let me see what Spinney has to say about what

we found. I have an idea, but I have to ask

Spinney about it first" smiled Preston. "What

are you thinking?" Carla questioned. "Maybe a sting. We'll see" Preston answered. "I will do some more research on Gene's psychopathy before I give a clinical diagnosis. Go ahead and run that evidence to the lab. I can hold down the fort here." "No. Not until Thomas gets here. I will not leave you ladies unprotected."Laughing, Carla patted Preston on the shoulder. "You are a decent man." "Thanks. I hope my wife agrees." "I am sure she appreciates you, Preston" Carla chuckled. "You truly care about the women in your group, don't you? Patricia was one of your patients, right?" "I met her many years ago. She had endured a lifetime of abuse. She survived many things. She was a great sponsor because she had survived all the same things the women had." "Do you think Gene killed Frank and Patricia?" "Based on the autopsies and what the medical examiner found, I would stake my life on it!" Carla exclaimed. Giving Carla a gentle squeeze, Preston looked into her eyes. "We will put him away." "I know, but you can't hate someone who is mentally ill. Gene is sick. The law doesn't fix these monsters. It just puts them away from public view. He is smart. He will do therapy and take medication so they will say he is all better. You cannot fix his problems. He has no empathy or moral compass to tell him he is doing wrong." "What do you think the judge should do?" "He needs to be in a hospital for the criminally insane. Getting sentenced to death will make him a martyr with followers."After a long pause, Preston said, "I understand now." "His symptoms probably started to manifest during his childhood. I am sure that he was a bully. He likely manipulated his mother into covering for him. He has had a lifetime to perfect his sickness into something that is entirely self-serving. There is no hope for him. A good psychiatrist could make their career on Gene." "Wow. He is truly a product of a system that's designed to fail" said Preston. A knock interrupted the silence between them. Thomas let himself into the apartment. "How did the night shift go?" Smiling, Preston pointed to the cassette players and the projector. The lab will be busy today. Carla will explain what we found. Later, partner!" "I brought you a little pick me up, Doc." "Thanks, Thomas." After Carla explained the night's events, Thomas began pacing. "That fucking prick! Oh, excuse me, Doc." "No worries. I felt the same way. He will get bail, won't he?" "With no traceable criminal record, it's a strong possibility." "Damn! I know I'm new at being an investigator, but Christ! He is a serial killer and he's going to waltz right out the back door! He wants that life insurance money. His ego will not allow him to let Patsy live. As far as he's concerned, he is invincible. Is he truly mentally ill? Or is he just a misogynistic prick with a God complex?" Carla patted his shoulder. "He is mentally ill. But if he is given the death penalty, he would have a cult following. Women would throw themselves at him. He really needs to be institutionalized."Carla read Thomas' questioning look. "In a hospital for the criminally insane. With bars and guards just like prison and a psychiatrist who will provide him therapy and medication." "Why not prison?" asked Thomas. "He cannot be put in general population. Gene, like most serial killers could sell you your underwear. They are snake charmers. Charismatic. Think Manson and family. Religious cult leaders have always been able to draw people in by offering unconditional love and acceptance. Most people need something or someone to believe in. People who feel unlovable are easy prey.

"Wow!" But as I explained to Preston, his symptoms/issues likely manifested in his childhood." "I do not envy your job, Doc. Mine is simple. If you break the law, we arrest you." "It's not always black and white, Thomas. "Boy, that's the truth. My mom told me being a peacemaker/ police officer was a noble career. If Mom only knew that it is not a simple job. I am sorry about Patricia." "Thank you, Thomas." Nurse Willetts came charging through the door in preparation for the shift change that was happening in an hour. Thomas smiled. "Hello, I'm Investigator Thomas." "I am Nurse Willetts." She looked at Carla. "I see there was a change of guard." "Yes. Preston took the evidence to the lab. We need to have it processed before we talk to Gene." "I spoke to Patsy's doctor. He is aware of what was found last night. He is not going to increase any of her medications." "Well, if you ladies no longer need me, I will head over to Spinney's office." Nurse Willetts looked at Dr. Sebastian with sympathetic eyes. "Call your secretary. Tell her to cancel all your appointments. Go home and get some sleep." "I just might take your advice. After all, you are in charge!" Nurse Willetts laughed. "Now, go home and rest. Nurses orders!" "Bye!"Thomas arrived at Spinney's office to find Preston crashed on the sofa in the outer office. Thomas moved a cup of coffee under Preston's nose. "Wakey, wakey!" "Asshole!" Thomas laughed. "I fell asleep waiting to hear from the lab. Spinney came through the outer office smiling. "I see we had a very productive overnight shift. I listened to your message, Preston. Seems our boy Gene is back at it. He set up the cassettes and projector while he helped move Patsy and Gertie into assisted living. It's safe to assume the tape was a tool to push Patsy over the edge so she would be heavily medicated. It would make her more accident prone. " "But what was he doing with the projector?" "It's still at the lab. "Guess that means we'll be visiting Gene today." "As per protocol, Nurse Willetts would have contacted Patsy's doctor and he would have increased her medication. What he had not planned was that two people normally don't share auditory

445

hallucinations. That's how Dr. Sebastian knew something was amiss. "Shaking his head, Spinney said, "He's a smart little prick! But I'm smarter! Thomas, head to the lab and light a fire under them." "Yes, Boss!" "That's right!" laughed Spinney. "Kids. You have to train them." "Let's move this into my office before my secretary kicks our asses!" Stretching, Preston grabbed his coffee and walked to the inner office. "Shall we give Gene a little heartburn for breakfast or lunch?" "Ha! Lunch. Make a big production of talking to him" cracked Preston. "Apparently, he gave a performance last night." "You're joking" laughed Preston. "No. He even asked that his audience applaud the C.O." "What a brown-nosing jerk!" "He knows exactly what he's doing. Never underestimate a sociopath with narcissistic features. He has no soul.""The Doc gave me a psychological breakdown of who he is. She said that if he got the death penalty, he would become a martyr and have followers." "Yeah, he would. In general population, no one would be safe from his manipulation. He would have an army in no time. He needs to be institutionalized where he can't prey on people. What happens after his arraignment?""We're going fishing." "Using Patsy as the bait?" "He wants that insurance money. Her death is the way for him to get it." "Do I even want to know?" asked Preston. "I can see your wheels turning." Spinney cracked an evil grin. "Gene has met his match. Let's just leave it at that. Hopefully the lab will have news for us. In the meantime, I'll put in a call to county and tell them to expect us." "Dr. Sebastian said we should let the C.O. question him about what we found in Patsy's apartment. We can claim that staff there found it and it was not authorized to be there. This way, it won't throw up any red flags for Gene." "He will be arraigned tomorrow. The litany of his charges is going to throw up a shitload of red flags. Physical and mental abuse, murder and attempted murder. I'd say he is going to be a bit nervous." With a knock, Thomas came bounding into the office. "The film on the projector is family stuff. But there's also what looks like a silhouette of a baby over a casket. It's a trick. The lab was able to duplicate the special effects that created the image. ""What about the cassettes?" asked Spinney? "They were several sound effects spliced together. A crying baby. Then a baby laughing and calling "Mama". It was timed to start playing at about the time that they would be entering R.E.M. sleep. It's about three minutes long and set to play every three hours starting at ten p.m. Because Patsy and Gertie are on medications that can cause hallucinations, no one would take them seriously when they reported what they were hearing. He planned this whole thing out and thought that he was free and clear because the rules of Patsy's facility don't allow overnight guests." "Let's go pay Mr. Superstar a visit. " "Dave thanks for coming in early to deal with this." After making a few calls, they made their way to the county jail, discussing strategies on the drive. Spinney and Preston hashed out the questions they needed to ask Gene. As they pulled into the jail's parking lot, Preston stared at the door. "I have to be honest, I may have trouble controlling my temper with Gene. " Spinney flashed a Cheshire cat smile. "Stick to the script. Do not show emotion. If Gene can get under your skin, he will use it to his advantage. Let's stop in and chat with C.O. Banes. He can bring us up to speed on Gene's behavior so far. It will give us an idea of what he's been talking to JJ about. Since JJ is a frequent flyer, I'm sure that he's full of advice for Gene.""Hello, Banes."

"Hey, Spinney." "This is Investigator George Preston." "How do you do? Come to see our resident superstar? "Of course we did. How is our boy doing?" "He performed for us last night. He seems right at home" "How about JJ?" "He's right in Gene's ear, making deals to get extra desserts and so on." "We need to talk to him about a projector that was found in his wife's bedroom wall." "I see. Is his arraignment still set for tomorrow morning?" "Yes. I called his lawyer and told him we were coming. Can you bring the guest of honor to the visiting room?" Barnes replied, "I'll help you break the ice with Gene." There was a clank. "Here he comes." Preston greeted him with a gruff

"Hello, Gene." "Hello." The guard handcuffed Gene to the table. "We've got a few things that we need to ask you about." "Sure. Shoot." said Gene. "Hold on. You may not question him without me present" Sam spoke up. "Nice to see you, Gene." "Yeah, yeah." Taking a seat across the table, Preston gave Gene a wide smile. Barnes said to Gene, "Hey, this guy's okay. He wouldn't be here, but that facility where your wife lives found something that wasn't authorized. They're here to ask you about it." "No problem, Barnes. Shoot." Preston looked to Gene's lawyer. He nodded in approval. "They found a projector in the wall behind Patsy's headboard last night. Can you explain that?" "Sure. I'm not allowed to spend

452

the night there and with Marge and Frank gone, I thought the old films of gigs, family picnics and good memories would help Patsy and Gertie not be so sad. No bad intentions, Preston. Honest." "Okay, but you do know that you needed permission to do that, right?" "Those fussy old busybodies just want to control everything! I could have taken care of my girls' just fine on my own! That place is just a fancy jail! Anything else?" "No. Thank you for your cooperation, Gene." "I hear your music was well received last night. The boys appreciate good music." Banes nodded to the guard to return Gene to his cell. "Okay, let's go" he said as he undid Gene's cuffs from the table. Gene gave his lawyer a questioning look. "I will see

you later, Gene" Sam reassured him. After
Gene was escorted out, Sam turned to face the
glass. "Spinney, I know you're there. Let's
have lunch and discuss the charges against my
client." "How about a late lunch? I have
appointments back at the office." "Sure. Let's
meet at the usual place at 1:30 this afternoon."
"Sounds good." As the mouthpiece left the
room, Preston turned to Spinney. "What's the
meeting about?" "He will ask what Gene is
being charged with. I'll say I haven't decided
yet. I want the element of surprise." "Got ya.
We'll discuss charges after your lunch with the
sleaze ball mouth piece." "I need to stop in and
chat with my boss first. Gene is being arraigned
at 10 a.m. tomorrow. I need to do the

paperwork on that." The drive back to the office was a quiet one. The wheels in Spinney's head were turning at full speed. "Do you know what Gene's charges are going to be?" "As many as I can find. Even if I can only make half of them stick, that egomaniacal prick won't be able to hurt anyone ever again. I can already prove a pattern of abusive behaviors that led him to murder in order to satisfy his own ego." Shaking his head, Preston asked, "Why not go for murder one?" "According to Dr. Sebastian's analysis, he has what they call IED. Intermittent explosive disorder. Generally, he has explosive outbursts of anger and violence to the point of rage. For instance, some woman laughs at your package when you drop your pants. Yes, it might piss you off, but it wouldn't make you angry enough to kill her. With Gene, any insignificant thing flips his internal switch and he has no control. The law says first degree murder is premeditated and intentional. Second degree murder means he didn't plan it. That he flipped the "crazy switch" with all those young girls." "But he did plan killing Frank and Patricia?" "I'm not a hundred percent sure. I believe he only intended to beat them senseless. But if they mocked him in any way at all, his ego could not handle it." "How many counts?" "I am thinking at least five counts of second degree murder, attempted murder, kidnapping and a few more" cracked Spinney. "All the leg work you and Thomas did will pay off."

"Thomas is concerned that he chose the wrong vocation." "This is his first case as an investigator. He will get a better understanding of things once he's been involved in a few trials" cajoled Spinney. "I don't want to lose the kid. He has good instincts. Back to the grind, Boss." "Here, you and Thomas have lunch on me. You both have logged a lot of hours on this case." "Thanks, Boss!" Walking through his outer office, Spinney stopped at Ms. Browne's desk. "Any messages?" he asked. She handed him a fist full of pink message slips. He headed for the inner sanctum of his office. "I have a 1:30 lunch with Gene Allen's lawyer." "Should I reserve your usual table?" "Yes, Ms. Browne." She picked up the phone. "One-thirty

457

reservation for two under Davis Spinney."

"You're all set, Boss." Spinney began returning

calls and updating his boss, Alexander Trenton.

"Well, Davis, I wanted you to go for murder

one, but I now understand why you chose to go

for Second degree. I have to review all your

evidence. You have built a strong case. How's

our star witness holding up?" "She's a rock.

Gene will totally lose control when he sees

her.""Keep her hidden." "In a safe house or

hotel?" "Hotel. I want her kept as comfortable

as possible. I'm sure we can get him to take a

plea, but in case we need her, she should be

prepared. I think I should be present for the

pretrial conference. Just as a show of strength.

His ego is large, but so are his self-preservation

skills. Sam is a smart lawyer. He'll advise him to take the deal. Are we on the same page, Spinney?""Yes, we are. I heard through the grapevine that Gene will be giving another performance tonight." "Good! Keep his ass out of the law library." "Do you agree that he's nuts?" "I think he is a sociopath and a narcissist who needs to be put away. I also agree with Dr. Sebastian's observations about what would happen if he was put in general population. He would have an army of assholes following his every move. He needs to be in solitary confinement so he can't prey on weak minded boys with too much time on their hands. I did some digging of my own, Spinney. Gene has been doing this stuff since he was a kid. He couldn't function in the military either. He has a very disturbed view of the world." "I glanced over your resources, Trenton. If this has been festering since his childhood, then he's a candidate for a psych defense." "Yes, he will be but we can push for him to be committed to a hospital for the criminally insane. He'll never be able to convince a shrink that he should be released.""Dr. Sebastian is concerned that he will try to kill Patsy. I agree with her. We have to get him get him to take the plea bargain." "Don't you have an appointment?" "Yes." "After the arraignment tomorrow, we'll meet to hash all this out. I'll give you a call after my meeting with Sam. Bye, Trenton." Washing his face, Spinney put on his best game face as he headed for his meeting with Sam. Walking in,

big man on campus Spinney nodded to the

waitress. "Sorry I'm late. Got held up on a long

call with my boss. I see you've already ordered

yourself a drink, Sam." "Yeah. I ordered the

best they had since it's on you." "Blue?" asked

Spinney. "Yeah. I was being kind to the D.A's

budget." "Kind of you, Sam." As the waitress

appeared, she smiled. "Do you need a minute?"

"No. Two surf and turfs and I'll have what he's

having to drink." "Should I bring the bottle?"

"No, we're on the clock." "What dirty trick did

you use to get Gene indicted?" "Your client has

been a bad boy, Sam. Anywhere Gene performs

on tour, they find bodies." "Circumstantial." "I

don't believe so. He didn't clean up all his

loose ends." "Come on, Spinney. Why so cryptic? I know things have happened that seemed suspicious but they could never prove he did anything!" "I know about the Adult Protective Services case." "He's a drunk with temper issues." "You are accurate." "His wife is not well, so a jury would despise you for putting her on the stand. You aren't about to make yourself look bad." "True, Sam. But you know me well enough to know that I don't indict unless I have a rock solid case. You know that the military threw him out because he liked substances a bit too much." Sam smiled, "Yeah, most men grow up eventually. Gene has issues. It's obvious when talking to him." "He had a great ruse, Sam. Underage girls who wanted to be singers auditioned for him. Get it?" "Okay so he solicited minors. Musicians don't check ID at gigs. Look, Dave. I never said Gene isn't a dirt bag. But that doesn't make him responsible for the disappearance of those girls." "He got a bit reckless. He left one for dead but she survived. We have her" Spinney snarled. "You know I will make her look like a two-bit harlot. So, we horse trading? cracked Sam. "We'll see how you feel after the arraignment." "If his tour was in a southern state, they start fucking at eight years old" snapped Sam. "Legally, the age of consent is eighteen" cracked Spinney. "Think about it, Sam. I laid my case before a Grand Jury. It only took fifteen minutes to indict Gene.

I have witnesses, physical evidence, and eye witness testimony. Your boy is up a creek without a paddle. Plus, one of his band members wrote a statement. This case is better than my birthday!" After a few more bites of food, Sam looked at Spinney. "Tell me what you're looking for on this one." Spinney drew in a sharp breath. "I have a pattern of behavior. I have a psychiatrist that has given her analysis of his issues. I have enough for murder one. I would love to cook him but it's obvious he needs to be where he can't hurt himself or anyone else." "The funny farm? I don't buy it." "Then he will die." "I would rather see him get the help he needs. The longer he is walking the streets, the more people are at risk. What do

464

you think, Sam?" After finishing his steak and another scotch, Sam smiled. "I will let you know after discovery." With a sigh of exasperation Spinney said, "You might want to read the psych profile before arraignment." The look on Spinney's face told Sam he would be burning the midnight oil. "I will assume this meeting is over?" "Yes. You have some reading to do." "It's been an enlightening lunch." Walking to his car, Sam wondered 'what the hell did I get myself into?' Spinney slammed through his outer office. "Lunch went that well?" chimed Ms. Browne. "Yes! I need you to put together a file. Put Dr. Sebastian's evaluation of Gene together and send it to Sam's office." Spinney made his obligatory call to Trenton to fill him in on what happened during lunch. "I'm pleased that you didn't give away our strategy. It was noble of you to give Sam the psychological profile." "I would not wish Gene Allen as a client on my worst enemy. Old Sam will earn his paycheck on this case for sure." "You better get some rest. Arraignment is in the morning."Spinney made a call to C.O. Banes. "How's our boy?" "Parading around like he owns the place. He's signing autographs. Hell, the other inmates are giving him pencils, paper, desserts, even their commissary." "Okay. His arraignment is early tomorrow morning. Have him ready." Spinney needed to wash away the events of the day. He took a hot shower and ordered some Chinese food to relax.He settled in to watch a comedy about aliens but fell asleep with the remote in his hand. At ten p.m. he awoke to a ringing phone. "Hello?" "You fucking prick!" "Sam?" "Yeah. I've reviewed the highlights of the file you sent me." "Why didn't you tell me?" "I tried." "We'll talk after the arraignment." Click.Spinney went back to sleep. His alarm started buzzing at six a.m. "Shit! I need coffee!" Spinney lazily went through his closet. He selected a blue pin-striped suit, red tie, white shirt, blue socks and black oxfords. This case is going to get me noticed, he thought as he headed to his office. This day could not end fast enough. By the time he reached his office, Spinney had all his motions ready. District

467

Attorney Trenton stopped him on his way to the courthouse. "I will be observing this morning." Jogging up the stairs, Spinney headed to the lawyer's room. Fifteen minutes later, the bus from county arrived bringing the inmates to their arraignment hearings. Gene was all smiles. JJ whispered, "This isn't a gig! Keep your eyes down!" The first few inmates went through the motions. "Gene Allen, Sr.? Step forward." "Samuel Dean representing Mr. Allen." "ADA Spinney for the prosecution." "What are the charges?" "Six counts second degree murder, one count attempted murder, one count kidnapping." "How do you plead, Mr. Allen?" "Not guilty, by mental defect" answered Sam. "WHAT?" Gene whispered angrily. "Shhh... I will explain" Sam soothed. "I will hear on bail." "I request bail be denied. He is a flight risk" Spinney stated. "Mr. Allen has no criminal record. He has a wife who is ill that he needs to support. He is a pillar of his community and a deacon at his church." "Due to the seriousness of these charges, I am setting bail at $150,000 cash or bond. The defendant will surrender his passport and wear an ankle monitoring device." Spinney added, "We also request a 4241 psychological evaluation of the defendant." "So ordered." Sam requested to speak with his client after the proceedings. Gene was escorted to a conference room. Once he was secured to the table, he looked at Sam and asked," What the fuck, Sam? A mental defect defense?" "I read the psychological profile. I read your history. This is your only prayer, Gene!"A knock on the door brought in a pile of paperwork that listed a potential trial date. "Can you make bail?" Sam asked. "I can put up the house and my truck as collateral." "Good. I'll call the bondsman. You'll be out by dinner time. I will need you in my office after I review everything they sent me in discovery." "Why did you plead me not guilty by reason of mental defect?" demanded Gene. "It was either that, or they can bump it up to murder one and give you the death penalty for Frank and Patricia! Let me get your bail taken care of. Then we can talk. Keep your mouth shut while I'm arranging things with the bail bondsman.

Those ankle monitors are no joke. They'll know when you're in the can." "Yeah, I got it. If I play any gigs, I gotta let you know where I will be." "I'll be back with papers for you to sign." Sam knocked on the door and was let out. Gene stood up, sticking his wrists out. As he was being cuffed, he casually asked, "So, what's for lunch?" Smiling, C.O Banes said, "I'm not sure, Gene" as he put him back in the cell with JJ. "Hey, man! You're back. What happened?" asked JJ. "They think I killed people. Second degree. But I got bail. I had to surrender my passport and agree to wear an ankle bracelet. So, no leaving the county for gigs." "Wow! Where would they get such a crazy idea about you?" "Who knows? It's a mix- up." "What does your

471

lawyer say?" "A bunch of stupid shit. I'll be here until dinner time." "I'll be arraigned later this afternoon. But I've been through this many times before.Clacking could be heard throughout the cell block. "The cook tried her hand at barbeque, Gene." "That sounds great. I'm starving!" "Glad we're able to appease you, Gene." After lunch, Gene stretched out on his bunk. Banes announced, "Gene, your lawyer wants to see you. You know the drill. He handcuffed Gene and escorted him to the rec room. After Gene had been cuffed to the table, Sam walked in with a stack of papers. "You need to sign here, there and initial here. Then you'll be fitted for your ankle bracelet. It will be synched to the Sheriff's Department computer system so they will always know where you are." It took twenty minutes of nerdy sheriff's deputies to get the monitor synched to the system. "Okay, let's get you dressed and processed out. There is a two hundred dollar setup fee for your ankle monitor and a daily fee of fifteen dollars." "WHAT?" screeched Gene. "It's better than sitting in jail for the next ninety days until trial." Sam replied. "Okay, I get it!" Gene snapped. Opening the door, C.O. Banes handed Gene his guitar. "We'll be seeing you, Gene!" cracked Banes. "Not if I can help it!" bitched Gene. "Gene, I'm taking you out to dinner so we can go over a few things" Sam said as he opened the door of the local bar. "May I help you? Table for two?" "Yes, away from the traffic, please." Once they were seated,

the waitress asked if they would like drinks. "I

will take…" Sam interrupted him. "Two Cokes

and two steak dinners medium well. Steak fries

and green salad with blue cheese dressing."

"Very good." "What gives, Sam? I needed

bourbon!" "That monitor also registers your

blood alcohol content through your sweat. It's

waterproof to allow bathing." "Thank you"

Gene said as he took a few sips of his soda.

"You also need to charge that thing twice a day.

If you let it die, they will bring you back to

court to show cause." "Jesus! It's as bad as

jail!" "Just because you got out on bail doesn't

mean it will be a cake walk." Gene smiled at

the waitress as she brought out their food.

"Anything else? Steak sauce plain or spicy?"

"Spicy" smiled Gene. "Can I refill your

drinks?" "Just bring a pitcher!" snapped Sam.

"Look, Gene. All gigs will have to be approved.

Stay out of the limelight, please. No alcohol.

You need to be available whenever I call you. "

"Geez, Sam! You act like they have me"

snarled Gene. "The psych profile is damning,

but they have an eyewitness who testified for

the Grand Jury. They accepted Spinney's

evidence without question. Plus, you were

indicted in fifteen minutes flat. I'll know more

after we get everything from discovery. They

have enough to request murder one, which

means the death penalty. You can eventually

get out of the hospital." "You mean the funny

475

farm?" "No, a hospital for the criminally insane." "What?! There's nothing wrong with me, Sam!" "I would take living in a hospital versus the death penalty any day" quipped Sam. "What about Patsy?" crowed Gene. "Look, I have heard Marge died accidentally and that you collected a life insurance payout on that. Do not think the same will happen to Patsy! Do what the fuck I tell you! I don't want to attend your execution!" "Fine!" "There will be a pretrial conference in a few weeks. That will be where we will do some negotiating." "What would happen if I fired you and defended myself?" "You might as well put your head in a noose!" "I want to be there when you depose this eyewitness." "Let's see what they present

476

in discovery. I will know more after that. Until then, behave yourself!" "Yes sir!""Dessert sir?" Smiling, Gene said, "Something chocolate and sweet." Sam scowled at Gene. "And for you?" the waitress asked. "Carrot cake, thanks." "I want you in my office in a week to go through what I get out of discovery." "Yes sir." "They executed a search warrant on your house and vehicles. I have no idea what they found. You need to be home by nine o'clock unless you're playing a gig. I will attend all of your gigs." "You gonna add that to my legal bill?" "Stop it, Gene. I'm trying to protect you!" "Are you gonna help me pleasure myself too?" "This is serious, Gene. If you won't cooperate, I will recuse myself as your counsel. "Sorry, Sam. I

477

just don't believe these charges. It seems like a

colossal joke at my expense." "Just go home.

Clean your house up. I'm sure they tore it apart.

Those social workers will be up your ass.

Behave. Be polite. Only visit your wife during

the day with nurses present so no one can say

you tried to hurt her. Don't give them any

reason to dig.""Fine, I'll be on church

behavior." "Church is good. Attend church.

Stay away from young girls, please?" "Jesus!

Should I join a monastery?" "No. Just don't do

anything to get your bail revoked! Go home and

dump any booze you have. I will have my

secretary call you with the date and time of

your appointment with the D.A's shrink and we

will have our shrink evaluate you, too. As they

left, Gene looked at his lawyer. "I don't have my truck." "Oh, sorry. I'll give you a ride home." As they pulled into the blackened driveway, Sam said, "I'll leave my headlights on so you can make your way inside the house." Unlocking the door, Gene flipped on the overhead light. He screamed at the top of his lungs, "Sam! Get in here! Look at this fucking place! They trashed it!" "Of course they did. Let's see what other damage they've done." Everything had been pulled out of every cupboard and cabinet. Gene ran outside to check on his truck. When he pulled on the door handle, he discovered that it had been left ajar. The battery was dead. Infuriated, Gene screamed, "How the fuck am I supposed to go see Patsy?""Do you have another vehicle?"

"Yeah, a van." "It doesn't seem to be here."

Sam grabbed the slip that had been nailed to the

door. "They have impounded your van." "What

the hell are they looking for?" "I'm not sure.

But I will call Triple A to have your battery

charged. On me" Sam said. "Let's go into the

house and call." "Let me run and grab a

disposable camera from my car. I always keep a

few of them handy for situations like this." He

returned a few minutes later with two cameras

in his hand. "Start here" he instructed Gene and

they went from room to room snapping pictures

as Sam took notes on the disarray. Sam wrote

some notes about the truck. They also had a

warrant for outside buildings. "Oh, shit! My

garage and tool shed" Gene said, glancing that direction. He opened the shed door and flipped on the light with a sigh of relief. "Not too bad. My tools are just out of order." As Gene made his way to the garage, a wrecker pulled into his driveway. Gene, wait!" yelled Sam. "Let's get your truck battery on the charger. After explaining that charging the battery was going to take a while, Roscoe smiled a toothless grin. "I was on my way home for the night. Lucky has the night shift. I recognized the address and volunteered to come."Sam looked deep into Gene's pitch black eyes. "I guess we need to check out the garage." Gene let out a sigh of anger and frustration. "I bet it's trashed, Sam." "They were looking for something specific"

Sam announced. "Do you own guns?" "Yeah, why?" "Are they registered? Damn it, Gene! I need to know everything!" "Ah, yeah. I carried a handgun when I traveled for protection. Some of those honky-tonks are dangerous places." Sam looked at Gene. "What about drugs? To make girls more cooperative?" "I don't have to drug girls! They fall for all of my charms!"Shaking his head, Sam cajoled, "Remember, anything you say to me is in confidence." "I know, Sam." Gene pulled out a ring of keys. "Hey, can I sue those asshole cops if they broke any of my band equipment?" "If we can prove they did it, I suppose we could." "Amplifiers and guitars are expensive to replace. They are my livelihood." As Gene

482

opened the garage door, he turned on the flood lights. With a scow on his face, Gene started to inventory the contents of his garage. "So far, all I can see is that they broke the backs off two amplifiers looking for drugs. I don't got none. I own a few pipes, but got nothing to put in them." "I'm sure they found them." Walking back toward the tow truck, Sam asked, "Why did you get released from the service?" "We'll say it was a mutual agreement. They lied about my job and didn't think I was trustworthy enough to travel around the world." "And?" "They said I have a personality disorder. Honestly, I did tons of self-medicating." "Okay. I need you to come to my office and sign some release forms." "Why?" "Look, Spinney is going to pull out all the stops to fry you. I have

to use whatever I can to stop that from

happening. There's a chance you can get

released from a hospital, but you can't come

back from being dead! I will give you the best

defense that is humanly possible, but you have

to help me whether you like what I say about

you or not. What I have read tells me the shrink

that wrote it thinks you have major problems

and prison is not the place for you." "But I have

to say that I'm crazy!" "No. If we can prove

that this pattern of behavior is caused by mental

issues, you will not be executed." "How long

would I be in the 'booby hatch'?" asked

Gene."I don't know, honestly. Roscoe looked at

Gene. "It looks like your battery is gonna need

a few hours on the charger. So, I'll just bill ya

for a new battery, Gene." Sam looked at Roscoe.

"How much for the battery and your time?"

"Two hundred bucks." Sam handed Roscoe his

money. "I'll need a receipt, please?" "Sure

thing.""Gene, you need to go plug your ankle

bracelet in." Roscoe handed Sam his receipt.

"I'll call you later, Gene. Bye!" "Sam, I'm

gonna need a crew to put my house back

together." "Do it yourself. Stay off Spinney's

radar." "What about Patsy?" "I will check on

her. You can call her. Stay home for a few days

until I get things rolling, okay?" "Yes sir!"

"Trust me, Gene" smiled Sam. "Guess I better

get to work." "Here is your stuff from lockup

and your guitar. I will call you to come in and

sign those release forms. Good night, Gene."Just as Gene was plugging in the bracelet, the phone rang. "Hello?" "Hey, man! It's me, JJ. I got sprung after you left. Let's go have a beer." "I have a house to put back together. The cops trashed it when they searched it. Fuck, man! I will need a crew to get this place back together!" "I can give you a hand" cracked JJ. "Once we get it put back together, we can practice." "Sounds good. Come over in the morning." "Will do. Night, Gene!Following the charging instructions, Gene checked the status of his ankle monitor. It was almost fully charged. He looked in the fridge. "Guess I need to do some grocery shopping." He opened the freezer and found several leftover casseroles from the funerals. He sat in front of the TV with his usual bottle of bourbon in his hand. He thought about his earlier conversation with Sam, but shook it off. One drink wouldn't hurt. After chugging half the bottle, Gene stumbled to bed.He was plagued by dreams of the loose ends he needed to tie up in order to walk away from the charges he was facing. He sat bolt upright in a cold sweat at three a.m. He walked into the kitchen and swilled water from the jug in the fridge. Wiping his face, he dropped back onto the bed and drifted back into the dark abyss of his tortured sleep. At eight a.m. Gene awoke and dressed for a day of house cleaning. He then made a full pot of coffee and formulated a plan of action.

He started with the living room then moved onto the kitchen while gulping down large cups of coffee. A loud thud on the screen door caught Gene's attention. "Hey, where are you?" Gene smiled. Come on in, JJ. I already started working on cleaning up the mess." "Jesus! They tore your shit up, man!" "Tell me about it." "Hey, I picked you up a few things. Milk, soda, beer and some odds and ends. Bread and cold cuts for sandwiches." "Thanks bud! Want some coffee?" "Sure, Gene. Lord! You need a turbo boost to get through this mess. I got just the thing." "What is it?" "My specialty. Bathtub crank." "I'm supposed to stay clean." "Well how the hell are you supposed to get this place put back together?" "Maybe I'll try a little. I had bad dreams last night." "This will fix you up. Plus, you will work at lightning speed." Gene perked up after a few lines. "Crank up some tunes! It's time to get this done!" The music was so loud you could hear it a quarter-mile away."Well I'd say we got a lot done. The kitchen, bath room, living room, music room and the den are now back in order." "Last on the list is my bedroom. Go make some sandwiches, JJ. I'll get started on this laundry. Fuck it; we'll just wash everything here. Those assholes threw it all on the floor." "Okay, now we can eat." Gene turned the stereo down. "Which of these casseroles should we have for dinner?" "Doesn't matter to me" said JJ. "Now I'm tired" Gene huffed. "Crank works really

well, but you're exhausted afterwards." "Beer
or bourbon to go with your sandwich, JJ?"
"Beer, of course." As he handed JJ a beer, Gene
opened a can of soda for himself. "What's
this?" JJ questioned. "This monitor can tell if
I've been drinking through my sweat. Sam says
I gotta lay off for a while. Oh, shit. I better plug
this thing in." "How are we supposed to go out
and play a gig?" "My lawyer has to notify the
Sherriff and he intends to attend all my gigs so I
don't get blamed for anything else.""You know,
if that monitor's not charged, they can't track
you, right?" "But then my ass will be dragged
into court to show cause. I could end up back in
jail. Supposedly they have an eyewitness that I
did all the things I was charged with. I did

490

nothing wrong. The D.A. already has a psych profile on me so I have to be evaluated by a shrink. This sucks!" huffed Gene. A knock on the door suspended Gene's rant. "Your lawyer needs you to sign these forms" said a man standing in the doorway. Being a bit blurry-eyed, Gene wasn't sure about signing anything until he recognized Sam's letterhead. Each release form was for different places. The military and previous employers. There was also one for Dr. Sebastian. "Oh, this will be interesting" chuckled Gene. After collecting the signatures, the courier took off down the drive on what looked like a moped. "Have you talked to your wife?" JJ asked. "No, Sam wants me to hold off on that. But he wants me to be there when he goes through the evidence from discovery." JJ thought about Gene's last statement. "Well, I guess he wants you to see everything they got against you." "I told him that I want to be there when he deposes this eyewitness. We'll see if they have the balls to accuse me to my face!" "I think that's called intimidating a witness, bud." "Call it what you will, it has always been very effective for me." "What is a "personality disorder", Gene?" "Well, I don't take orders well. I get pissy when I'm not treated like I deserve to be." "Wow. Okay. What about your band?" asked JJ. "They get to vote on music, but I have the final say on what and where we perform." "Okay" JJ responded. "Nothing in your world is democratic." "Sure it is. As long as you agree with me." "How did your family feel about that?" Laughing, Gene said, "They knew where the front door was. They were free to leave and easily replaced." "Boy, you're a tough taskmaster." "We will get along fine as long as you treat me the way I deserve to be treated. Patsy knows I am her God and she treats me as such." "Okay" JJ said as he glanced at the clock. "Crap! I have an appointment with my probation officer. I'll be back later." "Do you need a lift to town?" asked Gene. "Yeah. I can't pedal fast enough to get there on time" JJ said. "No problem" said Gene. "I want to check in on Patsy and Gertie." "Let's go then." Pulling up to the apartment complex with bouquets of roses, Gene bounded through the doors. In his pocket was a replacement micro cassette recorder and tape. He assumed that if the staff had found the projector, then they must have found the cassettes too. As he ran his hand along the recorder and cassette in his pocket, smugness washed over him. "I'll up the ante. If I'm not present, I can't be held responsible." He clicked the lock and wondered if anyone was home. Nancy was vacuuming the carpet. "I didn't hear you knock" she said, startled. "I brought my girls some flowers" Gene replied. Nancy looked at her watch and said, "Oh, I will be right back. I need to pick the ladies up from arts and crafts." Running out the door, Nancy had no idea that she had just given Gene the opportunity he needed to plant the recorders. Gene smiled devilishly as he set the loops to play in both bedrooms. "Let's play a game!" he laughed. The flowers adorned their nightstands and a sweet aroma wafted through the apartment. Nurse Willetts walked up behind Gene. "May I help you?" "Good afternoon, Nurse Willetts. I had an appointment in town, so I dropped off some flowers for my girls." "I would appreciate some notice before you drop in." "The flowers were an impulse." "I'm sure, since you are out on bail!" "Yes, you are correct. I even have an ankle monitor so everyone knows exactly where I am at all times. It's been a pleasure, as always Nurse Willetts." As Gene shut the door, Nurse Willetts went through both bouquets with a fine-toothed comb just in case he'd left any surprises for Patsy or Gertie. Nancy wheeled Patsy through the door, with Gertie hobbling beside her on her cane. "Where's Gene?" cried Patsy. "He had an appointment but he left you ladies a gift." Patsy walked into her room and shrieked with delight. "Roses! They smell heavenly!" Gertie walked into her bedroom to find roses adorning a spring bouquet. "Frank always got me this bouquet. Gene remembered. How sweet!" "Nancy, may I have a word with you?" "Yes, Nurse Willetts?" "How long was Gene alone in here?" "I was here when he arrived. Maybe ten minutes. I was here with him for five minutes." "Alright. He could not have done much in that amount of time. He is not to be alone with these ladies, understand?" "Yes ma'am."As Gene walked into the grocery store, he made his way to the personal care aisle for soap and shaving cream. "Oh, crap! I need razors too!" Leaving the store, Gene noticed a yellow light on his ankle monitor. He needed to get home soon. As JJ spilled everything Gene told him, Thomas listened carefully. "Look, this dude is twisted beyond repair!" Thomas laughed. "Maybe we should give you a matching ankle bracelet." "Why?" JJ protested. "So Gene believes that you are a dirt bag just like him." "I can't work on house arrest." "Yes, so would have to get permission to play gigs with the band too." "Fine."Preston piped in, "You should know

Gene killed Frank because he thought he was a rat." "WHAT?" "We are advising you to be careful. Try to avoid being alone with him." "He said his lawyer was gonna be at all his gigs." "That could be your saving grace. Call in tomorrow. You're dismissed." "Am I getting the ankle bracelet?" "Yes. We need to keep track of you." "Fine!" whined JJ. "Did you think you had a choice?" "We own your rat ass! Lay off the crank. You will need to be aware of your surroundings. Report to the Sheriff's office to get your bracelet." "What about the cost?" "It's on us for now."After having a shower and changing into clean clothes, Gene started making dinner. A light rap on the door derailed his train of thought. Hey, man! You look pretty good for just getting out of county."

"Not too shabby" laughed Gene. "We practicing tonight?" "Yup. After dinner. Hell, I even performed twice while I was in lock up!" "Christ, Gene! You can find an audience anywhere, can't you?" "I was well received, too." "We're gonna audition this new cat, JJ. See if he can hang with the big dogs!" "Okay. See you between seven and eight o'clock. Later!" "Bye!" As the band was leaving, the phone rang. "Hello?" "Thank you for the flowers!" "You are welcome, honey." "Did Gertie like hers?" "Yes, she loved them, Gene. Where have you been? I've been worried about you." "There was a mix up. Sam's been working on it." "Will there be a trial?" "There could be. Maybe Sam will have it taken care of at the pretrial conference." "So, you're out on bail?""Yes. I have a cool ankle bracelet that tells on me if I drink too much." "Oh boy. Did you get in a fight?" "No. We were a bit too rowdy on the last tour." "I see." "Well, I have to go now. It's time for my breathing treatment. I take less medicine now. I'm getting better. I can't wait to come home. Love you, Gene." "I love you too, honey. Give my love to Gertie. Bye."Checking on dinner, Gene walked to the music room looking around. Everything's ready. We'll see if JJ has the balls it takes to play with me! Setting the table, Gene looked up to see JJ hauling equipment up onto the porch. "Hey, where have you been? Practice is after dinner.

The boys were already here. I told them about you. Are you up to auditioning tonight? Your face is blood red. You been running" "My appointment was longer than I had planned and I had to go get my equipment." "Here, let me help you bring it in. Just set it there for now. Sit and eat." JJ guzzled down a few glasses of sweet tea. "What took so long at your probation appointment?" Gene questioned. JJ hiked his leg up to Gene's chair. "They felt I needed one of these and a piss test." "Ha ha! Well looks like they're gonna make their quota for the month." "Man, it's normally a fine or a lecture. Maybe community service." "I guess we're in the same boat. Dishes go in the dishwasher. Only my old lady washes dishes by hand. Go ahead and start tuning your bass. You have one of our songs you want to sing?" "Prison Blues sounds good." "Here come the boys."After introductions were made, Gene put JJ through his paces. He had to sing all parts of the song, not just the lead. "Grab a soda, JJ. I need to talk to the boys." "What do you think? "He needs some more practice with us, but he can play. He can also sing, so that's beneficial." "Okay, he's on a six month probationary period. If it works out, we make him a full member of the band." "His amps are new. That's a good thing.""Come back in, JJ. Six months of probation, then you can be a member of the band." "What do you say? The probation period is to see if we all work well together cohesively." "You want to make sure I'll show up!""Exactly! We need to give you time to learn our catalogue and we do take requests. We usually practice the most requested songs. We'll give you the catalogue. Gene writes new songs that will be introduced into the sets." "Okay, that's a wrap for tonight. We also have costumes but you and Frank are close to the same size. You can use his until you can afford your own."As everyone left, there were handshakes all around. "Have a seat. I'll grab the music for you." "Gene, can you get moving? This stupid ankle bracelet is blinking yellow." "Keep your pants on, JJ." "I'll end up back in jail if I don't plug this thing in!" Gene sauntered out carrying four binders of sheet music. "I need to memorize this by when?"

"Two weeks. Our first gig together will be at

the Black Oak Roadhouse." "Yes, Boss!" "Now,

get home and plug in!" Riding home, JJ was

sweating bullets. "Man, I don't know if I can

pull this off!" Sam was busy hauling boxes of

discovery evidence into his home office. "I

won't be doing anything this weekend"

grumbled Sam. After a shower and putting on

some sweats and a t-shirt, Sam phoned in an

order to his favorite Chinese takeout place.

Pouring himself three fingers of Scotch, he

opened the first box and pulled out Exhibit A, a

signed affidavit from Frank. As Sam began to

read, the color drained from his face. He went

back to the box that listed family and pattern of

behavior. He pulled out a new folder as he started reading about Gene's childhood. He shuddered as he perused the pages. He then looked at his calendar. The trial was in six weeks. The doorbell rang and shook his thoughts loose. As he opened the door, a small girl recited his order. "Twenty-five dollars please?" Sam smiled and included a ten dollar tip for the sweet delivery girl. Closing the door, Sam pulled out several containers of food and loaded it onto a paper plate. After four folders of Gene's history, Sam was swigging directly from his bottle of Scotch.He started talking to himself. "Gene's been fucked up since he was a kid. He was an abusive prick to his children and his wives. There's been too many unexplained

505

accidents. The military gladly threw him out and people have accidents around him. And this is only the first box!" As Sam replaced the files from the first box, he glanced at Frank's statement and quietly said, "Fuck it, I'm going to bed!" The sun began streaming through the cracks in the blinds, hitting Sam's eyes. As they adjusted to the bright light, Sam began thinking of a Saturday filled with golfing and drinks at the country club. As he stumbled to the kitchen to brew his morning coffee, Sam was full of possibilities. Grabbing his Harvard mug, he filled it to the brim with steamy goodness. As he wandered into the living room, he sat in his favorite easy chair. He grabbed the TV remote and flipped through the channels. His eyes glanced to the left and saw the boxes and folders that were strewn across the love seat and coffee table. He remembered there would be no fun this weekend. He had to go through every one of these boxes to save Gene's soul, or the pathetic life of a delusional man. Gene's delusions of grandeur made him believe that Sam owed him a five-star defense. His talent was meager at best. Throwing on a t-shirt and jeans, Sam knew that all he could do was try to get everyone to agree that a hospital was the best place for Gene. Pouring a second cup of Joe, Sam looked at the date on Frank's statement. Curious, he pulled out statements and interviews including the Adult Protective Services report. Shaking his head, he began to realize how long Spinney had been building this case. "Christ! If Gene doesn't take a plea bargain, they will fry his dumb, country bumpkin ass!" He finally got to the eyewitness testimony from the Grand Jury. Marissa's testimony would easily send him to death row. Reviewing all the other statements, he noticed that whenever Gene became upset or frustrated, he talked to himself in the third person and answered himself. He then looked back at Dr. Sebastian's psych profile. "I'll be damned! He truly does have issues. He needs to see our shrink, pronto. This explains why they would rather send him to a hospital for the criminally insane. Startled by the ringing phone, Sam answered. "Hello?" A familiar voice chuckled.

"We need a fourth for golf. You in?" Spinney was in a good mood. "I really need to go through these boxes of discovery evidence." "They will be there later. Come out and enjoy some fresh air and sunshine." "Sure, why not? See you in forty-five minutes at the club."

`Dressed in a polo shirt and casual dress shorts, Sam grabbed his golf clubs and got into his car. Arriving, Sam finds Spinney in the lounge. "Care for a mimosa before we start? How a muffin or a bagel? You don't look well." "I got friendly with a bottle of Scotch after reading about Gene's behaviors as a kid." "I thought you might need some relief after that." "Christ, Davis! You could have warned me!" "Have a drink and a bagel. Judge Benjamin will be

joining us." Sam gave Davis a questing look.
"It's just golf and chit chat, really." "Look, Sam
your client needs a quiet padded cell with a
shrink and plenty of drugs." "I have the video
of Marissa's Grand Jury testimony. He attacked
her after she mocked the size of his package
and his lack of prowess." "Oh, so if a woman
emasculates him or makes fun of his
performance, he flies into a rage and kills
them?" questioned Sam. "Exactly!" "I realize
he's a fruit basket, but damn!" "Frank told us
he helped Gene dispose of a body before the
band returned home from their last tour. Gene
stayed on tour playing solo gigs." "Okay. But
why would he kill Marge?" "We think he was
trying to kill both Patsy and Marge. Whatever

was in his homemade flu medicine reacted

badly with her other daily prescriptions. Gene

had life insurance policies on both women. Half

a million each." "Why kill Frank and Patricia?"

"Our investigators publicly hauled Frank in for

questioning. They got him to turn on Gene and

he figured it out. Patricia was Patsy's sponsor

from her Battered Women's group. She stood in

his way and was not swayed by his charm or his

intimidation tactics." "That fills in some of the

holes." "We found a micro cassette tape loop

that would play the sounds of a baby crying. It

was meant to push Patsy over the edge. She had

some issues with not being able to have

children. So, even with him out on bail, we

suspect he will try to get rid of Patsy so he can

collect the insurance money.""Hello, boys."

"Judge Benjamin." "It's Gerald out here. Let's

play some golf." On the first tee, the judge hit a

good drive. "This game is off to a good state.

Which one of you is buying drinks when I beat

your socks off?" "It would be just my luck"

whined Sam. "Nonsense, Sam. You have a

great opportunity to get your client the help he

needs and to make our streets safer." "I am not

sure Gene will agree with you, Gerald." "Well,

I'm sure you boys will be able to convince

him." "I told him he could only visit Patsy

during the day and when the nurses are

present." "He has already been to visit them. It

was recorded by the security system." "Shit!"

"He brought flowers for the ladies." "How long

was he there?" "Ten to fifteen minutes. There was a home health aide there when he arrived. She left and then he was surprised by Nurse Willetts." "Not enough time to do much damage. Luckily, Patsy and Gertie were attending arts and crafts in a separate part of the facility." "So, he was never alone with Patsy?" "No. We would have dispatched someone out to the facility if he had been there for too long." "So, what's the plan?" asked Judge Benjamin. "Well, I want him to see one of our psychologists for an evaluation. I have no doubt he or she will agree with Dr. Sebastian's analysis. He is even making his buddy JJ nervous." "JJ is a hardcore frequent flyer. Not much rattles him." "Gene wants to be present

513

when I depose Marissa." "Before that happens, you should see the tape of her Grand Jury testimony" chuckled Spinney. "Oh great! Another surprise?" "Just her closing remarks." "Christ! Will it send Gene over the edge?" "I'm sure it will. He has issues with women not giving him accolades and praise, so it will really get under his skin. You should watch the tape without Gene present first." "Looks like you boys are buying me drinks!" Judge Benjamin exclaimed. "Yes sir." "In my personal opinion, Gene needs a nice padded room. He would take over the weak minded saps in prison. He has the charisma of a cult leader. People would flock to him. He is a danger to everyone.""Let's grab some lunch.

514

The buffet here is pretty good." "I think a nice stiff drink is in order." "I dread going through the boxes from discovery" Sam scoffed. "The tape is in the bottom of the fifth box. Just relax, Sam. I am easy" laughed Spinney.Gene began putting away his laundry. At 1:00 p.m., he decided he was in the mood for a large sub. It was a short drive to town. He thought he could drop in and bring pizza to Patsy and Gertie. Nurse Willetts would be at the nurse's desk. He smiled, thinking to himself that he would bring movies and hang out. There was a knock at the door. "Patsy, are you here?" Gertie came out of her bedroom. "Oh, Gene! You came to see us!" "I brought your favorite pizza. Meat lovers and Hawaiian. I rented you Steel Magnolias and

Beaches. I'll set up the VCR. I got you a grape

and an orange soda."Patsy emerged from her

bedroom beaming because she heard Gene's

voice. "Here, let's get you comfortable, Patsy."

"This food isn't on our diet, Gene. Nurse

Willetts will be angry." "So, what? She's a

dried up old hag that no man would sleep with

voluntarily!" Giggling Gertie said," Behave,

Gene!"Starting the movie, Gene served them

pizza and drink on their TV trays. After

devouring his sub, he started on the pizza. "Oh,

I forgot, I also brought antipasto salad and

cannoli." "We can have the pasta salad later,

but cannolis sound delicious." Smiling, he gave

each lady dessert. "Here, I'll put in Beaches

now." Feeling full and satisfied, Patsy started

drifting off to sleep. Acting quickly, Gene bagged up all the garbage before helping Gertie to her room. He checked to see if the micro recorder was set. With a gentle shake, he helped Patsy get ready for bed. He tucked her in and kissed her goodnight. He put away the TV trays and bagged up the leftovers and the videos. He cleaned everything up so there was no trace that he had been there at all. He slinked out the door, thinking he had outsmarted everyone. He didn't realize that his ankle monitor was dead.He stopped off for a six pack of beer as he headed home. As he made his way into the house and sat down in his chair, he noticed that the green light on his ankle monitor was off. "Shit! I better plug this thing in!" He plugged in the

517

cable and found a Western on TV. After

downing half the six pack he had just bought,

Gene fell asleep.Nurse Willetts turned the key

in the door lock. It was awfully quiet in here.

With great concern, she made her way through

the apartment. Checking Gertie's room, Nurse

Willetts found her sound asleep. Curious, Nurse

Willetts quietly stepped into Patsy's room.

Walking to her bedside, she checked Patsy's

pulse. It was good. She tried waking Patsy to no

avail. She decided to return at 7:00 a.m.

Looking around, she noticed that the garbage

can was full. As she poked through it with her

pen, she found a wrapper for a sub sandwich.

This posed questions that only Patsy and Gertie

could answer. Nurse Willetts headed back to

the nurse's desk very confused about what was going on. The apartment was silent. The ladies were sleeping peacefully. At 11:00 pm, a soft cry played. As the decibel level increased, there was a child's voice asking "Mama, why did you kill me? Mama, help me!" As Patsy struggled to get out from under the sheets and blankets, the loop played again. "Mama, help me!" As Patsy was trying to find the crying child, she tripped over her oxygen tube and crashed into her nightstand. Her body bounced off the baby cradle and she crumbled to the floor. Her head was twisted opposite her body. Gertie hobbled to her side knowing something was very wrong. She used the intercom system to frantically call for help. Nurse Willets came bursting through the apartment door in a dead run. Kneeling beside Patsy, she checked her for a pulse. The ambulance was seven minutes away. As Nurse Willetts hooked up her oxygen, a low groan escaped Patsy's lips. Gertie was crying hysterically. "WHY!? We had a perfect evening!" The paramedics arrived, bringing in a backboard and cervical collar. They gently loaded Patsy into the ambulance and took her to the closest hospital.Preston arrived at the apartment, out of breath. "I heard it on the scanner." "What happened?" Nurse Willetts gave Gertie a glass of water. Preston looked into Gertie's eyes. "Tell me about your perfect evening, Gertie" Nurse Willetts coaxed. Gertie drew in a ragged breath. "Gene surprised us with pizza and cannoli. We watched movies just like we did before we moved here. He brought us flowers yesterday. We missed having him around!" sobbed Gertie. "What would have made Patsy get out of bed in such a hurry?" cried Gertie. Nurse Willetts and Preston exchanged a silent look. "I want to see Patsy!" Gertie exclaimed. "I'll drive you" announced Thomas, who had just arrived along with Dr. Sebastian. "Here, let me help you get dressed" offered Dr. Sebastian.Closing Gertie's bedroom door, Nurse Willetts stood still. "Shhh! Can you hear that?" The soft cry of a baby began to fill the room. Then "Mama, why did you let me die? Help me, Mama!" "Son of a bitch! He did it again!"Thomas drove Gertie and Dr. Sebastian to the hospital. As Nurse Willetts headed back

to the nurse's station, she turned to Preston.

"Tear this fucking place apart!" Gertie grabbed

Dr. Sebastian's hand, squeezing tightly. "I am

afraid, Dr. Sebastian." "I understand,

Gertie."As they walked past the reception desk,

Gertie asked where Patsy was. "She is in the

Intensive Care Unit. She broke her neck. We

can't do surgery yet. We need to contact her

next of kin. Did she have a Do Not Resuscitate

order? Who has medical power of attorney?"

"Gene does!" "We have called her husband. He

is on his way." Gertie begged to sit at Patsy's

bed side. "Of course! The nurse will take you to

sit with her. As Gertie walked to the side of

Patsy's bed and touched her hand, Gertie burst

522

into tears. "I love you more than anything! You can't leave me!"After bursting into her room, Gene went directly to Patsy's side, kissing her face. "You are my soulmate." Patsy's doctor asked Gene to step outside so he could speak to him. Shaking his head, he explained that Patsy would have to be kept alive by machines for the rest of her life. She wasn't going to get better. "We need to know if you want to discontinue life support." Gene nodded, his eyes filling with tears."Gertie needs to say goodbye" Gene said. Gertie screamed, "NO! She's not gone!" Gene hugged Gertie tightly. "I loved her too, Gertie. This is no life for her. We have to let her go." Sniffling, Gertie whispered, "I can't be here!" "I understand" Gene said sweetly. As he left the room, the doctor handed Gene the papers he needed to sign in order to discontinue life support. Gene looked into Patsy's face as the nurses disconnected her from the machines. Kissing her gently, Gene said "Goodbye my love." Exiting Patsy's room, Gene turned to Gertie and Dr. Sebastian. "It's done. She's gone." Gene walked out of the emergency room doors feeling as though he had just won the lottery.He could not contain his excitement on his way home. "I will get the insurance money! I can go on tour! Damn, I'm good!" Pulling into his driveway, he noticed a light on. "I turned everything off when I left." He cautiously opened the front door and grabbed the bat that he kept there. Gene crept into the kitchen, raising the bat. "What the fuck, Gene? I'm your friend!" "Why are you here?" "I heard about your wife on my police scanner." "I see" cracked Gene. "I just came to see if you were okay." "Thanks, JJ. I really appreciate it." "Do you need me to hang around for support?" "I will be fine. Go home. We have practice tomorrow night at 7:00 p.m." "Call me if you need anything. Later, Gene."As JJ left, Gene smiled to himself. "The money is mine!" While Gene celebrated Patsy's death, Preston found the micro cassette loop that Gene had set up. "He's gotten sloppy." He called Spinney at home. "We got Gene. I heard he pulled the plug on Patsy. He was completely cold and remorseless about it." "I'll call Sam and let him

know." The ringing phone jolted Sam awake.
"Hello? Christ, Spinney! It's late!" "Were you sleeping?" "Yes. I must have dozed off sorting through discovery boxes." "I've got news. Patsy fell and broke her neck tonight. Staff at the apartment facility found another tape he'd set up to mess with her mind. He happily pulled the plug on her an hour ago." "Shit! I guess I should tell you while he was having an unauthorized pizza and movie night with Patsy and Gertie, his ankle monitor was dead." "We will file for a just cause hearing. He refuses to comply with the terms of his bail and now Patsy is dead. Can we move up the pretrial conference so we can make a deal?" "Not for a week or two." "Talk to you Monday."As he packed up

526

all the boxes, Sam found the tape of Marissa's Grand Jury testimony. Watching the tape, he was mesmerized as Marissa listed off all the torturous things Gene had done and said to her. At the end of the tape, Marissa looked at Spinney and said, "Tell that miserable waste of sperm Gene that he hits like a bitch! Even though he left me for dead, I'm still here!" Sam chuckled slightly and called the psychiatrist that he would send Gene to. "It's a little late for phone calls, Sam." "I know Julian but this is important. Did you read the psych profile I sent you?" "Yes. I will do my own evaluation but if Carla Sebastian is slightly right, Gene has deep seated narcissistic tendencies and that is just a mild observation. I'll call you Monday

527

afternoon with a time and place that I can evaluate Gene. Good night, Sam."Sam made himself a cup of coffee from his single brew pot. He began drafting an outline of things to discuss with Gene. Frustration set in as he read through the statements from Gene's tours and gigs. Rereading Frank's statement, Sam knew he would need to travel. Flipping on the lights, Sam turned on his desktop. A soft hum brought the machine to life. He poured himself another cup of coffee as he sat at his desk and played the messages from his answering machine. A familiar voice said, "Sam, I know you're there. I can't sleep either. I'll be over in twenty minutes." Next message. "Hello. This is Nurse Willetts. I am calling to inform you that there's been an accident. Patsy fell and broke her neck this evening. Her husband took her off life support within her first few hours at the hospital. There were investigators at her apartment and they found another tape of a crying baby. Gene had been there delivering flowers. He also broke rules last evening by sneaking for a pizza party. He set up the loop so that Patsy would have an accident and he could collect the insurance money. I am on duty until nine a.m. if you would like to speak with me."Click.Sam had no choice but to let Gene go back to jail. By the time Sam had finished his second cup of coffee, he had put together something that he thought would get everyone in agreement to Gene going to a hospital rather than jail. Sam knew that if Spinney pushed for a just cause hearing, Gene would end up back in jail. Gene did not need to get his hands on Patsy's life insurance money. He wrote down all of his thoughts and carefully ironed out the details."Now I have a defense!" He said to himself. He was way too wired for sleep. He hit the coffee shop at five a.m. for breakfast. After devouring a large breakfast, Sam's sugar shakes stopped. "Can you fill my Thermos with High East, please?" he asked the waitress. "Sure thing. Got a long day today?" Sam nodded and collected his Thermos as he made his way to his car. The night guard on duty let him in when he arrived at his office. "Why are you here so early, Sam? Big case?" "Kind of." "The day shift will be here in forty-five minutes. I will let them know you're in your office." Bentley escorted Sam to his office. Sam unlocked the outer office. A deafening silence reminded him how early it was. He opened the door to the inner sanctum that was his office and thought to himself maybe he should speak to Gene for Gertie's safety. Spinney arrived with a box of donuts. "Thought you might like these" he said with a smile. "I am going to interview Gertie. Maybe when she sees her husband's statement against Gene she will talk to me." "I will assume that you have a plan" snarled Spinney. "Yes I do." "Well, I had the lab analyze the tape we found in Patsy's apartment. He put it there to fuck with her mind, just like the last ones."

As Sam listened to the latest tape, a burst of anger turned Sam's face crimson. "What the fuck is wrong with this man?! He has serious problems. I don't think he could tell the truth if you paid him to! I'm not sure that he can help in his own defense! In order to do that, you have to be able to differentiate between fantasy and reality. Gene isn't capable of that." "What do you want to do?" asked Spinney. "Arrest him. Hold him until we can get a just cause hearing. Once he's in jail, the psychologist can evaluate him." Spinney asked, "Do you have one in mind?" "Yes. I spoke with him late last night, Dr. Julian Michaels. He has a stellar reputation in the psych community." "Are you going to let me in on your plan?" "After I speak

with Gertie, I will sit down with Gene. I'm
going to play him the tape of Marissa's
testimony. That should make him come unglued
and have him committed to a facility until the
pretrial conference." "Would you like Marissa
to make an appearance at the pretrial
conference?" "I'll let you know. We need to get
him off the streets now." "I'll go file the
paperwork to get an arrest warrant." "Check the
computer system to see where he is." "If I had
to guess" said Spinney, "I'd say he's making
arrangements to have Patsy cremated. He's in a
hurry to submit her death certificate to the
insurance company so he can get paid." "Let
me do some digging. Maybe we can stop that.
We'll talk later!" Spinney cracked. Sam

exhaled a deep sigh. "Christ, Gene is a fruit basket. He truly believes he's the country version of a rock star. He's even got addictions, psychosis, narcissism, and sociopathy." Chomping down on a jelly donut, Sam began to think. 'I have always prided myself on my commitment to provide my clients with the best possible defense. My record reflects how hard I work for my clients. This is the first time I have ever felt that my client needs to be put away.' Finishing his donut, Sam called Nurse Willetts. "Hello, this is Samuel Dean, Esquire. I am returning your phone call. Would it be possible for me to speak with Gertie Snider?" "She took the news of Patsy's death hard. We had to sedate her." "Would it be possible for me to stop by this morning?" "Let me see how she's doing. Just a minute." Coming back to the phone, Nurse Willetts said, "She has agreed to come to your office. Nancy can have her there at nine a.m. ""That will be fine" Sam said as he hung up the phone.Now he had to prepare for her arrival. There was a knock on his door. "Boss, you're here early." "I've been here since a quarter after six." "I heard what happened to Gene's wife last night. Have you heard from him?" "No, I have not." The phone rang and the receptionist called out, "Line one, Boss! It's Davis Spinney." "They can't get the just cause hearing on the docket until Wednesday morning." "Shit!" screamed Sam. "I will contact the insurance company." "The judge

535

wanted to give Gene time to bury his wife." "Okay. I have an appointment with Gertie at nine." "Lunch?" "Okay. I'll see you at noon." "Make it one." "Same place as always?" "You know it."As Sam prepares for his interview with Gertie, Gene wakes with excitement. 'I have lots to do today!' Sipping his coffee, he looked at the list he made the night before.

1) Call funeral home about cremating Patsy

2) Take the death certificate to the insurance company

3) Check out dates for a summer tour

4) Check on Gertie

5) Accept condolence calls and gifts

'Guess I should call my lawyer. Ahh, later.' The phone rang. "Hello?" "Hello, this is Dr. Julian Michaels' office. Can you come in later this afternoon for your evaluation?" "Why?" demanded Gene. "Your lawyer arranged this." "Oh, yes. I remember. What time?" "Four o'clock." "Where are you?" "The fine arts building in Springville. Third floor, room 418. Please arrive twenty minutes early to fill out paperwork." "Yes ma'am."Hanging up the phone, Gene called the funeral home and made arrangements for Patsy's cremation. Plugging in his ankle monitor, he had a second cup of coffee.

537

Gene then called the insurance company.
They offered their condolences on his wife's
passing. "I will pick up the death certificate
from the hospital and bring it in to your
office" Gene said. "We can have your check
ready for you Thursday morning" the
receptionist replied. "That will be fine"
Gene said as he checked his ankle monitor.
It was almost green.'I need a shower before
I head out' smiled Gene. Gertie was escorted
into Sam's office by Nancy. "Have a seat. I
will let Mr. Dean know you're here" said the
secretary. She knocked on the office door
and announced, "Hey, Boss. Your nine
o'clock is here. She looks really fragile. Use
kid gloves." "I will" Sam smiled.He walked

538

to the outer office. "Hello, I am Mr. Dean."

"Hello. You can call me Gertie. Everyone

does." "Come with me." Nancy gave Gertie

a worried glance. "Stay here, Nancy. I will

be fine." "Have a seat, Gertie. I am sorry for

the loss of your friend, Patsy as well as your

husband, Frank." "It's because of Frank that

I have asked to speak with you. Did Frank

ever mention being questioned by the

police?" "Yes, and he had a meeting with

the police and our lawyer, Justin Alexander,

Esquire.""Yes, I have heard of him. He has a

fine reputation." "I have a deposition here

that was written by Frank. It's part of the

discovery I received from the Assistant

District Attorney. I represent Patsy's

539

husband, Gene. It seems there was an incident during his last tour. Do you remember Frank and the band coming home early?" "Yes. Gene can be difficult to work with at times.""I'd like you to read Frank's deposition, if you're up to it." Gertie shyly put on her reading glasses. "Can I get you something to drink? Coffee?" "Yes, please." Sam rang his secretary to bring in coffee and pastries for Gertie. "Oh, thank you" Gertie smiled. Sam slid a box of tissues within reach. As Gertie read the deposition, a storm cloud covered her sweet face with anger."That prick killed my Frank, didn't he?" "Frank and Patricia's deaths are included in his counts of murder" Sam said gently. "Your friend, Dr. Sebastian feels that Gene has psychological issues. Can you tell me what you know about him? If possible, I'd like to see him get the help he needs in a hospital, rather than have him end up on death row." "I heard he was charged with six counts of second degree murder. Why not first degree?" cried Gertie.Holding Gertie's hand, Sam looked into her sorrow filled eyes. "Second degree murder means it wasn't planned. Gene flies into a rage and he can't control himself." "Does he have anger issues?" Gertie asked. "Yes, he does." Sam answered. "If you don't cater to his whims, he becomes violent especially when he drinks." "Patsy was afraid of him but also

541

very dependent on him. He had her declared incompetent so he would be the payee of her disability benefits. He hated Patsy's sponsor, Patricia because he couldn't push her around." "I see" exhaled Sam. "Do you think Gene would try to hurt you?" "No. I took self- defense training. It would not be easy to hurt me" Gertie answered. "What makes Gene angry?" "If a woman dares to make fun of his manhood, he loses it. All women are supposed to believe his bullshit delusions about him being a country music God." "My Frank could sing and play circles around Gene." "You have really enlightened me as to how Gene behaves when he's angry. Thank you for coming in to talk to me,

Gertie." "I know you're Gene's lawyer, but everyone I loved is dead because of him. Gene needs to be put someplace where he can't hurt anyone or mess with people's minds." She looked at Sam. "You get this conversation for free. Next time you want to speak to me, contact Justin Alexander, Esq. I have to protect myself. There's no one left for me to depend on. Good day, Mr. Dean."As Gertie left, Sam understood. She knew Gene would kill her. He turned off the tape recorder he kept in his desk. He handed the tape to his secretary so that the recording could be transcribed and filed. Any concerns Sam had about Gene's mental defect defense melted away.Calling Dr. Michaels' office,

543

Sam needed to be sure Gene would show for the appointment. The Sheriff's office called to inform Sam that Gene had been to the funeral parlor to make Patsy's arrangements. He stopped at the hospital to pick up her death certificate and finally a stop at the insurance company. He was now on his way home."Well Gene is predictable" Sam grunted. Thinking for a moment, Sam knew that Gene was desperately trying to get his hands on the insurance money and if he did, Gene would be long gone. Spinney needed to get that arrest warrant soon. Sam kept thinking about the tape of Marissa's Grand Jury testimony and how he could get Frank's deposition admitted as evidence if they went to trial. Sam opened box three of the discovery evidence and reread the statements Preston and Thomas took from people who had dealt with Gene. Sam called Preston. "Can you and your partner come to my office? I need to speak with you." "Okay. We're on our way. Give us fifteen minutes." Sam scribbled some questions down and reloaded his tape recorder.Preston walked into Sam's office full of presence. "You wanted to see us?" "Yes. Have a seat. I have been reading all the depositions you took from people who dealt with Gene when he was on tour. Several people said similar things. That whenever Gene was angry or frustrated, he would talk to himself." "Yes,

545

they said he answered himself, sometimes in third person. Did you find this odd considering you think he's a serial killer?" Sam probed. "Most serial killers have delusions and many hear voices." As a seasoned investigator with years of experience, can you give me your opinion?" "He has no empathy. He feels nothing about killing or hurting someone. He is totally self-absorbed." "Have you spoken with his family?" "Yes." "Has this been an issue throughout his life?" "He has always thought he was King Shit. Discipline was not a deterrent. His parents were good, hardworking Christians. He was always looking for accolades and easy street. He was abusive to his children. Family

members hid his kids from him when he

drank. Some women got smart and ran as far

away from him as they could. He liked

young girls, drugs and alcohol. His wives

had accidents.""Okay. What about Marge?"

"I believe he mixed something with her

normal medications and it caused her death."

"Do you believe it was intentional?" "Yes.

He blamed her for the Adult Services case

being opened. That put him on the radar and

turned his life upside down. His music was a

hobby by their standards. They forced him

to get a paying job at the sewer treatment

plant. He thought that job was beneath him.

He killed Marge, collected the insurance

money and quit. They also questioned the purchases he made on his tour. Lingerie and gifts for underage girls." "Thomas, do you have anything to add?" "He's a dirt bag! He deserves death row." "Thank you, gentlemen." Heading out the door, Preston smiled at the secretary. Pulling the tape, Sam nodded. "Type it up." "Here's the transcription of the meeting with Gertie. After I type this up, I'm going to lunch, Boss." "That's fine," Sam answered. She appeared in his doorway twenty minutes later. "Here you go, freshly typed." "Thank you."Reviewing his pages, Sam began thinking about the fact that Gene had not contacted him. Not even to tell him about

Patsy's death. That prick was up to something! We'll see what the Doc has to say after talking to him. Gene had Patsy cremated without a service for friends to pay their respects and say goodbye. He wondered if Nurse Willetts had grilled Gertie.Gene was fuming to himself.' Guess I'm no longer responsible for the rent on Patsy's apartment. Those caseworkers are in for a big surprise! I paid for that furniture. It's mine and I want it back. Gertie can move in with me and take care of my house since I'll be on tour! All the witnesses are dead. I made sure of that. But Sam said there was an eyewitness. I'm sure they will get amnesia when they have to look me in the eye! Maybe I can light a fire under that insurance company. Plus, I can get that shrink to believe whatever I say! I'll pick up Patsy's ashes tomorrow. Sprinkle her around the backyard and she's gone. I need lunch, to plug in my ankle monitor and a nap before my appointment with the shrink.'Sam gathered his files, making a mental note to show up at Gene's appointment with Dr. Michaels. "I'll call Julian to let him know that I will be there." "Hey, Boss. You can go to lunch now. I'm back." "Thanks for permission" Sam chortled. "Shit, I'm sorry. That was obnoxious." "This client has your head a wreck, Boss." "Don't worry. He'll get what he deserves. Order yourself flowers because I was an asshole. Send Gertie a

bouquet to cheer her up." "I'm on it, Boss."

"I will be attending Gene's evaluation

appointment. Please call Dr. Michaels and

advise him to expect me. Now, I'm going to

lunch!" Laughing, Sam smiled at his

secretary.Dragging himself into the

restaurant, Sam searched for Spinney. "Yes

sir? Can I help you?" the host asked.

"Reservation for Spinney." "He hasn't

arrived yet. May I seat you?" "Yes."

Spinney walked in, just behind Sam. "Sorry

I'm late.""Drinks?" "An iced tea for me."

"Scotch and soda for me" Spinney

replied."What would you like to order?"

"The tuna lunch special" Sam replied. "And

for you?" "The seafood scampi and a green salad." "So, how was your morning, Sam?" "Not great. Gene is already having Patsy cremated and took the death certificate to the insurance company. They will pay out on the policy." "I have another meeting with the judge" Spinney said. "I need to explain that there won't be a burial because he is after the insurance money. I can prove he visited Patsy twice, despite being told not to without supervision. He knew his ankle monitor wasn't charged. Plus, that prick told Social Services that since Patsy is dead, he wants the furniture from the apartment!" Sam took a long drink of his iced tea. "Turn it around on him, Spinney. One of the conditions of his bail was that he had to support Patsy, correct? He broke the conditions of bail. The just cause hearing should send him back to jail." "It looks like our boy is planning a summer tour." Sam handed papers to Spinney. "I see he has been busy. I am including the evidence to show that Patsy's death should be investigated. This way, the insurance money will be held by the court until the investigation is complete. We'll have two years to prove he's guilty. If we can't, he gets the money. We charge people for causing others to commit suicide. He used those tapes of a crying baby to send Patsy over the edge. She was already in a fragile mental state. I will be filing new charges.""Do what you need to, Spinney." "You're too calm about this, Sam." "This is what I got from Gertie. I think Gene's visit with Dr. Michaels should be interesting. I will be there." "You know I will be getting a copy of the evaluation?" "Yes, under discovery. I have decided that Gene needs to hold onto his false sense of security for a little while longer." "Will you be filing new charges after you meet with the judge?" "Yes. And with any luck, the pretrial conference is tomorrow. So, hold on to your shorts, Sam." "This guy has me in such a foul mood. I got pissy with my secretary. You need to contact Gertie's lawyer, Justin Alexander so that Gene can't waltz in there and take the furniture." "Will they give her a new roommate?" "There's a good probability of that." "I hope Gene doesn't go after her." "She needs an Order of Protection in place so he can't just show up at the assisted living facility. Contact her caseworker, Ms. Lacey. We'll get the ball rolling on the Order of Protection." "Finish up. I need to get back to my office and make these calls. We should be able to get her an emergency Temporary Restraining Order." "Let me know when they're in the pipeline." Walking back to his office, Sam began to feel that there may be a flicker of hope. 'We might be able to have him committed to a hospital!' As Sam walked through the halls, electricity filled the air. "Boss, you've gotten a lot of calls" Rosie said as Sam flipped through the call slips. "Fax Justin Alexander the transcript from my conversation with Gertie. Be sure to include the phone message from Nurse Willetts. Send duplicate copies to Ms. Lacey and Mrs. Gibson at the assisted living facility. Send a fax to Spinney letting him know that I have no issues or argument with an Order of Protection for Gertie Snider against Gene Allen, Sr.""Spinney was able to have his appointment with Judge Madison moved up to two o'clock. You are required to be present." Grabbing his file, Sam headed to the courthouse. "Nice of you to join us, Mr.

Dean." "I'm sorry, your honor." "Let's take

care of the small things first. We need an

Order of Protection for Gertie Snider.

Multiple social workers have given many

reasons why this is necessary. Mr. Justin

Alexander is her counsel. She read Frank's

statement and explained that she was present

during the recent death of Patsy Allen. Patsy

is the spouse of Mr. Dean's client; Gene

Allen, Sr. Gertie also heard the first loop of

tape that Gene Allen placed in his wife's

apartment. She was alarmed and reported it

to Nurse Willetts. Gene used these tapes to

unravel an already fragile mind, which

resulted in his wife's death. He has already

been charged with six counts of second

degree murder. That number includes Gertie's husband Frank and Patricia Simpson. Patricia was Patsy's sponsor from her women's group."Spinney presented a print out of all the places Gene had been while he was out on bail. This was proof of his two unauthorized visits to Patsy's apartment. "His ankle monitor was not charged during his last visit. One of the reasons he was granted bail was so that he could support his wife. She is now deceased.""Anything else?" "Gene had a substantial life insurance policy on his wife. It will pay out soon. We would like the court to place a hold on those funds until we have had time to complete our investigation into

Patsy's death." "Anything else?" "We can prove he is planning a summer tour. He plans to be on the road." The judge nodded. "I'd like to listen to the tapes. I will grant the Order of Protection for Mrs. Snider. Mr. Alexander, see the clerk to obtain a temporary copy of that order until a permanent one can be sent to all parties involved."After listening to the tapes, Judge Madison agreed to place a hold on the insurance funds until Patsy's death was investigated. "Convene a Grand Jury. As for the just cause hearing, I will stick with Wednesday morning. Good day."Leaving Judge Madison's chambers, Spinney grilled Sam. "Where are you going?" "To poke the

bear." "What?" "You'll see." Sam dashed to
his office to grab the tape of his chat with
Gertie and his briefcase. He was on his way
to Dr. Michaels' office. His thoughts were
racing as he drove to Springville and pulled
into the parking lot of the Fine Arts building.
He took a deep breath. He knew what
needed to be done.The elevator ride took an
eternity. As Sam walked into the office, he
went to the window. After flashing his
credentials, he was told, "Dr. Michaels just
took Mr. Allen back."Julian Michaels
reviewed Gene's medical records. "Hello,
Gene. I'm Dr. Michaels. I've read your file
and have been asked to evaluate you. Let's
talk about what you enjoy. I understand

you're a musician." "Yes. I am a country music star. I have released CD's and I tour and play gigs." "I see. Tell me about your family." "I've been married a few times. Got a couple kids. Just a regular Joe." "Did you enjoy school?" "No. I had trouble with teachers and other kids." "Why?" "They were always jealous of my talent." "What was your best or most fulfilling experience?" "Performing my first solo in church. I received a standing ovation. Everyone was in awe of my talent." "I understand your wife passed away last night. That must be a shock." "She was in an assisted living facility. She had a lot of medical problems. She's better off now. No

561

more meds and breathing treatments." "I see. I have a test that I'd like you to take. Answer however you like." "How long will this take, Doc? I have things to do." Complaining, Gene did what was asked of him.Dr. Michaels was paged to the front desk. "I will be right back. Please finish the test." Dr. Michaels greeted Sam. "Why are you here, Sam?" "Do you still have a panic button under your desk, Julian?" "Yes why?" "I have a piece of discovery evidence for Gene to view. I'm sure it will bring his true colors out. But the orderlies need to be prepared and I should warn you he may try and attack you.""I have survived bigger and stronger men, Sam. Here is what Gertie Snider had to say after reading Frank's transcripts." Julian looked into Sam's face. Do you want him to lose it?" "Yes. He has no self -control when confronted with his inadequacies." "Okay. Let's get this done" Julian said.Gene sat with his arms folded. "Finished?" Dr. Michaels asked. "Yes," Gene grunted. "Hey Sam! Surprised to see you here." Gene, I'm sorry to hear about your wife." "Thanks, Sam." I hear you had to make the decision to end life support." "Yes. It's what Patsy would have wanted. She broke her neck." "I understand you made the same decision for Marge." "It was my duty as the man of the family." Dr. Michaels watched Gene carefully, studying his body language.

"Gene, this was part of the discovery from the ADA's office. I thought you should see it." "Okay. I guess it's movie time. Where's the popcorn, guys?" cracked Gene. Dr. Michaels started the VCR and the Grand Jury room came to life on the screen. Gene was emotionless until Marissa was called to the stand. As Spinney questioned her about the torturous things Gene had done and said to her, agitation filled Gene's face. Marissa told them how Gene said that he could help her become a famous singer if she would audition for him. At the end of the tape, Marissa stared into the camera and said, "Tell that waste of sperm, Gene that he hits like a bitch! Even though that pussy left me or dead, I'm still alive! He wasn't even man enough to do the job right!" As Marissa spoke those last words, Gene grabbed Sam by his neck. "You asshole! What have you been hiding from me!?" Gene bellowed as he punched Sam. Dr. Michaels tried to calm Gene, but received a punch in the face. Holding onto the desk, Julian hit the panic button. "Gene! I am your lawyer! I know what happened. Frank's deposition tells everything!" Before Sam could finish the sentence, Gene was on top of him, smashing his face into the floor. Gene screamed," I AM A STAR! I DESERVE IT ALL!" as the orderlies took him down, restraining him. Gene began talking in the third person.

Slowly standing, Julian removed the tape

from the VCR and slipped it into Sam's

briefcase before collapsing into his chair.

The orderlies gave Gene a dose of Thorazine

for his ride to the psychiatric ward.

Paramedics arrived on the scene. Sam was

put on a stretcher while Dr. Michaels was

patched up. "You need to go to the hospital,

Doc. It looks like a war zone in

here."Arriving in the emergency room, Sam

was tested, poked and prodded. While Dr.

Michaels had a cat scan, Spinney arrived. He

was demanding information on Samuel

Elliot Dean. Spinney pulled back the curtain

and stared at Sam. "Was that your plan? Or

did you actually poke a huge fucking bear?"

"Gene is on a psych hold" whispered Sam before passing out. Spinney patted Sam's hand. "I will contact the judge. That prick is going back to jail!" "Ouch, Spinney" whispered Sam leaning in. "What are you trying to tell me?" Sam whispered, "I have an idea." "Oh, really? Your last one landed you in here!" Sam whispered, "Trust me, Spinney. I need to tell the judge that I will not be able to attend the just cause hearing." Walking to the nurse's station, Spinney said," I need to ask about Dr. Julian Michaels." Julian spoke from behind Spinney. "I am fine. I just had a cat scan. My brain is still intact, thank you!" "Sam says he has another idea" smiled Spinney.

"Christ! His last one landed us all here.""Do you have any idea what he's talking about?" "Maybe. Just get me out of here!" Julian exclaimed. "I need to contact Judge Madison. We have a hearing Wednesday." "Can you contact Dr. Sebastian?" "Yes" replied Spinney."Why?" "Make your calls. We need to have an after- hours meeting." "Okay, Mr. Michaels, you have a slight concussion, but you'll be fine. Don't go to sleep for a while. No alcohol. Take ibuprofen for pain. Take it easy and follow up with your primary care physician in two days. Please sign your discharge papers" the emergency room doctor said.

"Excuse me, Doc. What about Mr. Dean?" "He'll be with us for a few days under observation." Spinney went off to call Judge Madison at home to fill him in on the day's events. He then called Dr. Sebastian for a meeting at his office. "Bring Preston and Thomas with you. I'll bring Dr. Michaels. Sam will be in the hospital for a few days." Then Spinney called to have Chinese delivered for the meeting. As Spinney was setting up for the meeting, his secretary asked, "How is Sam?" "He's got a head injury and a few stitches in his face. It will be a while before he's in good shape again." "Do you have everything you need, sir?" "Yes, thank you." "I will drop by the hospital and check on Sam. Hey, where's Dr. Julian?" "He's resting on the couch in my office." "You talk tough, but you really are a nice guy." "Jesus! Don't tell people that! They will expect me to be pleasant!" As

Preston and Thomas filed in, Spinney asked, "Where's Carla?" "She's coming. She stopped to send flowers to Sam." Carla spoke up, "I'm here. Sorry I'm late. Oh, you ordered food. Great! I'm starving!" "Let's have a seat. I'll go get Julian." "Hey, everyone is here." "Hello, all" Julian spoke in an octave that was just above a whisper. "Hey, Doc, how are you feeling?" "I have a massive headache. Oh, food. Great! Help yourselves and we'll talk." "Has everyone been brought up to speed on this afternoon's events?" "Yes." "Okay, Doc. The floor is yours." "Since Patsy's death, Gene has already contacted the insurance company. There are provisions in the law for us to get Gene some help since he clearly doesn't understand right from wrong. I suggest we use this. If Gene is unable to help in his own defense because we, the psychologists deem him incompetent, he will be committed to a psychiatric hospital for a year. If at the end of that year he is still deemed incompetent, he will be confined to the hospital. The first year gives you time to investigate Patsy's death and the court will hold the insurance payout for up to two years. It will cover all bases and keep Gene out of general population and medicated. What I am proposing here can be used at the pretrial conference in lieu of a regular plea bargain. A special pleas like this needs to be agreed upon by all involved parties. Does anyone object to this idea? Carla?" "I agree. This would be the most expedient answer to a trial." "Preston? Thomas?" "He needs to be off the streets and this buys us the time we need to investigate Patsy's death." "Spinney?" "This will suspend the proceedings on the six counts of murder. I can live with this." "We can't do a pretrial conference until Sam is back on his feet. Gene is currently on a seventy-two hour psych hold." "Will he be taken back to jail?" "Yes. He is not mentally fit for general population. He can be placed on an extended psych hold if he is deemed a danger to himself or others." "He meets those qualifications, I'm sure." "I guess we will see how he functions while medicated." "It won't help much. It may calm the voices in his head, but they won't go away entirely" replied Carla."Is he schizophrenic?" "No. He is a sociopath with narcissistic features and Intermittent Explosive Disorder. For his psych hold, he will be put into a cell-like room with a window so he can be observed.""Sam should be released from the hospital in a week, so I will set the pretrial conference for next Friday. Can you be prepared with your evaluations by then?" "Yes" they replied in unison. "I guess there's no need for

572

the just cause hearing" smiled Spinney. "Between us,

what set Gene off?" "The tape of Marissa's testimony.

Sam thought Gene should see it. Seeing Marissa alive

shocked him, but it was her last statement. The one she

directed at him that lit him up." "Oh, I remember that

part. Something like 'you hit like a bitch!'" "Oh, God! His

ego couldn't handle a blow like that. So he attacked Sam

and Julian. Those other women died because they

mocked his package and his sexual prowess. He believes

that he deserves praise and accolades. He needs to be told

how great he is." "So, is everyone okay with this?"

"Yes!" "But will the judge go along with our

recommendations?" asked Carla. "I believe he will see

that this is the best option." Preston offered to drive

Julian home. "Thomas can drive your car home for you."

"Carla, I called Melvin to accompany you home since

Gene attacked his own lawyer. I would prefer that you are guarded." "He is locked up." "He is still out on bail until it is revoked. The paperwork is just a formality. But just in case" "Alright, Spinney. I will trust your judgment." "Thank you, Carla." Preston helped Julian to his feet. "Let's get you home." "Get some rest" smiled Spinney. "Here, let me help you clean up since Melvin isn't here yet. Sam getting hurt scared you, didn't it, Davis?" "Truthfully, yes. But I will deny it if you tell a soul. Honestly, I have always assumed that clients who use a mental defect defense are full of shit with lawyers that are too lazy to defend them properly. Gene has shown me that some clients are twisted, sick men. Unfortunately, no one realized it until all those people died." A knock interrupted Spinney's rant. "You needed me, sir?" "Melvin, have you heard what happened to my colleague, Mr. Dean?" "Yes sir." "I want you to stay close to Dr. Sebastian until that maniac is put away!" "Yes sir." "Melvin knows his job, Spinney." "Get her home safely, please." "Yes sir." "Good night, Carla."Securing the office, Spinney cautiously walked to his car. A shadow seemed to be following him. As he unlocked his car door, the rustling sound behind him grew louder. Spinney turned around with both fists doubled. "Hey, it's me, JJ!" "Sorry, I'm a little on edge. What can I do for you?" "I heard about Sam. Did Gene really do that?" "Yes, he did." "Sam has represented me on a few charges. He was always a good guy." "I agree, JJ." "Tell me the truth. Did he kill Patsy?" "He may not have physically been present, but he caused her death just the same." JJ looked confused. "It would be the same if I bullied you into committing suicide. He played with her mind to cause her death. Preston explained to me what Gene has told you." "Look, there isn't much that intimidates me, but Gene sure as hell does. He has no soul. You can see it in his eyes." "Sounds like you actually have a conscience, JJ." "I am working on it, sir. Give Sam my regards. Tell him I hope he gets better soon." "Need a ride?" "No, I have my feet." Arriving at the hospital, Spinney went to look for Sam. "No visitors after eight p.m." Spinney flashed his credentials and the nurse relented. "Only for a few minutes." "Are you throwing your weight around again?" Sam sniped. "You know it!" Spinney said with a smirk. "Davis" Sam scolded playfully. "JJ sends his regards and hopes you get better soon.""So, how did the meeting go?" "The shrinks don't feel that Gene can assist in his own defense. He will be hospitalized for a year. Then they will decide whether he's competent to stand trial. If he isn't, the hospital will be his new home. Everything will be suspended for a year. Can you live with that? The pretrial conference is next Friday. Will you be ready?""No sweat." "Your face is a mess, buddy. Hopefully it will help sway the judge to agree with our recommendations. Get some rest." "Hopefully I can get out of here tomorrow." "Don't push yourself, Sam." "How's Gene doing?" "I will check on him. He deserves to spend his time waiting in jail!" screeched Spinney."I looked into his eyes as he was punching me. They were empty. No one was home. There is truly something mentally wrong with him, Davis!" "Rest, Sam. Later!" Driving home, Spinney breathed a sigh of relief. He was still concerned about Gene. He wondered to himself what would happen if Gene refused to cooperate. He made a mental note to research the mental health codes to ensure that their plan would go smoothly. Opening his front door, he went directly to the kitchen and retrieved a glass. He poured himself three fingers of single malt Scotch. It went down too easily. He poured another and sipped it much slower. Spinney dropped onto his bed and fell fast asleep. The following morning, he made phone calls to check up on Gene. He learned that Gene had to be restrained when the sedatives had worn off. That was not a good sign. As he was running to the courthouse to file his motion for the pretrial conference, Judge Madison asked to speak with him regarding the date of the pretrial conference.Spinney knocked on the judge's chamber door. "Come on in, Davis. How is Mr. Dean? "He's alright. He will be in the hospital for a few days." "In light of recent events, I'll assume that there isn't going to be a just cause hearing."

"No sir. Sam's client is on a psychiatric hold." "When were you planning to ask for the pretrial conference?" "Next Friday if the calendar permits." "Davis, I would like to take care of this as soon as possible. How's Monday? Will Mr. Dean be up to making an appearance on behalf of his client?" Yes sir" replied Spinney. "Be prepared to present your arguments about competency. Is nine a.m. good for you?" "Yes sir." "I have advised the court clerk to notify all concerned parties."Spinney ran back to his office to contact both psychiatrists about the new court date. He called out to his secretary, "Get Dr. Sebastian on the line." "Yes sir." "Make that a conference call with Dr. Sebastian, Dr. Michaels and Preston." "Yes sir. I have all parties on the line, sir." "Hello? What's going on?" "Judge Madison moved up the dates for our competency hearing and pretrial conference to nine a.m. Monday. Can you have your competency evaluations ready?" "I wrote my notes last night. We will be ready.""I'll notify Sam. Anything else we should know?" asked Dr. Sebastian. "Seems our boy had to be sedated after his medication wore off." "Noted!" Spinney ended the conference call and instructed his secretary to hold his calls. "I have appointments and I need to visit Sam." "Wait until lunch. He has tests this morning" reminded Ms. Browne. "You're right. Can you get me an interview with the treatment coordinator where Gene Allen is being held?" "I have arranged a meeting with you and Ms. Victoria Abigail Quinn at two o'clock. She is in charge of Gene's observation and treatment." "I need to pick up lunch for Sam. Hospital food is horrible!" "I will call your favorite restaurant. Two seafood specials and iced teas. Pick up at noon." "That would be great, Ms. Browne."Poring

through the mental health codes pertaining to Gene's

case kept Spinney busy. "Mr. Spinney, you have lunch

awaiting pick-up. See you later!" Spinney arrived at

Sam's room with food in hand. "Thought you might

appreciate some real food" Spinney crowed. "Thanks!

They keep trying to give me broth and Jell-O." "Ha ha!

That's not very appetizing" cracked Spinney. "I hear

Madison's upped our time table." "Will you be ready to

appear on Monday?" "Yeah. I'm ready now, but I can't

get out of here until all the scans come back clean."

"Take it easy. You have plenty of time to prepare." "I

want to see Gene.""Not without an armed guard, Sam!"

"He is my client. I owe him that much." "He will be

moved to the jail Thursday." "Well, there's my armed

guards." "I'll see you later. I've got afternoon

appointments." Spinney headed over to the psychiatric hospital to meet with the treatment coordinator. Standing outside of the Springville asylum, Spinney felt a cold chill crawl up his spine. As he walked the halls, a sick feeling grew in the pit of his stomach. "Excuse me; I am looking for Dr. Victoria Quinn." "You must be Assistant District Attorney Spinney." "Yes, I am." "I understand you have an interest in Mr. Gene Allen, Sr." "Yes, I do." "What is it you need to know?" "There will be a competency hearing. I need to know if you feel he can help in his own defense."He doesn't seem to have a very good grasp on reality. He needs to be medicated or he becomes explosive." "Could he handle a trial?" "No. I do not feel it would be fair to put him on trial. He has serious issues. We have to keep him medicated to speak to him right now. He hears voices and answers in the third person." "We are asking the judge to suspend all proceedings for a year so Gene can be treated. If at the end of the year he is deemed competent to stand trial, the proceedings will continue." "Would you like me to submit my findings to be included for the hearing?" "Yes, please. At this point, we feel that hospitalization is the best option for Gene." "I agree. I do not feel that moving him back to the county jail would be beneficial to him." "I see" replied Spinney. "I will have my findings sent to your office. Good afternoon." Driving back to the office, Spinney felt a flicker of hope. With all the doctors in agreement, the judge should concur. As Spinney walked into the office, Ms. Browne announced, "Judge Madison's clerk sent over the hearing notice complete with motions. All exhibits must be in his box by 3:00 p.m. on Friday. "Thanks Ms. Browne. Close up the office.

You're done for the day." "Thank you, Mr. Spinney."Grabbing his briefcase, Davis went home and had a nice hot shower. He put on a hooded sweatshirt and jeans and completed his ensemble with running shoes. Comfortable in front of the TV, Spinney started to doze off. He was awakened by loud ringing. "Hey, can you drive me home? My car is in the Fine Arts parking lot." "Sam? Are they letting you out of the hospital?" "I had to promise not to drive myself home. You can just drop me off at my car." "I will follow you home." "Deal.""I'll be there in twenty minutes." Click. Spinney arrived at the hospital and heard "I am fine! I can walk!" "You must ride in the wheelchair. Hospital policy." Laughing, Spinney barked, "Just get in the damn chair and I will push you out." The nurse scowled. "Follow the discharge instructions. Come back if you experience any of the symptoms listed on the paper." "I will. Thank you.

Spinney, get me the hell out of here!" As Spinney pushed

him out through the doors, the air hit Sam's face. "Get

the fuck in my car!" A short while later, Spinney pulled

into the parking lot of the Fine Arts building next to

Sam's car. "Thanks for the ride!" "Not quite! I will

follow you home!" "Fine, Spinney!" Pulling out slowly,

Sam drove very slowly but made it home. "Here, let me

carry all these damn flowers in for you!" Spinney put the

flowers on the table. "Do you have food?" Spinney asked,

opening the fridge. "Christ, Sam! It smells like ass!"

"Guess I should clean it out." "Good guess!" "Where's

your phone?" "On the stand next to the couch. Why?"

Spinney called and had groceries delivered. "Thanks,

Davis.""Can't have you starving, can I?" "I was planning

to go into the office tomorrow." "No. Give it another

day." "Yes Dad!" "Your groceries are here. Go bathe. You smell like your fridge." "I still intend to see Gene before the hearing." "Wait until he's transferred back to the jail. It's more secure." "How about if I bring Nurse Willetts? She was a Major in the Marine Corps. I bet she could kick Gene's ass! "Nice!" laughed Spinney. "There. I put away your groceries. Go fix your face. Take a shower. Watch TV. Get some rest." "Thank you, Davis. You're a good friend." "Bye, Sam." Closing the door, Spinney wiped his eyes. Damn tears, must be allergies.As Sam stepped out of the shower, he looked at his face in the mirror. "Shit! This beating is gonna leave a nasty scar!" Slipping into his favorite recliner, he started channel surfing as he dozed off. The sunlight streaming through the blinds woke Sam."What to do today?" Sam started the coffee pot while writing notes for the competency hearing. The ringing doorbell was a pleasant distraction. "Carla! What a pleasant surprise!" "Hey Sam. I thought you could use lasagna and some fettucine." "Thanks so much!" "Anything else I can do for you?" "Got a minute?" "Sure! Do I smell coffee?" "Sure do!" "What's on your mind?" "Well, I wanted to see Gene. I still feel an obligation to him as a client." "You also feel the need to prove you aren't afraid of him. That beating made you feel fragile and messed with your machismo. Basically, you need to stand up to Gene. It's a pride thing.""I get it." "He was your first client that you didn't have the upper hand with. You need to take charge of the relationship. This is why you need to see Gene.""Do you think Julian feels this way?" "Shrinks need to have control. That's why we have a panic button." Sam laughed out loud. "Now I don't feel so bad!" "I need to

587

get going before Melvin has a meltdown worrying about me." After his talk with Carla, Sam's worries melted away. Falling asleep, his nap lasted through the night. Thursday came and went. Sam was notified Gene had been transferred back to the county jail. On Friday, Spinney dropped off all of the depositions and evaluations pertaining to Gene. Spinney felt prepared and confident.As Sam pulled into the jail parking lot, his hands began to shake. Walking through the steel doors, Sam felt queasiness in his stomach. Signing in, Sam asked to see Gene Allen Sr. "Are you still his lawyer?" "Yes I am." "Wow. You're a glutton for punishment, aren't you?" kidded C.O. Banes. As Sam heard the clinking of keys and metal doors, Gene was escorted into the visiting room and cuffed to the table. "Good morning, Gene." "Wow! I can't believe you had the balls to come face me!" cackled Gene. "I came to inform you that we have a hearing Monday morning. The judge will hear arguments on your mental competency. All three doctors have given depositions and evaluations of your mental health. If the judge feels that you're competent, you will stand trial on all the charges against you. If not, you will return to the asylum for treatment until you are deemed competent to stand trial. If after a year you still aren't competent, you will be committed to the asylum. Do you understand everything I have explained to you?"You fucking little faggot! You sold me out! I deserve better than this! I'm a fucking star!" "If you're done, Gene." "Does your face hurt?" As Sam packed up his briefcase, he leaned in so that only Gene could hear him whisper, "You hit like a bitch, Gene!"Flying into a rage, Gene tried to reach Sam. Guards ran in to subdue Gene. "See you Monday, Gene!" Sam felt rejuvenated after finding his balls again. Things would work out. Gene's rage earned him a beating from the guards and a trip to solitary for the night. As Sam walked into Spinney's office, he received a standing ovation."Nice work, Sam! That earned you a steak dinner and a round of golf at the club tomorrow." "I think I may have to rest a bit. That took a lot out of me." "Go home and rest. Golf tomorrow at noon." Driving home, Sam felt exhausted. Walking into the house, he dropped into his recliner. Hitting the blinking button on his answering machine, Sam heard "Great job! I'm proud of you!" Smiling, Julian's words soothed him. Warming up the fettucine, Sam knew it would be an early night in. Once Gene was released from solitary, he was escorted to the dormitory where he received an icy reception. "Hey! Didn't you play a tour in

New Mexico?" "Yeah, so what?" "So what? You fucked my wife, you piece of shit! You fed her a load of bullshit about how you could help her career. That all she had to do was audition for you in your hotel room!" "Don't recall." Before Gene could finish his sentence, "You son-of-a-bitch! They found her dead! You're gonna die!" "She loved my big star quality dong!" Before the guards could break it up, Gene had been stabbed and his face stomped on. He was rushed to the infirmary to be stabilized. With no choice, Gene was transported to the emergency room. Four guards stood at attention while Gene was stitched up. The damage to his face was extensive. His jaw was wired shut. "He will need to be monitored for forty-eight hours in case of infection. We will put him in isolation. One of you can stay outside his room." C.O. Banes said "Hell no! I'll be in his room.

He's dangerous alright!"Each guard took a six hour shift watching over Gene. Barnes sniped, "Ah, the convict pipeline never fails me!" Kane shot him a questioning look. "I let Gene's past slip in front of JJ. Ha ha!" Sam enjoyed a restful night's sleep. He awoke the next morning and enjoyed a large breakfast. He was preparing for a pleasant Saturday of golf. Spinney arrived with pep in his step. He gave a quick knock on Sam's front door. "Hey Davis. Wow! Curb service!" exclaimed Sam. "Yeah, since you're feeble now! Get a move on. I want to hit the buffet before we tee off." "I'm coming!" "Here, give me those clubs." "In a bit of a rush, aren't you?" cackled Sam.Driving to the country club, Sam thought Spinney seemed anxious. When they arrived at the country club, Spinney literally sprinted through the lobby. "What the hell's gotten into him?" Sam thought as he slowly made his way to the polo lounge and sitting at Spinney's reserved table. "May I take your drink order?" "How about a caramel macchiato in a to-go cup? We're golfing today." "What happened to you?" "Nothing. You should see the other guy!" laughed Sam. When Spinney returned to the table, he looked out of breath and disheveled. Sam asked, "What happened? "I was paged." "New case?" "No. Gene was attacked last night. They had to transport him to the hospital. He is in isolation." "Looks like you will have to speak for him. He was stabbed by another inmate and had his jaw wired shut." A smile broke out across Sam's face. "Couldn't have happened to a nicer guy. Have some coffee and breakfast, Davis. I'm sure he's being guarded. A few rounds of golf will relax you. Who else is playing?" "Just us, I believe. I invited Julian but he wasn't sure if he would be able to join us." As the waitress returned with Sam's caramel macchiato, Davis looked at her. "A mimosa please." "Yes sir." "Can I get a bagel with cream cheese and lox?" "Yes sir. I will be right back." "Hey, buddy! Don't forget you owe me a steak dinner!""I know I do. I was already planning that." "Good, I'll be hungry by 6:00 p.m." After their brunch, the boys headed onto the golf course. Halfway through the game, Sam had to take a rest in the golf cart. "Maybe it's too soon for you to be golfing, Sam" Spinney said. "I hate to admit it, but I think you're right.Can we do dinner tomorrow?" "You look really pale, Sam. Let's get you home. You are sweating profusely. Do you need to go to the hospital? "No, I just need to lie down for a while." Spinney helped Sam back to the car and loaded him up. He drove at break neck speed back to Sam's house. Pulling up to the

594

curb, Spinney opened the door and helped Sam inside. "Where do your clubs go?""In the hall closet" replied Sam. "Lie down on the couch. I'll get you a cold compress. Do you want me to stay with you?" "Davis, go enjoy your Saturday. I'm going to take a nap." "I will check on you later, Sam.""Get out of here! I'm fine. I just got overheated." As Davis drove away, he had a bad feeling. Shaking it off, he headed home. Sam made his way to his bedroom. As he lay down, his head began to spin. After a few minutes, the dizziness subsided and Sam fell asleep. He awoke at 6:00 pm, had a glass of water and went back to sleep. Sunday morning, Sam lounged around drinking coffee and reading the paper.He began puttering around and picking up the house. Sitting down, he flipped on the TV looking for a ball game to watch. "There's nothing but racing on today! Guess I should do my laundry. Christ, I feel like I was hit by a truck!" Sam had some concerns about his health, but he didn't want to alarm anyone. 'Maybe I should call the emergency room and talk to the doctor who treated me' Sam thought. Finally, he picked up the phone. Once he reached a live person in the emergency room, there was a brief pause. "Hello. I am Dr. Stapleton. How can I help you?"Sam gave his name and explained that he had recently been discharged. "Let me bring up your chart, Mr. Dean. Looks like you had a nasty concussion and facial trauma. I'm not surprised you're still experiencing symptoms. Were you prescribed anything for your blood pressure?""No sir." "You need to take things very easy. Start out slowly returning to physical activities. High blood pressure can cause dizziness. Drink plenty of fluids. No beer. Drink less caffeine and more water. Rest in between activities. If you are not feeling better in a few days, make an appointment with your primary care physician. If you cannot get an appointment, come back to see us. Which pharmacy do you use?""Rexall on Eighth." "I will call in some prescriptions for you and ask them to deliver. No driving until your dizziness subsides." "Thank you, Dr. Stapleton." Click.'At least I know it's nothing major' thought Sam. "Maybe I should fold my laundry." He flipped the TV back on. Maybe there's a decent movie on! There were Westerns, bowling and crime movies that were nowhere close to accurate. Turning off the TV, he thought maybe some music would help him relax. He made himself brunch thinking food would also help. As he shoveled eggs into his mouth, the doorbell rang. He swallowed hard. "Who is it?" "Pharmacy delivery." Opening the door, he saw a boy around eighteen years old. "Twenty-five dollars please. Sign here." "Thanks" Sam said as he slid the kid a five dollar tip. Opening the bag, Sam studied the prescription bottles. Diuretics for blood pressure? He read the instructions. They were to help eliminate excess fluids. Take with water. Swallowing the pills with coffee, Sam finished his brunch. He pulled Gene's file from his briefcase. He added all the documentation of the injuries he had suffered at Gene's hands. Sitting back, Sam's thoughts drifted to Gene being in isolation at the hands of another inmate. Guess he's not so bad ass against a fellow psychopath. A warm, joyful feeling came over Sam as he thought about Gene enduring physical pain.Snapping back to the file, Sam worked on the motions for Gene's hearing. Judge Madison was a decent judge. Hopefully he would understand that Gene needed treatment. The fact that Gene required medication was proof of how severe Gene's issues were. He closed Gene's file and opened the next client's file. First time offender. Offered community service and counseling. The next client had three DWI's. He would be serving jail time. No license."I'll have to check and see if I have been assigned any new cases. This case load seems pretty light. A rap on the door distracted Sam's thoughts again. Spinney walked in. "So, what's on the agenda for today? You're looking better." "I slept after you left. Got up once for water and went right back to sleep. I must have been overdoing it. I spoke with the ER doc. He put me on diuretics for my blood pressure. Told me to drink more water to flush excess fluid out of my system. To take it easy and rest between tasks. You know.""I agree with them. Your client tried to make your face into steak

599

tartar!" "I've been puttering around the house. Did laundry and dishes. Worked on my case files." "I see." "Davis, I want to see Gene in the hospital." "He will be transported in the morning for the hearing." "I just need to see him. I know it's sick, but I want to see him in pain and cuffed to a bed."Shaking his head, Davis agreed to drive Sam to the hospital. "Hey, I bet you're still dizzy." "Kind of, why?" Davis gave an evil cackle and a smile. "I'm driving! You are at my mercy. Stuck going wherever I choose for your steak dinner! Haha!" Sam stared at Davis in awe. "You're a sick bastard!" "Yes, I know. That's why we're great friends. Let's roll! I've got a small cooler in the car for your water!" "You know damn well I've always been able to drink you under the table!" grinned Sam."Looks like it will be a while before we can test your theory!" sniped Spinney. "No worries. I will remain the undefeated champ!" "You mean chump, don't you, Sam?" "Fuck off, you prick!" "After you, dear!" cracked Spinney. "Fine! Hold up a minute!" Davis pulled into a convenience store parking lot, jumped out of the car and ran for the door. Shaking his head, Sam knew he was up to something. Davis returned to the car with two bags of soda and water. "I wasn't sure about your brand of water, so I got flavored. I got soda for myself. I figured I'd join you on the wagon!" "Gee, thanks!" "No problem" smiled Spinney. "So, how big is your hangover?" "See? You're an ungrateful prick, aren't you?" "No, I just know you." "You may be right, Sam." "You only drink soda when you have a hangover to settle your stomach. Did you have breakfast, Davis?" "Yes, mother! "Just checking. Can't have you puking!" "I am a pro, Sam!" As they pulled into the hospital parking lot, a

601

shiver crept up Sam's back. Davis smiled. "It will be fine. Here, take water." "I'd prefer a triple Scotch" croaked Sam. When the elevator stopped, Sam drew in a deep breath as he exited. Turning right, the C.O.'s were fully visible as they stood guard outside Gene's hospital room. Spinney asked," How is he?" "Obstinate as ever. We will transfer him in the morning." Looking at Gene's chart, the nurse put her fingers to her lips to keep Sam quiet. "We had to sedate him." "Why did you keep him?" "He was stabbed. We were concerned about infection. There was so much damage to his face that we had to wire both jaws shut and stitch up his face. Who are you?""I am Samuel Dean, Gene's lawyer. Will he be able to attend his hearing in the morning?" "Honestly, I am not sure. He is volatile and hard to control." "Thank you. Please tell him that I was here to check on him." C.O. Banes smiled at Sam. "Seems karma's a bitch!" Sam turned to

the nurse. "If it's possible, I'd like to get a written

statement that the doctor doesn't think he should attend

his hearing." "If we cannot keep him calm so he can heal,

we may have to transfer him to the psychiatric wing."

"Here's my card. Please ask his doctor to call me at home

this evening." Leaving the hospital, Sam was filled with

dread. Davis looked at Sam. "I know you're worried.""If

he can't attend the hearing, we may have to use video

conferencing for him to take part in the hearing." "The

judge could also represent his interests." "No, that's my

job!" "Alright, if you're up to it." "Now, I want steak!"

"You are too kind hearted, my friend. I couldn't represent

him after knowing all he's done." "My job is to get

justice for my client and his victims." "Damn, you really

believe in our judicial system!" "Yes, I do." "Wow! I am

truly impressed!" cracked Spinney. "Where are we going?" "It's a surprise" snarked Spinney. "Oh no!" "Honest, you'll enjoy it" Davis said as he pulled up to a house. "Hell, this neighborhood is too wealthy even for you, Davis!" Ringing the bell, they heard, "Come through the gate. We're out back!" Opening the gate, Sam was pleasantly surprised. It was a barbeque. "Hello, Sam!" "Dr. Carla!" "It's just Carla. Welcome to my home!" "I thought we were going to Spinney's favorite joint." "He told us about you not doing so well on the golf course, so I thought a barbeque in a home environment would be good for you." Spinney returned with the cooler. "What's this?" "My doc says my blood pressure's high and I need more water." "Well, help yourself to some of my lemonade. It's a family recipe." "He's on the wagon, Doc." "So am I" smiled Julian.

"Head injuries screw up your equilibrium. Who knew?" laughed Julian. Sam started to relax. "So, how's Gene doing?" "He got beat up in lockup. He is being kept under sedation because he has been violent and explosive. They aren't sure about him attending the hearing." "He should be okay for transport. A little Haldol and he should be good to go." "He was stabbed. His face was stomped. Both of his jaws were wired shut." Julian cracked, "Guess he can't complain in court!" "Exactly!" smiled Spinney. "So, what do we have for dinner?" "Steaks, salad and watermelon for dessert." "Who's grilling?" "Me!" Julian beamed. "Hell no!" screamed Spinney. "Move over, Doc!" "Boys!" laughed Carla. "No baked beans, Doc?" "Yes there is, thank God I don't have to share a bed with any of you tonight!" "Awe, Doc. Don't you think we're adorable?" Julian teased. "Yeah, like brothers!" Carla snapped back. After five hours of food, fun and relaxation, Davis announced "I better get Junior home. He needs his beauty sleep!" "You could use some yourself, buddy!" cracked Sam. "Carla thank you for your hospitality. I'll see everyone at nine a.m. in Judge Madison's courtroom. Good night!" Pulling into Sam's driveway, Spinney helped him into the house. "I'll put your water in the fridge. I'll pick you up at 7:15 tomorrow morning. We can stop by your office before court. Later!" "Good night."Closing and locking the door, Sam headed for the shower but noticed his answering machine flashing. Pressing the button, Sam heard "I am calling regarding Gene Allen, Sr. He will be able to attend his hearing. He will be transported at 8:00 a.m. If you have any questions, I am on duty in the emergency department until 7:00 a.m. Thank you."A smile spread across Sam's tired face. Now for a shower. Stretching out

on his bed, Sam set his alarm. Sleep came easy

tonight.Same awoke refreshed and ready to face the day.

After coffee and a bran muffin, Sam put on his best black

pin striped suit with a white shirt and a red tie and

handkerchief combo. At 7:15, Spinney rang the doorbell.

Sam smiled. "You're grinning like a Cheshire cat!"

Spinney winked. "I am ready!" "So am I. Let's get this

done!" Spinney explained. "Head to your office. Check

in and grab your files. I will do the same." Sam had a

confidence in his stride as he walked into his office. "Hey,

Boss! Looking good!" "Thanks." "I heard about the

water thing, so I took the liberty of putting a few in your

fridge." "You are a joy" smiled Sam. "I know!" Sam

noticed her smile for the first time. It was bright and

warm. "I put your files together for this morning's

hearing." Sticking his head in the doorway, Spinney said, "Let's head to the courthouse. Madison likes punctuality." "Yes sir!" There was a chill in the air at the courthouse. There was coldness to the air as they walked through the lobby. Sam thought to himself, I have been here many times before with uncertainty plaguing my soul. As he walked into the courtroom, his skin felt clammy. He had done this countless times before. Why the sudden anxiety? No! He was ready. The court officer called their docket number. I looked around as I walked in. I knew all the players. Everything had been planned down to the smallest detail. The judge called the court to order. Okay, show time! "We are here to discuss the competency of Mr. Gene Allen Sr. to participate in his own defense in a litany of charges. Is this correct?" Judge Madison asked. "Yes, your honor. Davis Spinney for the prosecution." "Samuel Dean for the defense.""Mr. Dean, where is your client?" "He will be here shortly. He was transported from the hospital, sir." Opening the doors, four guards escorted Gene to the defense table. "So glad you could join us, Mr. Allen. Has your lawyer explained the reason for this hearing to you?""Your honor, his jaws are wired shut. He cannot speak." "I see. Mr. Dean, can your client nod?" "Yes sir." "Mr. Allen, did you understand Mr. Dean's explanation for this hearing?" Gene nodded. "Let the court note Mr. Allen has answered yes. Mr. Allen, do you understand that if you are found incompetent today, you will be committed to the Springville asylum for treatment for one year? If you are deemed competent at the end of that ear, you will stand trial on all charges?"Gene nodded yes. "Let the record show Mr. Allen has answered yes. I have read all depositions and evaluations given by both the

prosecution and the defense. Is there anything else either

side would like considered before I render my decision?"

There was a unanimous "No, Sir.""After reading three

doctors recommendations, I have made my decision. But

first Mr. Allen, I want you to know that I strongly

disagree with the mental defect defense being used as

often as it is. I believe in our justice system and

accountability for our actions. But in your case, I concur

with the doctors findings. I had better not find out this is

a ruse to avoid jail time! My decision is as follows:

Gene Allen Sr. is incompetent to assist in his own

legal defense or to stand trial at this time. I sentence you

to be committed to the Springville asylum for one year to

undergo mental health treatment. We will revisit this case

in twelve months, pending the outcome of treatment. We are adjourned.Spinney and Sam shook hands. Sam looked into Gene's eyes. "I hope you get the help you need." The guards prepared to transport Gene to Springville. "Thank God it's over! The world is safe again!" smiled Sam.

Epilogue

Gene sat in a colorless room. Silence filled the air. He had only himself to converse with. The guards slid a letter through the slot in his cell door. It was fan mail.

Dear Gene,

I am Valeria A. Mann, Esq. I am your biggest fan. I would like to offer my services for your defense. I believe you belong on stage for your fans to enjoy.

Yours Truly,

Valeria A. Mann

A smile crossed Gene's face as he knew he would again be a star.

www.ingramcontent.com/pod-product-compliance
Lightning Source LLC
Chambersburg PA
CBHW060209030726
47499CB00004B/973